John Timpson was born i
Merchant Taylor's Scho
when he was sixteen. In
and they moved to Nor
reporter at Dereham for t
years. They have retained their affection for the county
ever since. When he joined the News Division of the
BBC they moved to Hertfordshire.

During nearly thirty years on the BBC staff he
reported for radio and television at home and abroad,
was deputy court correspondent, presented *Tonight* and
other news programmes on television, and from 1970
was co-presenter of the Radio 4 early-morning programme *Today*. He retired from *Today* to return to Norfolk at the end of 1986, and in July 1987 he left *Any
Questions?*, which he had chaired for three years, to spend
more time with his wife in their adopted county. They
have two sons.

In 1987 John Timpson was awarded the OBE for
services to broadcasting.

PAPER TRAIL

John Timpson

ARROW BOOKS

Arrow Books Limited
20 Vauxhall Bridge Road, London SW1V 2SA

An imprint of Random Century Group

London Melbourne Sydney Auckland
Johannesburg and agencies throughout
the world

First published by Frederick Muller 1989

Arrow edition 1990

© John Timpson 1989

Phototypeset by Input Typesetting Ltd, London
Printed and bound in Great Britain by
Courier International Ltd, Tiptree, Essex

ISBN 0 09 956220 0

To my Norfolk friends, who have helped me – albeit unwittingly – to write this book.

One

Charles peered out through the station entrance at the rain beating down on the cobbled forecourt. Above him an illuminated advertisement proclaimed to new arrivals: 'A FINE CITY, NORWICH'. Not today it isn't, thought Charles, and looked around for the bus to Toftham.

It had been a depressing journey. Any journey which involves Liverpool Street station starts under a handicap, and the first few miles chuffing through the bomb sites and junkyards of East London did nothing to help. Anxious to preserve the crease in his trousers and avoid a crease in his jacket, Charles had sat fairly rigid for most of the way, watching the Essex suburbs give way to boggy fields. The winter of 1951 had started wet and in January it was getting wetter. East Anglia was not looking its best. To Charles it looked quite awful.

On weekdays the express trains to Norwich with their new Britannia engines took little more than two hours. But Britannia only ruled the rails from Monday to Friday. The Sunday service was a much more leisurely affair, incorporating several lengthy stops, sometimes at a station but generally nowhere in particular. Charles had left London at ten and it was nearly one o'clock when he finally gathered up his mackintosh and his smart new leather brief-case and stepped out onto the platform at Norwich Thorpe.

He was late already. Now, looking out through the rain, it did not surprise him that there was not a bus in sight. The day had started badly, and was falling away. He watched morosely as other passengers were greeted and hugged and hustled away to waiting cars. The little cluster of taxis was dwindling fast. For a wild moment he contemplated taking one, then he remembered that

7

Toftham was about twenty miles out of the city. By the time he had calculated the likely cost the last taxi had gone.

No matter, he thought, the money would be better spent on something to eat. The Sunday train service did not run to a restaurant car and he had not had a bite since his early breakfast at home in Wembley Park.

He knew before he looked. The buffet was shut.

A solitary porter, leaning on a broom, was pretending not to watch him. Charles would dearly have liked to ignore him. He would look at his watch, perhaps, give an impatient shake of the head, and stride off purposefully towards the city centre, the seasoned business traveller hampered but not defeated by the incompetence of his colleagues.

He went over to the porter and asked him about the bus to Toftham.

The porter pondered. 'Tarf'm,' he said. 'That'll be out near We'lfud then.'

Charles was able to look knowledgeable. Until a month ago it would have been gibberish. But he had in his brief-case a recent copy of the *Toftham and Wettleford Journal*. 'That's the one,' he said.

The porter nodded. 'Nice little place, Tarf'm.' He fell silent, apparently savouring old memories. Charles waited for what seemed a decent interval, then tentatively asked: 'The bus?'

'Mind you,' said the Porter. 'We'lfud's a nice little place too. But thass a bit too quiet for me.'

Charles was beginning to get the hang of the conversation. 'Ah,' he said, and nothing more. The pair of them stood there on the deserted station in silent contemplation, while the rain beat down outside on the cobbles.

'So why d'you want to go to Tarf'm?' Charles almost jumped.

'I've got a job there, on the paper. The Toftham . . .' he corrected himself – 'The Tarf'm and We'lfud Journal.' Too late, he realised how patronising he sounded.

'The Tarf'm and We'lfud Journal, eh?' The porter's accent had stepped up a couple of notches. 'Why, thass a rum owld do, then. Blast me, that is.'

Charles knew now he would never find out about the bus. Just as he so often had been at school, he was being ragged unmercifully, and this time deservedly so.

'I'm sorry,' he said. He must have looked as dejected as he felt, and the porter mellowed slightly.

'The bus,' he said. I know, thought Charles to himself. I've just missed it.

'Thass the one, out there.' And the porter pointed. Parked on the far side of the forecourt was an ageing double-decker. The sound of its arrival had been drowned by the drumming of the rain. 'Dew you hurry, boy, thass a-goin' any minute.'

Charles thanked him hastily and dashed out of the station, not daring to pause to put on his mackintosh. His jacket was drenched in the downpour, his shoes and trousers soaked as he ran through the puddles. With great relief he leaped on board the empty bus.

When it eventually started, twenty minutes later, he realised that the porter had still not quite forgiven him.

The bus took him through the centre of the city, past the Norman castle and a glimpse of the cathedral spire, into the market place with the City Hall looming over it, then out on to the Toftham road. Charles noticed little of all this; he was too preoccupied with what lay ahead. He was due to meet the editor at two o'clock and it was now quite apparent he was going to arrive very late. He was also going to arrive very hungry and very wet. The only dry clothing he had was his mackintosh, still folded as neatly as when he left London. He neither looked nor felt like a valuable addition to the staff of the *Toftham and Wettleford Journal*. Certainly he would cut an unimpressive figure at his first meeting with Mr Juby.

All that Charles knew about his new boss was what he had been told at his interview in London by Jim Downing, personnel director of Anglian Press, the chain which owned most of the papers in East Anglia. It had recently acquired the *Journal* from Mr Juby, its sole proprietor since he took it over from his father in the 1930s. During the war he had carried on single-handed, and with minimal overheads, no pay-roll and much local good will it survived. But in the post-war world it all became too complicated. Readers were more demanding, printing in his own little works was more expensive, neighbouring papers already owned by Anglia Press were offering more competition.

So Mr Juby sold up. He retained the position of editor, but the final editorial control, with the printing, moved to Anglian's headquarters in Norwich. The unions indicated that Mr Juby should have a junior reporter; Charles answered the advertisement, and Downing gave him the job. But as a courtesy the company gave Mr Juby the final say.

Downing had assured him there would be no problem. 'Old Juby likes to think he's still lord of the manor out at Toftham, but he's not likely to argue if we recommend you. He knows which side his bread is buttered.' Downing was in his thirties, with the aura of a man determined to get a lot further before his forties. Charles decided he disliked him intensely, and marvelled afresh that he had given him the job. He had no journalistic experience, just some rather amusing articles in his school magazine, a good Matriculation pass in English, and no idea what else he could do. Could Downing have taken him on, he wondered, just to spite Mr Juby? In fact Downing had taken him on for a much less devious reason. He was the only applicant.

'Incidentally,' Charles asked before the interview ended, 'what's Mr Juby's first name?'

Downing thought for a moment, looked through some papers on his desk, and thought again. 'Do you know,' he said, 'I haven't the faintest idea. He's just Mr Juby. But I shouldn't worry; I don't think you'll be on first-name terms for a day or two.'

The memory afforded him little comfort as the bus

bounced and juddered its way through the city suburbs and out into the Norfolk countryside. The rain was still beating against the windows and Charles could only see an expanse of muddy fields and grey sky. Now and again they stopped by a cluster of houses while a handful of dripping figures climbed aboard. There was an occasional muttered exchange, but mostly the passengers remained deep in their own thoughts.

The conductor sometimes greeted a new arrival by name and attempted a joke about the weather, but he had said nothing to Charles since he took, his fare, except to warn him there was only one bus back from Toftham, at five o'clock. 'And you won't want to stay in Toftham overnight, I reckon,' he added, eyeing Charles's London suit and mackintosh, very conspicuous among all the old serge jackets and flat caps.

Charles did not attempt to explain that in a week's time he would be staying in Toftham not just overnight but indefinitely, if Mr Juby did indeed know which side his bread was buttered. In fact, as well as meeting his new editor, he was also due to meet his new landlady.

That was another solemn thought. Apart from his National Service, spent inconspicuously as an orderly room clerk in Aldershot, he had never lived away from his parents' neat little semi-detached in Wembley Park. Nor had he ever lived in the country, or worked in a newspaper office, or sat in a bus in a sodden suit on his way to one of the remoter outposts of the civilised world.

'What the hell am I doing here?' he asked himself in silent anguish.

The conductor tapped him on the shoulder. 'Toftham,' he said. 'Get you on t'gether.'

Charles got himself on together, and got off.

The bus had dropped him in Toftham Market Place, a long rectangle rather wider at one end than the other, with a bulge in each side which made it look the same shape as a coffin. The buildings around it were a haphazard assortment. Elegant Georgian houses, converted into

11

shops and flats, rubbed shoulders with ugly Victorian cottages, still privately occupied. Most were one or two storeys high, but each side of the Market Place was dominated by a more majestic building, lying slightly back behind a forecourt and thus creating the bulges.

They each bore notices and posters which made it clear that one was the combined Council office and court-house, the other a cinema called the Regal. The current attraction at the Regal was Johnny Weissmuller in *The Lost Tribe*. The current attraction at the council office, judging by the number of times his name appeared on the notices, was George Flatt, Clerk to Toftham Urban District Council.

At the narrow end of the Market Place was a war memorial inside a little fenced enclosure, with a couple of benches facing it on the pavement beyond for those who wished to study it at leisure. Charles counted four pubs in the square itself, and two or three more in the streets which led off it at each corner.

A few doors from the cinema separated by a butcher's, an estate agent and a florist and occupying a central position in the square, Charles identified the offices of the *Toftham and Wettleford Journal*. The ground-floor window was decorated with photos of weddings and dinners and small children in paper hats enjoying last month's Christmas parties. The curtainless window on the floor above bore the name of the paper in faded gold letters. The window on the second floor did have curtains, which were firmly drawn. The entire establishment was manifestly deserted.

There was a clock on the council office which indicated reassuringly that it was only half-past one, but Charles realised it must have stopped, or was still set at British Summer Time. It was actually half-past two, and he was half an hour late.

He went to the door of the *Journal* office, rattled the handle and banged on the panels, and peered between the photographs in the window, but he knew it was hopeless. Mr Juby had doubtless tired of waiting and had gone to spend his Sunday afternoon elsewhere. He was left marooned in a deserted market place in a deserted town. Even the pubs must have long since shut, if they had ever bothered to open.

He surveyed them sourly. On the other side of the Regal from the office was the Golden Fleece, a small and rather seedy establishment with a despondent yellow sheep dangling above the door. At the head of the Market Place, the opposite end to the war memorial, was the mock-Tudor Red Lion, and almost next to it a much older pub with flintstone walls and a low roof, the Bull's Head. Straight across the square from the *Journal* office, next to the council building, was the rather grander Dog and Partridge, and AA sign over the entrance displaying one lonely star.

Charles was contemplating this sign, wondering idly what amenities, or lack of them, qualified for such a modest accolade, when the door beneath it opened and Mr Juby emerged.

Charles knew immediately it was Mr Juby, though there was little to distinguish him at first sight from his former fellow passengers on the bus. He too wore a heavy serge jacket over a high-necked blue sweater, thick flannel trousers and what looked like lace-up boots. But he wore an old deerstalker instead of the regulation flat cap, and between a pair of bright-red cheeks, under a great blob of a nose and a bushy grey moustache, there emerged an incongruously elegant Sherlock Holmes pipe.

'Here we are then, boy,' he roared across the Market Place. 'Welcome to Tarf'm.'

It was the first friendly voice Charles had heard since he left Wembley Park. He hastened across the square and grasped My Juby's hand. 'Good afternoon, sir,' he babbled gratefully. 'I'm so sorry I'm late. I hope I haven't kept you waiting . . .'

'You're not late, boy,' said Mr Juby. 'I know what time that bus gets in by now. It was those folk at the Norwich office said two o'clock. I knew I'd have time for a glass before you got here.' He looked at Charles's bedraggled suit. 'You'd better come inside and have a drop too.'

'Are they still open, then?' asked Charles, checking his watch again. Mr Juby did not bother to reply.

They climbed the steps of the Dog and Partridge, walked through a rather faded entrance hall with a deserted reception desk – one star means there's a desk, two stars mean there's somebody behind it, thought Charles almost cheerfully – and passed through a door marked 'Farmers' Bar'.

It was comfortably full. There were settles around the walls, a big log fire, and rows of barrels behind the bar, where an ample lady of uncertain years presided. She was the only female in the room.

Charles expected that his arrival would attract some attention. He was, after all, a stranger in their midst, and it was long after the last drink should have been served. But he received only casual glances as Mr Juby led him to the bar. He was obviously under powerful patronage.

'A pint of old ale, Maggie, and another special for me.'

Maggie glanced at Charles, a slight and youthful figure beside the well-rounded and mellow Mr Juby. 'Are you sure he's over age?' she asked solemnly. Then she noticed his wet clothes and tut-tutted gently. 'You hang the lad up by the fire and dry him off a little.'

Charles spotted the hook in the fireplace and smiled nervously at Maggie. 'You're very kind, but I'm fine,' he assured her. Mr Juby chuckled quietly.

Maggie filled two tankards from a barrel behind her and poured something dark and strong-smelling from an unlabelled bottle into Mr Juby's. 'I'll put a drop in the lad's as well, to warm him up,' she said.

'I'm very much obliged,' said the lad. He took a few gulps from the tankard. It was much sweeter than he expected, and the after-glow was impressive. He had never drunk old ale before, let alone full-strength Navy rum. He found the combination exhilarating.

Mr Juby supped his own glass slowly and watched Charles draining his. 'I think that'll do for a start. I'll show you the office, then we'll go and meet Mrs Abbs.'

'Is he going to stay at Mrs Abbs', then?' asked Maggie, putting on a great display of concern. 'He'd better have another special, wouldn't you say?' Mr Juby just chuckled again, and this time Charles chuckled too. It sounded more like a snigger, but he pictured it as a chuckle. It definitely seemed a chuckly sort of occasion. Then he realised Mr Juby was regarding him rather solemnly. He found he had dropped his brief-case on Mr Juby's foot.

'Sorry about that,' he mumbled as he retrieved it, a little shakily.

'Ah', said Mr Juby, and led him to the door.

'Take care then,' Maggie called after them. 'And give Mrs Abbs my very best.'

'I will indeed,' Charles called back.

'You won't indeed,' said Mr Juby firmly. 'Maggie and Mrs Abbs don't quite see eye to eye. You'll find out.'

The rain had dwindled to a drizzle as they crossed the Market Place and Mr Juby unlocked the door to the office. Inside on the mat was a small heap of envelopes which he gathered up and stuffed in his jacket pocket.

'That's the way to fill the paper. The more people put this stuff through the letter-box the less I have to run around after them. Another year or two and I'll not need to stir out the door.'

Charles had already given up trying to understand the Norfolk sense of humour. He just nodded, and looked around. The front office of the *Toftham and Wettleford Journal* was not over-opulent. On the bare floor there was one rickety wooden chair by the counter for the comfort of customers. The counter itself bore a file of dog-eared old newspapers, a scattering of advertisement forms, and one or two pencil stubs. In the area beyond was a dilapidated desk and chair, the desk bearing a handwritten cardboard sign saying 'Miss Ellen Gruntling. Advertisement Manager'. The chair had an ancient patchwork cushion.

'This is Big Nellie's territory,' said Mr Juby as they headed for a door at the rear of the office. 'Linger here at your peril.' Again Charles thought it wise just to nod.

The door opened on to a narrow flight of stairs leading to the floors above. There was just one room on the next floor. It was lined along one wall with shelves bearing bound copies of early *Journals*, the faded dates on the covers starting from the First World War. There was another desk, devoid of any ornament and covered in a thin layer of dust, and a chair. The fireplace had been blocked up with hardboard, but there was a battered little one-bar electric fire, its original colour unrecognisable beneath its coating of rust. The room's only saving grace was the view from the window. It commanded the entire market place; no comings or goings could escape observation at the *Toftham and Wettleford Journal*.

'This used to be the reference library,' explained Mr Juby. 'When they told me you were coming they said I might like to share my office. I said I might not. So you're in the reference library.' He switched on the electric fire for a moment; the faintest of glows appeared on its solitary bar. 'There we are,' said Mr Juby. 'Nice and snug.'

They progressed up the next flight, past a door which all too obviously led to the staff toilet. Mr Juby's office on the top floor was rather less austere. It had a carpet, the desk had a lamp as well as a venerable Remington, and the chair behind it had padded arms and another patchwork cushion. There were a couple of cushionless chairs for visitors, a few books on the shelves, and the electric fire had two bars instead of one. Over it all hung the smell of Mr Juby's pipe.

'I doubt if Lord Rothermere would appreciate it, but it serves its purpose. Not that I'm here too much. I'm mostly in the Dog and Partridge.'

Charles got the feeling he was expected to offer some

comment. Should he express amusement, or surprise, or disapproval? The rum and old ale decided it for him. He chuckled.

Mr Juby's genial manner disappeared. 'Now hold you hard, young feller,' and his Norfolk accent thickened. 'That hent a joke, boy, that's good sense. You'll get narthing sitting here on your backside cleaning your fingernails. You need to be out there talking to people about their families and their jobs and how the farm's going and why they reckon the council's wasting their money, and who got knocked off his bike last night, and everything else that's going on in this town. And there's no better place to meet people than the bar at the Dog and Partridge. They won't bother to come climbing up here.'

He paused to take breath and Charles tried to gulp out an apology, but he was off again. 'Never you mind what they do in the city, boy, sitting behind their desks with their feet up, doing everything on the telephone. The way to get noos hent on the telephone, that's fairce to fairce, boy, and better still, fairce to fairce over a pint.'

The effects of the rum and old ale on Charles were dissipated completely by this broadside. He was amazed at the transformation from genial old buffer to stern-faced boss. The words of the unpleasant Jim Downing came back to him. 'I don't think you'll be on first-name terms for a day or two . . .'

'Yes, sir,' said Charles, much subdued. 'I'll remember.'

'Never mind the sir,' growled Mr Juby, calming a little. 'Mr Juby will do, same as everybody else. Now sit down and we'll have a mardle. Let's see what you've got to say for yourself.'

He sat down behind the desk and started refilling his pipe, while Charles pulled up one of the other chairs. He started to put his mackintosh and brief-case on the desk, then caught Mr Juby's eye and put them on his lap instead.

'Let me ask you straight,' said Mr Juby, and unnervingly he put the very question that Charles had asked himself on the bus. 'What the hell are you doing here?'

He had not been sure of the answer on the bus, and he was even less sure now. 'I want to work on a newspaper,' he said lamely.

'I'd hardly reckon Toftham the Street of Adventure. Why *this* paper?'

It seemed tactless to explain he had tried a lot of other ones rather closer to Wembley Park, but they all demanded some previous experience, if only as a tea-boy, and Charles did not even have that. He had gone straight from private school to National Service; this was his first attempt to earn a living.

'I wanted to get away from home,' he said truthfully; then less truthfully, 'I've always wanted to live in the country. This seemed a good chance to try.'

'Lots of quaint little rose-covered cottages, and the breeze rippling through the cornfields and a romp in the hay with a rose-cheeked dairymaid – that sort of thing?' Mr Juby pointed his pipe at Charles, and though it was curly-stemmed it was still menacing. Charles was to get to know that gesture very well.

'Those quaint little cottages have a copper in the wash-house and a bucket down the garden, boy. And that breeze can blow bitter in these parts. And the dairy-maids round here could eat you for breakfast!'

'That wasn't really what I had in mind.' Charles was beginning to feel he should be putting up a stronger show. Just as Mr Juby's accent increased under stress, so did Charles's private school drawl. 'It seemed a good idea to start out on my own, somewhere completely new, and try to learn a job properly from the bottom. I wanted to see if I could actually be good at something. I'm hopeless at making things, I didn't want to be in an office all the time' – that should please him, he thought – 'and the only thing I could do quite well at school was writing.' He started to open his brief-case. 'I did some articles for the school magazine . . .'

'Articles for the school magazine.' Mr Juby savoured each word.

'Mr Downing thought they were rather good,' said Charles a little hotly, then realised his mistake. He did not need Mr Juby's expression to remind him that there was little love lost between the personnel director and the editor of the *Journal*.

'In that case I've no doubt they were right little gems.' Mr Juby puffed fiercely on his pipe while Charles despondently re-fastened his brief-case. 'But never mind the writing, boy. You don't need any fancy English exams or any high-flown articles in a school magazine to write a report of a darts match or a funeral. How are you with people?'

Not too good, thought Charles, the way things are going. But he hardly felt this was a fair example. 'Normally I get along very well.' And he added, rather daringly, 'I'm just not very good when I'm shouted at.'

Mr Juby allowed himself a smile. 'Thass true,' he said. 'But it's not likely you'll be shouted at too often in Toftham; ignored, more like. The only one who'll do any shouting is me and you'll just have to put up with that. That's part of the job.' He leaned forward across the desk. 'Can you get people to talk to you, d'you think? It's no good coming that posh voice in these parts.'

'I did two years' National Service as a private. It was no good coming the posh voice with them either. I think I managed all right.' He had managed, he could have added, by laughing a great deal at everyone else's jokes and saying very little himself.

'Well, we'll give it a try.' Mr Juby knocked out his pipe and rose. Charles rose too. 'First of all, we'll try Mrs Abbs.'

The rain had stopped at last. A few people were out in the square, ambling about in little groups or leaning on walls. Mr Juby nodded to most of them as he and Charles walked past, and most of them nodded back at Mr Juby, but their eyes were on Charles. He could sense

19

the curiosity and the speculation. It was a very different atmosphere from the farmers' bar at the Dog and Partridge. His suit had dried out now and he felt a little more respectable. He assumed an air of nonchalance and hoped he looked like a city friend of Mr Juby's visiting him in his native habitat.

They took a lane out of the square beside the war memorial and passed a few small shops and yet another pub. In spite of Mr Juby's warning Charles began to look hopefully for Mrs Abbs's quaint old rose-covered cottage. He rather fancied a bedroom with sloping eaves and a lattice window looking out across a flower-bedecked garden. He tried not to think about the bucket.

They stopped at a row of red-brick council houses, facing the waterworks and backing on to the cemetery. Mr Juby noticed his expression as they paused at the gate of number 17. 'You should see the ones they built pre-war, boy. At least you'll have running water and an inside toilet.'

Charles had a vague memory of a court case about the sub-letting of council houses and illegal business use. 'Is a council tenant allowed to take lodgers?'

'Mrs Abbs doesn't take lodgers.' Mr Juby pronounced it 'lardgers' and his tone grew sharper. Charles detected the warning signs and realised he was entering dangerous ground again. 'She just has friends come to stay, and if they help out with the expenses then so much the better. Thirty shillun' a week, including dinner and high tea and your washing done once a week.'

'Very reasonable,' said Charles, and vowed to say no more.

A curtain in the front window twitched as they walked up the path, and along the row others were twitching too. Their arrival was not passing unnoticed. But they went through the formality of knocking on the door, and a decent interval elapsed before Mrs Abbs appeared.

If Charles had been expecting a motherly soul in a floral apron, with arms outstretched and a welcoming smile, he would have been disappointed. But Charles was beyond the stage of expecting anything. He met the cold eye of the angular figure in the black dress and the pink rinse and, without flinching, held out a hand.

'Mrs Abbs, I presume?' In spite of himself the private school accent came through.

'Of course I'm Mrs Abbs. Didn't Mr Juby tell you?' It was another inauspicious beginning.

She led them into the front room and sat them on chairs which were clearly built for show rather than comfort. 'I just use the front parlour for visitors and Sundays. You'll use the living room at the back. We eat in the kitchen, breakfast seven-thirty sharp, dinner one o'clock sharp, high tea six o'clock . . .' She paused. There seemed a certain flexibility about high tea thought Charles, but the pause was only momentary. 'And that's sharp too.'

'I'll make sure I'm on time,' he assured her.

'I'll give you a key but I don't expect you in later than ten-thirty, and it's no good you telling me you're out working for the paper because nothing happens in these parts after ten o'clock. So don't let Mr Juby keep you down at the Dog and Partridge talking to that Maggie after closing time.' Mr Juby seemed about to speak, but thought better of it. Mrs Abbs was now in full flow.

'And that's another thing. I'm a broad-minded person and I can't stop you having a drink or two. You're a grown man. Well, a grown young man. But I don't allow drinks in the house, not for guests. I take a small glass of sweet sherry in the evening, but I'm not having bottles of beer hidden away in the wardrobe. I'll have none of that.'

'Of course not, Mrs Abbs. Actually I rather enjoy a sweet sherry.'

She looked at him suspiciously. 'We'll have to see about that, won't we.'

Mr Juby was getting restive. His interest in sweet sherry was minimal. 'Shouldn't he see his room?' he suggested.

'I'll take him up.' They rose. 'And don't you light that pipe while I'm gone.'

The bedroom was decorated in dark green and beige, with a bed, a wardrobe, a chair and a table. On the table was a china jug and basin. 'I'll bring you the hot water in the morning,' she told him. 'I don't want you cluttering up my bathroom.'

'It's all very nice,' said Charles gamely. 'I'm sure I shall be very comfortable.'

Mrs Abbs pointed out of the window. It overlooked the cemetery. 'We've got very quiet neighbours,' she said coyly. Charles remembered his National Service lessons and laughed uproariously, to her obvious gratification.

But she had not quite completed the rules of the house. 'One more thing,' she said as they descended the stairs. 'No women in the bedroom. If you want to bring a young lady back here then I don't mind you sitting in the front parlour, so long as the door stays open. But you keep her away from these stairs.'

'Don't worry,' said Charles. 'There's not a chance.' And at the time he really believed it.

Back in the Market Place he waited by the bus stop while Mr Juby went back to the office and returned with a big brown envelope labelled 'Anglian Press, Norwich'. 'This is our highly technical means of communication with head office,' he told him. 'We put our copy in the envelope, and put the envelope on the bus, and they collect it from the bus station in Norwich. That's faster than the post and cheaper than the telephone. So you'll need to remember the bus times: twelve o'clock midday, five o'clock in the afternoon, and the late bus at nine o'clock on weekdays. Write those times on your heart, boy. They're as sacred as Mrs Abbs's meal times.'

It struck Charles that Mr Juby would not have bothered to tell him about the buses if he did not intend to approve his appointment. He hoped it was because he was satisfied with him, not just because of the butter on his bread.

It was still a few minutes before five o'clock when Mr Juby left him again, this time for the Dog and Partridge. It seemed a bit early to start again on the specials, and Charles was thinking rather virtuous thoughts about the perils of alcohol when Mr Juby reappeared, holding a brown paper bag.

'That'll be a long day by the time you're home, and you've missed your tea now as well as your dinner.' Indeed Mrs Abbs had not waived her rules about meal-times to offer them any refreshment. 'These are some of Maggie's ham rolls – keep you going until you get back to London.'

'I'm really most grateful.' And he really was. This went far beyond any duty Mr Juby might owe his masters in Norwich. He mentally apologised for the unkind thought about the special.

'See you in the office tomorrow week, nine o'clock,' called Mr Juby as he boarded the bus. 'Not sharp necessarily, just thereabouts.'

'I'll look forward to that,' Charles called back, and he meant that too. As the bus pulled out of the market place he looked round, poised for a farewell wave. But Mr Juby was already heading back for the Dog and Partridge.

Two

Toftham Market Place had woken from its Sunday slumber and resumed its normal weekday bustle. The central cobbled area was full of parked cars, the narrow roadways around it carried an equal mixture of cars and pedestrians, all manoeuvring around each other in what seemed to Charles, standing outside the *Journal* office, to be a quite suicidal manner. The shops on each side of him were open; the office was not.

The council office clock still stood at half-past one, but by Charles's watch it was nine-fifteen and he had already waited for twenty minutes. He had arrived promptly for his first Monday morning at work.

So far everything had gone surprisingly smoothly. The parting from his parents the previous day had not been greatly charged with emotion. Mr and Mrs Benson had got used to having the house to themselves while he was in the Army, and rather preferred it that way. They did express some surprise at his choice of profession, and even greater surprise at his choice of location. Mr Benson had commuted to his City office for many years, and he considered journalists rather vulgar fellows on a par with insurance salesmen and politicians. Mrs Benson, recalling Charles's school essays, took a more generous view and decided Charles had taken the first step to the editorship of *The Times*. That at least was what she told her bridge club.

So when he set off from Wembley Park, Mrs Benson put an extra woollie in his suitcase, Mr Benson gave him a couple of fivers to tide him over to pay-day, and they waved him goodbye, dry-eyed. Both of them privately forecast he would be home again within six months.

He had caught the same train and the same bus,

happily without encountering the same porter, and found his way safely to Mrs Abbs. High tea was a massive meal of sausages and bacon and baked beans with thick-cut bread and butter and dark brown tea in a cup the size of a birdbath. He had retired early, leaving Mrs Abbs with her sherry.

Breakfast was another major fry-up with thick-cut toast instead of thick-cut bread. A few weeks of Mrs Abbs's cooking, thought Charles, and he would be as portly as Mr Juby. He contemplated leaving some of the toast, but he felt Mrs Abbs's eye upon him and decided against it.

He did make one or two attempts at conversation but it became clear, rather to his relief, that Mrs Abbs preferred to eat in silence. Indeed she seemed to prefer silence most of the time. Her only observations the previous evening were to ask for his week's money in advance and tell him which hook on the hallstand he could use for his mackintosh.

He made a final gesture of civility as he left. 'Goodbye, Mrs Abbs,' he called into the kitchen. 'Dinner one o'clock,' was the only response. 'Sharp.'

As he waited outside the office he pondered on what a Mrs Abbs dinner might involve. Would it be thick-cut bread *and* thick-cut toast? Would he have his first encounter with a Norfolk dumpling, whatever that might be? And how could he cope with breakfast, and dinner, and high tea? Which would be hardest to endure, permanent damage to the digestive system or Mrs Abbs's displeasure?

'You waiting to get in then?'

A striking figure had appeared beside him, a young woman clad only it seemed in a knee-length fur coat. Peroxide blonde hair was piled above a heavily made-up face; the vivid red lips were set off by orange cheeks and green-rimmed eyes, as if modelled on a traffic light. But it was not the face which affected the traffic as much as the long legs in the fishnet stockings which emerged from beneath the coat. They did not actually stop it, but they distinctly slowed it down.

'You a bit early, aren't you?' she said, and produced a key from a shiny black shoulder-bag.

Charles took his eyes off the legs and checked his watch again. 'It's gone nine-fifteen. Don't you open at nine?'

'Well, there's not a lot of point really. Mr Juby don't get here till ten, and people can put their bits and pieces through the door. And if they want to see me about an advertisement' – she smiled complacently – 'they'll come back again.'

Charles followed her into the office. At close quarters the fur coat only slightly resembled real fur, but the legs were completely genuine and even more breathtaking from the rear. This must be Ellen Gruntling, Advertisement Manager, Mr Juby's Big Nellie. Big she might be, though the coat concealed the details. Leggy Nellie was more like it, thought Charles.

Then she took off the coat and Charles realised that Mr Juby had got his priorities right after all. Nellie was remarkably big. The dress, it seemed to Charles, had been made for someone much smaller.

She hung the coat over her desk, cleared a space on the counter and looked at him expectantly, quite undisturbed by his glazed expression. She was obviously used to the impact she made on strange young men.

'Now what can I do for you? Is it a small or a display?'

Definitely a display, thought Charles, but decided not to say so. He just gulped.

'A small ad in the classifieds or a page display?' she repeated, more helpfully. Charles surfaced at last.

'No I'm sorry, it's not an advertisement. I actually start work here today. Upstairs. I'm the new reporter.'

Nellie's expression changed, as much as any expression could change under all the paintwork. It was now distinctly unfriendly. She surveyed the neatly-pressed flannels and tweed jacket which Charles had decided upon in preference to the ill-fated and still wrinkled suit. She looked at the carefully folded mackintosh over his arm and the new and quite empty brief-case.

'Are you, indeed?' She leaned towards him over the counter, and he gulped again at the increased acreage of flesh. 'Now what does Mr Juby want with a reporter? You tell me that. He's managed all right before, hent he?' The antagonism in her voice was increasing, and like Mr Juby in times of stress her accent was thickening. 'That's those people in Narridge, no doubt. That hent enough to buy up his pairper, they want to get rid on him altogether.'

Charles was quite appalled. 'Its not like that at all. They're not going to get rid of him because of me. I've never even worked on a newspaper before.'

'Get him to teach you the job, then you take over. I know about you London people.' Nellie leaned even further over the counter, her bosom heaving. It was an awesome sight. 'How can you stand there, with your silly mackintosh and your fancy case, and take away the jobs of decent people like Mr Juby?'

Charles was nearly in despair. 'This is ridiculous. I tell you I'm just a very new, very junior, very inexperienced trainee reporter. I wouldn't dream of taking Mr Juby's job, I really wouldn't.'

'Why, that's a relief,' said Mr Juby from the doorway. 'I can breathe again.' Charles's discomfiture was complete.

Nellie also seemed to be taken a little off-balance by his sudden appearance. 'Whatever are you doing in the office this early?' she asked. 'You're not due in for a half-hour yet.'

'Had to look after young Charlie, didn't I? Just as well, I reckon. You might have frightened him back to London, going on like that. Come on lad, let's leave Nellie to calm down a bit. Mustn't have her bust something, must we?'

But Nellie was already calming down and her thoughts, it seemed, had gone off on another tack. As Charles followed Mr Juby towards the door at the rear of the office she put a hand on his arm and murmured, in a very different voice, 'Did you say – inexperienced?'

And she raised one black-pencilled eyebrow.

'Now let's see what we can give you to get on with.' Mr Juby browsed through the pile of papers on his desk in the top office, and produced some more from his pockets. 'Here's one for you. Mrs Maggs's report about the Methodist Women's Own. You take the typewriter downstairs and have a go at that. We don't want the names of the hymns but make sure you put in who the speaker is, and who served the tea and who ran the raffle, and all the prize-winners. It's names that sell papers in these parts, Charlie boy.'

Charles took the report, picked up the ancient Remington with some difficulty, and tottered towards the door. His own typewriter must be a first priority, he vowed; it was that or a hernia.

Mr Juby halted him for further instructions. 'If Mrs Maggs has left out any initials then you ring her up and ask her. And if she doesn't know, then ask her to tell you somebody who does. Initials are sacred, Charlie, just like bus times and Mrs Abbs's meals.'

'Yes, Mr Juby.' He made another bid for the door.

'By the way, how are you getting on with Mrs Abbs?'

'She doesn't say a lot.' Charlie finally got to the stairs. 'But she does cook a lot.' And he made his precarious descent.

It took some time to rewrite the report of the Methodist Women's Own. In fact Charles would never have dreamed that a couple of paragraphs could involve so much effort. Mrs Maggs had left out quite a lot of initials, and when he phoned her and managed to explain that he was Mr Juby's assistant, not some sort of salesman, she was still not too helpful.

'You've had all those names in the paper before. Just you look them up and put the same initials again.'

He did track them down eventually, all except one, a Miss Bodworthy who proposed the vote of thanks. At previous meetings, going back over several months, she had either been inactive or absent, and her name did not appear. In desperation Charles made a quick survey of the most popular initials among Methodist women and selected 'J' for Miss Bodworthy.

More reports came down from Mr Juby's office for rewriting. Charles toiled through a St John Ambulance Brigade demonstration, a darts dinner at the Jubilee Hall, three bring-and-buy sales, and a Conservative tea dance.

'Nearly time for the bus,' roared Mr Juby from upstairs. 'Let's have what you've done, boy.'

Charles took them up and Mr Juby read them swiftly, his only comment an occasional grunt which might have indicated approval or disgust. Finally he came to the report of the Methodist Women's Own.

'That must be old Arabella Bodworthy,' he said. 'Where did you get this "J" from?'

Charles thought fast. 'I must have misheard Mrs Maggs. "A", "J", very similar. Sorry about that.'

'You need to listen a little harder,' snapped Mr Juby. 'There *was* a Miss J Bodworthy, poor Julia. Got run over a few weeks ago. Nice for Arabella to read that the vote of thanks was proposed by her dead sister. Particularly' – Mr Juby's gaze was icy – 'particularly as she's a cousin of mine.'

He took a piece of paper and wrote on it in large capital letters. 'Here's some pins, now you put that on the wall where you an see it. I don't want any more of your "mishearings", or any more of your guesses for that matter, or you and I will fall out.'

Safely downstairs again, Charles sat at his desk and glowered at the piece of paper he had pinned on the wall. INITIALS ARE SACRED.

'Sod it,' said Charles.

He was very nearly late for Mrs Abbs's dinner.

The afternoon turned out to be even more humiliating than the morning. He had to cover his first funeral.

'It's quite straightforward.' Mr Juby had returned from the Dog and Partridge in rather more genial mood. 'You just stand at the church door and take down the names. If they say they're representing somebody else you put that down too. You won't have any problems, they'll be only too glad to tell you. Only reason they go, some of them, to get their name in the paper. Don't bother the family you can go round to the house afterwards when they feel a bit better. But don't miss any of the others. And what's the most important thing to remember?'

'I know,' said Charles. 'Initials are sacred.'

There was a steady drizzle outside, and the mackintosh was unfolded at last. Mr Juby offered him the use of a frayed black tie which he kept in his desk for such occasions, but Charles felt it was hardly worth it underneath the mac. A black umbrella would have been rather more useful, but that was beyond the *Journal*'s resources. He headed for the parish church, a couple of minutes' walk from the office, and took up his station in the porch.

He was relieved to find that the deceased did not have a wide circle of friends, and mourners were fairly thin on the ground. This gave him the time he needed to explain to each one who he was. He found that a full introduction: 'Excuse me, sorry to trouble you but I'm from the *Toftham and Wettleford Journal* . . .' was less effective than the more succinct: 'I'm with Mr Juby.' It seemed that several local readers had no idea of the paper's full name, but they all new Mr Juby.

One or two of them turned a little haughty, obviously expecting him to know who they were without asking. This included a Mr George Flatt, whose name seemed somehow familiar. 'Representing?' asked Charles routinely.

'Representing the Council, of course.' Mr Flatt was a thin, sour-looking fellow in a long black coat and a bowler hat. 'You'll need to remember that if you're going to work on the paper.'

It was the name Charles had seen on the notice outside the council office, vying for star billing with Johnny Weissmuller across the Market Place at the Regal. He wrote carefully in his notebook, 'Mr G Flatt representing Toftham Urban District Council and Mr J Weissmuller.' He was getting rather bored.

But the boredom ended abruptly when the funeral cortège arrived. He vacated the porch to leave more room for the bearers, and stood on his own half-way down the church path, head bowed respectfully as the coffin approached.

If he had kept it bowed all would have been well. But he glanced up and was transfixed by the sight of the undertaker, walking sedately ahead of the procession in his frock-coat, carrying top hat and black gloves, with his tongue extended to its full length. As Charles stared in amazement he withdrew his tongue, blew out his cheeks into two fat balloons, wrinkled his nose and quite noticeably twitched his ears. Then he sucked in his cheeks so that his mouth was compressed into a beak, and assumed a terrible squint.

The sheer incongruity of this astonishing performance was too much for Charles. Forgetting his own prominent position facing the oncoming cortège, he sucked on his cheeks, pursed up his lips, and squinted back.

The undertaker stopped grimacing and grinned cheerfully at Charles. He was still grinning, but more to himself, as the hapless Charles with sucked-in cheeks and pursed lips, stopped squinting and realised that he was being stared at with varying degrees of outrage by all the family mourners.

Hastily he resumed a more normal expression and tried to give an apologetic smile. It was too late. He got a glare from each mourner as they passed; one large lady seemed on the verge of striking him with her umbrella. He had never known such shame. The thought of calling on the family after the service to take down their names was too awful to contemplate. He lurked outside the church until it was over, hid among the headstones as the procession moved to the graveside,

31

then buttonholed some of the more helpful-looking mourners at the rear and managed to acquire the family names. For his own information he also acquired the name of the undertaker.

Back in the office he enquired casually of Nellie as he passed through, if she knew an undertaker called Pendleton.

'Freddie Pendleton? Everybody knows our Freddie. A proper laugh, he is. He's a great one at parties; you'd never think he made a living out of dead bodies. Have you met him then?'

'Oh yes,' said Charles. 'I've met him.'

He climbed the stairs to his office, debating whether to tell Mr Juby about his encounter with our Freddie, or whether it might escape his notice altogether. It was a vain hope.

He was half-way through the list of mourners – 'Mr J. W. Postlethwaite, representing Mrs Postlethwaite, Miss L. Postlethwaite and Toftham Golden Fleece Darts Club' – when there was a roar from the office above. 'Chaaarlie!' Then the ominous, heavily accented command: 'Come you here t'gether.' His heart sank, as he mounted the stairs.

Mr Juby glared at him through a cloud of pipe smoke. 'Just had a phone call from the grieving relatives. They say you stood in the churchyard making faces at them. Then you sniggered at them when they went by. Whatever were you playing at, boy?'

'I'm terribly sorry,' Charles stumbled. 'A most extraordinary thing happened. Mr Pendleton the undertaker . . .'

'I know, I know, Freddie made faces at you. He always makes faces at a funeral. He's done it to me many a time. That's how he cheers himself up a bit; it's a miserable enough job. And there's no harm done if the family can't see him – only if a stoopid young feller like you can't control himself.'

Charles writhed. This was worse than he thought.

Mr Juby continued relentlessly. 'I told them you'd just come up from London and you hadn't learnt any manners yet. That seemed to quieten them a bit. Now you'd better go round there and apologise.'

'Oh Lord, do I have to?' Charles looked so woebegone that Mr Juby addressed him a little more gently.

'You go round there looking like that and maybe they'll take pity on you. No need to say anything about Freddie Pendleton; you sort it out on your own. Off you go, boy.' And he gave him directions to the house.

Charles walked there as slowly as possible, desperately trying to devise some logical explanation for his behaviour. Could he have been grimmacing with grief, overcome by the sadness of the occasion? Did he have some uncontrollable facial twitch? Was he trying to suck something out of his teeth? When he knocked on the door, he still had no idea what he was going to say.

It was opened by the lady who had nearly assaulted him with her umbrella. Charles shuddered and began a blundering apology, before he realised that she was actually laughing. Behind her some sort of party was on progress; there were figures with bottles and glasses. Someone was holding forth by the fireplace, to the obvious amusement of the company.

'We thought Mr Juby would send you round,' said the lady at the door. 'Come you in, boy. There's someone else here you know.'

Indeed there was. The centre of attention was Freddie Pendleton.

'Here we are again, then,' cried Freddie. 'I thought I'd better come and tell our friends here why you behaved so daft in the churchyard. I think we're all feeling a lot better now.'

'We'd heard how Freddie goes on at funerals,' said the lady, 'but we never thought it was catching. You'd better get inoculated before you go to another one.'

Charles grasped Freddie's hand. 'I really appreciate you coming round to explain.'

Freddie grinned again, and Charles realised he was

much younger than he'd first thought, probably in his thirties. In these less formal surroundings the frock coat looked like fancy dress beneath the cheerful face.

'That was self-defence really. I thought you might blather out why you'd pulled that face, and I'd sooner they had the story from me than from a young feller they'd never seen before. That way we've all had a good laugh. But don't you slip up like that again, boy, not until you've been here a year to two and folk know you a little better.'

Charles hastened back to the office, feeling happier than he had been all day. He would just have time to finish off the list of mourners before heading home for Mrs Abbs's high tea. Nellie had already left, but he found Mr Juby browsing through the notebook he had left on the desk.

'It's all worked out all right, Mr Juby. Freddie Pendleton kindly went round and explained what had happened.'

'Ah,' said Mr Juby quietly. 'I told him that might be a good idea. Gave him ten minutes' start to get things sorted out before I sent you round there.' He looked up for a moment from the notebook. 'I don't quite see you as a Dan'l, boy. I wouldn't want you gobbled up on your first day.'

He chuckled to himself as he turned back to the notebook, while Charles marvelled at his kindly cunning. Then the chuckle suddenly stopped.

'What's this boy?' He was pointing at one of the entries. Charles looked over his shoulder and blushed. 'I'm sorry, that's just a joke, Mr Juby.'

'Another joke? One way and another, you seem to have had a very comical time at this funeral.' He thrust the notebook into Charles's hand. 'You make sure nobody else sees that – least of all George Flatt. You don't fall out with George in this town.'

He paused at the door. 'I suppose there's one thing I should be thankful for,' he growled. 'You've got Mr Weissmuller's initial right. Hooray for that.'

Three

Mr George Flatt, Clerk to Toftham Urban District Council, did not look up from his desk as Mr Juby led Charles into his office. They were on a tour of local contacts and Mr Juby had decided to start at the top.

'I'll be with you in a minute. Just signing these final demands. Some of these tenants have no idea how to look after their money. Feckless, they are.'

Charles occupied the time counting the fountain pens in the top pocket of Mr Flatt's navy blue suit. There were four of them, with a bulkier object which might be a clip-on comb, though this seemed improbable, judging by the sparseness of the Clerk's hair. Perhaps, he thought idly, it was a pocket thumbscrew to use on feckless council house tenants. He looked up from the crowded top pocket to find Mr Flatt's eyes upon him.

'Mr Juby's told you who I am, then.' Indeed Mr Juby had: 'He's a pompous old bully, is George, but he runs the Council and there's no way to avoid him.'

Charles nodded. 'I'm sorry about not knowing you at the funeral. I should have remembered the name from the noticeboard outside. Perhaps it needs to be painted a little bigger.'

My Juby looked at Charles sharply. The name of George Flatt was already the most prominent feature on the board. The Clerk, however, merely looked thoughtful.

'You may be right. It might help visitors to the town to know who's in charge. The locals know well enough, eh Mr Juby?'

'Oh yes, George, no doubt about that. Don't know where this town would be without you. Derelict, no doubt.'

This time Mr Flatt did look at them suspiciously, and

Charles concentrated on maintaining his composure. He could not face another Freddie-type incident. Mercifully Mr Juby changed the subject. 'I've brought young Charles here to meet you. He'll be in and out the front office fairly regular, but I've told him not to bother you personally unless it's something really top-level. I'm sure you'll give him a hand if need be. He's just come from London, so he don't know a lot.'

'I once met a young reporter from London,' Mr Flatt mused. 'Remember that time when we had all the trouble with the tenants coming into the council meeting to complain about the rents. He tried to tell me we couldn't go into closed session without proposers and seconders and all that squit. I'm glad you took him away, Mr Juby, before I set the police on him. All that stuff about the rights of the fourth estate – I hope we're not going to get any of that from our young friend here.'

'I wouldn't worry about that. He's only been in the fourth estate for five minutes. I doubt he even knows what it is. He won't do anything without coming to me.' Charles felt like a small boy being discussed by his elders and betters.

Outside he asked Mr Juby about the young reporter from London.

'He was a nice enough young lad, but he didn't know the ways of these parts. It's no good turning nasty with George, you just agree with him and then get on with things yourself. I got the lad out of the way and told him he ought to phone his office and tell them all about the uncooperative attitude of small-town officials. He did quite a good piece about it.'

'And what did *you* do?'

'What d'you think I did, boy? I went to the Dog and Partridge.'

Charles felt disappointed, and he must have shown it. Mr Juby explained. 'Most of the Council come into the farmers' bar after a meeting. I soon get a fair idea what went on at their closed session.' He chuckled. 'That hent easy to have a closed session in Toftham.' Charles nodded thoughtfully.

'Then I made a few phone calls to the London papers. Not the one that lad worked for, of course. Wouldn't want to embarrass him. Hope they weren't too hard on him when they saw the other papers. George thought the lad must have done it all, listening through keyholes or the like.'

'What's this about the London papers?' asked Charles with some interest. 'Do they pay for that sort of thing?'

'You don't need to bother about that,' said Mr Juby firmly. 'You concentrate on working for the *Journal*. Leave me to worry about the London papers.' And he led him into the offices of Dumble, Dumble and Burney, solicitors and commissioners for oaths.

The two Dumbles were long since deceased. Major Clarence Burney, the present head of the firm, had taken over from his father and guided it to an unassailable position as Toftham's leading solicitors. In so doing he had acquired the duties of district coroner and clerk to the magistrates. He was on the board of a number of local companies, and he served on several public committees. He was also president of Toftham and District British Legion, by virtue of the six years he had spent in the Army's legal department during the war. As that had involved much travelling into different war zones he had a most formidable collection of campaign medals, which he wore on Remembrance Day parades with enormous aplomb.

Mr Juby had already explained the essentials to Charles. 'He's all right, the Major. Knows his stuff, does his best for people. But don't forget to call him Major. There's a lot of ex-army people in these parts, and anyone who has higher than a lieutenant likes you to remember it.'

They were ushered into Major Burney's panelled office, furnished expensively and elegantly, and the Major rose courteously to greet them. Charles cast a quick glance at his top pocket. A red silk handkerchief was draped gracefully from it; there was not a fountain pen in sight.

'Ah, Mr Juby, glad to see you. Thought you did a good report of that inquest last week. Poor fellow was obviously drunk as a lord when he fell off the bridge. Good of you not to mention it. Saves the family's feelings a bit.'

'Seemed the right thing to do,' said Mr Juby. 'Now, this is young Charles Benson, my new reporter. I'll bring him along to court on Friday and no doubt we'll get him to an inquest in due course. I'd much appreciate it if you could give him a little advice if I'm not around. I think these days they give young chaps a lesson or two in the law before they let them loose, but with young Charles here I think it's just up to you and me to do what we can, if you wouldn't mind.'

'He'll be all right, I'm sure. Our cases aren't usually too complicated in Toftham. You'll soon get the hang of things.' Major Burney patted Charles on the shoulder. 'We'll look after you, my boy. If you're uncertain about anything, just ask.'

'I will sir, and thank you,' said Charles. He had rather taken to Major Burney. But in the Dog and Partridge later Mr Juby gave him a word of warning.

'That was good to call him sir. Don't try anything more familiar. He's county, is the major; and you don't take liberties with county.'

In the weeks that followed Charles learned quite a lot about the social structure of Toftham and its various attitudes to newcomers like himself, as Mr Juby sent him off on further perambulations around the town with a list of contacts to visit. The list had been drawn up just for his benefit, since Mr Juby had no need for any such *aide-memoire*.

He called on the Vicar, elderly and not too dynamic after twenty years in the parish, and the Methodist minister, young and quite new. They both received him patiently if not warmly, as another minor cross for them

to bear. He met the ladies who ran the Women's Insti-
tute and the British Legion Women's Section, and Mrs
Maggs of the Methodist Women's Own, all of mature
years, ample girth and few words, who obviously considered him to be a rather irritating and unnecessary
interruption to their household chores. They had run
their respective organisations for many years and needed
no guidance, in their view, on what to tell the press.

He met Mr Hurn, secretary of the Chamber of Trade,
in his hairdresser's shop placed strategically at one
corner of the council office, and thus rivalling the Dog
and Partridge as a centre for gossip and potential news.
Mr Hurn chatted to Charles while continuing a conversation with the customer in the chair, whom he was
shaving with an open razor. He seemed quite capable
of concentrating simultaneously on all three activities,
and the customer showed no disquiet as the razor
skimmed over his throat while Mr Hurn was looking
over his shoulder at Charles. Even so, Charles ardently
hoped his own safety razor would never let him down.

Mr Hurn made no attempt to introduce him to the
other customers who were ranged in chairs along one
wall behind a cloud of pipe smoke. They muttered quietly to one another, watching Charles through the smoke
and attending closely to every word exchanged. It was
an uncomfortable few minutes and he was relieved to
escape. He could hear the increased buzz of conversation
as he left; he felt fairly certain they were not just discussing his hair.

He was passing through the downstairs office of the
Journal after one of these sorties when Big Nellie called
him over. She appeared to have shed her earlier suspicions of him, but their exchanges were generally limited to a hallo in the morning, a goodbye in the evening,
and an occasional nod in between. She was normally far
too occupied to say any more. Customers were inclined
to linger for long periods after their actual business was
completed, the women to chat, the men to ogle. Her
desk was frequently surrounded by youthful admirers,

jockeying for the best view. She seemed to have no regular escort; Charles assumed she was playing the field. He did not hold any aspirations himself; the home team looked far too strong. But when she called to him he could not suppress a faint flutter of excitement.

'You got a visitor, Charlie. Mortimer from Wettleford.'

'Mortimer?' he queried. 'From Wettleford?'

Nellie became impatient. 'Mortimer Thirkle,' she snapped. 'Runs the Wettleford office. He's upstairs.'

'Of course.' He knew the paper had a branch office in Wettleford, but Mr Juby had not mentioned who ran it. 'What sort of chap is he?'

Nellie gave a disdainful shrug. 'He's a great old mawther, that's what *he* is.' Charles had not heard the word before, but its meaning was fairly clear. He nodded cautiously. 'What does he want?'

'To see what sort of chap *you* are, no doubt,' Nellie grinned.

He became daring. 'Did you tell him?'

'Oh yes. I told him.' And she turned back to her account books. He realised it was pointless to pursue it further; nobody could terminate a conversation more effectively than Nellie. But he would have loved to know what she had said.

Upstairs he found Mortimer browsing through his desk, a balding untidy figure in a shapeless blue suit. Charles was used to Mr Juby inspecting his work, but he saw no reason why his colleague from Wettleford should take the same liberties. His hackles rose.

'Good morning,' he said rather coldly. 'Can I help you?'

Mortimer straightened up from the desk, but having straightened up he was still stooping. He was also blushing, and very apologetic.

'I'm so sorry. I was just wondering if you had the report in for the Tittlesham Legion dinner. Tittlesham's just half-way between our offices and the correspondent there is never quite sure whether to send the report here or to Wettleford, and I hadn't seen it when I left so I thought I'd see if it had come here before I rang them up to ask for it, but I don't think you have, I'm so sorry . . .'

Charles felt as embarrassed as Mortimer. He obviously had the best of intentions, and was just thinking about his work. Actually Mortimer thought of very little else.

He made reassuring noises, much regretting his earlier sharpness, and confirmed that the Tittlesham Legion report had yet to appear. Feeling for once in charge of the situation – a feeling most people had when the situation consisted of Mortimer – he introduced himself more formally.

'I'm Charles Benson.' They shook hands awkwardly. 'I'm still very new, I'm afraid. I don't know much about anything yet.'

'I know,' said Mortimer. 'Nellie told me.'

Charles was immediately curious. 'What else did she tell you?'

Mortimer blushed again. 'What she actually said was' – and his barely detectable Norfolk accent thickened up – ' "He know narthin more about noospairpers than a crow know about a Sunday".'

Charlie wished he hadn't asked. Or at least that Mortimer hadn't answered. But Mortimer was quite lacking in guile or perception. If people asked a question he assumed they wanted an honest answer. Which was why he never did very well at job interviews, and in his mid-forties was still the Wettleford district reporter.

'Mr Juby asked me to take you around the area a bit, help you get your bearings.'

Charles was puzzled. 'I didn't see a car outside.'

'It's a motorbike actually.' Mortimer saw Charlie's look of surprise. 'It's quite a comfortable motorbike – and if we're lucky it shouldn't rain.'

Charles was still looking dubious.

'It's better than having to cycle.' Mortimer was showing signs of irritation, a trait which Charles did not

41

expect him to possess. 'It may look flat in these parts but you get on a bike and you'll soon find different.'

'I'm really very grateful,' said Charles hastily. 'I just didn't visualise you on a motorbike.'

The apologetic, self-deprecating figure suddenly came to life. 'You don't have to be a teenage tearaway to ride a motorbike. It's a very sensible form of transport – especially if you can't afford a car.' Mortimer's voice was rising. 'I don't suppose you're likely to have one of them just yet – not unless you're planning to take over from Mr Juby.'

Big Nellie, it seemed, was not the only one to nurse that theory. Or had she suggested it to him?

'There's no question of that, as you must well know.' Charles was getting a little irritated himself. 'How could I take over the paper? You ask Nellie – I don't know narthin more about it than a rook know about a Sunday.' He intended it as a joke, but Mortimer was unamused.

'Crow,' he said. Charles was baffled.

'That's a crow, not a rook. But never mind taking over the paper, what about taking over Wettleford? Maybe that's what they're thinking of, up in Norwich.' He was showing genuine anxiety, and Charles realised he must be one of Nature's worriers. He worried about the Tittlesham Legion dinner, and he worried about keeping his job. Charles did his best to reassure him.

'Of course they're not. They just think Mr Juby could do with a bit more help. They want to build up the paper, not sack people off it. They may want to give *you* an assistant too, for all I know.'

It was the second joke to go wrong.

'Why should they do that?' asked Mortimer quickly. 'Don't they think I can manage? I've managed all these years with Mr Juby, why shouldn't I manage now?'

'For goodness' sake!' Charles began to appreciate Nellie's description. 'Stop being such a great old mawther.'

Mortimer crumpled. 'I'm sorry. I've been a bit jumpy

ever since they bought up Mr Juby. I don't rightly take to them, those folk in Norwich. They're a rum old lot.'

'That they are,' said Charles sympathetically, his imitation Norfolk accent improving by the minute. 'Now. Where's that motorbike?'

He ushered Mortimer ahead of him down the stairs and through the front office. Big Nellie was deep in conversation with a couple of young men sitting on each end of her desk, and she spared them only a fleeting glance. Charles noted that Mortimer paused and beamed at her, and seemed about to go across and interrupt the conversation. Then he caught Charles's eye, blushed again and headed for the door. Charles made a mental note. Here was another sensitive area not to stray into with his Wettleford colleague.

The motorcycle was parked down an alley beside the office. It was a 500cc Triumph, quite a powerful-looking machine. When Mortimer straddled it he seemed to take on a certain authority. 'Ever ridden pillion before?' Charles confessed that he hadn't.

'Feet on the rests, grip with your knees. No need to hang on too tight, just put your hands on my waist to steady yourself. Lean into the bends, not away from them. And if you want to say anything, make sure you shout.' He was putting on a leather flying helmet and a pair of goggles.

'Very good, Cap'n Biggles,' said Charles. Mortimer just looked at him.

They rode sedately out of the Market Place, past Mrs Abbs's council house – Charles thought about waving, then decided against it – and left the town behind.

It was the first time he had seen the Norfolk countryside in the sunshine. The trees and hedges were still bare, but some of the fields were greening over, the winter wheat pushing through. On one field still bare and brown from the plough he saw his first pheasant, strolling unconcernedly along a furrow, and later he saw plenty more browsing beneath the hedges and even

43

standing at the roadside. They knew what he didn't: the season had just ended.

They were off the main road now and deep in the network of deserted lanes that criss-crossed High Norfolk. They rode through villages tucked away in little valleys, all flintstone walls and pantile roofs; lonely clusters of farm buildings, great houses tucked away in parkland behind endless low flint walls. They trundled warily around zig-zag bends between coppices of birch and oak, they rode gently over hump-backed bridges with cattle grazing in the water-meadows on each side.

Sometimes there was a pony leaning over a paddock fence, sometimes a flock of geese crossing the road from the farmyard to the pond. Occasionally they met a tractor towing one of the final loads of the sugar beet season to the concrete stand where the lorries would pick it up. Mercifully the lorries themselves were not about. When they passed a rider hacking along the roadside they would slow to a crawl; the rider would civilly raise a hand in acknowledgement, and just as civilly they would wave back.

Wherever they went, through villages or in open country, there was always a church in sight, one of Norfolk's great medieval churches, legacies of the wool barons, far too large for the communities they served yet still somehow preserved by faith and sales of work.

And over it all, as Charles looked out across the gentle hills and the woods and the scattered buildings, there was the vast Norfolk sky stretching to each horizon. He had never known such a sky in Wembley Park.

Mortimer must have sensed what he was thinking. As they reached the top of a rise he pulled off the road and switched off the engine. Charles walked across to a gateway in the hedge and looked around in silence. He remembered asking himself on that first bus ride from Norwich, what on earth was he doing there. He was beginning to find out.

'This is the boundary between your area and mine.' Mortimer had come up quietly behind him. 'From here up as far as the coast, I cover from Wettleford. I'd say we've got about a hundred and fifty square miles apiece, the same as the old Saxon chieftains. They called their territories the hundreds, and the rural district councils took over much the same areas, and so did Mr Juby, and now so has the Anglian Press. Yours is Launford RDC, mine is Empringham; and I suppose I've got the sea as well.'

Charles looked around again at his new empire. 'What's good enough for a Saxon chieftain,' he said, 'is good enough for me.'

In their new-found companionship, absorbing perhaps a little of the calm from their surroundings, they stood there for a few moments enjoying the quietness. It was Mortimer who moved first.

'We may as well call at Tittlesham while we're out this way and pick up that report. Then perhaps we can find a pub open.'

'From what I've seen of Norfolk pubs,' said Charles, 'that shouldn't be a problem. They never seem to shut.'

'That's in Toftham. It's different out in the villages. You'll see.'

They took a side lane and headed for Tittlesham, the frontier town as Charles pictured it, the last outpost before entering Thirkle country. But it seemed much the same as all the rest, a winding main street with a couple of little shops in the centre and a pub at each end, lanes running off each side with cottages clustered along them, the church set on its own by the small green, its grave-yard overgrown and most of the stones faded and worn, only the war memorial rising well clear of the long grass. Mortimer pulled up outside the Post Office Stores.

'Come and meet Mrs Boggis. She's been village correspondent here for as long as Mr Juby's had the paper, but she still doesn't know whether to send her reports to Toftham or Wettleford. She generally just puts "Mr Juby, The Journal" on the envelope and lets the post-man decide. It always turns up sooner or later.'

He led the way into the shop. Vegetables were lined

up in trays and open boxes, there were shelves of tins and bottles. Stacked in the middle was an assortment of fireguards and saucepans and crockery, in no particular order. A counter with a glass window and a posting-box was in the far corner. The place seemed deserted.

They walked over to the counter. Beyond the glass, but easily accessible through the gap beneath it, Charles could see sheets of stamps, a cashbox, and other official-looking papers. Mortimer reached through, and for a moment Charles thought he was going to get mixed up in a Post Office raid. But he only rapped on the counter and shouted through the gap, 'Come on, Mrs Boggis. Customers!'

'Hold you hard, then,' came a voice from somewhere beyond. 'I'm now comin'.'

The door behind the counter opened and Mrs Boggis appeared, a plump little soul in a headscarf and pinafore and carpet slippers. Charles guessed she was in her sixties, but he underestimated by nearly twenty years.

She beamed at Mortimer. 'Why, if that hent the boy Morty. I thought I hear that machine o'yourn. How are you a-goin' on boy?'

Mortimer assured her he was in good health, enquired after hers, and introduced Charles. Mrs Boggis beamed at him as she had at Mortimer. 'Nice to meet you, my man. You're in good hands with young Morty here. He's a good lad, like his father were. Up-'n-down straight like a yard o' pump-water, he is. You'll come to no harm with him.'

Mortimer blushed. 'You'll have to make allowances for Mrs Boggis,' he told Charles. 'She was at the same village school as my father. I think you rather fancied him, didn't you?'

'Never you mind, boy,' she admonished him, but she was still beaming. 'Yew keep to your writing, and let the past be gone. That's no concern o'yourn.'

Mortimer asked her about the British Legion report. 'Where did you send it this time?'

'I hent sent that nowhere yit.' Mrs Boggis was a

little put out. 'Blast, that only happened last Toosday. Whatever's the rush?'

'I think it was the Tuesday before last, Mrs Boggis. Have you done the write-up yet?'

'That I have. I just hent been able to get to the post.'

Charles looked at her in some puzzlement. The post-box was just beside the counter. 'Thass no use,' she explained. 'Old Henry lost the key to that a year or so back, so nobody posts anything in there. There's the other box at the end of the village.'

'Then shouldn't you block up the hole?' asked Charles. She looked at him in astonishment.

'Whatever for, boy? I just told you, everyone knows that hent to be used. And if one of Old Henry's inspectors come round and finds it blocked up, he'd have to explain he'd lost the key, and that wouldn't do him much good, now would it?'

'But couldn't you just hand him the letters when he calls, instead of posting them down the other end of the village?'

'How can I do that when he don't call? There's no point in him calling if he hent got to empty the box, now is there?'

The conversation was developing an unreal quality for Charles, but he persisted. 'Then what about parcels and registered letters and that sort of thing? He's got to call here for them, surely?'

'Well now, we don't get too many of them to worry about in these parts. People mostly go to Toftham if they want to post that sort o' caper. So long as they can buy their stamps and collect their pensions, that's all they want here. And that's the way I like it, my man. There's too many forms these days; I can't be bothered with them.'

'Quite right too, Mrs Boggis,' interjected Mortimer. He had become increasingly embarrassed by Charles's interrogation. 'Now how about that report?'

She went through the back to collect it. While she was absent Charles felt he had to make one more point, though more people had come into the shop and were taking great interest in the conversation. 'All that money,' he said, pointing at the cashbox and the sheets of stamps on the counter. 'Shouldn't she keep that locked up? Anybody could help themselves while she was out of the shop.'

Mortimer regarding him patiently. 'I suppose anybody could. But nobody would. You're a long way from London now.'

Mrs Boggis returned with an envelope and handed it to Mortimer. Inscribed on it in beautiful copperplate with hardly a waver was the address: 'Mr Juby, The Journal'. Mortimer thanked her and put it in his pocket.

'Anything interesting in the speeches?' he asked, as they prepared to leave.

'Don't be daft,' said Mrs Boggis. 'Who listens to the speeches? But don't you worry boy, I got all the names of the ladies that did the supper, and the winners in the raffle. You don't need to worry about no speeches.'

'Of course not,' said Mortimer. As they went out the door he murmured to Charles, 'Let's hope the chairman didn't say anything too important. He could have stood up and said "Heil Hitler" and I'd still be the last to know.' He was worrying again.

'Supposing,' said Charles, 'we try and get that drink. I've seen two pubs in the village. There's the Ostrich up one end and the Hero at the other. Which'll it be?'

'No use trying the Ostrich. The chap who runs it drives a tractor up at Manor Farm, and his wife works part-time in Toftham while the children are at school. They never open until the evening. We'd better try the Hero.'

They rode gently down the village street towards the Hero, where Lord Nelson glared at the world from above the door. Charles had seen many such portraits on their tour.

'A local lad?' he shouted over Mortimer's shoulder.

'Born in my area,' Mortimer shouted back, with a

hint of pride. 'There's more pubs named after Nelson in Norfolk than all your London kings and queens.'

Charles felt foolishly jealous. 'Any heroes from my area I ought to know about?'

'I suppose there's Boadicea,' replied Mortimer dubiously. 'But she was a woman, of course. She doesn't count for much round here.'

They pulled up in the empty forecourt of the Hero, and Mortimer bade him dismount. 'Better try the door before I switch off. It's just as likely to be locked. They don't get many tourists in Tittlesham.'

Charles was tempted to start a new discussion on the vagaries of Norfolk opening hours, but he tried the door first. It was open.

The public bar had dark brown walls, a darker brown ceiling and a grate full of cigarette ends. A few wooden chairs were scattered round the wall and an old piece of carpet led to an ageing dartboard. The bar itself bore a few dirty glasses, relics presumably of the previous night's excitements. On the shelf behind was a gin bottle, nearly empty, and a whiskey bottle, emptier still. There was also a cardboard carton marked Smith's Crisps, and some boxes of matches. The atmosphere was not so much musty as vault-like. It was all about as welcoming as a dentist's chair.

'At least it's open,' muttered Charles. 'We should be able to get something.'

'Not necessarily,' said Mortimer, and displayed a rare moment of humour. 'They could all be dead.'

They weren't. A large man appeared, in braces and collarless shirt, unshaven and so far as Charles could tell, unwashed.

'Yes?' he snapped. Mortimer gulped and blushed.

'Eh?' the man snapped again. Charles came to the rescue.

'Two pints of beer, please.'

'Only bottled. Light or brown?'

Charles ordered two brown ales. From below the bar the landlord produced two dusty bottles and two glasses, almost as grubby as those already on the counter. He rubbed them briefly on his sleeve and poured out the beer. In spite of holding the bottles at a considerable height he managed to produce only a vestige of froth. It seemed there was not a very fast turnover of brown ale at the Hero.

'Any chance of a sandwich?' asked Charles.

The landlord looked at him coldy. 'We don't do meals.'

'We'll have some crisps then, please.'

'No crisps.'

'What about the box?' Charles dared to ask.

The landlord looked at the box, then looked at Charles, then tipped the box over. It was empty.

'Anything else?'

They shook their heads. He took the money for the beer from Charles, put it in his trouser pocket, and leaned on the bar, looking at them. He did not speak, he just looked. In an embarrassed silence they drank their very flat brown ale, handed back the glasses, and with a mumbled word of thanks headed for the door.

'Ere', called the landlord. They turned.

'I've got some crisps coming on Friday.'

Norfolk hospitality was not quite dead.

As they rode back to Toftham Charles shouted in Mortimer's ear, 'Are all the village pubs like that at lunchtime?'

Mortimer nodded. 'Mostly.'

A thought struck Charles. 'Does Mr Juby ever go round the villages?'

'Never,' shouted Mortimer.

Charles smiled to himself and looked at his watch. They should just be in time for a ham roll at the Dog and Partridge.

Four

It was Friday morning.

Friday was the day of judgement for the staff of the *Toftham and Wettleford Journal*. It was the day the paper came out, and Charles's morning was generally occupied in fending off complaints, acting on guidance given by Mr Juby.

If it was an error in a report it was the fault of the printers in Norwich – 'out of our hands, sir.' If it was a report left out, it was pressure of space – 'that'll be in next week, madam.' Mr Juby was only called in for the more serious cases. One week it was a mix-up in the photographs on the wedding page; the blame, quite fairly, was laid on the printers, but Mr Juby still had to promise the weeping brides they would reprint the photos correctly the following week. There was also the embarrassing occasion when two paragraphs in adjoining funeral reports were transposed, and a repsected local spinster was credited with an extensive family of children and grandchildren. The apology next week was even longer than the original report. Fridays could be quite harrowing in the *Journal* office.

This Friday the rush had subsided and Charles was pondering, as he did about this time every week, on whether he should cut out his own contributions on the *Journal* and preserve them for posterity. He still had his opening masterpiece, featuring the Methodist Women's Own, and there was that first funeral with the final line that meant much more to him than the readers: 'Funeral arrangements by W. Pendleton and Son'. And there was the Tittlesham Legion dinner, which Mortimer had passed over to him with the gentle advice not to alter a word if he ever expected to get a report from Mrs Boggis again.

He also had an assortment of paragraphs from 'Round the Churches', some items about the Chamber of Trade gleaned from Mr Hurn, and a number of road accident reports which he acquired from his daily visits to the police station, in which he had been careful to follow Mr Juby's firm instructions. A vehicle never hit anything or anybody, it was always 'in collision with'. He still found it odd to report that a harmless pedestrian was 'in collision with' a ten-ton lorry, but he gathered it was something to do with legal liability, a field of knowledge he had yet to penetrate, so he followed his instructions blindly.

He browsed through the current week's crop of Benson gems. Mostly they were a couple of sentences, then the inevitable list of names and initials. Stallholders, prize-winners, officers elected, among those present . . .

Ridiculous, thought Charles, as he thought every Friday. Nevertheless they were his earliest printed works. When his story came to be told, these humble paragraphs could be collectors' items. He was reaching for the scissors when Mr Juby came down the stairs.

'Any problems?'

Charles knew the question was superfluous. Mr Juby could hear most of what went on below him. 'Just some raffle winners left off a W.I. report, and the Salvation Army house-to-house collection only raised £22, not £222.

Mr Juby tut-tutted. 'Printers, no doubt?'

Charles nodded solemnly. 'Printers.'

Mr Juby wandered across to the window and looked down on the Market Place. Friday was also market day, and the cobbles were covered with stalls and trailers. Cars and vans still struggled to get around them, much hampered by the pedestrians, who wandered unconcernedly on the roadways, tapping warningly on the bonnet if a vehicle came too close. Toftham Market had still not adjusted to the age of the motor car.

'You'll need to get out in the villages a bit more, now

Mortimer's shown you round. How do you reckon you're going to do that?'

Charles hadn't really thought about it. The railway line that came out from Norwich and linked Toftham with Wettleford wandered through some of the villages in his area, and there were a few buses to the other larger ones, but he assumed most of the contact would be by telephone. Mr Juby had seemed to get by on that principle.

'I don't think I could afford a motorbike just yet,' he said cautiously.

'No, no, we don't need a fleet of motorbikes. One's enough. I reckon a push-bike is what you need. Very cheap, very healthy. Do you a world of good.'

Charles remembered Mortimer's warning about Norfolk's deceptive terrain, but decided this was not the time to raise it. Instead he suggested that even a bicycle might be beyond his means.

'Nonsense,' said Mr Juby. 'Not if you get it in the market.'

Charles joined him by the window and looked down at the stalls. Some were draped with nightdresses and petticoats, others offered sickly-coloured sweets; there was any amount of crockery and china ornaments and bits of brass. The fruit and vegetables were at one end of the market by the war memorial, the fish and meat at the other. There was no sign of any bikes.

'Not down there,' Mr Juby told him. 'At the auction. Starts in the back yard of the Dog and Partridge at eleven. You'd better get round there; they sell the bikes first.'

Charles felt for his wallet. 'I don't think I have enough on me. Only five pounds or so . . .'

'Only five pounds?' Mr Juby was amazed. 'You won't need five pounds for that sort of bike, boy. A pound or two at the most. And perhaps a couple of bob for a few tools to hold the thing together.'

He took a pound note out of his own wallet and handed it over to Charles. 'That's office transport you're buying, so the *Toftham and Wettleford Journal* will go halves. I'll square it with Norwich later.'

Charles thanked him and headed for the door.

'Just remember, boy,' Mr Juby roared after him. 'Don't you go bloody mad.'

The back yard of the Dog and Partridge, normally used as a car park, was a scene of enormous activity. Set out in rows were pieces of dilapidated furniture, piles of garden tools, old trunks and suitcases, rusty lawn-mowers, dubious-looking cookers and washing machines, lengths of piping, rolls of wire, all manner of ancient farm machinery in various stages of disrepair. Milling about amongst it was a chattering crowd, trying out the chairs, sorting through the tools, peering into the cookers. Charles plunged into the throng and sought out the bikes.

There were about a dozen of them, propped up against a wall, some with flat tyres, some with bent handlebars, some short of a pedal or a chain, all of them coated with rust. He surveyed them without enthusiasm. Mr Juby's pound note, he thought, ought to buy the lot.

He examined them more closely. There was just one which might pass. It was a sit-up-and-beg affair, with a full complement of pedals, reasonable straight handle-bars, and both tyres fully inflated. There was only one drawback. It had a metal basket on the front, and slung from the crossbar was a metal plate which said:

Geo. Perkins: Purveyor of Good Meats

Charles was pulling at the nameplate to see if it was detachable when a handbell was rung vigorously just behind him. A little man in a brown coat was brandishing it; the crowd was thickening up around him. In the midst of the crush, head and shoulders above the rest, was a commanding figure in a bright green tweed suit under a leather jerkin, surmounted by a curly-brimmed brown felt hat. He carried a clipboard with a sheaf of papers. He shoved his way to the front of the crowd and stood beside the bikes. The auction was about to begin.

'Mornin'-mornin'-mornin',' he shouted. He was obviously used to shouting. He was also used to repeating himself. And he spoke in hyphens.

'Here-we-go-then-here-we-go-then. Lot-one-lot-one-lot-one. Cycle-in-need-of-repair.'

Lot one actually needed a lot more than repair. It needed half another bike to make up for the missing saddle, the missing chain, the two missing tyres, and the badly bent front forks.

'Who'll-gimme-two-gimme-two?' demanded the auctioneer. His voice made Mr Juby's sound like a whisper.

Two? thought Charles. He can't mean . . .

He didn't. 'Who'll-do-a-florin-a-florin-a-florin? Mr Futter? Thank you. Where's two-and-six-two-and-six?'

The bidding struggled up to four shillings, and died. The half-bike was sold to Mr Futter. So were lots two, three and four, none of them fetching more than ten shillings. Mr Futter, Charles deduced, was either in scrap business or marketed very unreliable reconditioned bikes.

'Lot-five-lot-five-lot-five. Delivery-bike-first-rate-condition, ready-to-ride-away. Who'll-gimme-ten-shillings-ten-ten-ten?'

'Yes,' cried Charles. He knew immediately he had made a tactical error. Every eye turned upon him, not least the eye of Mr Futter, whom Charles had picked out by now in the crowd, a formidable figure with a beard and a flat cap.

The auctioneer paused. He very nearly licked his lips.

'Ten-I-have-ten-I-have-ten-where's-fifteen-fifteen-fifteen? Thank you Mr Futter, fifteen-fifteen. Do I have a-pound-a-pound-a-pound?' He was looking directly at Charles.

Charles nodded.

Mr Futter went to twenty-five shillings, Charles to thirty. Mr Futter hesitated before going to thirty-five. Charles nodded for two pounds, and felt victory within his grasp.

'I have two-pounds-two-pounds-two-pounds. Do I hear more? It's in the front at two-pounds-two-pounds.'

Charles looked across at Mr Futter, but Mr Futter had turned his back. I've-got-it-I've-got-it, he thought exultantly. The auctioneer's style was catching.

'It's going-at-two-going-at-two . . .'

'Fifty bob', shouted someone at the back of the crowd. Charles was stunned.

'At-fifty at-fifty at-fifty!' The auctioneer stared expectantly at Charles. Everyone else stared expectantly at him too. A surge of resentment overcame him. The bicycle, he felt, was morally his. He had fought Mr Futter in bid-to-bid combat and emerged triumphant. Now some outsider was robbing him of the spoils of victory. Hoping he looked calmer than he felt, he nodded again.

'I have three-pound-three-pound. Three-fifty-three-fifty. Four-four-four. Four-fifty-four-fifty . . .'

It was all moving too fast for Charles. He found himself nodding helplessly. He had no idea who had bid what. The auctioneer spotted his confusion.

'It's against you at four-fifty, going at four-fifty, going at four-fifty . . .'

He could sense the entire yard willing him on. The bizarre thought struck him that if he gave up now, he would never hold his head up in Toftham again. His nod was almost imperceptible, but it was enough.

'I have five-five-five.' A murmur of appreciation went round the crowd. Charles waited, half of him eager for victory, the other half longing for another bid to release him from this expensive folly. He recalled Mr Juby's parting warning: 'Don't go bloody mad!' It was too late.

'Sold at five pounds!'

A considerable hubbub broke out. Charles stood in a daze as the auctioneer leaned towards him. 'Mister . . . ?'

'Benson,' muttered Charles.

'Benson!' roared the auctioneer. The whole of Toftham knew who had bought Geo. Perkins' delivery bike.

For the first time in his life, Charles was experiencing notoriety. It was not an unpleasant sensation.

'Well done, Charlie boy,' said a voice behind him. It was Freddie Pendleton, undertaker, face-puller and practical joker. 'That must be a world record for a butcher-boy's bike. You done well there.'

Realisation dawned. 'Was that you bidding at the back?

'Naturally,' said Freddy. 'Just what I needed, that bike. Lot cheaper to run than the hearse. Might have had to make the basket a big bigger, of course, but I'd only have to change Perkins to Pendleton and that could still be "Purveyor of Good Meats". The relatives would really appreciate that.'

'You realise,' said Charles bitterly, 'you made me pay three pounds more to get that bike, just for a laugh.'

'I didn't make you.' Freddy was serious for a moment. 'You could have stopped any time, then you'd have landed me in it instead. That's what auctions are all about, Charlie boy. You'll learn. Come on, you can settle for the bike later. I'll buy you a drink.'

Charles was still in the farmers' bar when Mr Juby came across for his lunchtime refreshment. Freddy had bought him a beer, then departed, presumably to go about his macabre business. Charles felt he needed to fortify himself further before facing the world with his new acquisition.

'How d'you get on then?' Mr Juby asked, as Maggie poured his usual special.

Charles decided to get it over. 'Come and see,' he said, and ushered him to the rear yard. Some of the lots had already been removed but the bicycles were still propped up against the wall. Mr Futter had been refreshing himself also.

'Which one do you think I bought?'

Mr Juby seemed strangely amused. 'That's pretty obvious, I should say.'

Puzzled, Charles looked more closely at the bikes. He

57

realised that Freddie Pendleton had not had an inter-
ment in mind when he left the Dog and Partridge. The
name-plate on the delivery bike had been repainted, in
an amateurish hand. Parts of the original inscription had
been blotted out, and replaced with the new lettering.

It now read: *Chas Benson: Purveyor of Good News.*

'Tel you what, boy,' said Mr Juby. 'I'll give you
another pound towards the fiver you paid for this old
heap. It's worth it for the advertizing.' He was still
chuckling as they headed back towards the bar.

'How did you know I paid five pounds?' asked
Charles.

'George Perkins came in and told me, him that sold
the bike. He couldn't believe his luck. So he left a little
present for you, by way of appreciation.'

They reached the bar and took up their drinks.

'What's the present?' asked Charles.

'That's a bicycle pump. He bought it specially, just
to give it to you.'

Charles felt a little better. 'That's very kind of him.'

'Well, not entirely.' Mr Juby took another sip at his
special. 'He thinks you may need it very shortly. He
only pumped up those tyres just before the auction. He
reckons they'll both be down again by this afternoon . . .'

Charles's first public appearance on his bicycle created
quite a sensation. He had handed over his five pounds
and collected the pump from the office to blow up the
tyres which as Mr Perkins had predicted were quite flat.
He had a trial spin around the yard, his balance only
slightly impaired by his lunch-time libations, then rode
boldly out into the Market Place.

As he emerged he was startled to hear a ripple of
applause from the customers at the nearest stalls. It
followed him as he circled the Market Place, weaving
between walkers and traffic. Word of his profligate
spending had obviously got round.

Somewhat exhilarated, he made another circuit before
pulling up outside the *Journal* office. Awaiting him on

the pavement were some of Big Nellie's followers, young men in crew cuts and jeans who whistled and cheered as he drew up beside them. Then Nellie herself emerged from the office, bearing a laurel wreath made out of green cardboard file covers stapled together, and hung it ceremoniously round his neck.

'The winner!' she announced. 'Safely home, and not another rider in sight.'

'Give him a kiss, Nellie!' shouted one of her entourage, and Nellie did, with great panache, both her hands behind his head and her magnificent chest pressed firmly against his, quite crushing the cardboard file covers.

'Oh stop it, Nellie,' gasped Charles, hoping she wouldn't. 'Or at least let me get off this bike.'

In this moment of triumph a terrible roar came from a window two floors above. It almost silenced the Market Place. 'That's enough of that nonsense. Get you up here, boy, there's a job for you. Nellie, you put him down.'

Charles smiled at her sheepishly, put his bike in the alley beside the office, and went off to report to Mr Juby. Behind him he would hear Nellie and her friends laughing, but he did not feel too despondent. For a moment or two he had been part of the fun. It was the first time Nellie had treated him with familiarity. Was it a breakthrough, or would it be back to 'hallo', and 'goodbye', and 'there's someone to see you in the office'? He was still deep in such thoughts when he entered Mr Juby's office.

'Take that stoopid thing off and clean up your face.' Mr Juby's lunch-time good humour had disappeared. Charles removed the cardboard laurel wreath and wiped away the lipstick round his mouth. He noticed that some of the white paint Freddy had used on the name-plate had come off on to his trousers, and he tried to wipe that off too.

It was not Nellie's attitude he should be worrying about, it was Mr Juby's, he thought miserably. And Mr Juby was in no mood for suffering bedraggled fools gladly.

'Did you make the police call this afternoon?' Mr Juby's tone made it clear that he already knew the answer. In the excitement of the auction and the events that had followed, he had quite forgotten.

'Then you won't know about Mrs Boggis. Luckily the sergeant gave me a ring to let me know. Poor old lady's been robbed. All her Post Office takings gone, and she's had quite a scare herself. They'll want this one in Norwich for the *Morning News.*' The *East Anglian Morning News* was the daily paper published by Anglian Press. District offices were expected to supply it with any news of general interest to the county. Unlike the London papers, no extra payments were involved.

'Is that Mrs Boggis at Tittlesham?'

'Of course it is.' Mr Juby was already putting some paper in the typewriter. 'I'll write a holding piece from what the sergeant gave me and put it on the five o'clock bus. You get on that bike of yours and go and talk to her, and some of the neighbours, and the local PC. That's Billy Dugdale, he's a helpful lad.'

Charles remembered the empty shop, the open cash-box, the gap between the counter and the window. And Mortimer saying, 'Anybody could – but nobody would.' Now somebody had.

As he started down the stairs he barely noticed Mr Juby shouting after him: 'And don't forget to take your pump . . .'

The Norfolk countryside did not look as idyllic from the saddle of a pushbike as it had from Mortimer's pillion. The saddle itself was wrinkled and lumpy, and the gentle undulations which the motorbike had sailed over so effortlessly now seemed dauntingly steep. Mercifully it was not raining, but the winter afternoon was chilling off and the light started to fade. Charles realised gloomily that Geo. Perkins must have made all his meat deliveries in daylight; there were no front or rear lights on the bike.

He had studied the map on the office wall before

leaving to remind himself of the route, and fortunately the signs to Tittlesham were fairly clear. But it was a good hour before he saw the cluster of houses with the church towering above them, and rode past The Hero and down the village street to the Post Office Stores.

There was a little group of women outside the shop. They eyed the name-plate on his bike with interest.

'That must be a long ride from Fleet Street, my man,' said one of them, with some concern. He forced a smile. 'Most of it was downhill,' he assured her.

She did not smile at all. It occurred to him, for a nasty moment, that she was probably quite serious. In Norfolk he would never be absolutely certain.

'What a shame about Mrs Boggis,' he said, changing the subject. 'I thought it would be easy for anyone to reach over that counter and take the money.'

A little ripple ran through the group. The woman who had spoken to him first looked at him more closely. 'You been here before, then?'

'Oh yes, just a few days ago. The cashbox was on the counter, and Mrs Boggis wasn't about, and none of you ladies was in the shop. I could have taken it then, if I'd wanted.'

'Could you indeed?' There was a touch of menace now in the woman's voice, and her companions were exchanging glances. Suddenly, suspicion hung heavily in the air.

'But I didn't, of course,' Charles added hastily.

'Not that time you didn't,' said the woman with deep significance.

'Not any time,' Charles insisted desperately. 'Really, not any time.' He wondered rather wildly if there were still cases of lynching in deepest Norfolk. 'I came here with Mortimer Thirkle.'

It was as if the clouds had suddenly lifted.

'You came with Morty? Why didn't you say so, you great pillock.' The woman relaxed, and so did Charles.

'May I go in now, please?' he asked meekly. They

ushered him towards the door. Inside was Mortimer Thirkle.

'What on earth are you doing here?' asked Charles, genuinely surprised.

Mortimer blushed deeply. 'I'm terribly sorry, I knew you had no transport, and we're never quite certain whose area this is, and anyway Mrs Dugdale rang me up to tell me about it, and we don't often get a robbery, and I just thought I ought to come out.'

Mortimer was getting more and more miserable as he reeled off his explanation. Charles actually had no doubt which area Tittlesham was in – Mr Juby had made it very clear when they returned from their motorbike ride, which was why Mortimer had handed over the British Legion report. Mr Juby had instructed him personally to cover the story, and he had cycled several uncomfortable miles to do so. There was no reason for Mortimer to be involved.

He looked at Mortimer's downcast face. The stoop, always slightly there, was now more pronounced. He may have been over-zealous, but he had probably waited years for a story like this, now it looked like slipping away from him.

Charles made a decision. 'I just came out to help,' he said cheerfully. 'Mr Juby thought I'd pick up a few tips if I saw how you handled it.'

Even then Mortimer could not shed his worries. 'You mean he sent you to keep an eye on me,' he muttered.

Charles could not conceal his exasperation. 'Nothing of the sort,' he snapped. 'Morty, do grow up.'

Mortimer, twenty years his senior, swallowed and stood up a little straighter. 'I'm sorry. Ever since those Norwich people took over . . .'

'I know. Let's not worry about Norwich just now. Shouldn't we be talking to somebody?'

Mortimer had already talked to most people – PC Dugdale and Mrs Dugdale, and all the women outside. He was waiting now to talk to Mrs Boggis, who was still with PC Dugdale in the back room. Apparently she had been there when she heard a noise in the shop and found someone by the post office counter, reaching through for the cashbox. She had shouted at him and he had waved his fist at her, then he had run out of the shop with the cashbox and she heard him drive away.

'Any idea who he was?'

'That's what I want to find out,' said Mortimer.

A young policeman emerged from the back room, putting away his notebook. He nodded at Mortimer and looked enquiringly at Charles. Mortimer introduced PC Dugdale, and asked how he had got on.

Mrs Boggis, it seemed, was still very upset. She hadn't been able to give a description of the intruder, except that he was a young man with no distinguishing marks. Mortimer asked if they could have a word with her, and PC Dugdale said he had no objection; it was up to her, and he would go back and ask her.

It transpired that Mrs Boggis would talk to the boy Morty, but not that other young feller. Charles mused wryly that he would have had to hand over the story to Mortimer anyway; he was glad he had made the gesture first.

He chatted with Billy Dugdale and found he had only just been posted to the village, but had lived in the area all his life and knew Mortimer well. 'But then, everyone around Wettleford knows Morty,' he said. 'The Thirkles have been in these parts since the Domesday Book. You won't find their name in it, of course. They came under the heading of "serfs and villeins".'

Mortimer reappeared, looking almost cheerful. He was hardly stooping at all. 'I think I can help you a bit, Mr Dugdale,' he said. 'The young chap who did this didn't need to have any distinguishing marks. Mrs Boggis knew who he was anyway. It's that lad that delivers the vegetables from Mr Nicholson up at Manor Farm. He must have thought he could get in and out of the shop without her seeing him.'

PC Dugdale was grateful, but somewhat annoyed.

'Why ever didn't she say all that when I talked to her, then?'

'She said she was nervous about telling you in case you didn't believe her. She thought you might be a friend of his, or it might get her in bad with Mr Nicholson, and he wouldn't let her have vegetables any more. She's not quite thinking straight at the moment. But I said you and I were old friends, and it would be all right if I told you.'

Dugdale shrugged. 'I'd better have another word with her, then I'll be off up to Manor Farm. I'm much obliged to you, Morty. Perhaps if I'm here another twenty years or so, people will talk to me too.' Charles knew how he felt.

'What happens now?' he asked Mortimer as the young officer went back to see Mrs Boggis.

'I'll go up to Manor Farm with him and see how he gets on up there. Then I'll go back to Wettleford and phone through the story to Norwich – if that's all right with you?' Mortimer was worrying again.

'Of course it's all right with me. It's your story. I'd better be getting back to Toftham before Mr Dugdale notices I haven't got any lights.'

He pointed out of the shop window at his delivery bike, propped against the kerb. 'Unless I can give you a lift,' he offered. 'I owe you one for that ride you gave me. Can you fit into the basket?'

'That's very good of you,' said Mortimer seriously. 'But actually I do have my motorbike.'

Charles looked at him carefully. No, in Norfolk he would never be quite certain.

Back in Toftham, aching and saddlesore after his ride through the darkened lanes, he found Mr Juby ensconced as usual in the Dog and Partridge, enjoying his second special. He told him what had happened and Mr Juby accepted his explanation with an equanimity above and beyond the effect of two specials. It turned out that Mr Nicholson of Manor Farm had phoned his old friend and drinking companion to advise him about the transgressions of his employee, while Charles was still cycling back. And he had some further information.

'Seems his lad was in the shop some days back when he heard some feller say how easy it would be to take the cashbox off the counter. Says that's what put the idea in his head. Some London feller, he said. Now I wonder who that could've been.'

'I can't imagine,' said Charles, and by the way of counter-attack he observed a little sourly, 'No doubt you've telephoned the story to London?'

'No doubt at all,' said Mr Juby.

Charles made his way home to a late meal and the wrath of Mrs Abbs, reflecting ruefully on his first major assignment. Mortimer had the story, Mr Juby had the money, he had the guilty conscience and a sore backside.

Would it be ever thus?

Five

'Samuel Jesse Johnson, you are charged that on the night of March 25th last at approximately eleven-thirty p.m. you were drunk and disorderly in a public place, namely outside the Golden Fleece public house in Toftham Market Place. Do you plead guilty or not guilty?'

Charles had been struggling to decipher his notes on the previous case, but at the mention of the Golden Fleece he looked up to study the defendant. The pub was only a few doors away from the *Journal* office, much frequented by the less desirable elements of the town, who also frequented the pavement outside the office hoping for an encounter with Big Nellie.

He recognised Samuel Jesse Johnson as one of the regular members of the group. They had often exchanged glances as he made his way in or out. The glances were not over-friendly. His privileged position as occupier of the office above Nellie's did not make him too popular with Sam and his friends.

'Not guilty, sir.'

In the dock Sam wore an ingratiating smile instead of his usual belligerent scowl. He also wore a blue serge suit, a fairly white shirt and a tie, none of which was normal gear for the clientele of the Golden Fleece.

'You may sit down Mr Johnson,' said Major Burney. The Clerk seemed as impressed by this metamorphosis as Charles.

He called the first witness and Charles concentrated. It was the first time he had covered Toftham Court on his own. Mr Juby had accompanied him up to now, explaining the basic rules of evidence, the distinction between a summons and a charge, the different procedures for pleas of guilty and not guilty, the need to insert 'alleged' into almost every sentence. Toftham

Court rarely had to handle anything more complex than speeding cases, outdated dog licences, and the occasional indecent exposure, so it was not too long before Charles was allowed to fly solo on the reporters' bench. The case of Samuel Jesse Johnson was his biggest yet.

PC Malcolm Blewitt was the only witness for the prosecution. He had had some difficulty, Charles gathered, in persuading Sam's drinking companions to provide corroborative evidence. But the facts seemed straightforward. He had been called to a disturbance outside the Golden Fleece, and arrived to find Sam standing on the pavement, singing very loudly, and not terribly tunefully, 'I've got a lovely bunch of coconuts'.

'His breath smelt of alcohol and he was unsteady on his feet. I came to the conclusion he was drunk.'

PC Blewitt, a veteran of such encounters, did not arrest him immediately. He suggested instead that he might end his serenade and retire to his bed. Sam's response was to wave his arms in a threatening manner and offer to demonstrate the full size and beauty of his coconuts. He also fell down a couple of times. PC Blewitt then took him into custody.

Sam elected to conduct his own defence. It was true, he said, that he had been humming quietly to himself when the officer arrived, but that was no reason for Mr Blewitt to adopt such an offensive and provocative manner. He did not threaten him with coconuts or anything else, he merely raised his arms in supplication, and in doing so misjudged the height of the kerb.

Major Burney allowed him to give his explanation then enquired how much he had to drink prior to his encounter with PC Blewitt. Sam did not care to hazard a guess. 'No more than usual,' was as far as he would go. On further questioning, however, it transpired that he had been in the Golden Fleece from the time it opened until it eventually shut. Allowing for the variability of licensing hours in Toftham – the doors were probably only closed with PC Blewitt appeared – this meant a period of anything up to five hours.

Major Burney pursued the matter no further.

The three magistrates on the Bench went through the motions of having a consultation. Charles did not bother to take a bet with himself over the outcome. He suspected that Sam Johnson was already well-known to them; and in a straight test of credibility between Sam and PC Blewitt, there was little doubt who would be believed.

The fine was £10 with £2 costs. Sam was given a month to pay.

As he left the dock he caught Charles' eye. The look he gave him was calculating, instead of the usual glare. Charles felt a certain unease. He kept his eyes on his notebook until the next case was called.

When he emerged into the Market Place, Sam Johnson was waiting for him.

'Can I have a word?'

Charles was not sure about the ethics of the situation, but he could see no way of avoiding it. 'What is it?'

Sam nodded towards the Golden Fleece, on the other side of the Market Place. 'Fancy a drink?'

Charles was taken aback. He had never been inside the Golden Fleece. To make his debut as the guest of Samuel Jesse Johnson would be as gratifying in its own way as being introduced by Mr Juby into the Dog and Partridge. He was torn between a natural inclination to be civil and a growing suspicion about Sam's motive.

'I'm afraid I have to get back to the office. I've got these court cases to write up.'

'That's what I wanted a word about,' said Sam. Charles's suspicions were confirmed. 'Fact is, my mum's very poorly at the moment. Could be fatal, the doctor says. I wouldn't want her to be worried when she sees the paper on Friday.'

Charles was not sure how to handle this. In theory he knew he should brush Sam aside; but Sam was not looking very brushable. Instead he suggested tentatively that if Mrs Johnson was so poorly she would not want to see the paper anyway. It appeared however that she was one of the *Journal*'s most avid readers. Even on her sick-bed she liked to read it right through. She would think it very strange if this week's issue failed to reach her.

Charles tried another tack. 'It's not really my decision. You'd better ask Mr Juby.'

Sam's ingratiating smile disappeared; he assumed his customary scowl.

'I'm not talking about Mr Juby, I'm talking about you. You don't need to tell him about it at all.'

Charles guessed it would be no use trying to explain that Mr Juby knew everything that went on in Toftham, particularly in Toftham Court. Sam was obviously determined to make him personally responsible for his mother's survival.

'I'll see what I can do,' he muttered. He knew he should be taking a firmer line, but even in a suit Sam was quite a daunting figure.

'You do,' growled Sam. 'I'd appreciate that.' And he added, to Charles's increased discomfiture, 'So would my mates.'

He accompanied him to the door of the office, and gave him a final nudge.

'One more thing,' he said. 'Watch out with Nellie.' And he headed off for the Golden Fleece.

Inside the front office Nellie looked at him suspiciously. 'What you been up to with Sam?'

'I haven't been up to anything. It was just – business.'

'Funny sort of business that must be,' she sniffed. Then her manner changed. The sniff turned to a smile, almost an ingratiating smile. For a moment Charles thought she must be in league with Sam and was going to plead with him about the ailing Mrs Johnson. His heart sank. To refuse an appeal from Nellie would be even more difficult than fending off Sam. But he was wrong.

'You doing anything Saturday night?'

Saturday night! The traditional night for romance in

Toftham, for lovers' trysts and the pledging of troths. Charles had come upon them frequently on his way home from the Dog and Partridge, sometimes in shop doorways, sometimes in the alley next to the office, sometimes quite blatantly on the seats beside the war memorial. In his mind, birds began to sing.

'I think I'm free,' he said. 'Why?'

'How do you fancy the Young Farmers' Club dance?'

'I fancy it very much.' He could not conceal his enthusiasm. That bit of fun over the delivery bike must have done the trick. Nellie had accepted him at last.

'You mean you'd like me to escort you?'

'Well, not exactly.' She seemed a little taken aback. 'It's just that I've got to sell six tickets and I've only got rid of five so far. Would you like the other one? I've tried everyone else. They're three-and-sixpence.'

Charles was crestfallen, but not crushed. At least he was being offered a sporting chance, albeit not too graciously. At five-to-one the odds were not too overwhelming. Three-and-sixpence was a small price to pay for a foot in Nellie's door.

He went upstairs to his office in buoyant mood, clutching his three-and-sixpenny passport to unknown adventures on Saturday night. But as he put it in his pocket he felt the notebook and remembered he had a more pressing matter to resolve.

There was no point in trying to keep Sam's court case from Mr Juby. He always asked to see the court list, and would certainly notice a case of drunk and disorderly. But after all it was a minor offence, no harm had been done to anyone, and Sam's mother might actually be quite ill. Sam was already being punished to the tune of £10 with £2 costs – was there any need to punish his mother too? They could always argue that the report had to be dropped because of space.

Charles marshalled all these arguments to put to Mr Juby – and knew before he even started up the stairs to the second-floor office that there was not the faintest hope they would be accepted. He could not put the most cogent argument of all – the reaction of Sam and his mates if the report went in.

Mr Juby was putting on his coat. It was nearly time for lunch.

'Anything out of the ordinary?'

'Just a drunk and disorderly; got fined ten pounds.' Charles took a breath. 'Chap called Samuel Jesse Johnson. Asked me to keep it out of the paper.'

'Ah, they often do that.' Mr Juby buttoned up his coat, quite unconcerned. 'Generally it's the indecent exposure cases. Can't face the wife and kids, that sort of thing. What excuse did Sam have?'

'It's his mother. Supposed to be at death's door. He's worried if she sees it in the paper the shame might kill her.'

'The shame!' Mr Juby roared incredulously. 'Ashamed of young Sam having a drink? Blast, boy, Annie Johnson hent had a day sober since she was sixteen. She don't give a damn what he drinks. She'd only be ashamed he didn't thump the copper that arrested him.'

'She's not ill, then?'

'I wouldn't like to vouch for her liver, but otherwise she's right as ninepence.'

Charles was mystified. 'Then why is he so keen it shouldn't go in the paper?'

Mr Juby was heading for the door. 'No idea. But it makes no difference anyway. If it's in the court, it's in the paper. Don't you take any notice of Sam, boy' – and he shook his pipe at Charles significantly – 'whatever he may have said.'

Charles realised that Mr Juby probably knew all about Sam's methods of persuasion.

'Any trouble, you let me know. But he's all talk, is Sam, just piss and wind. You get that report done for the five o'clock bus.'

'Yes, Mr Juby.' Charles was resigned to his fate. He turned his mind to a happier topic as he followed him down the stairs. 'By the way, what's it like at the Young Farmers' Club dance?'

Mr Juby paused and looked over his shoulder. 'The Young Farmers, eh? A word of advice, Charlie boy, if that's where you're off to. You make sure you call at Mr Pollitt's first.'

He carried on down the stairs, chuckling. Charles grasped what he meant. Mr Pollitt was Toftham's leading chemist.

It was another Friday morning at the *Toftham and Wettleford Journal*, another day of judgment. Prominent on this week's front page was a court case headed: 'Market Place Disturbance Leads to £10 Fine: Disgraceful Conduct, says Magistrate.'

Charles sat in his office, waiting. What form would Sam's wrath take? Would he come storming up the stairs and beat him to a bloody pulp? Might he even have a shotgun? There were plenty about. Or would he lie in wait for him somewhere, on the way to Mrs Abbs's perhaps, or in the alley where he kept his bike?

His bike! Would he find it a mangled wreck – if he found it at all?

Lunch-time came, and still nothing had happened. He looked out of the window, along the pavement to the Golden Fleece. There was the usual cluster of youths around the door; Sam was not amongst them.

'Any problems?' asked Mr Juby as he passed the door. Both of them knew what he meant.

'No problems,' said Charles.

It was well into the afternoon when he decided to take the initiative. He would go down to the front office and ask Nellie about her friend Sam. He might also be able to pave the way for the following night's dance.

It proved to be an inauspicious moment. Nellie had some of the Golden Fleece regulars around her desk. They all turned and stared at him. His heart sank.

''Ere's the little creep,' said one of them, a smaller version of Sam Johnson. It was his brother. 'Chas Benson himself – Purveyor of Bad Bloody News.'

The others joined in the jeers. It was a very different

reception from his triumphant arrival on the delivery bike.

He turned to Nellie for explanation and support. 'What's wrong with them?' He thought he knew; but there was more than he expected.

'Lost Sam his job, haven't you, putting in that report. Might've known his boss would see it. He'd already warned him about boozing. Really done him up, you have.'

Charles understood at last. That was why Sam had been so anxious to keep the report out. Presumably he thought Charles would be more moved by the vision of an old lady on her deathbed than an angry employer.

'I'd no idea,' he said, in all honestly. 'But there was nothing I could do about it. Mr Juby said it had to go in.'

He was beginning to feel very uncomfortable. It was not just because of the glares and the jeers. He had never been responsible for anyone getting the sack before.

Sam's brother took a step towards him. The others stirred too. 'Mr Juby said it had to go in,' he mimicked into Charles's face. 'Mr Juby says, Mr Juby says . . .'

'I'll tell you what Mr Juby says,' roared a familiar voice from the foot of the stairs. The editor, it seemed, could not only hear what went on in Charles's office, he could hear what happened in Nellie's office too.

'Mr Juby says get your backsides out of this office. Now.' Sam's brother started to speak, but Mr Juby ignored him. 'Go on, the lot of you. Hent y'got no wuk to do?' His voice rose, and the Norfolk accent thickened. 'Nellie, you want to keep these young fules out o' here, they're a damn noosance.'

'Don't you go a-mobbin' me, Mr Juby.' Nellie had also shed her genteel accent. Feelings were mounting alarmingly. 'They hent come to see me, they come to see him.' And she pointed at the hapless Charles.

'Well *he* don't want to see *them*, no more'n I do.' Mr Juby paused as a thought struck him. 'Anyway, you'll all be seeing each other tomorrer. That should be a rare old party, down at the Young Farmers.'

He shoo-ed the group out of the door, gave Charles a nod, and went back upstairs.

Charles was left alone with Nellie. Her splendid chest was still heaving after the altercation, and he could not help being fascinated by it, in spite of the strained situation. But Mr Juby's comment was just sinking in.

'Is that lot really going to the dance?' he asked.

'Course they are. They've got my other five tickets.'

'But they're not Young Farmers!' he cried desperately.

'No more are you,' she snapped, and turned her back on him.

'Oh God,' said Charles. His cup was full.

Toftham Jubilee Hall was *en fête* for the Young Farmers' Club annual dance. The Christmas bunting had been resurrected and strung around the walls, coloured crêpe paper festooned the front of the stage, and a revolving multi-faceted silver ball hung from the ceiling, a notice above it bearing the legend: 'Kindly Loaned by Evans Electrics'.

Card-tables and chairs were ranged around the hall, and the vacant floor area had been treated with French chalk giving the uneven boards a spurious gloss. Ensconced on the stage behind their music stands were Tom Twite and his Toftham Troubadours, the big drum bearing the four intertwined 'T's which formed their emblem. Jim Bloxham, landlord of the Golden Fleece, who was regularly granted the licence for Jubilee Hall functions because he was used to handling most kinds of trouble, presided behind the bar.

The ticket had said 'Dress Optional', an unhelpful instruction but for Charles there was no option anyway. He had no dinner jacket, and had to fall back on his London suit, newly cleaned and pressed. But he need not have worried. Dress ranged from black ties and stiff white collars to crew-necks and leather jerkins. The suit merged inconspicuously into this sartorial confusion.

The girls displayed just as much variety, from strapless boned dresses to woolly sweaters. Hemlines varied from ankle to knee. Dress at Young Farmers' dances was very optional indeed.

He was not looking forward to the evening after the events in the office, but he felt he had better turn up or he could never look Nellie in the eye on Monday morning. He did not expect any problems from Sam and his friends at the actual dance, but he had taken the trouble to locate an escape route through a fire exit behind the stage, just in case.

He had taken another precaution too, involving a visit to Mr Pollitt the chemist. But in view of the state of war that currently existed between him and Nellie, he saw little hope of needing it.

Very few people were actually dancing when he arrived. Most of the men were in the bar, most of the women were sitting around the hall, glaring at the men in the bar. Charles edged his way in that direction. He was half-way round the hall when the music stopped, there was a desultory round of applause, and Tom Twite of the Toftham Troubadours announced a Paul Jones. 'Everyone on the floor, please . . .'

The men in the bar became even more deeply engaged in conversation. The women however surged on to the floor, taking Charles with them. He observed others making sorties into the bar and dragging out their menfolk. In the midst of one group of drinkers being cajoled away from their glasses Charles was not too surprised to observe Big Nellie, the bar's only female occupant. She had the lowest neckline and the highest hemline in the hall, a vision of red satin and bare flesh. Her hair, normally piled high, hung over her shoulders; her make-up was comparatively restrained. Her legs, as usual, were devastating. Charles decided he was glad he had come, after all.

Under the firm guidance of Mr Twite the ladies formed a circle facing outwards; the men formed another facing them. 'Hold hands,' cried Tom, and the music began.

''Ere we are again, then.' Charles immediately recognised the voice. He was holding the hand of Samuel Jesse Johnson. His other hand was being grasped, with increasing firmness, by Sam's brother.

Thus linked, they pranced ponderously round the hall. Charles was not sure whether he wanted the music to stop or continue indefinitely.

'I'm sorry about the job,' he shouted at Sam above the blast of Tom Twite's trumpet.

'I dare say you'll be sorrier,' was the ominous reply.

The music stopped, but the grip on Charles's hands remained as firm as ever. He had a ghastly vision of himself being led away by the brothers to some place of execution, the distant trumpet of Tom Twite sounding the Last Post.

'Come on then,' said the girl in front of him. 'It's a quickstep; it's quite easy.'

On each side of him the brothers were being accosted too. Grudgingly they released his hands. Charles watched them disappear among the dancers, then concentrated on the quickstep. Slow, slow, quick-quick slow . . .

As they danced he discreetly inspected his partner. She wore what he considered was a proper dance frock, hemline just below the knee, nipped-in waist, strapless top. He had a close-up view of the freckles on her shoulder, but the long hair obscured her face. She danced very well.

'You don't look much like a Young Farmer.' Her voice had no trace of a Norfolk accent.

'I'm not. I'm with Mr Juby.'

'Who's he?'

He was flabbergasted. This was the first person he had met in Toftham who had never heard of Mr Juby.

'He's the editor of the *Journal*,' he explained, and waited for her to ask, what *Journal*? 'Oh, that,' she said. It was almost worse.

'I'm the new reporter.' After three months he no longer felt very new, but he appreciated that to most people in Toftham he always would be.

The girl pulled away for a moment and stared at him. He observed that she had freckles on her face as well as her shoulder, and her eyes were very blue.

'You're not the one that goes around on that ridiculous bike?'

Charles blushed. He had thought more than once of obliterating the name-plate on his bicycle, but he found that many people found it rather endearing, and he was coming to enjoy the feeling it gave him of being something of a Character. Now he resolved to remove it forthwith.

He explained briefly how he had acquired it, and asked a few questions himself. Her name was Rebecca and no, she wasn't a young farmer either, she was the daughter of a doctor at Remingham, one of the larger villages about three miles outside Toftham. She was in her second year at university, and home for the Easter vacation. She was hoping to get a degree in politics, philosophy and economics, but she had no idea whether she wanted to be a politician, a philosopher or an economist.

He was about to ask what her involvement with the Young Farmers was when the music stopped. From out of nowhere Sam Johnson loomed up beside him once again.

'Having fun?' Sam enquired. 'Make the most of it.' He took Charles's hand and squeezed it painfully as they set off in the circle. Charles tried to console himself with Mr Juby's words: 'He's all talk, that Sam, just piss and wind.' But he did seem to have a very powerful grip.

The music stopped again. Charles hoped that by some miracle he would find himself opposite Rebecca. Instead, his partner was Big Nellie.

Or so he thought, and so did she. They moved towards one another, Nellie with a disdainful stare, Charles with a wary smile. Then Charles felt himself barged aside as

Sam Johnson took his place, and put a hand firmly on Nellie's waist. 'Mine, I think,' he grinned.

'Hang on,' said Charles. The dancers nearest to them had seen what happened and were waiting for his reaction. 'I think you were the next one along.'

Sam let go of Nellie and turned to face him. To Charles he looked rather like a lion that has just been thrown a plump Christian.

'What did you say, boy?' Sam raised a hand and pushed him, quite hard, in the chest, propelling him backwards into one of the bystanders, a sturdy figure in a dinner jacket, with a ruddy face and large hands. He was the first person Charles had encountered in the hall who actually looked like a Young Farmer.

'Now stop that,' remonstrated the Young Farmer.

'You shut up,' snapped Sam, and advanced on Charles.

The ruddy-faced man became ruddier. 'If you don't quieten down you'll have to get out. We don't want any of your sort here.'

'My sort!' Sam lost interest in Charles. All his attention was on the Young Farmer. 'What yer mean, my sort: What sort is that, then? And what's your sort, eh? Lord Bloody Muck is it, waiting to take over your old man's farm when he pushes off . . .'

The Young Farmer hit Sam on the nose.

Tom Twite and the Toftham Troubadours were working hard on a valeta, but nobody was dancing. Sam was holding his nose in astonishment, but showed no sign of retaliating as the Young Farmer shaped up to hit him again. Full marks to Mr Juby, thought Charles, it looked as if Sam really was all piss and wind.

But Sam's brother wasn't. He emerged from the crowd of spectators, observed Sam's plight, and hurtled himself at the Young Farmer. More dinner jackets came to the rescue. Sam's friends from the Golden Fleece joined in.

It was another lively Saturday night at the Toftham Jubilee Hall.

Charles edged away from the fracas and looked

around for Big Nellie. With Sam's friends heavily occupied this seemed an ideal opportunity to try his luck. But Nellie was engrossed in the battle, shouting encouragement to the Golden Fleece contingent and occasionally taking a swing at a dinner jacket herself. He found himself next to Rebecca instead.

'I say, did you start all that?' She seemed mildly impressed. He admitted that he had been rather involved.

'Well, Daddy would say it's all good for business.' She looked more closely at some of the dinner jackets, now locked in close-quarter combat on the floor. 'That's my group under there. I think I'll leave them to it; I don't suppose they'll feel like dancing any more.'

Charles felt a flicker of excitement. 'How are you going to get home?'

'I can take one of their cars,' she said casually. 'There are two or three here from Remingham. They'll manage.'

'But what about keys?'

'I expect they've left them in the cars. They get so used to leaving them around on the farm, they never bother to take the keys out. This isn't London, you know.'

Charles thought of the robbery at Tittlesham. That hadn't been London either. But perhaps Young Farmers were different from Mrs Boggis; they probably assumed that nobody would dare.

'Can I go with you to the car, then?' he asked, without much hope.

Rebecca surveyed the scene of battle. 'Well, when they get to this stage you never know who they'll hit next. Perhaps you'd better stick with me, in case they decide it's you.'

It was not quite what he had meant, but the result was satisfactory. 'I know a way out the back,' he said, and led her past the stage, where the Troubadours had just embarked on a slow foxtrot. But he noticed that Jim Bloxham had emerged from behind the bar and was removing his jacket. The situation had presumably reached crisis point.

He led the way through the grubby passage backstage to the fire exit. Rebecca had brushed against something oily and was trying to clean it off her skirt. She asked if he had a handkerchief.

'Of course,' said Charles and pulled it from his pocket with a flourish. With it came Mr Pollitt's precautionary packet. It fell to the floor between them.

The doctor's daughter looked at the packet, and looked at Charles. She wiped her dress, handed him back his handkerchief, and opened the door.

'You'd better get that nameplate changed on your bike,' she said. 'Chas Benson, Purveyor of Rubber Goods.'

She smiled, and was gone.

Behind him, above the sounds of battle, he heard the strains of the National Anthem. Tom Twite and the Troubadors had decided to call it a day.

Charles took the hint.

Six

'That's high time,' said Mr Juby, 'you came to a Council meeting.'

Charles felt gratified. Council meetings were always Mr Juby's personal preserve. He attended them, not only to report the proceedings, but to keep in touch with what went on behind the scenes. These gatherings of the Great and the Good were technically open to mere mortals, but in practice the public rarely attended. To be asked to accompany Mr Juby on such an occasion was almost like being asked to join the Masons.

'Ever been to one before?'

'Never.'

'Then today's your big day.'

Charles glanced in the office diary, open on Mr Juby's desk. Today's page was blank. Mr Juby intercepted the glance.

'No point in putting those down every month. Ought to know by now when they are: Toftham first Tuesday, Launford second Thursday. Been the same days ever since they started. Not likely to change now.'

Charles made a quick calculation. It was the second Thursday.

'We'll start you off with Launford. They're a little easier to follow than this lot in town. George Flatt's inclined to run the meetings so nobody knows what's going on except hisself. Launford is a little more' – he paused to consider the right word – 'a little more homely, you might say.'

Toftham Urban District Council, Charles knew, met in the courthouse across the Market Place. He had visited the modest offices of Launford Rural District Council on his regular round of contact calls, but they seemed to have nowhere large enough to hold a council meeting. Mr Juby enlightened him.

'They meet at the workuss.'

Charles blinked. He had learned by now that Norfolk was not the most dynamic or forward-looking of counties, but did it still have workhouses in the 1950s?

'Well, that hent a workuss any more. They call it an old people's home these days. They've cleaned it up a bit and put a few armchairs about, and the ladies from the village take a trolley round, but that's hard to tell the difference really. You'll see.'

Launford Old People's Home, formerly Launford Workhouse, was some miles outside Toftham, and this was one of the rare occasions when Mr Juby got out his car. Indeed Charles had only recently discovered he had a car at all. He knew he lived on his own in a rather bleak Victorian house on the edge of town, but the edge of town was just a few minutes' walk away, and the only other journey Mr Juby made regularly was across the Market Place to the Dog and Partridge, for which a car was equally superfluous.

However, after the Tittlesham Post Office affair Mr Juby had considered it appropriate to visit the village personally, to express his sympathy to Mrs Boggis over her ordeal, and to thank his friend Mr Nicholson at Manor Farm for passing on the information. He had parked his car briefly outside the office, and Charles had been much impressed. It was a pre-war Standard, splendidly preserved, with spacious running-boards, handsome silver headlamps, and the original Union Jack emblem on the bonnet. Mr Juby had a simple method of maintaining the car's pristine appearance. Unless absolutely unavoidable, he never took it out in the rain.

Fortunately on this second Thursday the skies were clear, and Mr Juby had brought his car to the office for the Launford expedition. He climbed into the driving seat and sat majestically behind the wheel. Charles started to get in the other side.

'Hold up, boy,' growled Mr Juby. 'That'll need a crank or two.'

His dry-weather policy kept the car in the garage for long periods, which benefited the bodywork but did the battery no good at all. Anyone who travelled with Mr Juby needed a sound back and a strong arm.

Charles took the starting handle and got the engine going on the third turn. He climbed back into the car and Mr Juby drove slowly out of the Market Place. He drove slowly out of Toftham. Then he drove slowly.

Charles appreciated another reason for the car's immaculate paintwork. There was no likelihood of a stone flying up from the tyres. Any stone driven over by Mr Juby hardly twitched. He also avoided any spray or mud splashes from roadside puddles by driving permanently in the centre of the road.

Remembering the sort of reception this would have had from other road users back in Wembley Park, Charles huddled down in his seat in embarrassment, hoping not to be recognised. But he need not have worried. Oncoming cars pulled on to the verge to let them by, the drivers raising their hand in friendly salute. Cars behind them slowed down to their pace; not a horn nor a hooter was heard.

Mr Juby's car, it seemed, was as widely respected as Mr Juby himself.

They drove through the sunlit Norfolk countryside, and Charles felt the same contentment creeping over him that he had experienced on his first motor-bike ride with Mortimer Thirkle. It was spring now, and though there was still a nip in the air the leaves were beginning to show on the trees and the hedgerows, the fields had greened over, the muddy farmyards had dried out and the farm buildings were looking cleaner and fresher. He began to enjoy the car's gentle pace; this was a world in which to motor, not to drive.

They passed through a village of flintstone walls and pantiled roofs, with a pond in the centre and the church towering behind it. The only sign of life was the ducks, scattered around the pond or paddling gently across it. It was an idyllic scene, and even Mr Juby seemed taken with it.

'Take a good look, Charlie,' he murmured. 'The view round the next corner hent quite the same.'

They rounded the corner and Charles saw what he meant. Straight ahead of them, on top of a slight rise and dominating the whole landscape, was a massive red brick building. It had a central entrance block with two wings running back on each side, rows of small windows, a plain slate roof with a little turret in the centre, and on the turret a spike. To Charles it looked as though the architect had started out to build a stately home and finished up with a prison.

'There it is,' said Mr Juby. 'That's had a lot of names in its time. A House of Industry it was first. Then they called it a workuss. A lot of people just called it the Spike. Then we got a little more fancy and called it a Reception Centre. Now they reckon it's an old people's home. But I'll tell you the best name for it, boy. The Pauper's Palace. That's what it is.'

The name seemed to suit it exactly. Charles was impressed. 'Is that just your name for it, Mr Juby?'

'No, no. Old feller called George Crabbe thought o' that. Saw them all being built back in the 1770s. Didn't fancy them much.' And Mr Juby surprised Charles by pulling over on to the grass verge, causing an unprecedented mud stain on the nearside wing.

'Here's what he wrote,' said Mr Juby. 'I had to lun it at school. Every time I come here, I remember it.' He stared at the gloomy building ahead.

' "Your plan I love not; – with a number you
Have placed your poor, your pitiable few;
There in one house, throughout their lives to be,
The pauper-palace which they hate to see:
That giant building, that high-bounding wall,
Those bare-worn walks, that lofty thund'ring hall!
That large loud clock, which tolls each dreaded hour,
Those gates and locks and all those signs of power:

It is a prison, with a milder name,
Which few inhabit without dread or shame" '

He recited it extremely well. Charles marvelled again at
the different facets of the man, concealed beneath that
bucolic exterior.

'That's not so long ago they were still taking in tramps
at the Spike,' Mr Juby mused. 'They got a night's shelter
and a bit of food, but they had to work in the fields or
chop some wood, and the women had to do the scrubbing and the cleaning. They let them stay a day or two,
then they moved on to the next Spike over Empringham
way.

'I remember one of them telling me, when I was about
your age, they didn't have beds, they slept on the stone
floor with just a couple of blankets, and they got eight
ounces of bread and water twice a day. That wasn't
Victorian times, that was just about thirty years ago.
Things are better in there now, but somehow the smell
don't seem to change.'

He started to pull back on to the road, just as a large
Bentley came round the corner at considerable speed.
For the first time that morning Charles heard the blast
of a car horn, then the Bentley swept past them. The
driver, an elegant middle-aged man in a camel-hair coat
and a brown felt hat, did not give them a glance.

Mr Juby grunted. 'There's other things don't change
in these parts too, boy. You'll have to watch out for
that.'

'Watch out for what?'

'In some ways we aren't just in Victorian times, we're
still in feudal times.' He called it 'foodal' and Charles
noted the warning sign. This must be a subject on which
he felt strongly.

'That feller in the Bentley, he's part of them. Lord
Remingham.'

The name rang a bell. Remingham, Rebecca. 'Isn't
that a village?'

''Course it's a village. His Lordship owns it. He owns

most of this part of Norfolk – the land, and the farms on the land, and the cottages on the farms. The Reminghams have owned it ever since one of 'em did some dirty work for Henry the Eighth. It was one of the Reminghams who knocked down all his servants' cottages because they spoiled the view from his front windows. Rebuilt them a mile away, mind you, and a lot better than the ones he knocked down, but I doubt he asked the servants if they wanted to move – and they had an extra mile to walk to work.

'This one we've got now hent quite so drastic, but he follows the same principle. He'll look after his tenants all right so long as they don't cause no trouble. You'll find that's the general rule, out of the towns. They don't actually touch their forelocks any more, but my heart alive, they have a job to stop themselves.'

Mr Juby spoke with increasing vehemence. They drove the remaining distance quite fast.

The Bentley was in a space marked 'Reserved', immediately beside the front door. 'I forgot to tell you,' said Mr Juby. 'He's chairman of the council too.'

Inside the stone-flagged corridor with green-painted brick walls which lay beyond the doorway, Charles understood what Mr Juby meant about the smell. It was a mixture of carbolic soap, cheap floor-polish and over-cooked cabbage which he had not encountered since his army days. But there was an extra ingredient too, the mustiness of clothes which had been worn too long.

The corridor itself was deserted, but in the rooms which opened off it he could see elderly figures slumped in chairs around the walls. Nobody seemed to be talking; very few were even moving. Charles tried hard not to think of them as people waiting to die.

Launford Rural District Council held its meetings in the dining-hall, which ensured that meetings ended by noon so the trestle tables could be rearranged for the midday meal. Now they were laid out in a rectangle with simple wooden chairs around them, except for a magnificent high-backed affair with leather-padded arms which had once been occupied by the workhouse master. It was now occupied by Lord Remingham.

The figure beside him with the imposing naval beard was the Clerk to the Council, Commander Bludgen, who had spent the war in various administrative posts in the Admiralty and had now found a pleasant niche in which to augment his pension and occupy his declining years. Next to him, almost hidden behind piles of books and papers, was his assistant Mr Grind, insignificant and retiring but enormously efficient. Without him the council's affairs would long since have drifted into chaos.

But it was the other characters around the table that fascinated Charles as he took his seat with Mr Juby at a separate trestle rather grandly labelled 'Press Table'. Several of them looked as though they qualified for the rooms along the corridor. Most of them were old; some of them were very old indeed.

They wore suits of varying vintage, but the 1930s seemed the most popular. A fair proportion wore mufflers tucked round their necks instead of ties, the traditional Norfolk 'rarper'. A notable exception was a gentleman in a wing-collar, a wide grey tie, and a tiepin so dazzling that if the stone had been real it could have paid for the complete rebuilding of Launford Old People's Home.

'That's Fred Knock,' whispered Mr Juby. 'Great character, Fred. Generally livens things up a bit. The rest don't stir too often.'

'So how did they get elected?' Charles remembered some jargon from the last general election. 'Are they just put in by the party machine?'

Mr Juby spluttered quietly. 'Party machine, boy? There hent no parties on Launford Council – unless it's the Remingham party. Most of 'em belong to that, only they go down on the form as Independents. Fred Knock's the only real Independent, but he calls himself

87

Labour. And they get elected because nobody else wants to do it.'

He pointed out one or two of the councillors wearing ties. 'You've got to be your own master, like one or two of these farmers, or else retired. Nobody who's in work is going to lose a day's pay coming along here; and if they've got a shop or they're in trade they hent the time anyway. Might not be so bad if they met in the evenings, like Toftham, but it's always been in the mornings and it always will be. His Lordship likes to keep his evenings free.'

His Lordship was also anxious to get the meeting under way. He had shed his felt hat and camel-hair coat to reveal an immaculate grey suit and a Guards tie. He was a picture of languid elegance, but Charles caught the cold glance he gave Mr Juby, whose noisily whispered commentary was obviously beginning to irk him. He decided he would try to steer clear of Lord Remingham.

'Time to kick orf, I think.' Charles had never heard anyone say 'orf' outside a Whitehall farce, but nobody else seemed to notice anything unusual. An immediate silence fell.

'No apologies. We'll take the minutes as read. Now committee reports. Finance first. Mr Nicholson.'

One of the collar-and-tie councillors raised a hand. 'I move,' said Mr Nicholson.

'Any comments? Any questions? All agreed? Thank you Mr Nicholson.' The finances of Launford Council, it appeared, were in safe hands.

'Housing Committee. Anything to say, Glubb?'

Glubb was in a 'rarper'. Anyone without a tie, Charles deduced, did not rate a 'mister'.

'No your Lordship, thank you very much.' The chairman of the Housing Committee bobbed briefly to his feet as he spoke, then bobbed down again.

'Thank you, Glubb. Any comments? Any questions? All agreed . . .'

'Hold hard, Mr Chairman. You're a rattlin' on too fast again.'

All eyes turned to the figure in the wing collar, the grey tie and the dazzling tie-pin. Fred Knox had risen to his feet. Charles waited for a bolt of lightning to strike him down; or at least a blast from the chairman. But Lord Remingham was apparently used to interruptions from this quarter.

'Well, what is it, Knock?' In spite of the collar and tie, Knock was classified among the rarpers.

'Page 11, paragraph 4.'

Mr Juby showed Charles his copy. The paragraph was headed: 'Expected rate of council house building 1952–53'.

'That says we expect to complete ninety new houses in the coming year, Mr Chairman. Is that right?'

'Of course it's right. And a very good effort too. I'd say. Wouldn't you say so, Glubb?'

Glubb bobbed up again. 'Yes, Your Lordship, a very good effort, no doubt about that.'

'Why thass a terrible effort and well you know it, Horace Glubb, and you know it too, Mr Chairman.' Fred Knock drew a piece of paper from his pocket, covered with notes.

'I've got here the figures for last year. We finished 48 houses in the first half, and 46 houses in the second half. That's 94, which hent a lot anyway. Now you say we can only build 80 in the whole of next year. That's wuss and it's getting wusser. What are yew a-doin' on that committee, Horace?'

This time Glubb did not bob up. Instead he looked appealingly at the chairman.

'There's a simple explanation,' said His Lordship sharply. He turned to the beard beside him, 'Commander?'

'One moment, Mr Chairman.' The commander turned to his assistant and they disappeared together behind the piles of papers. There was much muttering before he re-emerged.

'I understand from Mr Grind that it's a simple matter

of finance, Mr Chairman. The money just isn't available.'

Lord Remingham's eyes gleamed. 'Quite so. And of course we've already approved the Finance Committee's report, so we can't go back over that again.' In his moment of triumph he granted a minor courtesy. 'Anything else, *Mr* Knock?'

'Yes, Mr Chairman. There's no mention of housing in the Finance Committee's report. I move to refer back this paragraph for further consideration by both committees.'

'I think you'll find that after further consideration the committees will come to precisely the same conclusion.' The chairman's voice was icy.

'No matter,' said Fred Knock cheerfully. 'Thass worth a try.'

Lord Remingham surveyed the comatose figures around the table. 'I doubt you'll find a seconder,' he said with some confidence. For a moment, nobody moved.

'Yes, I think I'd like to second that.' It was Mr Nicholson, Chairman of the Finance Committee. 'I don't seem to remember those figures for last year being mentioned when we talked about this. Might be worth another look.'

Mr Juby's chuckle at the Press Table must have reached Mr Nicholson. He turned and, surprisingly, winked.

'That will do Juby.' The chuckle had reached His Lordship too.

Charles was quite scandalised. He had never heard his editor addressed as Juby before. Forgetting about journalistic impartiality he aligned himself wholeheartedly with the persistent Fred Knock. He was quite delighted when the vote was taken. Not many hands went up in favour of Mr Knock's motion, but only the obsequious Glubb actually voted against.

'Good old Nick,' muttered Mr Juby. 'That's his own farm out at Tittlesham so he don't have to worry too much about His Lordship. But that takes a bit o' doing

to cross him, just the same.' Now Charles could understand the wink. Mr Nicholson must be his editor's old
friend and informant at Tittlesham.

Lord Remingham meanwhile was moving on through
the agenda at his usual speed. Committee reports were
announced, proposed, approved and apparently forgotten. Only one subject aroused any discussion. The
Public Health Committee proposed the appointment of
an extra rat catcher.

Nobody but Fred Knock had been roused by finance
or housing programmes. These were matters to be left
to the experts. But everybody knew something about rat
catching. There was much discussion over types of
poison, methods of laying bait, and reasons for the
increase in the rat population, before Lord Remingham
drew attention to the intensifying smell of cabbage from
the kitchens and called for a vote. In spite of a protest by
Fred Knock – 'Why give 'em another month to breed?' –
the proposal for an extra rat catcher was referred back.

Lord Remingham declared the meeting closed and
chatted to his Clerk while Mr Grind produced an old
suitcase from beneath the table and started packing
away his books and papers. The councillors broke up
into groups and Mr Juby went to have a word with his
friend from Tittlesham. Fred Knock came over to
Charles at the Press Table.

'So what do you reckon to this lot, then? Not quite
the House o' Carmons.'

'Not quite,' agreed Charles. 'But I thought you did
splendidly over that housing business.'

'Don't you go havin' me on, boy.' Charles assured
him he meant it, and Mr Knock shrugged. 'I doubt
that'll do a lot o' good, but thass a pity not to try.'

Lord Remingham was passing them on his way to the
door. 'Good day to you, Knock.'

'Good day to you, sir.'

'Yes, good morning, sir,' said Charles. His Lordship
eyed him in slight surprise, gave a barely detectable nod,
and passed on.

Fred Knock watched him go. 'There's some situations, boy, where you don't speak till you're spoken to. That was one of them.'

'You don't seem to mind speaking up to him.'

'Well, I do different, don't I. I can do it because I hent beholden to His Lordship like all the others here. It's more like he's beholden to me. Couldn't do without me, up at the Hall; no more could a lot o' these.'

He took a card from his pocket and gave it to Charles. 'I might be of service to you one of these days, do you get a place of your own.' He headed for the door, leaving Charles studying the card. FREDERICK KNOCK AND SONS: NIGHT-SOIL COLLECTED: CESSPOOLS DRAINED.

'Fred trying to drum up a little business?' Mr Juby had returned. He gathered up his copies of the reports.

'Always an eye for a new customer, has Fred. You know, when he went on about those housing figures he wasn't just thinking about giving people nice new homes. More houses means more business, at any rate until they get the sewers into the villages, and that won't be for a while yet. Even His Lordship has only got a septic tank – and that can make a nasty mess if Fred decides he don't have time to empty it. There's nobody else'll do it.'

Another councillor came over to the Press Table. Charles assumed he wanted to talk to Mr Juby and he started to move discreetly away, but the councillor called him back.

'I think you know my daughter.'

Charles stared at him. Big Nellie's father? This well-spoken, rather handsome figure in the neat dark suit with the expensive-looking watch-chain across the waistcoat?

'I'm Doctor Bateman. From Remingham. His Lordship is one of its councillors, I'm the other.'

Rebecca's father. Charles shook his hand. 'It was a pleasure to meet her, sir. I'm sorry it turned into such a rowdy evening.'

'About average, by the sound of it. But I gather you

escorted Becky out of the hall. She told me about it; I'm very grateful.'

Not all, Charles hoped; not the incident with the handkerchief.

'We're having a little garden party in aid of the church on Saturday week. Becky suggested you might like to come out and report it – if that's all right with Mr Juby. I was going to drop you a note.'

Mr Juby had been listening with considerable interest. 'That's fine with me. But he'll have to make his peace with Mrs Curson.'

'No problem there. She'll be glad not to have the bother.' Mrs Curson, he explained to Charles, was the Remingham village correspondent, but she was doing the teas at the fête. Charles would have a clear field.

'And this was Rebecca's idea?' Charles wanted to make quite sure.

'Certainly. I told her it was a long way for you to come, but she said you had a particularly good bike. See you Saturday week . . .'

The trestle tables were being moved into line and the smell of cabbage was becoming quite overpowering. Charles followed Mr Juby back down the corridor and out into the fresh air. From the front door of the old workhouse the open Norfolk countryside beckoned. He swung the starting handle with enthusiasm, and they headed back for Toftham.

'Not a lot in all that,' he commented on the way.

'Don't you believe it. We've got four columns to fill from Launford RDC; we never have less. I'll write up that housing business and the rat catchers. You can get the rest out of there.'

He passed him the committee reports. 'Milk 'em, boy. You got to milk 'em dry. That's what council reporting is all about.'

The committee minutes of Launford Council were not the stuff that scoops are made of. Charles waded through the road-repairs programme of the Highways Committee, the budgetary juggling of the Finance Committee, and the vaccination arrangements of the Public Health Committee with increasing depression. He would much rather be thinking about Saturday week.

He managed to fill up several paragraphs with a list of minor roads to be resurfaced in the forthcoming financial year, and as a gesture of solidarity with Mr Knock he expanded in some detail on the reduced cost of night-soil collection. Since Mr Juby was handling the housing debate he spent only a few moments on the Housing committee report; he was about to move on to the General Purpose Committee when his eyes was caught by the final paragraph: 'Allocation of council houses for the preceding three months'.

The list of successful applicants seemed to have a curious feature. He pondered it for a moment, then gathered up the minutes and climbed the stairs to the editor's office. Mr Juby was contemplating the ceiling, obviously as enthralled by the affairs of Launford Council as Charles was himself. Charles coughed.

'Do you happen to know a family called Tucker in Withersett?'

'Ben Tucker? What about him?'

'Does he have an exceptionally large family, would you know?'

'Ben? Not too many for these parts. Three or four children – must be in their teens by now. Got a lot of brothers but they don't live around here. They're down in Suffolk somewhere. What's Ben been up to?'

'Well, unless his teenage sons have matured very early, I think he may be getting more than his share of council house accommodation. There are three houses allocated to Mr John Tucker, Mr Philip Tucker and Mr Herbert Tucker, and their present addresses are all given as care of Mr Benjamin Tucker, Estate Cottage, Withersett.'

Mr Juby was no longer contemplating the ceiling. Instead he was contemplating Charles with the look of a man who has just been brought tidings of great joy.

'Let's have a look.' Charles handed him the minutes. He read the list of names out loud, savouring each one. 'Mr John Tucker, Mr Philip Tucker, Mr Herbert Tucker. You know who they are, boy? They're Ben's brothers from Suffolk. And you know who Ben Tucker is? He's the foreman on Lord Remingham's Withersett estate. And you know what you've hit on here, boy? You've hit on a little bit o' fiddling, or my name's Horace Glubb.'

Charles had suspected as much, but it all seemed too transparent. 'Surely somebody else would have spotted those names, in the committee for a start.'

'The committee does what Horace says, and Horace does what His Lordship says. That fool of a Clerk never reads the minutes anyway, and poor little Grind wouldn't dare say narthin.' Mr Juby's accent was thickening with excitement. 'Yew done hully well here boy, I tell you. Now let's see how we handle this little booty.'

'Don't we just print it, and point out who all these Tuckers are, and why should they get priority on the housing list? You could put a piece in Waysider.' The Waysider column was Mr Juby's weekly commentary on local affairs, generally devoted to praising the organisers of charity collections, with an occasional complaint about litter in the Market Place or a call for united action to cut the grass in the churchyard.

'Don't be daft, boy. We need somebody else to say all that. This hent the *Daily Express* and I hent Lord Beaverbrook' – Mr Juby paused and sucked his teeth thoughtfully – 'though we mustn't forget them in all this, of course. But first things first. You get on to Ben Tucker at Withersett – he's in the book under Remingham Estates – and just ask him how his brothers are and when he's expecting them to move in. And you might ask him what they'll be doing there. I did hear His Lordship was looking for a couple more pigmen and a tractor-driver. That all falls into place, Charlie. Off you go.'

He had already lifted the phone and was dialling a

number. As Charles went down the stairs he heard him asking to speak to Mr Fred Knock – 'and tell him to take another look at the housing minutes . . .'

That Friday the *Toftham and Wettleford Journal* carried its equivalent of a splash headline. Charles had mentally devised something more in the shock-horror-probe tradition: 'Council Chairman's Foreman in Housing Scandal: Is It a Case of Family Favourites?' What it actually said was: 'Councillor Complains about Housing Allocation: Chairman's Explanation.'

A councillor had indeed complained.

'Mr Frederick Knock told the *Journal* he was disturbed to note that three council houses in Withersett had been allocated to members of the same family, and that none of these applicants had resided in or near the village for several years.'

That was not all that Mr Knock had said; he had waxed eloquent on the connection between the Tucker brothers and the Council Chairman, but Mr Juby did not need to consult the Anglian Press's solicitors to know he could not print it. Instead he had asked Charles to contact Lord Remingham for his comments.

The comments were conveyed through his foreman, Ben Tucker. They were short and to the point. The Tucker family had lived in Withersett for generations. The brothers had had to move away to find work, but they were entitled to return if work became available, and it had. Nobody on the waiting list had raised any objection. What on earth was the point of all this. And what was your name again, son?

It all looked pretty tame in the *Journal*, thought Charles, but it was enough. There were a great many callers at the office that Friday morning, all of whom insisted on seeing Mr Juby, not to complain but to hear more. Charles was called up more than once to be congratulated on his successful study of the minutes, an accolade which, remembering Ben Tucker's final question on behalf of Lord Remingham, he would gladly have done without. Being a crusading newspaperman, he thought, was all very well if you could do your crusading at a distance.

This thought was reinforced when Commander Bludgen appeared in his doorway, beard vibrating with rage, and demanded to know who was responsible. He directed him hastily to the second floor and made his escape.

Later, in the Dog and Partridge, Mr Juby and Charles were the centre of attention. Everyone was eager to confirm what they had read between the lines. Mr Juby was the soul of discretion – just an expressive shrug, a raised eyebrow, the hint of a wink. The name of Horace Glubb was frequently mentioned; there was talk of demanding his resignation.

There was no talk at all of demanding Lord Remingham's resignation. The Day of the Revolution was not quite nigh.

That afternoon Mr Juby spent much time on the telephone. On Saturday, as Charles wandered through the Market Place, he observed that the editor was still active in his office, a most unusual occurrence at the weekend. On Sunday morning it all became clear.

Most of the national papers carried the story of the Withersett council houses in far more explicit terms than the restrained version in the *Journal*. One of them, Charles noted wryly, even carried the headline: 'Council Chairman's Foreman in Housing Scandal: Is It a Case of Family Favourites?'

He might make a newspaperman yet.

Seven

Garden fêtes did not generally hold any great mystique for Charles. From a reporting point of view they shared the same category as bring-and-buy sales and church bazaars: the struggle to dredge a few lines from the opener's remarks, the weary round of name-gathering at the stalls while fending off the offers of home-baked cakes and hand-knitted tea-cosies, the succession of phone calls next day to discover how much they had made, and the inevitable complaints on Friday about the key helpers he had left out.

He always nursed the hope that something dramatic might happen. The official opener could fall through the platform and break a leg. A riot could break out over the jumble stall – not such a wild surmise, he had seen some quite vicious individual encounters. There could be a rare first edition among the tattered second-hand books, or a choice piece of Doulton in all that old crockery. So far, he was still hoping.

The Remingham garden fête, however, offered quite a different element. Somewhere among the cakes and the tea-cosies and the Agatha Christie paperbacks there would be Rebecca Bateman. This called for a new approach.

Charles debated over what to wear – which was a new approach in itself. For these occasions he rarely gave the subject much thought. He did make a point of wearing a tie to uphold the dignity of his profession, but it generally went with his oldest jacket and his baggiest slacks. He had once worn a suit and been mistaken for the official opener. He was hustled on to the platform and put in the chair of honour before the genuine opener came to his rescue. It was a nasty moment, which he did not wish to risk again.

On the other hand, Rebecca's presence did merit something a little special. He decided on the smarter of his two sports coats, the more respectable of his two pairs of flannels, a white shirt, and his old school tie. The old school was quite unknown in Norfolk, or indeed outside Wembley Park, but the colours were quite dashing and it might provide a talking point. He made sure he had a comb to repair the ravages of the journey, and set off on his bicycle for Remingham church fête.

He was now quite used to the delivery bike after many excursions to the villages around Toftham. He had padded the agonising saddle, located the slow punctures in the tyres, and bought front and rear lights. The nameplate he had decided to leave unchanged. It was after all the reason Rebecca had first known about him; it had acquired a certain sentimental value.

The three miles to Remingham should not have offered much of a challenge, but it was a hot day, the Remingham road had more than its share of undulations, and the smarter of his two sports coats was also the heavier. For once the specialised equipment on his bicycle came into its own; half-way to Remingham he took off the jacket, folded it neatly and put it in the big basket on the handlebars. He completed the journey in shirt-sleeved comfort.

Remingham was a pleasant village of perhaps five hundred people. It still had its own village school, its pub, its stores and of course its church. It also had Remingham Hall, an imposing eighteenth-century mansion built by an earlier Lord Remingham in open parkland beyond an ornamental lake. The long gravel drive from the Hall emerged on to the road through splendid wrought-iron gates, just outside the village. As Charles cycled past them an elderly figure – an Aged Retainer, Charles assumed – was hauling them open.

'That's very good of you, but I'm not calling on His Lordship today,' he called out. The Aged Retainer looked at him as if he had just cycled down from another planet. Charles waved cheerfully and rode on.

Dr Bateman lived in the Old Rectory, alongside the church. Part of the stable block had been converted into a surgery and the coach house was now a garage, but otherwise the rambling house and its extensive gardens were much the same as when an earlier and more affluent breed of parson cared for the souls of the Remingham faithful. The present Rectory was a modest red-brick villa at the other end of the village.

Today the front garden of the Old Rectory was decorated with bunting and balloons, there were stalls on each side of the drive and teas were being served on the lawn. Notices advised that round the back one could throw ping-pong balls for goldfish, play hoop-la, or bowl for a pig. There were groups of women looking at the stalls, groups of men looking at their watches, groups of children looking for trouble. It was the archetypal English fête.

Charles propped up his bike in the lane and reached for his jacket. As he attempted to pull it out of the basket he realised he had made his first mistake of the day. He had forgotten about Samuel Jesse Johnson.

After the Jubilee Hall fracas Charles had not met Sam again. He heard that he had found a new job on another farm, and hoped that might end the matter. But if Sam was out of sight, his friends were not out of mind. Unpleasant anonymous messages were sometimes left on his desk. Nellie denied all knowledge of them, but he could not imagine how else they got there. He often had catcalls directed at him from the Golden Fleece as he crossed the Market Place. And he had to give up leaving his bike in the alley beside the office after finding the saddle soaked in what he hoped was only water.

Now he kept it in Mrs Abbs's garden shed when he was not actually using it, but he still automatically checked the saddle. He did not however check the basket. As he tried to extract his jacket it became apparent that Sam's friends must have visited Mrs Abbs's shed. The wires of the basket were coated with something transparent and sticky, possibly from the *Journal*'s supply of office glue. The jacket was firmly attached.

Charles pulled harder. Some of it came free, but one sleeve refused to budge. Even if it did, the coat was unwearable – the pattern of the wires was etched on to the cloth.

Charles contained himself. Happily it was the sort of weather in which shirt-sleeves ought to be permissible. As he walked through the gate he assured himself that Dr Bateman would probably be in shirt-sleeves himself.

Dr Bateman was actually in a dark suit, complete with waistcoat and watch-chain. He was pacing the drive, inspecting the stalls as a commander might inspect his troops, with a word of congratulation here, some gentle advice there. In spite of Charles's jacketless condition he greeted him with reasonable cordiality.

'Here you are then, young man. You're in time for the opening ceremony after all. His Lordship has been slightly delayed.

'His Lordship?' So that was why the gates were being opened. Charles had not expected to meet Lord Remingham again so soon. Indeed he had no great desire to meet him at all after the Tucker affair. It seemed to have died down, but he knew that Norfolk memories were long.

'He should have been here at two o'clock; but held up by something at the Hall. Couldn't expect all these good people to wait, so we've carried on. Not unusual, really; last hospital I was at was actually running for two years before it was opened officially. Lot of nonsense really, but people like to have a little formality.' He saw Charles's eyes wandering. 'I think you'll find Becky doing the teas.'

Charles made his way through the groups scattered around the lawn. The women, he noticed, were in quite elegant dresses and most of the men had jackets. This was obviously a rather superior fête; the expected presence of Lord Remingham must raise it a few notches on the social ladder.

101

Rebecca was behind a long trestle table, wielding an enormous metal teapot which bore the legend 'Remingham WI' in green paint. She wore a light summery dress, cut low enough to reveal a delightful expanse of freckles.

'Excuse me, miss, I'm from the *Journal*. Could I have your name and initials please?'

Rebecca looked up and smiled. 'Miss Bateman, initials R. I. My parents took Adam and Eve quite seriously.' And as Charles looked at her blankly: 'R.I.B. I'm a spare rib too.'

'And what does the "I" stand for?'

She looked at him with mock coyness. 'Surely the *Journal* doesn't need to know that.'

'We like our reports to be accurate and comprehensive, Miss. We leave no detail unturned.'

'Then I think you'd better get some of the other names, not just mine.' She started filling up more cups. 'Come back and have some tea later on.'

Reluctantly Charles started to move off. 'Thank you for asking me to come.' She smiled up at him again. 'We needed an accurate and comprehensive report.'

Charles set off along the stalls, taking down names and initials but thinking mainly of Miss Bateman, R.I. He was half-way down the drive when a familiar Bentley turned in through the gates and drove past him up to the front door. Dr Bateman hastened towards it as Lord Remingham emerged, immaculate as always in grey tweed suit and brown curly-brimmed felt hat, gripping a shooting stick.

'Sorry I'm late Doctor. Spot of trouble at the Hall. Had a break-in, I'm afraid. Very tedious.'

Charles stopped writing down names and initials. A break-in?

'Ladies and gentlemen, gather round please for the opening ceremony.' Dr Bateman rallied his troops as he ushered Lord Remingham to the centre of the lawn. From the back of the house a young clergyman appeared and came over to join them. He wore a clerical collar but no jacket. Charles immediately warmed to him.

Dr Bateman cleared his throat; Charles turned a new page in his notebook.

'May I welcome you all to the Old Rectory again for this year's church fête. As you know we still have to raise a great deal of money to repair the church roof, and as churchwarden I am very grateful to you for your support. I am sure we all much appreciate Lord Remingham being with us again – and as usual he has kindly donated the pig for the bowling competition. I will now ask him to declare the fête officially open.'

There was a ripple of applause – mostly for the pig, thought Charles.

'Delighted to be with you today, and my apologies for being late.' Charles hoped for further explanation, but none came. 'Excellent cause, this. Got to keep the church watertight – if only to keep the rain off my ancestors!' There were dutiful chuckles at what sounded like a familiar annual quip. The young Rector, however, failed to smile.

'Very good of the Doctor and Mrs Bateman to allow the use of their grounds – and of course our thanks to the lovely Rebecca too.' He bowed gallantly in the direction of the enormous teapot. Charles felt his lip curl.

'Mustn't hold you up any longer. Keep the money rolling in, spend as much as you can. Got to keep this young feller happy, haven't we?' The Rector realised he was being referred to and this time he did manage to muster a smile, but only a fleeting one. Charles warmed to him again. This young feller, he suspected, did not have a lot of time for Lord Remingham.

'I have much pleasure in declaring this fête well and truly open.'

Another ripple of applause and a small girl was persuaded to hand Lord Remingham a small posy of flowers for his buttonhole. He patted her head and thanked her, and with some difficulty attached the posy to his elegant lapel.

'Just time for a quick look round the stalls, doctor, then I'll have to get back to the Hall.'

They set off round the lawn and Charles introduced himself to the Rector. He took down his name and initials – Cranmer, J. B. – and filled in a few details about the roof. It was a standard story of too small a congregation trying to preserve too big a church. The Rector himself, however, did not seem quite so standard; in most villages around Toftham parsons ranged from the elderly to the venerable. Charles ventured a thought.

'Rather an overwhelming character, Lord Remingham. Can't be too easy, having him as a parishioner.'

John Cranmer looked at him levelly. 'He's a very generous man. He's given a great deal of the money we've raised so far. I think it's quite understandable if he looks on the parish church as his own family chapel.'

'Mr Juby has a word for it,' said Charles. 'Foodal.'

The Rector grinned. 'It does take a bit of getting used to. But it has its good points. If his Lordship supports the church, so does the village, at least on occasions like this. Unfortunately he finds it rather difficult to come to church every Sunday, with shoots and house parties and the like. And if he doesn't come, a lot of the villagers follow suit.'

'How many do come?' asked Charles.

'About a dozen regulars. A lot more than that at Christmas and Easter, of course.' He grinned again. 'Those are the ones his Lordship comes to.'

Charles grinned back. 'I assume you're not a local yourself?'

'Hardly. If I recognise that tie correctly, I come from the same area as you. Wembley Park?'

It was the first time anyone had recognised his tie, in Norfolk or indeed in Wembley Park. He was amazed. 'How on earth do you know it?'

'Because I have one just like it. I must have been there about six years ahead of you. Small world . . .'

They continued chatting, recalling masters they had both known, catching up on what had happened since.

John Cranmer had gone to theological college, spent a short time as a curate in North London, then came to Remingham, his first incumbency. Lord Remingham was patron of the living, and he rather suspected he had been appointed because His Lordship assumed he was a descendant of the Archbishop, and would thus add a little tone to the parish.

They discussed social life in the country, or the lack of it, and John mentioned he was a member of Toftham and District Round Table, a body that Charles had heard about but not yet encountered. 'You'd be welcome to come along as my guest if you're interested. There's an age limit of forty, so we keep fairly lively. We're limited to two members from any one occupation, but Mr Juby doesn't quite qualify, I think, so you'd be the only journalist if you wanted to join.'

'And does that mean you're only allowed two Young Farmers?' asked Charles hopefully.

'In theory, yes. In practice we have two dairy farmers, two arable farmers, two sheep farmers, and so on. It's unavoidable in an area like this. But there's enough of the rest of us to balance them out.' Charles thought that sounded reasonable; he agreed to come to the next meeting.

He had one other enquiry to make of his new friend. 'What's the situation with Rebecca Bateman? I was thinking of asking her out, but I don't want to tread on any toes.'

John Cranmer grinned again. Indeed he grinned rather a lot, except at Lord Remingham's jokes about the church.

'So that's the interest in Young Farmers, Well, there's quite a few who've made a bid. And there was one scion of the local nobility from the other side of Wettleford who used to be around quite a lot. But I think she might find the Wembley Park approach a refreshing change.'

As they parted Charles assured him, in case he had any misgivings later, that he would not print any of his comments about Lord Remingham. John Cranmer became serious. 'I never thought you would. But one day somebody will have to start speaking out about the situation in the villages, and try to drag them into the second half of the twentieth century. It could be the Church that does it; it could be the Press.' Back came the grin. 'Or it could be the two of us together – the Old Boy Network. One foodal system against another!'

Outside the front door the engine of the Bentley revved up. Lord Remingham had completed his tour of the stalls, and in a carton on the seat beside him were jars of jam, a bag of cakes, a fretwork teapot stand and a hand-embroidered cushion. He had also bought several raffle tickets and bowled unsuccessfully for his own pig. His duty was done, his conscience was clear. He was orf.

Charles and John stood beside the drive as he drove past. He was smiling benevolently until he saw Charles, then the smile faded. The look he gave him was cool and thoughtful. John noticed it and looked at Charles curiously, but said nothing. The last they saw of the Bentley as it went off down the lane was something being tossed out of the driver's window. The posy's duties were over too.

When Charles returned for his cup of tea Rebecca was missing. Instead there was a tall, efficient-looking lady behind the teapot. Charles automatically opened is notebook and asked for name and initials.

'Mrs Bateman, wife of Dr Arthur Bateman,' came the crisp response.

Charles gave a little bow. 'And mother of Miss Bateman, R. I. I'm Charles Benson.'

'I thought you must be. Where's that marvellous bicycle?' Geo. Perkins' delivery bike might have seemed expensive at five pounds, but in publicity terms it was proving to be worth every penny. Charles told her where he had left it, and in turn asked where he could find Rebecca. Mrs Bateman said she was dutifully attempting to win a goldfish, or a pig, and Charles headed for the back garden.

Rebecca was bowling for the pig. The pig itself, which had earlier been grunting encouragement to the competitors from its small pen nearby, had now got bored with the proceedings and was dozing peacefully in the sun. There was plenty of activity however among the helpers hovering behind the numbered target board, waiting to retrieve the balls. Charles realised they must have a pleasant view of the freckles each time she stooped down to bowl. Indeed, the chief helper volunteered to pay for an extra go. To their general disappointment she saw Charles and declined. 'Let the press have a go instead.'

Charles tossed the balls at the board without noticing much where they went. He was too busy framing his crucial question to Rebecca. The helpers melted away; the chief helper did not offer him a second go.

As they walked from the pig to the goldfish he took a breath and put the question. It came out much more abruptly than he had planned. 'Are you free tomorrow?'

They reached the goldfish stall and Rebecca paid for some ping-pong balls. 'There's church in the morning, but I might be free in the afternoon.' She lobbed a ball at the rows of goldfish bowls. It bounced off.

'I wonder if you'd care to come for a bicycle ride?' Lacking a car, or even a motorbike, it was the best he could do. Another ping-pong ball bounced off the bowls.

'I'm sorry, I don't have a bike,' Charles hopes slumped. 'But I do have a pony.'

'Oh Lord,' said Charles. 'I'm afraid I don't ride. In fact I don't know anything about horses.'

'You don't have to,' she explained. 'I'll ride the pony; you could ride your bike.'

The idea had not occurred to him, and he seized upon it. 'Wonderful. The bike's not very good at clearing fences, but I should keep up with you on the flat.'

'Whoopee!' cried Rebecca. It was not the thought of the ride; she had just lobbed a ball into one of the bowls. But Charles took it as a good omen all the same.

They agreed that he should cycle over to Remingham after lunch. She would be ready with the pony. And she had another idea. 'I'll make up a picnic and you can carry it in that basket on your bike.'

'Wonderful,' said Charles again. Then he remembered about the basket, and came down to earth. He would have to do something about the jacket. He also remembered that he had other work to do, for which shirt-sleeves would most definitely be inappropriate. Without going into detail about Sam Johnson he told her about his predicament, and together they went out to the bike.

This time they managed to ease the whole jacket free and Rebecca took it indoor to see if the marks of the wires would come off. Meanwhile Charles made his fare-wells to Dr Bateman and his wife and explained about his assignation with Rebecca on the morrow. The doctor merely nodded; Mrs Bateman surveyed him carefully, then said she would lend a hand with the picnic.

She found John Cranmer totting up the early takings from the stalls, and arranged to call in next day for the result. 'You'll be in Remingham again tomorrow, then?' asked the Rector, with his customary smile.

'And not a Young Farmer in sight,' said Charles.

Rebecca reappeared with the jacket. Some of the worst stains had gone but it was not looking its best. The mixture of glue and rust would take a lot of shifting. But he thanked her fulsomely nonetheless.

'By the way,' she said, 'you'll be glad to know that this time nothing fell out of the pockets . . .'

Things are looking promising all round, thought Charles, as he mounted his bike and waved her farewell. But first there was a less palatable appointment to be kept. He headed down the lane and through the still-open gates of Remingham Hall.

The closer he got to the Hall the more imposing it looked. The roof was battlemented, the great windows had elegant carved surrounds, there was a broad flight of steps up to the massive front door. He parked his cycle at the foot of the steps, climbed them and hauled on the wrought-iron bell-pull, feeling like a character in a horror movie. Would the Mad Professor answer the door, or the Monster itself?

It was actually a tall thin man in a black frock-coat and pin-stripe trousers. His hair was as black and shiny as his boots. He looked at Charles's stained jacket and raised one eyebrow. Then he looked beyond him at the bike propped against the steps, and raised the other.

'The tradesmen's entrance,' he said coolly, 'is round the back.'

Charles swallowed hard, and stood his ground. 'I'm from the *Toftham and Wettleford Journal* I understand you've had a burglary. I wonder if I could have a word with Lord Remingham?'

'The *Toftham and Wettleford Journal?*' The butler made it sound like a brand of toilet paper. Charles decided to take a chance.

'I also represent the *Daily Telegraph, The Times*, and the *Manchester Guardian*.' And so he did, indirectly, since he represented Mr Juby, who represented, as far as he knew, the whole of Fleet Street.

The butler tried not to look impressed, but it had obviously been a shrewd move. He pondered for a moment.

'I am not sure His Lordship would wish to see you at the moment. He has been greatly distressed.'

'I wouldn't worry too much about that. He put on a very brave face at the church fête this afternoon; I think he may have recovered quite well.' Of all the thin excuses, he thought: Lord Remingham 'distressed'!

The butler took his point. 'Kindly wait here while I consult His Lordship. And while you're waiting, please be good enough to move that machine. It could be most dangerous for anyone leaving the house.'

It also spoils the view, thought Charles, but he moved it away from the steps and returned again to the front door, now firmly shut again. From this vantage point he admired the beautifully kept park, the ornamental lake, the immaculate drive and the distant wrought-iron gates. It was a scene from a film set – where was the carriage bringing James Mason and Patricia Roc home from their honeymoon? He had to admit that his old bike hardly fitted in.

The door opened. 'Is your name Benson?' Charles admitted it was. The butler nodded, and the door shut again.

This is it, he thought, he's going to have me flung in the dungeons. Will it be the thumbscrew or the rack? he joked to himself rather desperately; his apprehension was real enough.

'His Lordship will see you. Come in.'

It was a vast hall with a vast staircase. The ceiling was vast, and so were the walls. The architect must have had one simple instruction. Make it vast.

They walked across the hall and entered one of the rooms. It was vast. Lord Remingham was standing at the far end.

'So you're Benson.' It sounded like a sentence of death.

Charles tried to keep the tremor out of his voice. 'Yes I am, sir. We met at Launford Council.'

'I don't recall meeting you. But I remember seeing you. And I recall what happened afterwards. The Tucker affair.'

The moment had come. Charles waited for the axe to fall.

'I gather you spotted all the names in the minutes. Very sharp of you. Very sharp indeed.'

Charles still waited.

'You jumped to the wrong conclusion, of course. The Tuckers were perfectly entitled to the houses – one of the oldest families in the village. Very reputable lot, good workers, good for the village. But I can understand how it must have looked. Surprised the Clerk didn't spot it. He could have put an explanatory note in the minutes and saved a lot of ill feeling, unnecessary embarrass- ment. Told him so; stirred him up a bit.'

Charles remembered the vibrating beard in the doorway of the office. Commander Bludgen had certainly been stirred up a bit. He began to feel he might survive the interview after all. Lord Remingham continued.

'Poor old Glubb has been given a rough time – talking about resigning. Never was strong enough for committee chairman. I think I might suggest Fred Knock for the job. What do you think of that, Benson?'

Charles was dumbfounded. Instead of being put to the torch, he was being consulted about the appointment of a new housing chairman.

'I think Mr Knock would do the job splendidly,' he ventured.

'So do I. Trouble is he prefers to stand back and criticise instead of pulling his weight. He likes to knock, does Fred Knock.' And Lord Remingham gave a short, sharp laugh. Charles was convinced he was dreaming; he would wake up back on the front steps, with the butler inviting him in.

'Now look here, Benson.' This sounded much more like reality. 'You did well to spot those names. That's the sort of initiative I can appreciate. But make sure you check all the facts before you go rushing off to Juby. He's a good man but he's got some old-fashioned views. Still thinks in terms of wicked landowners grinding the faces of the poor.'

Charles couldn't resist muttering a word under his breath. 'What was that you said?' demanded Lord Remingham.

'Just one of Mr Juby's words, sir. Foodal.'

'Feudal?' There was another short, sharp laugh. 'Well, possibly. I prefer paternalistic. Try that one on your Mr Juby. There's a lot worse things than paternalism, Benson, and don't you forget it. Now, about that report.' The sternness returned. 'I've had a word with your Chairman; told him what I've told you. Use your initiative properly and you might get on. Fail to check your facts properly and you might get the sack. Understood?'

'You know the Chairman, Sir?' It was more than

Charles did. He had seen his name on some of the office literature, but that was his only contact.

'Of course I know him. He's my first cousin. That's another fact you should have checked.' He should have known anyway, of course; among the county, as in the villages, everybody seemed to be related to everybody else. He hoped this was an appropriate moment to change the subject.

'About this burglary, sir . . .'

'That's another thing. How did you know about that? The police said they wanted it kept quiet.'

'It wasn't the police, sir. It was you, at the fête. I heard you talking to Dr Bateman.' Charles grew overbold. 'I suppose you could call it initiative, sir.'

'I call it damned eavesdropping, never mind initiative, young man.' He knew he had gone too far. Another of Mr Juby's maxims came to mind: *You don't take liberties with county.*

'Now listen, Benson. I want you to be quite clear on this. There's a very good reason the police are keeping quiet. There's just a couple of pictures taken – rather good ones, but they're quite small and they were in one of the rooms I don't use much. It was quite a fluke I noticed they'd gone. The police think it'll help if the theft is kept quiet for the moment – let the thieves think they haven't been missed yet. They'll explain it all to you – and I suggest you do as they advise.' Or you'll have another word with the Chairman, thought Charles.

'Let them know you've seen me, and tell them I agree to them giving you the information once they're ready to release it.' How could you stop them, thought Charles, then realised it was a foolish question. The Chief Constable was probably a first cousin too.

The interview was obviously over. Charles murmured his thanks, suppressed an urge to back out of His Lordship's presence, and turned for the door.

'By the way,' Lord Remingham called after him. 'What was all that nonsense about representing the *Telegraph* and all the rest? Was that initiative too?'

'Not entirely sir. Once I get the story, they'll get it too.' And this time, he vowed to himself, Mr Juby could give him a share of the payments as well.

The butler ushered him out and he rode off down the drive in good heart. He was going to get a story into the nationals, he was going on a picnic with Rebecca, he had made a new friend in John Cranmer. And his jacket didn't really look too bad.

As he cycled past the Old Rectory, where they were packing up the stalls and clearing up the litter, Dr Bateman called to him from the gateway and completed his day.

'Lucky you've got that basket on your bike, young man.'

'Why is that, Doctor?'

'You've won the pig.

Eight

Charles spent much of Sunday morning scrubbing the glue off the basket of his bike. To his relief he had not been expected to use it for his bowling prize. Few pig-winners on such occasions actually kept the pig. It had been sold to the local butcher and Charles received the cash, which would be more than enough to cover the cleaning of the jacket and the modest expenditure on cups of tea and raffle tickets. For once he had come away from a fête with a profit.

And with a story. He had visited the police station when he got back to Toftham, and Detective-Sgt Collier of the local CID had been most helpful, once he had heard about the conversation with Lord Remingham. A group of London art thieves who had been operating in Suffolk now seemed to have moved further north. His colleagues in London were watching out for them and wanted the theft kept quiet for twenty-four hours. But he saw no reason to suppress the news any longer than that, and if Charles cared to see him on Sunday evening he could have all the details.

Charles was quite happy about the delay. The Norwich paper was not published on Sundays anyway, and he would have time to negotiate with Mr Juby before the story went to the nationals for Monday morning.

He finished work on the basket, cleaned himself up and rode to the *Journal* office. He locked the bike inside, beyond the clutches of Sam Johnson and his friends, and at twelve noon precisely he entered the farmers' bar of the Dog and Partridge.

Mr Juby had already started on his first special. He nodded to Charles, gave another nod to Maggie, and a fresh pint appeared on the bar. The ritual rarely changed, since Charles never managed to get in the bar ahead of Mr Juby to order first, no matter how skilfully he timed it. He rather suspected he had his own key.

'Here's a bit o' noos that'll interest you, young Charlie. Horace Glubb is resigning from the Council. All because of that story of yours.'

Charles nodded. 'I know,' he said nonchalantly. 'Lord Remingham was telling me only yesterday.'

'Fancy that now.' Mr Juby's disbelief was manifest. 'I suppose he told you who'll be taking over the Housing Committee, then?'

'He's going to ask Fred Knock, but he doesn't think he'll take it. Likes to criticise, he said, but won't take the responsibility himself.'

Mr Juby, to Charles's delight, was much impressed. 'You couldn't have dreamed that up on your own, young Charlie. What have you been up to?'

Charles told him.

Mr Juby chuckled over the butler and his reception at Remingham Hall. He did not chuckle over Lord Remingham's view of the Tucker affair, even though Charles omitted His Lordship's comments on Mr Juby himself.

'He may say that looked above board from where he sits up at the Hall, but that don't from where I sit. Don't you let him have you on, boy.'

Charles promised he wouldn't 'But you might have warned me he was related to our Chairman.'

''Course he's related. They're all related. They're county. You tread careful when you're dealing with them, boy.'

'But why should we have to tread careful?' Charles was remembering his conversation with John Cranmer. 'We can't go on treading careful indefinitely. Somebody will have to stand up to them sooner or later – the Press, or the Church, or even the two together.'

Mr Juby had looked increasingly astonished at this outburst, until Charles mentioned the Church. Then understanding dawned.

'That's it, then. You been talking to that young

Cranmer out at Remingham. Lively young feller, hent he? Wants to change the world by next Toosday. But perhaps you'll need to give it another couple o' days, seeing you'll be busy writing up that fairte.'

Charles ignored the warning signs. 'I really do think people should stand up for themselves. It's ridiculous having this Lord of the Manor situation in the nineteen-fifties.'

'Thass what Robert Kett thought in the fifteen-fifties. Thass taken four hundred year to git this far; take a little longer dew we get rid on 'em altogether.'

Charles's exasperation increased. 'But I thought you felt the same way. You complain enough about the county having it all their way. Why don't you do something about it? You've got the *Journal*; why not use that?'

Mr Juby put down his glass and looked at him solemnly. Charles had said much more than he intended – he half-expected to be ordered out of the bar.

'How long you bin in Norfolk now, boy?'

'Four or five months, I suppose.'

'Four or five months,' Mr Juby repeated slowly. And he laughed. It was not his usual cheerful chuckle. Charles knew the word for it: mirthless.

'Thass not four or five minutes in these parts, and already you know all the answers. I've lived here near sixty years and I don't know hardly any. What I do know, boy, is that long after you've come and garn, and you're sitting in some smart office in Lunnon telling your fine Lunnon friends what a rum lot o' gormless old fules you wukked with in Norfolk, we'll still be living here, trying to get things right, little by little, because thass the only way you do get things right, hereabouts.'

Charles tried to protest, but Mr Juby had not finished.

'No doubt if you come back in thutty year's time you'll find His Lordship sitting up there at the Hall, or his son maybe, and he'll still have all that land and all that money, but there'll be stronger councils with more power and more guts than they got now, and there'll be other folk about in the villages, not just farming folk beholden to the likes of him for their jobs and their homes, and maybe we'll have new laws about wrongful dismissal and victimisation, and we might even have a chairman of the company what hent his fust cousin. But until then, boy, all I can do on the *Journal* is print stories like the Tuckers and hope that'll dew a little good. Dew I dew any more and that'll be the finish, and then what kin I do? Thass why I tread careful, boy, and if you want to stay in these parts, thass what you do too.'

If he wanted to stay. Charles had not really thought about it before. There were plenty of arguments against it, once he started totting them up. He had long since wearied of Mrs Abbs's establishment, but he could find no other haven. There was the continuing harassment by Sam Johnson's friends, and the boredom of writing up whist drives and church socials and Mothers' Union meetings. And there was the 'foodal' system which according to Mr Juby he could do nothing about.

But there had been the excitement of the Tucker affair, and the way people now greeted him as he crossed the Market Place, and the strange draw of the Norfolk countryside. And now there was Rebecca . . .

'I take your point,' said Charles. 'And I think I'll stay.'

'Right,' said Mr Juby. 'Then I'll have another special, and dew you tell me about this burglary.'

Charles remembered now the point of the meeting. This seemed an inauspicious moment to suggest taking a cut of Mr Juby's linage payments, but time was slipping away, and he would soon have to leave for Remingham.

He reported his discussion with Detective-Sergeant Collier and the agreement they had reached about delaying the announcement of the theft. Mr Juby was unsurprised; arrangements with the local police, to their mutual advantage, were part of his way of life.

'So I'll have the story this evening and I'll phone it through to Norwich for tomorrow morning. There's just the matter of the nationals. I expect they'd like a few lines.'

'Yes,' said Mr Juby. 'I expect they would.'

There was a long pause, while Mr Juby sipped his special.

'I wondered,' said Charles, 'as I found out about the story, whether I might take a share of the linage.'

'Did you now?' said Mr Juby. 'Well now, I don't rightly think so.'

Charles felt the resentment mounting inside him. 'I think that's a bit much,' he snapped.

'Hold hard, boy. You wait till I finish. Never mind sharing. Thass your story, you get the linage.'

Quite abashed, Charles mumbled his thanks. And Mr Juby chuckled – his old familiar chuckle. 'By the time you've phoned eight or nine pairpers, with the same story over and over, then tomorrow morning you find only a couple a lines in any on 'em, you'll have earned every penny, boy.'

Remingham was enjoying another fine afternoon as Charles parked his bike outside the Old Rectory. The sun always shines in Remingham, he thought blithely.

He heard the rattle of hooves down the drive and Rebecca rode out off the gateway on quite the biggest horse he had ever seen. It was a grey and white skewbald of noble proportions. Rebecca sat level with Charles's head, in jodhpurs and riding cap and thin white shirt.

'Don't look so terrified. Thunder doesn't eat reporters on Sundays.'

He tentatively patted Thunder's neck. Thunder flared his nostrils and eyed him contemptuously. The best that could be hoped for between them was an armed truce.

Rebecca handed down the wicker basket she was carrying and he put it in the basket on his bike, now pristine and glueless. 'If it's all right with you,' she said, 'I thought we might go down to the river and have our picnic there. It'll give Thunder the chance of a little exercise.'

'The bike could do with a canter too,' said Charles. 'Lead on.'

They set off through the village, Rebecca and Thunder leading the way, Charles bringing up the rear. Remingham seemed deserted, but he had no doubt their progress was being followed by most of the population. Horse and rider made a magnificent combination; riding behind them on his delivery bike he felt like Pancho Villa following in the footsteps of Don Quixote. He refused to let it depress him.

They left the village and Thunder broke into a gentle trot. Charles pedalled gamely behind. They'd never believe this in Wembley Park, he thought; a few months before, he would never have believed it himself.

Rebecca turned off the road along a wide, straight drift, slightly uphill with high hedges on either side. She slowed Thunder to a walk so that he could come abreast. The road had been quiet enough; the drift was so silent and empty, the hedges so high, they seemed completely cut off from the outside world.

They talked quietly as they rode. It was difficult at first because of the difference in height. Seated on his bicycle, all he could see at eye level was Rebecca's right thigh. But it was not an unattractive thigh, and he decided it was a satisfactory subject to study while she talked down to him, and he talked up to her.

He had tried to talk to people on horses before. Invariably they made him feel an inferior being – especially the very small children. Once people got on a horse, it seemed, like getting behind the wheel of a car, their character changed completely. Rebecca, he noted with relief, did not change at all.

They talked about the fête and his success in bowling for the pig. They talked about Toftham, and Remingham, and what life was like in both. Charles told her how he had come to Norfolk, she told him how her family had moved there from the South Coast at the beginning of the war and stayed on when it was over. Charles told her about his National Service in Aldershot, she told him how she had gone to university because there seemed nothing much else to do, except for Thunder. Her riding brought her into contact with the local farming gentry, and after twelve years or more in Norfolk she was just beginning to be accepted.

That led them to talking about status. The village doctor, it seemed, rated rather higher than the rector or the schoolmaster, and because of his indispensable services – valued even higher than Mr Knock's – he was included in county guest lists, though he would never quite rate as county himself. A local reporter, on the other hand, came several rungs lower, on a par with insurance salesmen, bank clerks and the junior ranks of estate agents. But at least he wasn't 'in trade' . . .

They laughed together about such distinctions, as knowledgeable people of the world who had experienced life outside the social constrictions of East Anglia. And they laughed about other things too – about Charles's disastrous encounter with Freddie Pendleton at his first funeral, about the inordinate sum he had paid for his bicycle, about Mrs Abbs's domestic discipline and Mr Juby's homely homilies. They even laughed about Samuel Jesse Johnson. All the way up the drift there was much laughter. Charles could not remember when he had enjoyed himself so much.

Then the hedges ended and they were out in the open, on the summit of a gentle rise. The Norfolk countryside stretched away in front of them. There were great rolling fields of young beet and barley, little ponds and coppices, long lines of hedges, an occasional narrow lane twisting through the fields, some scattered farm buildings, two or three churches on the horizon. The drift they were following led down to the river, winding through bright green watermeadows. In the whole of this great panorama, there was not another person to be seen.

They paused there for a minute, taking it all in, the girl on the skewbald horse and the young man on the delivery bike. This was not picture postcard stuff, thought Charles, this was a working landscape, productive, practical, utilised to the full, with its own special

Norfolk qualities – sturdy, honest, unsophisticated. For some reason Charles thought of Mr Juby.

'Race you to the river,' cried Rebecca, and was off down the hill at a gallop.

'Oh God!' muttered Charles. He did not even try. Apart from the effort, Thunder was scattering dust and pebbles in all directions. If Charles did manage to keep up with him it would be a most unpleasant ride. Instead he followed sedately at his own speed, and caught up with them eventually some way along the river. Rebecca had put Thunder on a long tether, and was sitting on the grass, still panting a little.

'Who's a cissy?' she mocked.

'Didn't want to risk losing the basket,' he replied loftily. He put it on the grass, lay the bike on its side, and sat down beside her. They looked at each other.

'I know a local reporter is several rungs lower than a doctor,' said Charles, 'and I know that a doctor's daughter who rides a very large horse is several rungs higher still, but would it mean the collapse of the social system if I kissed you?'

'So long as nothing falls out of your pocket,' said the doctor's daughter.

The remnants of the picnic had been cleared up and put back in the basket. They were sitting in a companionable silence. Charles would happily have sat there forever, but there was the visit to Detective-Sergeant Collier and a long evening ahead on the telephone. He was about to suggest making a move when Rebecca forestalled him.

'Thunder's getting very bored. I think it's time we went. I wonder if I could just ask you something. Are you going to stay in Norfolk?'

It was the second time the question had arisen that day. He avoided an immediate answer. 'Why do you want to know?'

'Because if you're not, this looks like the start and the finish of another beautiful friendship. I go back to college later this week.'

He had not realised it would be so soon. It helped to make up his mind.

'I think I'll be staying. I might win another pig.'

'Or something,' said Rebecca.

'Yes. Or something.' And he kissed her again.

They walked back up the hill side by side, Rebecca leading Thunder, Charles pushing the bike. Rebecca seemed to be meditating, then asked him about Mrs Abbs. 'You were talking about trying to find somewhere else.'

He turned to her eagerly. 'You've got a spare room at the Old Rectory? What a splendid idea. Would your parents agree?'

'Certainly not. They'd think it was highly improper – even when I wasn't there. No, I was thinking of John Cranmer. He lives on his own in that three-bedroomed house. The last rector had quite a big family, but John must have a couple of rooms to spare. I don't know what the Church Commissioners' rules are about lodgers, but any extra money would be a big help for him – he gets a lousy stipend.'

Charles immediately liked the idea. 'I'm sure we'd get on – and the Church Commissioners are a long way away from Remingham. But do you think he'd want to give up his privacy? I'm not sure I would.'

Rebecca nodded rather seriously. 'I think he'd be very glad of the company. There's not a lot of people he can talk to in Remingham – not really talk to. Most of the villagers are still a bit suspicious of him – they're not used to having a bachelor rector. There's father of course, but he's much older and they're not really on the same wavelength. And I don't think he has many cosy chats with His Lordship at the Hall. I think you'd do him a lot off good.'

'Well, let's see what he thinks. I've got to pick up the result of the fête anyway.' Another thought struck him. 'It'll mean biking to work each day. That won't be too bad in the summer, but I may have to think again next winter.'

'By next winter,' said Rebecca, 'anything can have happened.'

'Very true, very true,' said Charles with heavy significance.

'I mean, you might have bought a car.'

'Ah,' said Charles.

They mounted their respective steeds, and rode off down the drift.

John Cranmer greeted them at the door of his house with his cassock over his arm. He explained he only had ten minutes before evening service. Charles would have left it at that, but Rebecca asked straight away if he might like a lodger.

The Rector grinned. 'Are you running away from home?' he asked her. 'I'd be delighted.' But he knew what she meant, and to Charles's relief he did not hesitate.

'It sound an excellent plan – but the rent goes to the church, not to me. I need to keep the study to myself, but we can share the lounge and the kitchen, and one of the spare rooms upstairs is big enough for you to use as a bedsitter, if you feel like a little peace yourself. You do your share of the cleaning – and if you can cook, so much the better.'

Charles couldn't, but he promised to learn. They agreed on the rent – thirty shillings, the same as at Mrs Abbs's, which would not include a midday meal as he would be in Toftham, but the compensations far outweighed that. He would give Mrs Abbs a week's notice and move in on the following Sunday.

'Have a look round now if you like,' said the Rector. 'Don't bother to lock the door when you leave. By the way, here are the figures from the fête – we really did rather well.'

Charles took the slip of paper. 'Just one more thought. What time do you eat in the evening? Would it be six o'clock sharp?'

'Whenever I feel like it. Is that all right with you?'

'That is most certainly all right with me.'

John Cranmer walked off to the church, and they went into the house. The kitchen was neat and clean, the lounge comfortably untidy. The larger spare bedroom looked out over open country, first a wheatfield, then parkland, then Remingham Hall in the far distance. This is more like it, thought Charles. It was a world away from Mrs Abbs and the cemetery. There was no thatch, and no oak beams, and no ingle-nook fireplace – but he might plant a rose-bush to grow round the door.

'This is great,' he said and, quite without thinking, sat on the bed.

Rebecca looked at him coolly. 'Don't get carried away,' she said, and went downstairs. He followed her down and out through the front door. 'I really didn't mean anything, you know.'

'I don't suppose you did,' said Rebecca as they closed the door. 'I just thought I'd make things clear.'

You've been going out with too many Young Farmers, thought Charles, but had the sense not to say so. Instead, as they stood by the front gate with Thunder and the bike, he asked when they could meet again. She had a full week: on Monday she was gong to Norwich with her mother, on Tuesday she was spending the day with an old schoolfriend, on Wednesday she was riding in a point-to-point. She went back to university on Thursday morning.

'Then it looks like the point-to-point,' said Charles cheerfully. 'I'll see you there.'

She hesitated. 'Do you think that's really a good idea?'

'I think it's an excellent idea. I'll ask Mr Juby if I can cover it – then I can combine business with pleasure, and get in free to boot.' He paused. 'Why shouldn't it be a good idea?'

'Well, you know.' Rebecca looked uncomfortable. 'I'll have to look after Thunder, and there are some people I've promised to meet . . .'

Light dawned. 'And the place will be teeming with Young Farmers, no doubt.'

She smiled at him. 'No doubt at all, I'm afraid.'

'Any particular Young Farmer?' He tried to sound flippant, but he found himself quite tense as he waited for the reply. But she smiled again. 'Not that I can think of, offhand.'

'Then think no more. There'll be a particular reporter there instead.'

She shrugged. 'Just so long as you don't set off any more pitched battles. They fight with horsewhips at point-to-points, you know.'

'In that case I should get another good story for the nationals. Try and egg them on if you can.' He mounted his bike, and for a moment he thought of kissing her goodbye, but there were one or two people on their way to church and doubtless many other eyes were on them too. He shook her hand politely.

'Thank you for a lovely day,' he said, as his mother had taught him.

She was equally proper. 'Thank you for taking me.'

Charles gave her the basket and rode away towards Toftham, humming happily as he went. The sun still shone over Remingham.

It was seven o'clock when he reached Toftham police station, rather later than he intended but still in good time to phone Norwich and then London. At the desk he asked for Detective-Sergeant Collier. The desk sergeant shook his head.

'He's been called away. We won't see him back tonight. But Mr Juby came round earlier – they had a long chat together.'

'The old devil!' cried Charles, and rushed out of the door. The desk sergeant shook his head sadly at the impetuosity of youth. He had not been able to give him the full message; young people had no patience these days.

Charles cycled to the office in a state of considerable rage. After all that talk at lunchtime and the generous gesture – 'you take the lot, boy' – old Juby had pinched his story and was no doubt phoning it through even now. Well, he'd demand a share anyway; it was still his story.

The office door was locked, but Charles assumed Mr Juby had fastened it to avoid being disturbed while he was phoning. He unlocked it, left the bike in Nellie's office, and stormed upstairs.

'Mr Juby!' he yelled.

Nobody answered. Mr Juby's office was empty. Baffled, he went down to his own. There was a typed sheet of paper on the desk, and a note:

'Charlie: Bill Collier tried to contact you when he had to go out, but you left no number so he called me. Here are the details he gave me, and the phone numbers to ring in London. If you want me, I am in the D. and P.'

And there were the details – a description of the stolen pictures with their value, how the thieves had broken in, how Lord Remingham discovered what had gone. It gave the police theory as to the thieves' whereabouts, the reward Lord Remingham was offering for their arrest and return of the paintings, a footnote about the other robberies in Suffolk of a similar nature.

It was a good story, and Mr Juby had handed it all to him on a plate.

Much later that evening, Charles joined him in the farmers' bar of the Dog and Partridge. Mr Juby had obviously indulged in several specials, but Charles ordered him another. 'I owe you that, and a lot more,' he said.

Mr Juby looked at him a little glassily, and chuckled. 'Have you put the world to rights yet, boy?'

'Not quite,' said Charles. 'But I think it's getting better.'

Nine

'Didn't know you fancied horses,' said Mr Juby as he handed over the press pass for the point-to-point. 'I generally let Mortimer look after this one – you wouldn't think he was a racing man either, t'look at him.'

'I wouldn't want to deprive him,' said Charles hastily.

'You won't deprive him. He's got his own pass after all these years; if he wants to go, he'll go. He just won't need to write the report, Tittlesham's not in his area anyway.'

The point-to-point was on Mr Nicholson's land at Manor Farm, which lay to the north of Tittlesham, and Charles suspected that if Mortimer wanted to be difficult, he could argue that while Tittlesham was in Charles's area, Mr Nicholson's farm was in his. But Mortimer never wanted to be difficult. Charles took the press pass and left.

The ride through the lanes to Tittlesham was not as peaceful as usual. Horse-boxes and trailers kept overtaking him, passing so closely that in the end he dismounted every time he heard one coming and climbed up on to the verge. It's not their fault, he kept telling himself, these are narrow lanes and those are wide vehicles. But it was an ignominious experience nonetheless. He arrived at Tittlesham dusty, weary, and in rather a bad temper.

He would feel better, he decided, after a drink. And he headed for the Hero.

But could this be the same deserted Hero where he and Mortimer had drunk their flat brown ale under the eye of the surly landlord? The forecourt was crowded with cars and horse-boxes and trailers. Tables with coloured umbrellas were set around the open front door, and the doorway itself was jammed with customers carrying empty glasses in and full glasses out. There was much shouting and laughing and cries of 'Mind your backs!' and 'One for the road!' It was point-to-point day at Tittlesham, and the Hero was jumping.

Charles tucked his bike out of sight behind a horsebox and fought his way inside. The surly landlord was transformed too; he was scuttling about behind the bar, exchanging cheerful banter with the customers while two young assistants filled up the glasses from a barrel in the back room. On the shelves behind the bar, instead of an empty crisp carton, there were pies and sandwiches and sausage rolls.

It took a little time for Charles to get a drink. Whenever he tried to order, some louder voice caught the landlord's ear, or a burly tweed shoulder blocked his view. After some minutes of jostling and shoving and increasing frustration, he altered his tactics. After all, he thought, the Hero himself would never have stood for this.

'Pint of bitter!' he roared. And when nothing happened, he roared again. 'Pint of bitter, over here!'

The customers around him, instead of being annoyed by this forceful approach, regarded him with some admiration. The landlord nudged one of his assistants. A pint appeared in front of him.

'And a ham sandwich,' he snapped. The sandwich appeared too. He began to feel better.

'Come up from London for the racing then?' asked his neighbour, an elegant young man in a brown and green check jacket and gaiters. Charles wondered if it was his London accent that had given him away, or just his belligerent behaviour.

'Actually I'm from the *Journal*,' he explained.

'A racing journal, is that?'

'No,' said Charles, trying not to sound defensive. 'The *Toftham and Wettleford Journal*.'

The elegant young man looked at him blankly. 'Can't say I know it.' And he turned away.

'I expect It'll survive,' muttered Charles, but not loud

128

enough for his neighbour to hear. He was beginning to feel bad-tempered again. He struggled outside with his pint and drank it in the comparative peace of the car park.

He left the empty glass on one of the tables and collected his bike. He was pushing it out onto the road when the elegant young man emerged from the bar and caught sight of him. He intercepted Charles to study the nameplate on the bike.

'Chas Benson: Purveyor of Good News,' he read out slowly. 'Well, well.'

'Well, well indeed,' Charles replied, his hackles rising. 'Anything wrong?'

'Nothing at all, dear boy. Very worthy occupation. Keep it up.' He patted Charles's shoulder, gave another amused glance at the name-plate, and wandered back to the bar.

You patronising bastard, muttered Charles as he mounted the bike and headed for Manor Farm. He hated the elegant young man with a deep and terrible hatred.

The course for the point-to-point races was laid out over two fields, separated by a low hedge which provided two of the jumps. Others had been constructed from poles and brushwood and barrels. Cars were parked two or three deep on each side of the course or scattered around the first field. More were queuing outside the entrance gate as Charles arrived. He cycled past them loftily, showed his pass, and started riding around the field in search of Rebecca.

It was not easy. People and horses were everywhere, milling about between the cars and vans. A few were wandering about on the course, a great many were gathered in groups beside open car-boots full of baskets and bottles. There was cut glass and gleaming cutlery, set out on folding tables with ice containers to cool the wine. There were very thin sandwiches, and very attractive pâtés, and a great deal of smoked salmon. One group was actually carving a cold roast chicken. Charles remembered the simple picnic by the river at Remingham, and thought he understood better why Rebecca had been reluctant for him to come. This was a very different world.

He cycled slowly from group to group, ignoring the curious glances at his bike. He decided to brazen it out. If any of them reacted in the same way as the elegant young man, he told himself, he would not just mutter, he would say it straight out. But nobody did.

There was no sign of Rebecca in the first field. He rode his bike through a gap in the hedge beside one of the jumps. The second field was not so crowded, and in the distance he spotted Thunder's familiar grey and white patches. Another familiar figure was leading him. He set off cautiously across the bumpy field. Rebecca waved as he approached.

'What are you doing right over here?' he asked, a little out of breath.

'Just walking the course, to see what the jumps are like. They're rather a stiff lot this year.'

To Charles they looked completely unsurmountable, but Rebecca was obviously not too worried and Thunder, as usual, looked capable of anything. He got off his bike and paused. He would have very much liked to kiss Rebecca, but there were others wandering nearby and he feared he might embarrass her. They rather awkwardly shook hands.

'Have you eaten yet?' she asked as they walked on round the course. He told her about the Hero and the battle for the pint and the ham sandwich. He did not tell her about the elegant young man. 'How about you?'

'I'm due to meet some people for a quick bite. They've brought a few bits and pieces in their car. I don't expect they'd mind you coming along.'

'I've seen the bits and pieces,' said Charles. 'They don't exactly rough it, do they?'

She looked at him rather sharply. 'Why should they? Most of them work quite hard, you know, they're entitled to enjoy themselves. For goodness' sake don't get a chip on your shoulder, Charles.' She relented slightly. 'You wouldn't begrudge a Young Farmer the odd slice of smoked salmon.'

'The odd slice? They're eating it by the pound!'

'Well, I'm sure there'll be some left. You can have some fish with your chip. Are you coming or not?'

'I suppose so,' he mumbled ungraciously, refusing to rise to her banter. They walked back into the first field in silence.

As they approached the line of parked cars by the course Rebecca asked casually, 'Do you have to take that bike everywhere?'

'Yes I do,' said Charles. 'It's essential equipment. Suppose there was a ghastly murder, or a bomb outrage, or a hold-up by a gang of smoked salmon thieves. I'd have to dash off and hold the front page. Why? Do you mind?'

'I don't mind. It's just that people might think it was – well, a little odd.'

'It wasn't odd at Remingham. Why should it be odd here?' Charles had given up his brief attempt at levity. He was really getting quite angry. And so was she.

'Never mind. It's too late now anyway. Just try not to scratch anybody's car with it.'

They had reached a group of people sitting on folded chairs behind a large station wagon. The back of it had been converted into a bar, with rows of bottles and glasses. An open hamper was on the grass, with plates and cutlery neatly strapped to the inside of the lid. Inside the hamper were sandwiches, sausage rolls, chicken legs – and smoked salmon.

The people in the group were mostly in their twenties, dressed either in riding gear or tweeds. The women were in twin sets and headscarves, the men in sports jackets and flat caps. One of the sports jackets, Charles noted with a sinking heart, was a brown and green check.

'Hallo Becky,' said the elegant young man. 'And I think I know your friend.'

The others greeted Rebecca with handshakes or kisses.

The elegant young man got a kiss. 'How do you know Charles?' she asked him.

'I met him at the pub. He was taking the good news from Aix to Ghent.' And he pointed out the nameplate to the others. There were one or two titters, but mostly just polite smiles.

Rebecca made a general introduction. 'This is Charles Benson, he's reporting the races for the *Journal*. And Charles, this is Harry Burton. I expect you can guess what he does.'

'I think I can,' said Charles. 'Where's your farm?'

'My father's got a patch near Wettleford,' said Harry Burton. Charles was going to ask how many thousand acres made a patch, but he caught Rebecca's eye and stayed silent.

She recited the names of the rest of the group, and they nodded to him, and he nodded back. None of the names was familiar, but he did recognise one of the men, Jim-something – he missed the surname. He was the Burly Young Farmer who had punched Samuel Jesse Johnson on the nose at the Jubilee Hall.

The recognition was mutual. 'You're the chap Sam Johnson was pushing around at the dance,' said Jim-something. 'You started a rum old punch-up there, Charles boy.' His accent was much broader than Charles remembered. There were in fact quite a number of broad accents around. If you farmed a few hundred acres and you rode a horse, he mused, you were in.

'I didn't exactly start it, I think Sam did that. But I'm sorry if it caused any trouble.'

'No trouble at all, boy. Sam and his mates need keeping in order now and again. Blasted noosance, they can be. But he's working for me now, so I can keep an eye on him. You let me know if he causes you any more trouble.'

'I'll manage, thanks.' His attitude towards Young Farmers was mellowing a little, but putting himself under their protection was going a little too far. However, he was interested to discover what had happened to Sam. It was another surprising feature of Norfolk paternalism, no doubt, that you could punch a man on the nose and then offer him a job. It was just as surprising that, having been punched, the man could accept the job.

Rebecca tethered Thunder nearby and Charles propped his bike, very carefully, against the station wagon, though there was little danger of scratching it. It was already covered in dents and mud. Charles deduced that, like Jim-something who owned it, when it was not at point-to-points it was working on the farm.

He joined the circle and was plied hospitably with food and wine. The wine was pleasantly chilled; the smoked salmon, he had to admit, was delicious. Most of the group were reasonably civil to him, though they were largely engrossed in their own conversations. The only real irritant was Harry Burton, who monopolised Rebecca and kept calling her Becky in a proprietorial fashion which Charles found highly offensive.

They had reached the coffee stage – the coffee was in vacuum flasks which fitted neatly into slots in the hamper – when Charles recognised another familiar figure wandering aimlessly among the parked cars. The figure was in a dark blue suit, which even Charles could appreciate was not quite standard wear for a point-to-point. It was also carrying a leather flying helmet and a pair of goggles.

'Mortimer!' called Charles.

Mortimer Thirkle saw him in the group around the hamper surrounded by bottles and glasses and empty plates, and raised a tentative hand, but made no effort to join him.

'Excuse me a moment,' said Charles and went over to him. Apart from being sociable he also wanted to make sure he had not caused Mortimer any offence by asking to cover the point-to-point. Mortimer seemed about to back away, but changed his mind.

'Hallo, Charles. Didn't want to butt in on your party.'

'My party?' Charles laughed at the thought. 'It's not

133

my party, Mort. I'm just a gatecrasher.' He had taken to calling him Mort rather than Mortimer which he thought sounded pompous, or Morty which just sounded awful. Mort did not seem to object; but then, he never did. Charles continued, 'I hope it was all right, my asking to do this. Mr Juby said you wouldn't mind.'

'Not at all,' said Mortimer, and he repeated Mr Juby's comment, 'I didn't know you had a fancy for horses.'

'It's not exactly the horses,' Charles confided. 'There was somebody here I wanted to meet. But come to that, I didn't know you were a horsey chap either.'

'Ah,' said Mortimer slowly. 'Well, I suppose you could say we're both here for the same reason, really.'

'You're here to see Rebecca?' asked Charles, astonished. 'I don't believe it.'

'Rebecca?' said Mortimer blankly. 'I don't know who you mean. No it's – er – somebody else.'

'Get away.' Charles was fascinated. 'Who is it?'

'I think I'd rather not say, if you don't mind.' Mortimer was beginning to look around furtively. He obviously wanted to escape from Charles before his mystery friend appeared. 'We arranged to meet over by the bookies. I think I'd better get over there, if you'll excuse me.'

Charles bade him goodbye, but made a mental note about the bookmakers. He realised how inquisitive he was feeling about Mortimer's assignation, and had a quick vision of all those lace curtains twitching when he first arrived at Mrs Abbs's. It must be catching, he thought guiltily, and returned to the group at the station wagon.

They were just starting to move off, some to get mounted, others to get near the course for the first race. Rebecca was still talking to Harry Burton – or more accurately, Harry was talking to her. She looked up and caught Charles's eye. It was all he needed.

'Excuse me, Harry.' It sounded like 'Harreh'; that must be catching too. 'Rebecca offered to show me where everything is. I've never been to one of these things before.'

134

'I rather thought not,' Harry drawled. Yes, thought Charles, you really are a patronising bastard. But Harry had turned back to Rebecca. 'Don't let him too near the course with that bike, Becky. He might frighten the horses.'

Charles was about to explode, but Rebecca got in first. The elegant young man had gone too far. 'As far as I am concerned,' she said, almost haughtily, 'he can take his bike wherever he likes. I think it's quite splendid,' And she smiled at Charles, who smiled gratefully back. All seemed to be well again.

'Actually I'll leave it here, if that's all right.' He nodded towards Harry Burton. 'I don't think there's going to be a ghastly murder after all.'

Rebecca untethered Thunder and they walked off together, leaving behind a still elegant but now slightly bewildered young man. 'Where do you want to go?' she asked.

Charles remembered Mortimer's secret tryst. 'Perhaps we could go and look at the bookies,' he suggested. 'By the way, that was jolly good of you to stand up for the old bike.'

'Harry can seem a little rude sometimes, but he doesn't really mean it.'

'Of course he means it,' said Charles and unwisely he blurted out, 'He's a patronising bastard.'

'He's nothing of the sort.' Rebecca stopped and glared at him angrily. 'How can you say that when you've hardly met him? He happens to be a friend of mine.'

Charles was mortified. It had seemed they were getting back to the pleasant atmosphere of the Remingham picnic, and now he had spoilt it again.

'I'm so sorry,' he said abjectly. 'I'm sure he's an extremely pleasant fellow.'

'Now who's being patronising?' She was not to be placated.

They walked on along the lines of cars. Rebecca sometimes exchanging greetings with other strollers, Charles sunk in a gloomy silence. He did occasionally recognise a face from Toftham, and was somewhat disconcerted to see Mr Philpott the chemist, who smiled at him and then at Rebecca. He assumed chemists were sworn to silence about the prescriptions they dispensed; he hoped they were equally discreet about their other sales.

'I'd better give Thunder a little exercise,' said Rebecca brusquely as they approached the bookmakers' stands. 'You'll need to find out about starting prices and so on.'

'I don't even know which race you're in,' Charles muttered miserably.

'There's only one Ladies Race. You can hardly miss it.'

'Should I have a bet on you?' he asked, intending to anyway.

'All life is a gamble,' said Rebecca airily. 'Please yourself.'

She mounted Thunder and rode off without a backward glance. Charles watched them go. There are times, he pondered, when it must be rather nice to be a horse. He blotted out the thought and turned to look for Mortimer.

It occurred to him that he might find him on one of the stands, taking the money or chalking up the odds. That might account for the dark blue suit. But there was no sign of him. Even on this day of surprises it would be too much to discover that Mort was a part-time bookie.

Charles gave up the hunt and got a racecard. The Ladies Race, he discovered, was third on the card. He thought he might have a look at the runners in the first race and perhaps risk a few bob if there was one he fancied.

The horses in the collecting ring varied in size and colour but he could deduce very little about their speed. He glanced through the names but found nothing that caught his eye. He noticed however there was a horse called The Scribe in the second race; that must be worth supporting. It also reminded him that he had a few duties to perform, which Mr Juby had carefully outlined.

As well as the results he had to record the starting prices and the distances between the first three. That was straightforward enough; the information was broadcast over the loudspeakers and written up outside the stewards' tent. He also had to get the attendance figures from the stewards on the gate, and somebody had to give him an official description of the going.

'Thass no good coming back and saying, "I did not notice the going thereof"',' Mr Juby had warned with one of his rare literary flights. 'And don't try to make it up; people know about such things in these parts.'

He had given him one more instruction. 'Don't describe any races off your own bat, Charlie. You don't know one horse from another. Just listen to the common terry and write a few lines from that.'

So he stationed himself beside one of the loudspeakers as the common terry started for the first race. It was not too complicated; one horse led all the way. Quite a lot of people watched and cheered, but quite a lot more, he noticed, kept on strolling and chatting without sparing a glance for the race. Perhaps, like him, they had come to see people, not horses.

He had collected the attendance figures on the gate and was on his way back to put a bet on The Scribe when he saw yet another familiar figure – and this time it really was the figure that caught his eye. The magnificent chest was quite unmistakeable. Amazingly, Big Nellie was at the point-to-point. Even more amazingly, she was on a horse.

'What-ho, Nellie!' he cried, in great surprise. 'What on earth are you doing here?'

'What's it look like I'm doing?' said Nellie belligerently. 'You can't be as stoopid as all that.'

Charles gazed up at her. Her face was not coated with its usual layer of make-up and she looked quite young and vulnerable. The splendid legs were not so eye-catching in jodhpurs and riding boots, but the chest, seen from below, was quite devastating.

'I'd no idea you rode a horse. Is it yours?'

'Course it's mine.' She was highly indignant. 'Why shoont it be? I've as much right to ride a horse as anybody else. I've been riding since I was seven.'

Charles apologised. He was not having a very good day with the ladies. He realised that he must be sounding rather like the appalling Harry Burton. So he tried again.

'Are you in the Ladies' Race, then?'

'Yes I am.' He was clearly still not doing very well. 'I suppose you think I'm illegible for a ladies' race.'

'Of course not, Nellie. You know I didn't mean that. I must make sure I have a bet on you. Will you tell me the name of your horse?'

'Fat chance.' He had not expected her to be quite so abrupt. 'Anyway, you don't want to waste your money on betting.'

'All life is a gamble,' quoted Charles. 'I'll look up the name on the card. Good luck anyway.'

Nellie gave a grunt and rode off. Charles heard some shouting from the course and realised he was missing the second race. As he hurried over to catch the final words of the common terry he glance across at the route Nellie had taken. She had stopped again and was leaning down to talk to somebody else, who was gazing up at her with rapt attention. It was a man in a dark blue suit, carrying a leather flying helmet and a pair of goggles.

It really was turning out to be a most remarkable afternoon.

Back at the stewards' tent Charles collected the result of the second race. The Scribe had won by several lengths. He was disappointed not to have backed it, but encouraged by the omen. Perhaps it would turn out a good day for scribes after all. Feeling a little more cheerful he headed for the collecting ring in the hope of a word with Rebecca. As he went he checked through the names of the six runner on the card, and soon found Nellie's; it was called Fat Chance. So he had got that wrong too.

But Fat Chance? Not a name to encourage the punters, thought Charles. On the other hand it might be intended to deceive them. He went over to the bookies and found that names count for little in the racing world. Fat Chance was odds-on favourite; Thunder was second favourite at two-to-one. He put five shillings on Thunder, then remembering his promise to Nellie he put another two shillings on Fat Chance.

When he got to the collecting ring Nellie was just riding in, with Mortimer walking beside her. They were no longer talking but Mort was still gazing up at her, and he continued to gaze from the rails as she started to circle the ring. Charles tapped him on the shoulder.

'I know you get all sorts of horses at point-to-point, but you must be the darkest of the lot.'

It took a moment for Mortimer to withdraw his attention for Nellie and grasp what he was getting at. Then he grinned sheepishly. 'I suppose I should have told you, I always come here to see her ride. I have a sort of interest in her horse.'

'An interest in her horse?' Charles was determined to hear the whole story, and it gradually came out. Mortimer had known Nellie since she was a small girl. Her father had been a groom for Lord Remingham and she was allowed to ride the horses. When her father died they had to leave the tied cottage on the estate and move into Toftham. What was worse from her point of view, they had to leave the horses.

Mortimer helped her get the job in the *Journal* office, but she still pined for them. In the end he made enquiries among the local riding fraternity and found somebody with a foal to dispose of. On Nellie's eighteenth birthday he took her to see it. 'How would you like to have that?' he asked her.

'Fat chance,' said Nellie. But Nellie got her birthday present and the foal got its name.

She managed to pay for its keep out of her office salary. Mortimer did not actually say so, but Charles guessed that he covered all the extra expenses.

'She's lucky to have an old friend of the family who's so generous,' said Charles warmly. 'More like an uncle really.'

Mortimer gave him a rather odd look. 'I'd rather not think of it that way. I'm not all that old, you know.'

'Of course not, Mort.' Charles remembered the look that Mortimer had given Nellie in the front office, the way he had gazed up at her earlier that afternoon. Indeed he could see how he was watching her now as she rode around the ring. 'Silly of me,' he said, and changed the subject.

'What do you think of that big skewbald?' Rebecca was just riding Thunder into the ring, but she had not noticed him. 'Think it's got a chance against Nellie's?'

'They're old rivals,' Mortimer told him. 'They've met two or three times; Nellie's never been beaten yet. But there's always a first time.'

'Indeed there is.' And judging by all the other odd things that have happened today, he thought, this could be the time.

The horses moved out of the ring and headed for the start. Nellie ignored them, but Rebecca gave him a quick wave, which Mortimer was quick to observe. 'So that's the Rebecca you were talking about. Dr Bateman's daughter.'

'Well actually I bought her that horse,' said Charles solemnly. 'We were going to call it Lightning, it was so fast, but we thought that would give the game away so we called it Thunder instead.'

'That's amazing,' said Mortimer, equally solemnly. 'I thought she'd had Thunder for years.' Charles was not sure whose leg was being pulled by whom; he never was, in Norfolk.

As they followed the horses to the course Mortimer scratched his head reflectively. 'I thought Miss Bateman was going out with Harry Burton.'

'Did you really?' said Charles grimly. 'Who is this Harry Burton anyway?'

'By rights he's the Honourable Henry. His father owns

the Burton estates; they cover most of my area between Wettleford and the coast.'

So much for the 'patch', thought Charles sourly. And that is what John Cranmer must have meant about a 'scion of the local nobility'. But hadn't he said he *used* to be around quite a bit? He clutched at the straw. Then the starter's flag went down, and the Ladies' Race was off.

It was two circuits of the course, starting and finishing in the field where they stood. They watched the runners take the first couple of jumps, tightly bunched, then clear the hedge into the next field. Until they reappeared they had to rely on the commentary. Apparently all six horses were evenly matched at this stage, there was little to choose between them.

Then they were back over the hedge again and heading for the last fence to complete the circuit. They were still in a bunch but Rebecca was in the lead, just ahead of Nellie. Both of them were easy to spot, Rebecca because of Thunder's distinctive colouring, Nellie because of her own distinctive proportions.

'Come on Fat Chance!' yelled Mortimer, waving his flying helmet.

'Come on Thunder!' shouted Charles, jumping up and down. He had no idea it was going to be quite so exciting.

The field swept past and started on the second circuit. As they headed for the hedge again one or two of the runners showed signs of flagging. Perhaps they had only expected to go round once, thought Charles sympathetically.

There was an 'Oh!' from the crowd. A horse had fallen as it jumped the hedge. From where they stood it was impossible to see which one. An ambulance started up.

'Just a precaution,' Mortimer tried to sound reassuring. 'They don't often hurt themselves too badly.'

'It looks worse than falling off a roof,' said Charles unconvinced. But the commentator had identified the horse and rider; they were unknown to Charles. Neither was hurt.

The commentator picked up the race again. Thunder and Fat Chance were ahead of the field and drawing away steadily. But there was nothing to choose between them. All eyes were on the hedge where the horses would reappear.

'I've never really bothered about horse-racing before,' Charles confided, 'but this is a real gripper.'

Mortimer gave him a gentle smile. 'It's not exactly the Grand National – but it'll do.'

The first horse appeared above the hedge. Or rather, the first chest. Nellie and Fat Chance sailed over and headed for the final jump, Rebecca and Thunder followed, a good ten yards behind.

'One to go,' breather Mortimer. 'Come on Nellie, you're nearly there.'

'Come on Rebecca!' shouted Charles, his voice rising to a scream. 'Go, go, go, Becky. Go, go, *go*!'

As he screamed Nellie looked over her shoulder. It was a mistake. When she looked back she was almost on the jump. Fat Chance took off with Nellie still gathering herself. The horse seemed to hesitate in mid-air; its back legs caught the top of the jump, it landed awkwardly and jolted Nellie off its back before regaining its balance and running on. Rebecca was far enough behind to take avoiding action and Thunder cleared the jump well away from where Nellie was still lying. They raced on alone to the finishing line. Charles cheered Rebecca over the line, then turned to find that Mortimer had ducked under the ropes and was running up the course to where Nellie was now sitting up, apparently still dazed. Charles started to follow, then decided against it.

He watched Mortimer kneel beside her and cradle her against him. He took off her riding cap and stroked her hair. They made an incongruous but somehow touching couple, the forty-year-old in his dark blue suit, the pretty girl in her riding gear, sitting alone together in front of hundreds of spectators. Charles appreciated that there was very little of the avuncular about Mortimer at that moment.

Then the little tableau ended. Nellie got to her feet, waved Mortimer away with obvious irritation and started walking along the course to where Fat Chance was being held. She got a sympathetic round of applause from the crowd. Relieved to see she was all right, and not anxious to meet Mortimer again at that moment, Charles headed for the winner's enclosure.

The Honourable Henry Burton was already there, with a bottle of champagne. So were other members of the luncheon party, full of congratulations, and waving glasses. Rebecca dismounted, and disappeared from sight. Charles hovered on the edge briefly, then left them to it. He was beginning to wish she had come in last. Then he remembered his bets, and found that while he had lost two shillings on Fat Chance, he had won ten on Thunder. He took the money and headed for the beer tent, deciding he would catch up with Rebecca later. There he found Mortimer, in equally sombre mood.

There was no need for words. Charles bought the first round.

'You'll have to leave now, gentlemen, we're closing the bar.'

Outside the beer tent the last race had been won, the last winnings had been collected, the last betting slips had been torn up. The last horses were being coaxed into their trailers, the last cars were queuing up at the gate. Inside the tent, only Charles and Mortimer remained.

'Are you going to be all right on that bike, Mort?' Charles had made an occasional sortie to collect the race results and a few other details, but Mortimer had remained at the bar throughout. Neither of them had set eyes on any actual racing after Rebecca's victory. Charles felt he was getting the hang of these point-to-points.

'I shall ride,' said Mortimer slowly, 'with enormous

care.' He donned his leather helmet, which miraculously he had retained throughout the events of the afternoon. Combined with his dark blue suit it gave him the appearance of an absconding bank manager. He looked imposing enough, thought Charles, to cow any traffic policeman.

'What about *your* bike?' asked Mortimer in return. 'Where is it, anyway?'

'Oh dear,' said Charles, and hastened out of the tent. He looked along the lines where the parked cars used to be. Now just a few were dotted along the course, the spaces between them littered with paper bags, old cans and crisp packets, and empty bottles.

Where-Jim-Something's station wagon had been parked the area had been cleared quite efficiently; Young Farmers, it seemed, had some respect for other farmers' land. All that remained was Charles's delivery bike, lying forlornly on its side. A note was attached to the nameplate: 'Have to go. Sorry you're not about. Hope you're not sulking. See you in the summer. Rebecca.'

And there was a postscript. 'All life is a gamble.'

The cycle ride back to Toftham was even worse than the ride out. The remaining horse-boxes were travelling much faster and they seemed much wider. He had some quite alarming moments as they thundered past, particularly as the bike seemed to wobble more than usual, but he refused to take to the verge. Instead he waved his fist at their retreating rear bumpers, a precarious exercise in itself. When he finally reached the office and climbed the stairs to his room he felt in no mood to write the report, but Mr Juby was waiting for it upstairs.

When he eventually took it up to him, he knew it was not one of his finer creations. Mr Juby's expression as he read it suggested he shared the same view.

'You've waxed a bit lyrical over the Ladies' Race, boy. "Miss Bateman and Miss Gruntling fought out a magnificent race on Thunder and Fat Chance. The crowd rose to them as a man, as they headed for the final jump".' Mr Juby interrupted himself. 'There hent narthin to sit on at a point-to-point; how could they rise, then?'

'It's metaphorical,' said Charles weakly.

'That's may be metta-farricle, but it hent the *Journal*.' Mr Juby struck out the sentence and went on reading.

' "Fat Chance, ten yards clear of Thunder, took the last jump badly and unseated its curvaceous rider . . ." ' Mr Juby stopped again. He did not need to speak; he just looked at Charles, and shook his head sadly. 'Curvaceous' was firmly crossed out.

' "As she lay prostrate on the ground she must have heard the thundering hooves approaching, but with great skill Miss Bateman succeeded in avoiding her. She took the jump perfectly and rode Thunder past the winning post, an elegant and worthy victor".'

Mr Juby looked up at Charles again, his face solemn. 'Why blast my eyes, boy,' – he was laying on the accent heavily – 'you fair got my hart a-thumping there. Thass better than that Barbrer Cartland and no mistairk.'

As Charles watched, humiliated, he struck out the entire paragraph and wrote instead: 'Miss Bateman took the jump safely and rode on to win by a distance.'

'I suppose Nellie weren't hurt?' Mr Juby enquired. Charles said she was fine. 'That must have been a nasty moment for Mortimer, I'll be bound.' The link between Mortimer and Nellie had obviously not escaped him. Fat Chance, thought Charles appropriately.

'We'd better put our readers out of their misery too,' observed Mr Juby as he added another line: 'Miss Gruntling was unhurt.' Then he resumed his reading.

'You don't say much about the later races. Fairly dull, were they, after all that excitement?'

'Yes,' said Charles. 'Fairly dull.'

'Or couldn't you hear the common terry in the beer tent?' Charles's breath was still fairly potent. Fortunately Mr Juby did not seem to expect a reply. He reached the final paragraph.

'There's one thing you've left out, Charlie, and I partickerly told you about it. How was the going?'

Charles thought back over his disastrous day: the first encounter with the abominable Harry Burton at the Hero, the row with Rebecca, the crowd of her friends in the winners' enclosure which prevented him getting near her, the unwise sojourn in the beer tent, the laconic farewell note, the uncomfortable journey home, Mr Juby's dissection of his report. And now he foresaw a further reprimand and a tedious round of phone calls. He gave up.

'The going,' said Charles, 'was bloody awful.'

Ten

They were sunning themselves in the little back garden of Lambeth Palace – Charles's unofficial name for John Cranmer's modest Rectory – when John suggested that he might like to come to morning service next day.

He had not suggested it before in the weeks since Charles had moved in. He had rather hoped that Charles might suggest it himself. Charles, on the other hand, liked to keep his Sundays free. It was the only day of the week when his services were not normally required by the *Journal*. Apart from Remembrance Day Parade and the final of a Sunday Cricket League, Sunday was in the office diary a newsless day, a welcome blank. It was the day when Chas Benson, Purveyor of Good News, was able to leave his bike undisturbed in the shed.

This was not a good moment for John to make the suggestion. The afternoon had been spent on the usual tour of fayres and fêtes which occupied every Saturday during the summer. There had also been the Toftham Baby Show, an horrific affair involving a great deal of screaming. The babies were quite well-behaved, the screaming came from infuriated mothers whose offspring had failed to win a prize. It was the only event Charles had been to where the judges refused to give their names.

He had cycled back to Remingham tired and depressed, wondering not for the first time why had got himself into a job where he had to work at all hours, on six days of the week, with little to show for it except a few columns of names on a Friday morning. He thought enviously of some of his fellow members of Toftham Round Table – kindred spirits who had welcomed him to their meetings and speedily enrolled him. Most of them were nine-to-five men, from insurance agents to junior council officials. There were farmers too, of course, but he had never fathomed how they spent their days . . .

Now he was sprawled in one of the Rectory's ancient deckchairs, enjoying the sunshine and looking forward to his first pint at the Remingham Arms. Tomorrow, he was thinking, he might stroll down to the river where he had picnicked with Rebecca, and wallow in nostalgia and misery. He had not heard from her since she had returned to university after the ill-fated point-to-point.

So he was not wildly enthusiastic about spending Sunday morning in church. He was still trying to think of a convincing excuse when John enlarged on the invitation.

'To be quite honest, I'd be glad of your support. I'm trying something a little new tomorrow morning, and trying anything new involving the church is quite a major undertaking. People don't seem to like changing the established way of things.'

Charles could sympathise. He knew what he meant. Soon after he had arrived in Toftham he had suggested to the elderly Vicar that he might call on Wednesdays instead of Tuesdays, so that more of the week's news could go into Friday's paper. The Vicar insisted on consulting the parochial church council before he would agree.

'What do you plan to do? Sacrifice a goat? I could make a bob or two out of that.'

John grinned. 'Very nearly as dramatic. I'm going to have a family service.'

'A family service? For families?' Charles raised his hands in mock amazement. 'Does the Archbishop know about this?'

'It may not sound very revolutionary, but some of my parishioners seem to think so. Anything outside the Book of Common Prayer could be the work of the Devil. For them it must be 1662 and all that. They're not the ones who actually come to church, of course. I think my regulars are game to give it a go. It's the ones who don't come who are making the fuss.'

Charles was baffled. 'If they don't come, what's it got to do with them?'

'Even if they are not church members it's still their church,' John explained patiently. 'They may never come into it except to be christened, and married, and buried, but the church belongs to the village and the village wants a say in what goes on in it. And that has to be what went on in their father's day, and their grandfather's; the old prayers, and hymns that everyone knows, and a sermon that's nice and short so that, if they do happen to come along, they can be sure to be out by twelve o'clock. Then the men have time for a pint while their wives cook the dinner. It is a plan ordained by God, tried and proved over the years, and thus it ever shall be, world without end. Except that tomorrow I'm having a family service.'

'But what's the difference?' Charles could still not understand the problem. 'Are you going to read the first lesson from the *Beano*? Or do a little juggling in front of the altar? Or a couple of somersaults out of the pulpit? Or what?'

'I might, if it made a point. Actually I've got Willum to play the guitar.'

Now Charles appreciated why John might need support. Willum was the lad who took round the deliveries from the village shop. It was about all he could do, because Willum was a simple soul who had never worked out how to read or write, but Mrs Curson at the stores put little drawings on all the boxes of goods he had to deliver, so he knew where they had to go. He hauled them round in a little wooden handcart, and rarely made a mistake. He was also inclined to do little dances in the roadway, and sing very suddenly and very loudly. Strangers found this disconcerting, but nobody in Remingham took any notice. In a town Willum would have been an oddity; he might even have been put in an institution. In a village, he was just part of the scenery.

And Willum had two great attributes. He was always smiling, and he could play the guitar.

Mrs Curson had given it to him some years before as a Christmas bonus. It had belonged to her son who had long since left home, and it was still in reasonable order. She had shown Willum how to play it, and Willum revealed a remarkable natural talent. Without being able to read a line of music he could now play any tune that he heard just once. He was a great attraction at village concerts, but he refused to stir further afield. Indeed he had only been to Toftham a handful of times in his life; he had never been to Norwich, and London could have been on another planet.

'He should be a great success, if he doesn't do any of his dances,' said Charles.

'I think it's worth the risk. The children will love him. And I thought if you were fairly handy you could quieten him down if he got too excited.'

Charles resigned himself to a Sunday morning in church. It might be quite a lively one at that. 'But what's he going to play? He can hardly know any hymns.'

'He does now. I spent last evening with him, humming the tunes for him, and he can play them without a falter. Just simple ones that the children can understand. The real problem is getting the children.'

Charles could understand that. There had not been a Sunday School at Remingham for many years. The Rector visited the village school regularly to take the scripture class, but that was the nearest that the children came to attending church, except for the compulsory turnout at Christmas and Easter. John calculated that the average age of his regular congregation was nearer sixty then fifty, and getting older all the time. This was his first attempt to reverse the trend.

'I mentioned the service at the last scripture class, and I asked the children to tell their parents, and I've put up a notice in the porch, but it's touch and go whether any of them come. So I thought if you came along, apart from keeping an eye on Willum, at least I'd have somebody there from the younger generation.'

150

'Thanks very much,' said Charles. 'I'll bring my teddy.'

'Make sure it knows the hymns,' said the Rector.

It was the first time Charles had entered Remingham's splendid parish church, and it looked even more impressive inside. Massive stone pillars soared up to the fine hammer-beam roof, now alas in urgent need of repair. The rows of pews seemed to stretch away into the distance. Beyond them, in the chancel, he could just see the ornate memorials to the Reminghams, the showpieces of the church, much treasured not only for their artistic value but because they helped to hold up the walls. They were also the symbol of the continuing influence of the Reminghams of Remingham Hall; but Charles noted there was no sign of that particular family today.

Nor indeed were there any other families. From the doorway he could see a handful of worshippers in dark suits and sober dresses, presumably the regular congregation, but there was no sign of any children. Poor old John, he thought.

'Welcome, young man. Nice to see you.'

Dr Bateman was handing him a prayer-book and a hymn-book. 'I'm not sure if you'll need these – not quite certain what the Rector's up to today. But you'd better be on the safe side.'

It was the first time they had met since Rebecca's departure. Although they were near neighbours there was little occasion for their paths to cross. Charles spent most of his days out of the village, and a good many evenings too. John Cranmer did the household shopping so he rarely visited Mrs Curson's shop except to collect her village news. In Remingham, as in Tittlesham and many other villages, the *Journal* relied on the local shopkeeper as its official correspondent, and Charles wisely left all the routine newsgathering to her.

So his only regular forays into the village were to have a drink at the Remingham Arms, and not surprisingly he had yet to meet Dr Bateman in the bar. It had not occurred to him that the church was a much more likely place to find him.

He took the books the doctor was offering him. 'I hadn't realised you were a sidesman, sir.'

'Churchwarden, actually. Another of the duties I share with Lord Remingham, though I'm afraid we don't see much of him. Busy man, of course.'

'And – how is Rebecca?' He tried not to sound too eager.

'I suppose she's very well. No doubt we'd hear if she wasn't. But she's not a great letter writer.' The doctor looked a him quizzically. 'I was rather wondering if *you'd* heard from her?'

'Me?' Charles was quite startled. 'Why should I have heard?'

'Well, she seemed to be talking about you quite a bit after you went on that picnic. But I gather you had some sort of row over at the Tittlesham point-to-point. She seemed a little upset when she came back.'

'It was only a minor row. I never got the chance to put things right.'

'She said much the same thing. Looked for you all over the place, apparently. That's why I thought she might have written.'

'Oh damn,' said Charles. Then, realising his surroundings, he apologised. But he was furious with himself; he should never have gone off to that beer tent.

'Perhaps I could write to her, if you'd let me have her address.'

'Newcastle University should be enough. Now you'd better find a seat.' He ushered Charles towards the central aisle.

That shouldn't be too difficult, thought Charles. The rest of the congregation were all occupying the rear pews. There was a vast empty expanse between them and the front of the church. In other circumstances he would have tucked himself away with everyone else to be as inconspicuous as possible. But he could not be much help to John, or to Willum, from there. He walked the length of the aisle and sat himself in the front pew on the left.

There was a murmuring from behind him, but he assumed it was because he was a newcomer, and thought little of it. After a few moments, however, he heard footsteps coming down the aisle and Dr Bateman tapped him gently on the shoulder.

'Sorry about this,' he whispered in Charles's ear, 'but you're in Lord Remingham's pew.'

Charles was mystified. 'I didn't know he had a personal pew. But anyway, I thought you said he wouldn't be here.'

Dr Bateman's whisper grew a little louder. 'It doesn't really matter whether he's here or not. This is his pew. I wonder if you'd mind sitting somewhere else.'

Charles felt a wave of embarrassment and anger. For a moment he was on the brink of storming out altogether. But it would be letting down John Cranmer, it would mark him out in the village as an eccentric, just when he was beginning to be accepted, and anyway this was Rebecca's father. No point in stirring up trouble there. He rose slowly.

'Where do you suggest I do sit?' he asked, trying hard to keep his voice calm. 'Would I be all right over there?' He pointed to the other front pew, on the right of the aisle.

'Actually,' said the Doctor, 'that's my pew. But as I'm on my own today you are very welcome to share it.'

Honoured, I'm sure, thought Charles sourly, but he thanked him, and they both took their seats in the pew.

At that moment there was a minor commotion at the back of the church. Two small children had come in, a boy of about ten and a girl slightly younger. The girl was carrying a woolly shawl containing a very small baby. The children's clothes must have seen many a jumble sale, but they were clean and tidy, and the children themselves looked well-scrubbed.

They had been talking together happily as they

entered, but as every head turned towards them they fell silent, and stood uncertainly in the middle of the aisle.

'Ah, it's the Gibsons,' said Dr Bateman, and hastened up the aisle. He said hallo to the children, gave them prayer-books and hymn-books and led them down to the front. For a moment Charles thought he was putting them in Lord Remingham's pew; could these be his offspring, travelling incognito? But they were ushered into the pew behind, where they sat looking around wide-eyed at the memorials in the chancel, the pillars, the lofty roof. It was obviously their first visit too.

So this was the sole result of John Cranmer's canvassing, thought Charles. At a family service he might also have hoped for the rest of the family, but half must be better than none.

The Rector emerged from his vestry and came down the chancel to stand beside the front pews. Charles had not seen him in his vestments before. They gave him a little extra presence, he did not look quite so young.

Behind him was Willum with his guitar. As always, he was smiling broadly. His suit was rather too large for him – another inheritance from Mrs Curson's absent son – and his hair had been flattened down with something very greasy. He wore his usual battered black boots, but today they bore the trace of a shine. Willum, in short was in his Sunday best – and as with everything that happened to him in his untroubled life, he was enjoying the experience hugely. Charles poised himself in case he broke into one of his little dances.

The Rector surveyed the distant members of the congregation, nodded to Charles and the Doctor, and smiled at the children.

'Welcome to this family service,' he announced. 'Some of us may find it a little different from what we are used to, but it is nice to see some new faces who have joined us, and I am sure that with Willum's help we shall manage very well.'

Willum's smile grew even broader. 'Hair we go then,

marster!' he cried, and struck a chord on the guitar, as the Rector hastily announced the first hymn. Charles detected some more murmuring from the rear pews, but ignored it. They launched into the first verse of 'There's a Friend for Little Children'.

The two little children in the pew opposite did not attempt to sing, or even open their hymn-books. They were fascinated by Willum's energetic strumming. Willum sensed their interest and ambled happily to the end of their pew, still playing. John Cranmer winked across at Charles, and they kept singing.

They came to the end of the first verse and Willum looked round at the rector. 'How many more, marster?'

'Five more, Willum,' replied the Rector.

'Five that'll be,' agreed Willum, and started again.

By the end of the second verse he had lost count again. 'How many more, marster?'

'Four more, Willum.'

'Four that'll be.'

And it became a ritual. After the next verse the children joined in with Willum. 'How many more, marster?' they chorussed.

'Three more, Willum,' the Rector dutifully replied. And they all responded, 'Three that'll be.'

Finally the Rector had to answer: 'No more Willum.' And Charles could not resist joining in too, as Willum and the children called out together, 'No more that'll be.' The family service had got off to a rollicking start.

It went on in much the same vein. There were some simple prayers, and a little talk from the Rector about the value of family life, and being members of God's family. He illustrated it with drawings on a blackboard which he produced from inside the pulpit and propped against the lectern. From the back of the church, where they had no doubt assumed he had climbed into the pulpit to preach a more orthodox sermon, there was another bout of muttering.

They sang a couple more hymns, played with great panache by Willum, who had followed the drawings on the blackboard just as closely as the children. Charles had been watchful for any signs of an impromptu dance, but Willum had remained absolutely engrossed throughout. In fact the only disturbance occurred when the baby woke up and started wailing, but the little boy produced a dummy from his pocket and passed it to the little girl, who stuffed it in the baby's mouth. It was obviously a familiar routine.

The last hymn ended. John Cranmer pronounced the blessing and walked back to his vestry. Willum was about to follow when the little boy called after him, 'Can you play "Roll Out The Barrel"?'

Willum beamed with delight. 'That I can,' he cried, and began to strum the tune. The two children joined in lustily. 'Roll out the bar-rel, we'll have a barrel of fun, roll out the bar-rel, we've got the blues on the run . . .' At the rear of the church the murmur increased.

Dr Bateman was rising to interrupt the singalong when John Cranmer reappeared, now just in his black cassock. He caught Charles's eye and they exchanged a grin before he tapped Willum gently on the shoulder.

'Ease up, Willum. Why not play the rest of it outside. The children can go with you.'

Willum agreed happily. He stopped playing and waved at the children. 'Come you on, my bootys. Come you on t'gether.' And taking one child in each hand he led them up the church. As he passed the soberly-clad figures in the rear pews he broke into one of his little dances and shouted a greeting. Then the little group was outside the door, leaving a stunned silence behind. The strains of 'Roll Out The Barrel', with two piping voices sounding over the notes of the guitar, receded into the distance.

Two figures left the rear pews and came down the aisle towards the Rector, an elderly couple whom Charles remembered seeing running one of the stalls at the church fête. The wife was in a big black hat and long black coat, the husband in a black suit and a black tie.

The ensemble presumably doubled for Sunday best and funerals.

'Could we have a word, Rector?' asked the husband. From their expressions it was not going to be a very pleasant one.

'Let me say goodbye to the others, Mr Browning, then I'll be glad to see you,' said John Cranmer quietly.

The lady in the big black hat looked back up the aisle. 'Seems like they've already gone,' she observed. And indeed the last of the congregation were just disappearing through the door.

'What a pity,' John murmured. For a moment his shoulders slumped and he looked a little older. Then he straightened up and smiled determinedly at the elderly couple. 'Right, then I can see you straight away. Come into the vestry. Good-day, Doctor, and thank you. And Charles, I expect I'll see you back at the house.'

'I suggest the Remingham Arms,' said Charles firmly.

The Rector gave a wry grin. 'Perhaps you're right,' he said. Then he led the way into the vestry.

Charles helped Dr Bateman gather up the hymn-books and put them on the shelves at the back of the church. Each of them was waiting for the other to speak first.

'I thought that was rather a good service,' said Charles at last.

Dr Bateman did not commit himself. 'I'm afraid it didn't go down very well with our regular worshippers. They're not used to having guitars and blackboards in church.'

'I don't suppose they're used to having children in church either,' commented Charles rather shortly. 'Or babies for that matter, except when they're christened.'

'These folk are the mainstay of the church. They're good people.' The Doctor was getting annoyed. Charles realised with regret that he seemed to have the same effect on the father as on the daughter. 'Those two that have just gone in to see the Rector: Mr Browning is the church treasurer, Mrs Browning always comes into the church first thing Sunday morning in her old clothes to give it a sweep through, then goes back home to change for the service. They've come to this church all their lives. You don't just start having guitars and blackboards instead of the organ and a proper sermon, and you don't let Willum play the fool during the hymns, good lad though he is. And you certainly don't end the service with "Roll Out The Barrel". Young Cranmer will have to go a little slower. I think he's probably finding that out even now.'

Charles could see his point, but he could see John's also. 'Surely it's a good thing to try to attract young people to church. The Brownings won't go on forever.'

'Of course it's a good thing,' agreed Dr Bateman. 'That's why I backed him on this service. And I'll go on backing him – it's good to have a lively young parson in a village like this – they're mostly in their dotage. But it's no good antagonising your faithful supporters for the sake of attracting two extra children – and a baby.'

'Who were the children, by the way?' Charles felt it was time to change the subject. 'The Gibsons, did you say?'

'Now there's something it would be useful for the Rector to get involved in.' Dr Bateman looked at him speculatively. 'You too, possibly. It would do no harm to let some people know how the other half has to live. You ought to go and see the Gibsons.'

'Why didn't the parents come – or aren't there any?'

'Oh yes, there are parents. Good people, the Gibsons, but Dan is crippled with arthritis and his wife won't stir far from him, even though the children are old enough to look after him now.'

Charles raised an eyebrow. The two little children seemed to cope well enough with the baby, but they hardly seemed capable of looking after an invalid. The Doctor smiled, and explained.

'No, not those two. They're the youngest. There are four more of them, the oldest is about fourteen. Very fertile lady, Mrs Gibson; and Dan seemed to manage very well up to a year or so back, in spite of the arthritis. But it doesn't make for very gracious living, nine of them in a two-bedroomed cottage.'

Charles was aghast. 'Nine of them in two bedrooms? How on earth do they manage?'

Dr Bateman patted him on the shoulder. 'Why not go and see, lad? You need to meet a few more people than doctors and parsons to find out what country life is all about.'

'But hang on,' said Charles. 'You're on the local council, sir. Can't you do something about re-housing the Gibsons?'

They strolled towards the church door. 'It's not as simple as that. They've been on the waiting list for years, but we've no empty council houses in Remingham and anyway they've only got three bedrooms. We couldn't fit all the Gibsons into one of them.'

'Then why not give them two?' asked Charles. 'After all the Tuckers over at Withersett got three.'

'The Tuckers were three separate families, even though they were all related. One family, one house, that's the rule. Anyway, how could you split the Gibsons between two houses? Half the children in one, and half in the other, and poor Mrs Gibson running backwards and forwards in between?'

'But there must be some answer,' said Charles, a little desperately.

'If there is,' – Dr Bateman looked at him with great solemnity – 'If there is, then I'm sure you'll find it. Now I must be off. If you're writing to Rebecca, do send her our love.'

As Charles watched him set off down the path the Brownings emerged from the church behind him and went past with only the slightest of nods. John Cranmer came out behind them looking a little flushed. Charles gave him a sympathetic smile, and they walked down the path together. As they reached the gate Willum and the two children came into sight down the street. They had apparently made a tour of the village, and they were still singing. 'Now's the time to roll the bar-rel . . .'

The two young men looked at each other and they both started laughing. Without a word, they turned towards the Remingham Arms . . .

Eleven

The cottage at the end of the long rutted track seemed on the brink of collapse. The flaking brick walls were discoloured by damp and one of the side walls was bulging ominously. A number of the pantiles on the roof were broken or out of place, one or two windows had boarding instead of glass, and there was a long crack down the side of the chimney. The front door, its paint flaking, hung lopsidedly open.

A few yards from the cottage was a ramshackle washhouse, and beyond that a smaller structure, the smell from which made its purpose quite clear. The area in front of the cottage, once presumably a garden, was now bare earth; by the front door was a well with an oldfashioned pump. Charles noted wryly as he pushed his bike up the lane that this was one country cottage without any vestige of roses round the door.

It had taken him a little time to get around to the Gibsons, but this was a Thursday afternoon, always the quietest time in the week, when it was too late to get anything else into Friday's paper, and he had suggested to Mr Juby that he might pay them a visit. He assumed Mr Juby knew all about them, and of course Mr Juby did.

'Remarkable woman, Betty Gibson, coping with all those kids, and Dan as well. Very handsome woman in her day. Dan was a good man too, but fit for nothing now. Has to live on the Welfare.'

He took much the same view as Dr Bateman about the difficulty of moving them. Unlike Dr Bateman, he did not seem greatly concerned. 'There's a lot of folk out in the villages living too many to a house. There are some big families hereabouts, five or six children some of 'em. The only house big enough to take them are all owned by the gentry. There's not a lot you can do there, boy.'

Charles feared he was probably right, but he felt he owed it to Dr Bateman at least to visit the Gibsons. So, having cycled about a mile out of Remingham and negotiated the rutted track – almost impassable in winter, he guessed – here he was.

For such a large family the place seemed uncommonly quiet; then he remembered the children must still be at school. The only sign of life came from the wash-house. There was a plume of smoke drifting from its squat little chimney, and somebody moving about inside.

He propped his bike against the pump and walked over to it. Mrs Gibson was on her knees on the floor, blowing the fire that was burning underneath the big copper. The copper was full of clothes, and the wash-house was full of steam. Charles felt he had stepped back fifty years.

Mrs Gibson paused at her blowing and looked up at him. She was only in her forties but she looked older, her bare arms thin and wrinkled, her hair prematurely grey, but the lined face was still attractive and the blue eyes bright and keen. Mr Juby was right; she had been a handsome woman.

'Yes?' she asked, getting to her feet. She was quite tall.

'My name's Charles Benson. I'm with Mr Juby on the *Journal*.' He gave his customary introduction. She was uninterested and unimpressed.

'You must have come to the wrong place, then. There's no news here.'

She spoke pleasantly but firmly, with only the trace of a Norfolk accent. She turned back to the copper.

'Dr Bateman suggest I might call.'

She looked round at him again. 'You're a friend of Dr Bateman?'

'Well, yes,' said Charles. 'Actually I know his daughter quite well.'

'Now there's a nice girl.' He had made an impression

at last. 'Wait till I get this fire going, then I'll make a cup of tea.' She was down on her knees again. Charles noted appreciatively that she had very shapely ankles.

'Do you always do the washing at this time of day?' he asked curiously. He assumed everybody did their washing on Monday morning.

Mrs Gibson smiled up at him. 'With a family like mine you do the washing at all times of the day, every day.'

She led the way into the cottage. The front door opened directly into the sitting room. There was a frayed carpet, a mixed assortment of battered chairs and an old table, a bed along one wall and a cot in the corner. The baby was in the cot and Dan Gibson was sitting up in the bed. He was older than his wife, in his mid-fifties, a big man but Charles could see that his hands were gnarled and twisted, and he could hardly hold the book he was reading.

Mrs Gibson introduced them and went through into the kitchen, apparently the only other downstairs room. Charles shook one of the twisted hands, and nodded across at the baby. 'We've already met.' He explained about the family service.

'Those were our two youngest,' said Dan Gibson. 'A couple of bright ones, they are. Heard about the service at school and asked if they could go. It was their idea to take the baby – they're very good with it. The older ones weren't interested, I'm afraid. I told Betty she ought to go but the others had all gone out and she wouldn't leave me. She's a good woman, Betty, but she ought to get out more.'

'Why should I want to get out more?' called his wife from the kitchen. 'I've got all I want here.'

Dan shrugged. 'No good trying to say anything private in this place. Not unless the children are all home. Then nobody can hear anything anyway.'

Charles followed up the opening. 'That's really what I came about. How on earth do you all manage here? I mean, where does everybody sleep?'

He sensed immediately that he had made a mistake. Dan Gibson glared at him from the bed. 'What's that to do with you, then?'

Mrs Gibson came in with a tea-tray. More quietly she said, 'I don't really think it's any of your business, Mr Benson.'

Charles apologised. 'I'm sorry. I wasn't just trying to be nosey. I thought I might be able to help. It seems all wrong to have to cope with such a big family in such a small cottage. I wondered if I might contact the Council for you.'

'The Council!' Dan's resentment had given place to disgust. 'Whatever's the Council going to do? They've had us on their list for years. They've got nowhere to put us, and they never will have.'

'It might be worth another try. And the *Journal* might be able to help – give it a little publicity, put on a little pressure.'

'Pressure? The *Journal?*' Dan was obviously amused. Mrs Gibson was obviously not. 'We don't want any publicity,' she said sharply. 'That's the last thing we want. That'll only do harm, not good. I won't have anything in the papers, that's definite.'

'Why not?' asked Charles bewildered. 'Why should it do any harm? You can't be worse off than you are.'

'Of course we could,' cried Betty Gibson. 'They could take the children away. That's what could happen if you put us in the papers. And I won't have that; I want my children with me. So just you forget all this, Mr Benson, and leave us be.'

It was an aspect that had not occurred to Charles, but he realised she might be right. If he caused too much of a stir and the authorities were forced to take action, it might well finish up with some of the children being taken into care. He could understand Mrs Gibson's concern.

'I see what you mean. And of course I'll do as you say. But there must be an answer.' He remembered saying that before.

Betty Gibson poured the tea. 'I'm sorry if I was rude,' she said, 'but I meant what I said. Now have a cup of tea before you go.'

They drank their tea, exchanging polite observations about nothing of consequence, with Charles still trying to think of something he could do for the Gibsons. It seemed all wrong just to go off and forget them. Apart from anything else, it had the makings of quite a story.

He was making his farewells when he heard the sound of children shouting and laughing as they came up the lane. The young Gibsons were on their way home from school. As he and Mrs Gibson emerged from the front door the two youngest, who were in the lead, caught sight of him and whispered to the others, three girls who looked very like their mother, and a boy of about fourteen who seemed to be the eldest. they giggled together for a moment, then marched in a group towards him. As they marched they sang lustily, 'Roll Out the Barrel'.

'What's all this about?' asked Mrs Gibson, but before he could explain they were surrounded by the children, the two little ones seizing Charles's hands, the girls taking their mother's, and with the oldest boy watching rather sheepishly they were marched around the garden, still singing. It was impossible for the two grown-ups not to join in.

'. . . and the gang's all here!' The young Gibsons gave a cheer and poured into the cottage. Charles could hear them greeting their father and thundering up the stairs. The two little ones appeared in the bedroom window which still had glass in, and waved down to them. Charles waved back.

'My word, they're a cheerful lot,' he exclaimed to Mrs Gibson.

'Not always. But they do seem to get on very well together.' She was smiling after them affectionately, but when she turned to Charles she was quite serious again.

'I'm not just being selfish, wanting to keep them. They'd hate to be split up. I know it'll have to happen when they get a little older, but they're not ready for it yet.'

'I wonder if we could make an agreement,' said Charles. he had been thinking hard. 'I'd still like to see if there's something that can be done, but I promise to go about it carefully and I won't print a word unless I can find somewhere better for all of you. If I do, then once it's all safely settled I'd like to write the story. And not just for the *Journal* – I'm sure some of the London papers would be interested. People down there ought to know about families having to live in cottages like this. But I'll only do it after you've moved. What do you think?' As she still hesitated, he added: 'It was Dr Bateman's idea I should try to help.'

'I don't know,' said Mrs Gibson. 'I really don't know.'

Charles looked around for inspiration. He found it in an unlikely quarter.

'I suppose that's the privy.' He indicated the little building beyond the wash-house. 'How do nine of you manage with just one chemical closet?'

Mrs Gibson gave a wry smile. 'Nothing quite so sophisticated as that,' she said. 'It's just the old bucket. The night-soil men come and empty it once a week – if they can get up the lane. But it fills up before that, of course. There's hole round the back of the cottage I empty it into. "Burying the donkey", the children call it.'

Charles grimaced. 'That can't be much fun. And then there's that old wash-house, and I suppose just the pump of water. Do you think it's fair to keep the children here, if there's a chance of a modern house with proper sanitation?'

Betty Gibson smiled at him again. 'You know,' she said, 'you talk just like that young Rector.'

He was taken aback. 'John Cranmer? Has he been round?' He had not yet mentioned the Gibsons to John.

'He came some time ago, soon after he first arrived. But I told him what I've told you, and he promised not to say anything in case we were split up. He's a very understanding man, the Rector.'

'Well I do understand too, and I'll be very careful. And with the Rector on our side as well as the doctor, I'm sure we'll get somewhere.'

The eldest boy came out of the cottage and started walking to the privy. Then he realised Charles was watching, and blushed with embarrassment as he hurried the last few steps and dived inside. Mrs Gibson saw him too. She turned back to Charles.

'You're quite right, of course,' she said quietly. 'It's not just the privy. He has to share one of the bedrooms with the two youngest at the moment. The three girls share another. They're all growing up. They can't go on like that much longer.'

Charles had guessed that must be the situation. 'So you have to sleep downstairs?'

She nodded. 'We put up a camp bed each night in the sitting-room and I sleep down there with Dan and the baby.'

She looked around them at the bare garden, the tumbledown cottage, the wash-house with its chimney still smoking, the privy. The blue eyes were bleak.

'Yes,' she said, 'you're quite right. It would be good not to spend any more winters here. Please go ahead, Mr Benson. Do what you can.'

As he set off down the track with his bike he was halted by a shout from one of the bedroom windows. It was the two smallest Gibsons, calling out in chorus the line they had learned in church with Willum.

'How many more, marster?' It seemed strangely appropriate after Mrs Gibson's comment.

He took up the cue. 'No more, Willum,' he called back. At least I hope not, he added to himself.

The answering chorus from the children followed him reassuringly down the lane.

'No more that'll be.'

Back at Lambeth Palace Charles greeted Mrs Clegg, the lady who came in once a week to clean through the house. He saw John Cranmer through the open door of his study, gazing reflectively into space. There was a letter open in front of him on the desk. Charles decided this was not the time to raise the matter of the Gibsons, but the Rector called him in. 'Have a look at that,' he said, and passed him the letter.

It formally requested the Rector of Remingham to call a meeting of the Parochial Church Council to consider a resolution that 'family services' – the quotation marks were heavily emphasised – should be discontinued, and that all services in the parish church should be conducted according to the Book of Common Prayer. It was signed by H. Browning, M. Browning and C. Smith.

'I know the Brownings. Who's C. Smith?'

'The secretary of the PCC. He also happens to be Mrs Browning's cousin. He's obviously been boning up on his handbook. You need one-third of the council to call for a meeting, and we have eight members altogether so three's enough.'

'But is it up to the PCC to tell you how to run your services?' It was all a new world to Charles. His only previous contact with the administrative procedures of the Church of England had been as a member of a church youth club back in Wembley Park. The PCC had forbidden the playing of music in the church hall after ten o'clock. When all appeals to the Vicar had failed he had become an acting Free Churchman and joined a Presbyterian youth club where dancing went on until eleven. But there was no such solution available to John Cranmer.

'It's all down in the book. Even if the General Synod approves a different form of service, and the Bishop endorses it, the parochial church council still has the last word. It's quite right really; why should they be dictated to by the Synod, or the Bishop – or me, for that matter.'

'But how did you get the OK for the last one, if they object so strongly?'

'Technically the PCC approved it at the last meeting. We had a quorum, three of us, Dr Bateman and

Cuthbert Smith and myself, and Cuthbert raised no objection.' John looked a little uncomfortable. 'Perhaps I didn't explain too clearly what I had in mind – I just said I hoped to encourage more children along. The Brownings couldn't get to the meeting; I suppose they could argue it wasn't a valid decision.'

Charles shrugged. 'Well, if they want to do it by the book, let's see what else the book says about calling special meetings. Let's have a look.'

John passed him the little volume, *A Handbook for Churchwardens and Parochial Church Councillors*. He turned to the section headed 'Notices Relating to Meetings' and read it carefully.

The Rector watched him. 'I can tell you what it says. If I refuse or neglect to call a meeting within seven days of receiving the formal request, they can convene a meeting themselves.'

'But it doesn't give you a deadline for the actual date of the meeting. It says there has to be at least ten days' notice, but I can't see anything that says you have to hold it within a certain period.' Charles looked up triumphantly. 'Why not call it for, say, Christmas Day?'

John smiled and shook his head. 'I don't think that would be quite acceptable. But it's a kind thought.'

Charles tried again. 'At least give yourself time to hold another family service before they get the chance to vote against it. It's worth another go. Now, it's Thursday today. You're allowed a week to call the meeting so you can wait until next Thursday. Then if you give three weeks' notice, that won't be until after next month's family service. Three weeks doesn't seem too excessive.'

John was not convinced. 'Is it worth all that deviousness just to get in one more service, if they're going to stop them anyway?'

'Perhaps if they have another one they'll get more used to the idea. Or perhaps we could get some more support from the village, to show them they're in the minority.' Charles was warming to the idea. 'Why don't you have a go at the head teacher at the school? Give her a note for all the children to take home to the parents. Then have a go at the parents. I could have a word with some of the chaps at the Remingham Arms.' John laughed out loud and Charles took his point. 'Perhaps that's a bit too optimistic, but you're around the village all day, you could do a little house-to-house canvassing.'

'Oh come on, Charles, calm down.' The Rector was still smiling. 'I don't think we want to turn Remingham into a battleground over this. I don't quite see that as my pastoral role.' He became thoughtful again. 'But it would be nice to have another try. I learned one or two things from the last service. A little firmer control on Willum, perhaps, and bringing the grown-ups into it more instead of making them feel it's all for the children and nothing to do with them. And I could get the children to join in a bit more, instead of me doing all the talking . . .'

A new voice joined in. 'That's right, Rector. You give that another go, sir.'

They both looked round. Mrs Clegg was standing in the study doorway. She had been following the discussion with interest. 'Pardon me for butting in like, but I was there on Sunday and I thought you and Willum did a rare good turn between you. I reckon my little granddaughter would enjoy that singing with the guitar, and that story you told on the blackboard. Next go off, I'll bring her along.'

John Cranmer was almost blushing. 'Well thank you, Mrs Clegg. I'm glad you thought it was worthwhile. I'm sorry I didn't have a word with you afterwards. I got a bit involved with Mr and Mrs Browning.'

She nodded sympathetically. 'I saw them coming after you, so I didn't hang about. But don't you take too much notice of them; they're a little set in their ways. That was a good old do, that service. You keep a-goin'.'

Mrs Clegg went off into the kitchen and Charles grinned at John. 'I believe that's what they call an unsolicited testimonial. You'll have to carry on now.'

'Actually,' said John, 'it's rather more than just a testimonial. Mrs Clegg is on the church council too.'

Charles was delighted. 'That's one vote you've got, then. And I think you have a vote, so that's three out of eight. You only need two more.'

'As it happens I only need one more. I'm the chairman. If it's four all, I have a casting vote.'

'Better still.' Charles started making a list. 'Who else have we got?'

'As well as the Brownings and Cuthbert Smith, there's Cuthbert's wife. She does the church flowers. She's a nice soul but I don't think she'd vote against her husband. So you might call that a block vote really; they'll all go the same way.'

'But that's only seven members,' said Charles. 'There must be another one.'

'Of course there's another one.' John smiled wryly. 'My other churchwarden. Lord Remingham.'

'Ah,' said Charles thoughtfully.

'Ah indeed,' said John Cranmer.

'Do we know if he supports the idea?'

'Well, he didn't oppose it. But that's not the point. Apart from the annual meeting he never comes to the PCC. And I don't think we can take a proxy vote. Unless we can swing that block vote, it's 4–3 against.'

He was getting depressed again.

'Don't worry,' said Charles, with more confidence than he felt. 'We'll swing it. A lot can happen in four weeks. It's worth a try anyway.'

He put the *Handbook for Churchwardens and Parochial Church Councillors* on one side and sat down opposite John Cranmer. 'Now. Let's talk about the Gibsons.'

They did for some time. John advocated caution; it would break Mrs Gibson's heart to have the family split up. Charles still felt something ought to be done, and they debated at some length the various possibilities. But in the end it was not the Rector who gave him the idea for how to help the Gibsons.

It was Willum.

*
171

Before he cycled into Toftham next morning Charles made a point of stopping at the shop for a word with Mrs Curson about the family service. 'If you haven't written the report yet, I'd be glad to look after it for you.' He knew very well that she hadn't.

'I heard from Mrs Browning that were a bit of a disaster,' said Mrs Curson.

'Not at all,' Charles assured her. 'It was a great success. If you like, I'll write a few lines for next week.' The news would be nearly a fortnight old by the time it appeared, but in the section of the *Journal* headed 'Round The Villages', time was not exactly of the essence.

'Well if you wus there, I suppose you might as well,' she said grudgingly. It was a couple of shillings out of her pocket.

'Don't worry,' said Charles, 'I'll put your name on it. They'll still pay you for it.' This was strictly against the rules, but he felt it was worth it to keep her on his side. He had plans for getting her to put up a poster about the next service in her window.

As he came out of the shop he found Willum on his knees beside his handcart, sorting out the cartons and boxes. The youth beamed up at him. 'That were a good owld do at the church, marster. Are we goin' to have anarther?'

Charles smiled back. 'Indeed we are, Willum. You were really great with that guitar. I expect the Rector will be teaching you some more hymns.'

Willum broke into one of his little dances. 'Dew you tell him I'm ready and wairtin',' he declared, then got back on his knees beside the cartons. He took one with cardboard divisions for bottles and started tearing out one of the middle sections.

'What's the problem?' asked Charles.

'Why, that hent no problem' said Willum happily. 'I got to get this gurt owld bartle in.' He waved a fat bottle of salad cream. 'These holes hent big enough, so that'll have to be two holes into one, like.' He tore off a piece of cardboard and triumphantly fitted the bottle into the

172

enlarged hole. 'Thar she go, marster, snug as a ferret in a drairnpipe.'

The idea was so obvious that Charles had quite over-looked it. He slapped Willum on the back. 'Two holes into one, Willum! I tell you what, you're a bloody marvel.' He dug in his pocket and found a sixpence. 'You get an ice cream for yourself, old son. I'm very much obliged to you.'

He got on his bike and headed for Toftham. Behind him he heard Willum push the shop door open and shout inside: 'D'yew know what, Mrs K? That young marster, he say I'm a bloody marvel . . .'

As Charles entered the front office he offered his usual greeting to Nellie and Nellie gave her usual grunt in return. Relations had been even more strained since the point-to-point; she seemed to be nursing some new grudge. He thought perhaps she was annoyed that he had found out about her link with Mortimer, or it might have something to do with her fall and Mortimer's unwanted attentions in such a public situation. What-ever it was, she had hardly exchanged a word since. He shrugged, and went upstairs to find Mr Juby.

The editor was ensconced with Fred Knock in his office, discussing the latest titbit from Launford Council. Horace Glubb had bowed to public pressure and resigned as Housing Chairman.

'He would wait until that's too late for the paper,' grumbled Mr Juby. 'Cussed to the last, old Horace.' He nodded to Charles, then turned back to Mr Knock. 'Well now, Fred, what are you going to do about it?'

'Nothing at all,' said Mr Knock. 'That's His Lord-ship's worry, not mine. He'll have to find somebody else to hand out council houses to his men.'

Charles would not resist joining in. 'That's just why you should be doing something, Mr Knock. Why don't you take on the job? There'd be no more talk of favourit-ism after that.'

Mr Knock looked at him in some surprise. 'That's

not my cup of tea at all, lad. I'm not cut out to be a chairman. I do better keeping an eye on 'em from down the table.'

Charles took a breath. 'So Lord Remingham was right, then. He said you'd never take it on.'

The councillor stiffened, and glared at Charles. 'Did he, then? You been hob-nobbin' with His Lordship, have you? There's a fine thing.'

Mr Juby came to Charles's rescue. 'Now quieten down, Fred, he was just doing his job. And he's quite right, you know. You ought to take it on.'

But Mr Knock was still glaring at Charles. 'What else did he say about me, then?'

'He said you preferred to stand back and criticize rather than take on any responsibility yourself.' Charles did not mention that Lord Remingham also said he would make a good chairman.

'Did he, be damned. What the devil does he know?'

Mr Juby winked discreetly at Charles. 'Why not take it on then, just to show him?'

'I might at that, Mr Juby. I might at that.' Mr Knock pondered the thought for a moment. 'But somebody's got to propose it. That hent something you just volunteer for.'

Again Charles refrained from mentioning that Lord Remingham might well propose it himself. If Mr Knock knew he had his blessing that might well put him off. Mr Juby answered instead.

'No problem about that, Fred. Nick Nicholson from Tittlesham can propose it, and no doubt Charlie here can get Dr Bateman to second. They're very thick these days – share a pew, no less.' The bush telegraph had been buzzing again. 'I can't see anyone putting up any argument. Congratulations, Mr Chairman.'

'Hold on, Mr Juby, that's a bit early for that,' said Fred Knock, but he was obviously gratified at the idea.

'Perhaps I can give you the first case for your consider-ation,' ventured Charles, thinking this was as good a moment as any to test out his plan. They both turned to him.

'Don't tell me you're looking for a house, young Charlie,' Mr Juby chuckled. 'I didn't know you were getting along that fast with the gal Becky.'

Charles blushed. 'Of course not, Mr Juby. It's nothing to do with me. It's the family I was telling you about at Remingham. The Gibsons.'

'I told you there was no chance there, boy. Not with all those children.'

Mr Knock did not know of the Gibsons, and Charles explained about the conditions Dan and Betty Gibson were living in with their seven children. His first reaction was not encouraging.

'I suppose they're Catholics, then? They're always in trouble like that.'

'Now come on, Fred,' remonstrated Mr Juby. 'I know you're a Primitive Methodist, but we got over that sort of talk a long time ago, even in Norfolk.'

'Well then, why don't they put some of the children into care? That's the answer.'

'No, it's not the answer, Mr Knock,' Charles protested. 'They're a very close-knit family, very fond of each other. It would be a tragedy to break them up.'

'Well, what is the answer then, lad? We hent got a council house big enough, that's for sure.'

'But you could have.' Charles could not resist pausing for effect. This was the crucial moment. 'Launford Council always builds three-bedroomed, semi-detached houses. Why not knock two of them into one?'

Mr Knock looked at Mr Juby, and Mr Juby looked at Mr Knock. They both looked at Charles. He hastened on. 'It shouldn't be much of a job. Knock a door in the dividing wall upstairs and down; I doubt it's very thick. Block up one of the front doors if you like, then you can fairly say it's just one house, if anybody complains you're giving two houses to one family. They'll need the six bedrooms; the boy ought to be on his own at his age, and the three elder girls are growing up fast, and the baby shouldn't have to share Mr and Mrs Gibson's room, especially with Mr Gibson so ill. It seems the ideal solution.'

'Now hold you hard, Charlie.' Mr Juby was making a note or two. 'Let's just think about that for a moment. Even if Fred here got the council to agree, you'd still need to find two empty houses next to each other. That don't often happen these days.'

'It might be difficult in Remingham itself, but I don't expect the Gibsons would mind living in a different village if they had to. They don't see much of Remingham anyway; the cottage is quite isolated and they hardly ever get out. The children would have to change school, but they wouldn't have a mile to walk each way, like they do now.'

'What about the waiting list?' asked Mr Knock. 'Poor old Horace has just resigned because the Tuckers jumped the waiting list. You don't expect me to allow that.' He was already talking as if he were Chairman, Charles noted.

'There's no problem there, Mr Knock. They've been on the list for years. If there hadn't been so many children they's have had a house ages ago.'

The Housing Chairman-in-waiting had one more question. 'Why are you interested in the Gibsons, lad? What's in it for you?'

Charles decided to be frank. 'I like the Gibsons; I think they deserve better than they've got. But not only that. It would be a great story for the *Journal* if it happens. And it'll show that Launford RDC had got an imaginative, go-ahead new Housing Chairman . . .'

'None of that soft soap, lad,' said Mr Knock, but the point had sunk in. 'I'll tell you what I'll do. The Council meets next week. If they appoint me Chairman, I'll raise it at the next Housing Committee. We'll see how we get on.'

'You won't mention it elsewhere, Mr Knock? The Gibsons are very anxious in case the children get taken away, if too many people start talking.'

Fred Knock headed for the door. 'You ought to know, lad,' he said majestically, 'all such matters are strictly confidential. It is the duty of a chairman to make sure they remain so. Good day to you, Mr Juby. I'll see you at the meeting.'

Mr Juby waved him goodbye. He waited until Mr Knock had gone into the front office, then he gave Charles a long, calculating look. Charles wondered what was going to come next.

'You crafty young bugger,' said Mr Juby. 'You're lunnin' something at last.'

Twelve

There were only three days left before the second, and crucial family service at Wellingham, and Charles had to admit it, the preparations were not going very well.

They had started promisingly enough. John Cranmer had followed his suggestion about the timing of the church council meeting, so it would not take place until after the service. If the Brownings had any objections they did not voice them. Meanwhile an enthusiastic paragraph had appeared among the village items in the *Journal*.

'For the first time in Remingham a very successful family service was held in the Parish Church, the Rector (the Rev. J. Cranmer) officiating. A number of children were in the congregation' – Charles did not specify what number – 'and the Rector gave a special illustrated talk for their benefit instead of the usual sermon. Music for the hymns was provided by Mr William Eke on the guitar' – Charles had had no difficulty in establishing Willum's full name; half the village were Ekes – 'and this proved particularly popular with the children. The Rector plans to hold further family services each month, and he is confident they will receive strong support as they become more widely known.'

The problems had started when the Rector started seeking that 'strong support' in which the *Journal* said he had such confidence. Mrs Curson at the shop, unimpressed by the report she was supposed to have written, regretted that she had no room in her window for a poster. The headmistress at the village school declined to allow the Rector to distribute letters for the children to take home – it was not a Church of England school, she said, and if a precedent were set then the Methodists would want to give out letters, and the Salvation Army, and the Jehovah's Witnesses, and where would it all end?

More significantly, parents whom he approached in the village were uniformly unhelpful. They pleaded an assortment of illnesses or previous engagements. None of them actually spoke out against the family service; nevertheless Charles detected the hand of the Brownings behind this consistent lack of enthusiasm. He began to realise that, where the village politics were concerned, he still had much to learn.

On top of all this, Rebecca had still not replied to his letter. He had worded it with great care; it was conciliatory without being abject, amusing without being facetious, warm without being sloppy. Or so he thought. Clearly it had not worked.

So he was in suitably sombre mood when he settled down in his office to write an obituary notice for the market tolls collector, Jonathan Clapp. It was not an easy obituary to write. Mr Clapp had been universally detested in the town for his servility towards the gentry and his officiousness towards everyone else, and his passing was a particular blessing to his much-bullied wife. It was an occasion for carefully selected euphemisms, and Charles was making what play he could with phrases like 'unswerving devotion to duty' and 'meticulous attention to detail'.

Outside, the Market Place was slumbering in the sunshine. It was just after lunch on early closing day. Just after lunch was pretty quiet on most days in Toftham, with the lunchtime drinkers still ensconced in the pubs over their cheese and pickles, the children still trapped in school for another hour or so, and their mothers relaxing over a cup of tea at home. On Wednesday afternoons not even the occasional shopper was about. The only activity was in Mr Hurn's hairdressing establishment on the other side of the Market Place. He stayed open on early closing days for the benefit of his shopkeeper neighbours, and they congregated there whether they needed a haircut or not. Knowing this, other customers tended to stay away, so that Mr Hurn could hold his informal Chamber of Trade with interruption.

It was therefore only Mr Hurn and his select clientele, and Charles himself up at his first-floor window, who saw the motorcade drive into the Market Place from the London road and draw up beneath him. A little white sports car was in the lead, two station waggons were behind it, and a battered van brought up the rear.

All four vehicles came to rest in the narrow roadway outside the office, regardless of the empty parking spaces in the centre of the Market Place. Inside the station waggons and the van nobody moved, but two figures emerged from the sports car and surveyed the offices of the *Toftham and Wettleford Journal*. They did not seem enormously impressed. One was a blonde young woman in trousers, shirt and waistcoat, and a brown trilby hat. She wore a complicated pendant round her neck, slung very low. It thumped against her stomach as she straightened up.

Her companion, who took rather longer to struggle out of the passenger seat, was middle-aged and male. In spite of the sunshine he was wrapped in a shapeless check overcoat. He obviously had some trouble standing upright after the constrictions of the journey.

The young woman marched briskly into the front office; the man limped along behind. Charles heard the chatter of conversation below and wished, not for the first time, that Mr Juby spent more time on editorial administration and less time gathering news in the Dog and Partridge. The situation seemed to have all the makings of a major development requiring a decision, and Charles relished neither.

Downstairs at her front counter Big Nellie was trying hard not to be cowed by the brown trilby. 'I'm afraid the editor hent in just at this partickler moment in time,' she enunciated in her best Toftham High School voice. 'What might be the parpus of your enquiry?'

Brown Trilby switched on the smile she obviously

180

reserved for very small children, very old men, and market towns with a population of under five thousand. 'We're from Television Documentaries,' she said, pronouncing the longer words slowly and clearly. 'We'd very much like to meet someone on the staff who might possibly assist us with a story we are interested in, involving a family in your area.'

Upstairs, Charles's heart sank. Oh lord, he thought, they've found out about the Gibsons. Damn, damn, damn.

Below, Brown Trilby was still being terribly charming. 'As the editor is not available, could there possibly be somebody else who might spare us a few moments.' She paused to glance past Nellie at the magazine she had been reading. 'I know you must all be terribly busy.'

Nellie noticed the glance, and bridled. 'I'm checking the 'vertisements, as a matter of fact,' she said belligerently. 'Thass my job, 'vertisements. There's a lot of work goes into that.'

'Yes, of course,' said Brown Trilby soothingly. 'And a most important job it is too. How could newspapers survive without 'vertisements? But perhaps you have an assistant who deals with the news side, whom I could have a word with.'

Nellie had not considered the office staffing arrangements in that light before. She mellowed.

'There's young Charlie, he's a reporter. But he only come up from London a few days back, he don't know narthin much about these parts.' Charles had actually been there six months by now, but time was measured by different standards in Toftham.

'I'm sure he'll do very nicely. May we go up?' And Brown Trilby was halfway up the stairs before Nellie could reply. The man in the shapeless overcoat paused by the counter and gave her a wry little smile.

'When she takes that damn silly hat off,' he said, 'she can sometimes behave quite normally.' He started plodding wearily up the stairs, but Nellie called after him.

'Is she really in television then?'

He did not pause. 'Isn't it obvious?' he said.

Charles was back behind his desk, and deep in the last tributes to Jonathan Clapp, when Brown Trilby marched into his office. 'At the funeral service on Wednesday,' he typed, as she crossed the room and stood in front of him, 'those present included the widow and Mr Frederick Doy, representing the Market Committee . . .'

'Good afternoon,' said Brown Trilby. 'You must be young Charlie, who don't know narthin much about these parts.'

'Not exactly,' said Charles, looking up and discovering that the pendant which was now at eye level against Brown Trilby's stomach, was actually a stop-watch. 'My name is Charles, and as it happens I know quite a lot about funerals. Excuse me a moment.' He studied his last sentence, decided to put accuracy first, and replaced 'those present included' with 'those present were'.

'We're from Television Documentaries,' said Brown Trilby a little sharply. 'This is my reporter James North, and I am Cynthia Grayley. James, this is Charlie, who prefers to be called Charles.'

'Hallo, Charles,' said James North. 'Actually I prefer to be called Jim, but it only confuses them when they put up the credits.'

'Hallo, Jim,' said Charles, and in a final gesture of defiance he added to Brown Trilby, 'and hallo Cynth.' Then Television Documentaries took over.

'We are here,' said Cynthia Grayley, 'to cover a rather disturbing story that has reached us about a local family in your area. It involves a mother and the difficulties she is having over her children.'

Charles wondered desperately what he could do to head off this purposeful young woman. But he already knew the answer: absolutely nothing.

'I expect you know about it,' said Cynthia. Charles nodded glumly.

'Then I'm sure you can help us. We have a camera crew outside, we plan to recce this afternoon, try and

182

do a little shooting before the light goes, stay overnight here in Toftham – no doubt you can recommend a good hotel – then we'll get the bulk of the shooting done tomorrow. The whole thing should be ready to go on air next week. We plan to call it "The Skilliton Scandal" – it rolls off the tongue nicely.'

'She wanted to call it "Skilliton in the Cupboard" but thank goodness they talked her out of it,' explained James North. But Charles was still staring at Cynthia Grayley.

'Skilliton? Why Skilliton? Don't you mean Remingham?'

'No I don't, I mean Skilliton. You could hardly confuse that with Remingham.'

'Indeed you couldn't,' said Charles with enormous relief. He had never heard of a village called Skilliton; it must be one of the more obscure hamlets on the edge of his area, or even in Mortimer's. Certainly it was nowhere near Remingham. The Gibsons were still safe. But what on earth was she talking about?

'Is there some way I can help?' he asked guardedly, hoping there wasn't.

Cynthia took a notebook from her bag and started checking through a list. 'We need to meet the chairman of your local council, somebody representing the education committee, a few local parents and perhaps some teachers and a tame left-winger who can rant a bit to camera. Anything you can lay on for us would be very much appreciated. ' She gave him the benefit of her under-five-thousand-population smile.

Charles glanced across at Mr Hurn's shop, where he recognised some of the inquisitive faces lining the windows, including Mr Hurn's. Haircutting had been temporarily suspended.

'At the moment,' said Charles seriously, 'I can offer you a newsagent, two greengrocers and an assistant postmaster. And there's a chemist too, if you don't mind him being half-cut. His hair, that is.' He beamed at Cynthia.

Cynthia failed to beam back. 'I don't think I quite understand. How can the assistant postmaster be involved in the Skilliton Scandal? Or the chemist.' She stopped, and her eyes widened. 'Do you mean drugs are involved?'

'I don't honestly know,' admitted Charles. 'I'm afraid I've been a bit involved in Mr Clapp's funeral today. What's actually been happening at Skilliton?'

'Nothing has been happening *at* Skilliton,' she said coldly. 'It's what has been happening to the Skilliton family. You must know about it, surely? It has all the makings of a *cause célèbre*.'

'Ah,' said Charles carefully. This was getting dangerous again. Could she have confused Skilliton with Gibson after all? 'I wonder if you could refresh my memory? I was out covering a sheepdog trial all yesterday. Perhaps that's why I missed it.'

James North chipped in. 'Not yesterday, nor the day before. Television Documentaries don't move quite as fast as that. Show him the cutting, Cynthia, then we can all start level.'

Cynthia delved in her bag again and produced a crumpled newspaper cutting. Charles realised guiltily that it originated from the *Journal*. 'It comes from your own paper, only four weeks ago,' she said rather pityingly. 'I'd have thought you knew *something* about it.'

Charles remembered Nellie's comment earlier in the front office. 'I've only been here a few days,' he said smugly. It silences Cynthia while he read the cutting. It was headed: 'Mother Refuses to Send Children to School. "I Can Teach Them Better Myself", Court Told.'

At Toftham Magistrates Court on Friday Mrs Jean Skilliton (35) of Church Cottages, Little Crunham, was fined £10 with £5 costs for failing to send her four children to school. Mr John Prodger, prosecuting, said every effort had been made to persuade the defendant to send her children to Little Crunham School, but she insisted that she could educate them better at home. She had ignored all the correspondence from the local education authority and had refused to speak to officials who called at her home.

Mrs Skilliton, who pleaded not guilty, said there was more education than the three Rs, and she was educating the children herself in the widest possible sense.

Announcing the fine, Mrs Godfrey Bleddington (chairman) said: 'You must abide by the law of the land.' Mrs Skilliton said she would appeal.

'So,' said Cynthia Grayley. 'What about that? An extraordinary story. Not just a matter of children's education, it's the whole principle of human rights. Here's a mother who's prepared to stand up and be counted in defence of what she feels is best for her children, against all the bureaucracy of the local education authority, and the magistrates' court, and the Mrs Godfrey Bleddingtons of this world.'

Now she was really under way. 'Mrs Jean Skilliton could be the flagbearer of a campaign against the standardisation of our society by the faceless men at County Hall. It's a classic case of the individual against the state.'

'And what's more,' said James North solemnly, 'it should make some quite nice pictures – especially if Cynthia can get her to break down, on camera.'

Charles stared dazedly at the cutting. Why hadn't *he* thought of all that, when he actually wrote the story four weeks ago? He remembered the case now. Mrs Skilliton had struck him as an argumentative and unprepossessing character who only kept her children at home because she was too idle to get them off to school. Her idea of 'educating the children in the widest possible sense', he suspected, would include plenty of practical experience in every aspect of domestic science. He had taken an instant dislike to her, and the fine she got seemed to him to be richly deserved.

'A remarkable woman,' he said to Cynthia sagely. 'I was impressed by her straight away. Matter of fact, we were thinking of following up the story this week. But what happens if she's sent the kids back to school?'

James North smiles patiently. 'A little thing like that doesn't stop Television Documentaries. Cynthia will soon have them out again.'

'James is joking, or course,' said Cynthia. 'He always gets a little difficult after these long drives. Now what we would like to do is have a chat with Mrs Skilliton at Little Crunham, wherever that might be. The office told me it's only a few miles from Toftham. But first we want a shot of the magistrates' court while the light holds. Can you direct me to it?'

'That's not too difficult,' said Charles, going to the window. 'That's it across the Market Place. It's that room over the hairdressers; part of the council offices. I'm afraid it doesn't look very exciting – we don't run to a statue with a pair of scales, or anything like that.'

'I'm sure we'll manage,' said Cynthia briskly. 'James, you'd better think up a piece to camera while I round up the crew. Charlie, you've been a great help. You'll be here of course when we come back.' And she was off down the stairs. Don't bet on it, he thought.

'Mind if I use your office?' asked James. 'They'll take ages to set up, and Cynthia has to do her bit with angles and zooms and things, to keep the cameraman confused.' He started getting some crumpled pieces of paper out of his pocket. 'She's not a bad soul really, but she does take it all so seriously.'

'What's this piece of camera, then?' asked Charles.

'It's my moment of glory,' James explained. 'They stand me up in front of something and I sum up the state of the nation in twenty-five seconds. It's mainly to let the viewers know what's happening in case they can't make head or tail of what comes next. Most directors hate it because it gets in the way of their beautiful pictures. Cynthia only suggested this one because your magistrates' court would look so bloody boring on its own. If she could get a pack of hounds to go

186

past it, or a steamroller or something, she'd much prefer that. Now if you'll excuse me, I'd better write out my spontaneous commentary.' He started scribbling on his pieces of paper, and Charles took another look out of the window.

Below him, Cynthia was assembling her crew. Two young men in jeans and T-shirts were unloading camera gear from one of the station waggons, a wizened little man in a flat cap was getting microphones and cable out of the other. A fourth man in overalls was unloading lamps and reels of wire from the van.

Charles glanced round the sunlit Market Place and looked again at the growing heap of lighting equipment below. 'What do they need all that lot for?'

James looked up from his scribbling and saw what was happening. 'It's in the rules, he said. 'You must have a lighting man, just in case. I remember we had to film a sunrise once, and we took a lighting man for that – I suppose in case it was cloudy. Don't think it would have looked very convincing, though.' He grinned at Charles. 'Anyway, by the time they've decided where to shoot from, it'll probably be dark enough to need him.' He resumed his writing, mouthing the words quietly to himself as he wrote.

Charles wondered whether he should join Cynthia and her crew to record their activities for Friday's issue or maintain the dignified detachment of one professional who does not encroach on the work of another. The decision was taken out of his hands.

Out of the Dog and Partridge on the other side of the Market Place emerged the slightly roseate figure of Mr Juby. He caught sight of the activity outside his office and headed purposefully towards it. As he approached he saw Charles peering out of his first-floor window and his familiar roar boomed upwards. 'What in hell's a-goin on, boy?'

'It's Television Documentaries,' Charles shouted back. 'They've come to do some filming.'

'They hent come to do deep-sea diving, thass for sure,'

roared Mr Juby, now on the pavement beneath Charles's window and only a yard or so from Cynthia and her crew and the heaps of equipment. 'What do they reckon to film, then?'

'It's the Skilliton Scandal,' said Charles nonchalantly. He allowed himself a moment of satisfaction at the blank look on Mr Juby's face, then hastily explained. 'Mrs Skilliton and the children she won't send to school, out at Little Crunham. They say it's a *cause célèbre*.'

'Cause celaber?' roared Mr Juby. 'All that young mawther causes is trouble. Why take pictures of her?' He turned to one of the young men handling the camera. He had an exposure meter dangling round his neck, a cousin to Cynthia's stop-watch. 'You, boy,' said Mr Juby, 'what's all this squit about a cause celaber?'

'You'd better ask her. I just turn the handle.' The young man set off across the Market Place with his camera while his assistant laboured along behind with the tripod. Cynthia attempted to follow.

'Hold you hard, young lady,' said Mr Juby, catching her by the arm. 'What are you chasing that Jean Skilliton for? She hent wuth a row o' beans.'

Cynthia glared at him coldly and disengaged her arm. 'I presume you are something to do with the local authority,' she snapped. 'I am afraid you can't intimidate Television Documentaries. We intend to report the full facts of what appears to be a most deplorable case of bureaucratic bumbledom.'

'The only deplorable thing about this case is that she weren't brought to court before,' Mr Juby snapped back. 'Those kids of hers are growing up more ignorant than their father. The only sensible thing he ever did was leave her.'

'If I may say so,' said Cynthia, her voice now icy, 'that is a typical male attitude. We hope to give a more balanced picture.'

'If you don't like male attitoods,' responded Mr Juby in tones that could be heard all round the Market Place, 'then why in the hell are you wearing that weskit and trousers and that dam' silly hat?'

'Well played,' said a quiet voice behind Charles, up in the window. James North had put aside his spontaneous commentary and was following the action outside. 'Who is that splendid man?' Charles told him.

'Wonder if he'd like a job in Television Documentaries,' murmured James. 'We're getting over-run with these women – we could do with a chap like that.' He smiled sweetly down at Cynthia, who had just caught his eye.

'If you've got your piece ready,' she called, turning her back on Mr Juby, 'we'd better get on with it before the light goes completely.'

James North shaded his eyes from the still dazzling sunlight. 'Absolutely right,' he called back genially. 'Better warn the Sparks, just in case.'

He slapped Charles on the back and headed for the door. 'Make the most of Mr Juby,' he said over his shoulder. 'One day you could be working with Cynthia.'

Mr Juby's voice echoed up from the street again. 'Charlie, get you on across there and keep an eye on these folk. That could be an eddication for a young reporter.'

As Charles crossed the Market Place a goodly crowd was beginning to assemble, including a substantial contingent from the Golden Fleece. Cynthia was dividing her time between marshalling the spectators and instructing the cameraman.

'Somehow,' she was saying, 'we must take in the courtroom without showing the hairdresser's underneath. That would just confuse the story. Is that practicable?'

'Entirely practicable,' said the young man with the exposure meter. 'It just means that James will have to do his piece to camera half-way up the wall. He may not like that.'

'Very amusing,' said Cynthia. 'I know. We can put him in a window.'

'Just like a bloody aspidistra,' muttered James, but only Charles heard him. Cynthia was already in the hairdresser's shop, demanding the way up to the court-room. Mr Hurn had never had a woman in his shop before, even one wearing a waistcoat and trousers, and it took him some time to explain that the entrance was round the corner, and that not even in Toftham did magistrates have to approach their place of duty through a heap of hair clippings. His customers, equally dumb-founded, formed an open-mouthed guard of honour beside the door as she re-emerged, displaying a rather faded version of the under-five-thousand-population-smile.

She went round to the little side entrance that led to the council offices and the court, and Charles pictured her progress through the outer office, past Miss Marsh the telephonist, and up the stairs to the courtroom, which he now remembered was being used this afternoon for a meeting of the General Purposes Committee.

He allowed ten seconds for Cynthia to deal with Miss Marsh, another ten to get up the stairs, and perhaps thirty to oust the committee chairman. George Flatt, the Clerk, would be the toughest nut to crack. That might well take another couple of minutes, but he had no doubt of the outcome.

In fact, less than a minute had passed before a window was flung open and a triumphant trilby appeared. 'Come up here, James,' cried Cynthia. 'They've kindly agreed to suspend their meeting while you do your piece to camera from this window.'

'My God,' mumbled James as he headed wearily for the side door. 'Not so much a piece to camera, more an address to the nation. She ought to be working with the Pope.'

When he eventually appeared in the window the crowd in the Market Place had grown considerably, and there was an appreciative cheer as he gave a mock-regal wave.

'Do stop arsing about, James,' said Cynthia beside him. She signalled to the cameraman. 'Go ahead.'

'Ready, James?' shouted the cameraman. James nodded.

'Ready, Fred?' The wizened man in the flat hat, his head now clamped inside an enormous pair of head-phones, nodded.

'Ready, Cynthia?'

'Ready,' shouted Cynthia.

'Then do get out of shot, dear,' said the cameraman. She very nearly blushed, and disappeared.

'Running,' said Fred from inside the headphones.

'Mark it,' shouted the cameraman. And to the delight of the crowd, the second young man held up a clapper-board and, just like they had seen in the movies, cried: 'Skilliton Scandal, Slate One, Take One.' He banged the clapperboard shut and retreated.

'Go, James,' the cameraman instructed. And James went.

But this was a transformed James, no longer huddled in a shapeless overcoat but revealed in a smart city suit, his hair smoothed back, the shoulders straight, the voice crisp, commanding, incisive. Charles watched in open admiration as the camera whirred beside him.

'Here in this remote courtroom in a quiet corner of East Anglia, a drama has been acted out which could change the course of our educational system. Here a young mother defended the principle she holds sacred, that she has the right to educate her own children. Through her own personal teaching and example she maintains she can instil in them a better appreciation of the world around them than anything they can acquire through the routine classwork of the local school. Here she defied the might of the education authority; she remained true to her resolve even when the chairman of the Bench gave her the grim warning: "You must abide by the land of the law" . . . Land of the law? Sod it!'

'Cut!' shouted Cynthia. 'Bad luck, James, you were nearly there.'

'Law of the land, law of the land,' mouthed James angrily. 'How the devil did I get that wrong. Law of the land, law of the land . . .'

'Ready, James?'

'Law of the land . . . Yes, all right.'

'Ready, Fred?'

'Running.'

'Mark it, then.'

'Skilliton Scandal, Slate One, Take Two.'

James started again. 'Here in this remote courtroom in a quiet corner of East Anglia . . .'

'Cut!' Sorry, James. Aeroplane. Give it a moment, then try again.'

'Skilliton Scandal, Slate One, Take Three.'

'Here in this remote courtroom . . .'

'Cut!' This time it was the cameraman. 'Hold it, James, the sun's just got round on to that window. Can you close it a bit? Splendid.'

'Skilliton, Slate One, Take Four.'

'Here in this remote corner-room in a quiet court of East Anglia . . . Damnation!'

'Cut!'

The crowd had been behaving remarkably well, but Charles detected a certain element of hysteria developing amongst the group from the Golden Fleece. As James North's commanding voice rang out for the fifth time from the courtroom window, a chorus joined in from the pavement below.

HERE IN THIS REMOTE COURTROOM IN A QUIET CORNER OF EAST ANGLIA . . .'

And before Cynthia even appeared in the window, the entire Market Place shouted with one voice: **'CUT!'**

'That does it,' said James. 'I'll write it into the voice-over instead.'

He turned to the crowd just once more. 'Here in this remote courtroom, in a quiet corner of East Anglia, we're packing up for tea. Cynthia, let's go.'

*

At seven o'clock that evening James North, the camera crew and Charles gathered in the farmers' bar of the Dog and Partridge, as guests of Mr Juby. Cynthia had driven out on her own to Little Crunham to recce Mrs Skilliton. Charles had been delighted to see her go; Little Crunham was a long way from the Gibsons at Remingham.

The beer was flowing well, and Mr Juby was in mellow mood. 'Thass a rum do, that Skilliton business,' he observed to James. 'I daresay you checked up with the gal Jean before you come all this way?'

'Couldn't check, really,' James explained. 'The only telephone in Little Crunham is in the village stores, and apparently they're not on speaking terms with Mrs Skilliton. It seems there's another principle she holds sacred beside home education – not paying her grocery bills.'

'Pity about that,' said Mr Juby. 'Not checking, that is. Still, your young lady should have found out by now, no doubt.'

'Found out what?' asked James.

'Found out about *Mister* Skilliton,' said Mr Juby.

James was disconcerted. 'There's a Mr Skilliton?'

Mr Juby took a sip at his special. 'Well, sometimes there is and sometimes there hent. But just at the moment I rather think there is.' He took another sip. James, who had already grasped the basics of Norfolk conversation, waited patiently.

'He can't stand that wife of his, y'see, but he's very fond of the kiddies. Comes back every so often to make sure she's treating them right, and sending them to school regular, and the like. It could just so happen he saw that report in the *Journal* as well as your Cynthia.' Mr Juby chuckled darkly into his glass. 'Don't reckon he'll take a shine to her, somehow. Especially in that hat.'

He was still chuckling when Cynthia appeared in the doorway. She surveyed the group at the bar coldly, with a special glare for Mr Juby. There were mud splashes

193

on her trousers, the waistcoat was slightly awry, and the trilby looked as though at some stage it had been thrust down over her ears; it was only partially restored to its normal jauntiness. But her step was as firm as ever, as she marched across to them.

'How did it go?' asked Charles solicitously, since nobody else made a move.

She ignored him and went up to Mr Juby. 'I suppose you knew the Skilliton fellow was back home?'

'Thought he might be,' said Mr Juby gently. 'Funny sort o' chap, hent 'e?'

'He's an ignorant lout,' snapped Cynthia, the poise momentarily slipping. 'He refused to let me see his wife, he told me the children had been back to school for a fortnight – and he kept addressing me as Burlington Bertie.'

Charles spluttered slightly into his beer. Mr Juby studied the ceiling. But James North, perceiving that the end of the Skilliton Scandal was in sight, was inclined to be more sympathetic. He would, after all, have to work with Cynthia again.

'Bad Luck, old girl,' he said. 'Good try, but you can't win them all. Let me get you a drink, then we'll all head back to town.'

Cynthia was still seething. 'The wretched fellow got quite worked up when I wouldn't go away. He kept rambling on about a woman's place is in the home, and why didn't I wear proper clothes, and wasn't it time I found a husband and settled down . . . I gave up trying to talk sense to him in the end. I thought that sort of attitude went out with the Victorians.'

'It hasn't gone out in these parts, believe me,' said Charles quietly.

'Oh come now,' said Cynthia. The semblance of an under-five-thousand smile crept back on her face. 'I can't believe you're all in the Dark Ages in Norfolk.'

'You'll believe it when you try to have that drink,'

said Mr Juby, downing his special. 'They don't serve women in the farmers' bar.'

Charles and Mr Juby stood outside the Dog and Partridge in the late evening sun, watching Television Documentaries disappearing down the London road. Mr Juby had consumed more than his usual quota of specials, and his Norfolk burr had thickened accordingly.

'Fust thing tomarra,' he said to Charles, 'get you along to Little Crunham and see that Skilliton gal. I think you'll find she'll have the kiddies staying at home again. Then we'll send off a line to the Sunday pairpers.'

Charles looked at him in bewilderment. 'But what about Mr Skilliton?'

'He'll be gone by now,' said Mr Juby confidently. 'He on'y went home because I told him that young mawther was going out to see his missus. Just happened to have a mardle with him while they were playin' gairms up over Harry Hurn's shop.'

'You just happened to see him?' asked Charles suspiciously.

'Well,' Mr Juby admitted, 'he did tairke a bit o'finding, I grant you. But it was wuth the trouble. Blast me, those Lunnon folk can't have all the fun, now can they?'

For the first time since he had arrived in Toftham, Charles felt part of the community. For the first time, Mr Juby had not included him in the Lunnon folk; he had been accepted as an ally against a common foe. He experienced a gentle glow, not entirely attributable to Mr Juby's hospitality in the Dog and Partridge.

'Ah,' he said slowly and thoughtfully, in the way that Norfolkmen have of making a simple syllable sound slow and thoughtful. He ventured a stage further. 'That they can't, Mr Juby. That they can't.'

Mr Juby gave him a quick glance. 'Quite so,' he said, but there was a warning note in his voice. 'Now thass high time you got back to Remingham. Fare y'well boy.'

For a moment Charles was tempted to repeat the farewell, then wisely he realised how far he could go. He was no longer a foreigner, but only just.

'Goodnight, Mr Juby,' he said. Mr Juby nodded silently, and went his way.

As he cycled home to Remingham, Charles's glow began to dissipate and his earlier gloom returned. The Gibsons had escaped detection by the awful Cynthia, and they now had the new Housing Chairman, Fred Knock, on their side, but he had made it clear that the chances of two adjoining houses falling vacant simultaneously, anywhere in the district, were quite remote. His brilliant solution to the Gibsons' plight was not turning out so brilliantly after all.

There was also John Cranmer's family service. Short of bribery or blackmail he could see no way of persuading any families to attend it. He had failed there too. The modest victory over Television Documentaries seemed unimportant by comparison.

When he got back to Lambeth Palace was in darkness; John Cranmer had already gone to bed, so he wandered into the kitchen to make a cup of tea. He was surprised to find a bottle of beer and a glass awaiting him on the table. It was unusual for the Rector to encourage him in this way; he had more than once indicated a certain disquiet at Charles's condition after his evenings at the Dog and Partridge. But perhaps, thought Charles, he guessed that I needed cheering up.

Then he noticed the envelope propped against the bottle, and when he saw how it was addressed he realised that the beer was not for consolation, but celebration. The address read: 'Chas Benson, Purveyor of Good News, Lambeth Palace, Remingham, Norfolk.' The postman had commendably managed to interpret it correctly. The postmark was Newcastle.

Charles opened the bottle and poured out the beer very slowly, savouring the moment. Then he read the letter.

'Dear Charles,' it said. 'Thanks for the letter. See you

when I get home. And it's your turn to bring the picnic. Love to Mum and Dad. Rebecca.'

Dr Bateman had been right; his daughter was not a great letter writer. Elizabeth Barrett Browning might have added a few extra touches. But for Charles it was quite enough. He had never enjoyed a beer more.

Thirteen

On the morning of the Remingham family service the atmosphere at Lambeth Palace was fairly fraught. This was entirely Charles's fault; the Rector, after his many disheartening encounters in the village, had now enveloped himself in a fatalistic calm. He had prayed quite a lot, and left it at that. But Charles felt a great burden of responsibility. He had urged him to make the stand, he had acted as his campaign manager, and if it all ended in disaster it would be his fault.

'Do cheer up,' urged John Cranmer as he left to prepare for the service. 'They don't burn heretics at the stake any more, even in Remingham. You'll have a few hours in the stocks, and that'll be it.'

'Nothing would surprise me,' said Charles morosely. Then he managed to summon a smile. 'Good luck anyway. And if it doesn't work out, you can have the first choice of holes.'

Ten minutes later, as he made his own way to the church, all his apprehensions returned. Even the rustle of Rebecca's letter in his pocket failed to soothe him.

There was nobody ahead of him on the path up to the church. He wondered if the entire village had decided to boycott the service. But when he went inside Dr Bateman was at his regular post beside the hymn-books, and there was the customary scattering of dark-clad figures in the rear pews.

And that was all.

'Not a big turnout yet,' said Dr Bateman, guessing his thoughts. 'There's a little time yet – we may get some more. But you can't expect miracles – even at a family service.'

Charles put off the moment for walking down the aisle under the eyes of the Brownings and their friends. They no doubt knew about the part he had played, and he did not exactly expect a burst of applause. Instead he told the doctor about Rebecca's letter.

'That sounds quite a major literary effort, by her standards,' her father commented. 'You're quite honoured.'

'Any idea when she's due home?' asked Charles.

'She's always a bit vague about that. Quite often goes and stays with her friends before she comes back to Norfolk. You'd better consult Thunder; he always seems to know she's on her way before we do.'

'So that's what they mean about "straight from the horse's mouth",' said Charles, trying to be jovial, but it was depressing news. He had hoped she would come straight home; now it was impossible to make any plans.

'Morning, Doctor. Morning, Mr Benson. This is my grand-daughter Jenny.' It was Mrs Clegg the cleaning lady; she had kept her promise.

Charles welcomed her warmly, and even patted Jenny's head. It was not his usual practice to pat the heads of small children, but this seemed a special occasion. Jenny did not seem too impressed; she eyed him suspiciously over her shoulder as Dr Bateman led her and Mrs Clegg down the aisle towards the front of the church. Mr and Mrs Browning, who had turned to inspect the new arrivals, were also staring at him coldly. That'll be an extra day in the stocks for child molesting, thought Charles almost cheerfully.

Then Mrs Bateman arrived. 'I am sorry I can't bring the third member of the family,' she smiled, 'but at least we'll have two out of three.' She went and took her seat in the front right-hand pew.

It's building up, thought Charles hopefully. And indeed it was. Up the path came Mrs Gibson, carrying the baby, and surrounded by five of her six other children.

'I don't usually leave Dan, but I thought you might need a little support,' she explained. The eldest boy had stayed behind to keep his father company.

'Marvellous. Really marvellous.' Charles felt quite touched. Dr Bateman was at the front of the church, talking to his wife, so Charles issued the hymn-books and led the Gibsons down the aisle, past the watchful gaze of the Brownings. He distributed them in two rows behind the empty pew on the left-hand side. The two youngest children explained knowledgeably to the others what was going to happen.

Charles looked back up the church. In spite of the two pews of Gibsons and Mrs Clegg with her grand-daughter, the front part of the church still looked piti-fully empty, and the service was about to start. He caught the eye of Mr Browning in the rear pew; even at a distance he thought he detected a gleam of triumph.

All right, he thought savagely as he sat down behind the Batemans. All right, so you've won. Just don't take it out on John Cranmer.

Dr Bateman looked round and saw his expression. 'Don't look so grim,' he murmured. 'There might be one more.'

Charles shrugged. 'Just one more won't make much odds, will it?'

'It depends,' said the Doctor, 'which one it is. Excuse me.'

There *had* been another arrival, who was now walking briskly down the aisle. The doctor hastened back to greet him. He escorted him the rest of the way and ushered him into the front left-hand pew.

The newcomer glanced across at Charles and nodded.

'Good morning,' said Lord Remingham.

'Good Lord,' said Charles.

The service went very well. Rather to the disappoint-ment of the two youngest Gibsons, Willum did not indulge in any chanted exchanges with the Rector in between the hymns – John Cranmer simply held up his fingers to indicate how many verses were left.

To illustrate his talk he distributed scissors and sheets of paper, and showed how to fold and cut the paper to make stars; Charles noted that even Lord Remingham had a go, though he did not dare look round to check on the Brownings.

It ended, not with 'Roll Out The Barrel', but with an equally cheerful rendering of 'All Things Bright and Beautiful'. Even some voices from the rear pews joined in. 'How great is God Almighty,' sang Charles lustily, 'Who has made all things well.'

Lord Remingham did not linger. As soon as John Cranmer had taken up his position at the church door he was the first to walk back up the aisle, nodding briefly to each of the congregation as he passed. He shook hands with John.

'Good service, padre. Enjoyed it. Keep it up.' The Brownings, a few feet away in the rear pews, could not have failed to hear him. Then he went off briskly down the path; the Bentley was parked across the gateway.

Charles walked back up the aisle with the Batemans. 'I thought you said we couldn't expect miracles,' he murmured. The doctor just smiled. 'And how did you know he was coming? I thought he never turned up except at Christmas and Easter.'

'There's still a thing or two you don't know about Lord Remingham,' said Dr Bateman quietly. 'His wife died in a riding accident years ago. His son has gone abroad with his wife and children; he rarely sees them. He lives on his own up at the Hall. He may have a lot of land and a great deal of money, but he has no family life at all, something he misses a great deal. And he feels very strongly that those who do have a family around them should make the most of it.'

'But how did he know about the service?' Charles was still baffled.

'Because I told him. You're not the only one on the Rector's side, you know; and there's more than one way of helping things along in a village like this. You can't just do it with fanciful newspaper reports.'

Charles blushed, but fortunately they had reached the church entrance, where John Cranmer was surrounded by cheerful young Gibsons, insisting on showing him the excellence of their paper stars. Hovering to have a word with him, Charles noted with some misgiving, were Mr and Mrs Browning.

He turned back to Dr Bateman. 'We're not out of the wood yet, are we? I can't imagine you've persuaded Lord Remingham to come and vote at the PCC meeting.'

'Somehow I don't think that'll be necessary,' said Dr Bateman. 'The Brownings know when to take a hint.'

Mr Browning had caught the Rector's eye and was talking to him quietly. The Rector nodded, and smiled, and shook Mr Browning's hand as they parted. Mrs Browning shook hands too; she even nodded to Charles.

Charles felt a tug at his sleeve and found Willum beaming up at him. 'Thass a good piece you put in the pearper, marster. Mrs Curson, she read it out for me. Mr Willum Eke, that say. I hent never been called that afore. You goin to write that each time I play at the sarvice?'

'I'll try, Willum. I'll certainly try. But I think I'll have to leave it to Mrs Curson from now on.' He smiled across at Dr Bateman. 'At least I seem to have done one thing right.' He remembered what Mr Juby had said, and added; 'Maybe I'm lunnin' at last.'

Dr Bateman smiled back. 'It's a start, Charles. Just a start.'

John Cranmer came over to them. He was smiling too. 'Mr Browning reckons we needn't hold that PCC meeting, if that's all right with me. He seems to think family services might be acceptable after all. A wonderful change of heart. Mrs Browning too. I wonder if I shall ever understand these good Norfolk folk. I'm afraid I've been misjudging them.'

Charles patted him gently on the back. 'Tell you what, boy, thass just the foodal system for you.' He dropped the bogus accent. 'Maybe there's something to be said for it after all.'

'You bin causing more trouble then.'

Charles had been feeling quite cheerful as he rode into Toftham on Monday morning. The family service crisis had been resolved, he had Rebecca's letter in his pocket, and a couple of the Sunday papers had used the story of the Skilliton Scandal, toned down from the Television Documentaries vision of it but still good Sunday paper material. Now Big Nellie was casting a damper once more.

'What have I done this time, Nellie?' he asked patiently.

'Stirring up the folk out at Remingham with your friend the Rector over some silly play-acting in the church. My uncle's told me all about it.'

'Your uncle?' He knew of no Mr Gruntling in the village, but he made a guess. 'Would that be Mr Browning, then?'

'How'd you know that?' demanded Nellie.

'I think he was the only one who was really bothered. And it's all been sorted out now.' He decided to sort something else out too, now that Nellie had actually opened a conversation with him.

'By the way, why have you been so sour with me since the point-to-point? You really did ride extremely well – it was awfully bad luck you fell.'

He had obviously touched a nerve. 'That weren't bad luck, that were you,' hissed Nellie. 'Lost me the race, you did.'

He had no idea what she was talking about. 'Lost you the race? Why me?'

'You and your stoopid shouting for that Bateman girl. All that "Go, go, go" stuff. I thought she must be just behind me – I'd never've looked round otherwise, that close to a jump. And there she was, yards away, nowhere near me. Then when I look back we're right on the jump and thass too late. I'd never've come off if that hent been for you.' Charles observed with alarm that she was close to tears.

'Nellie, I'm so sorry, I'd no idea. I just got carried away a bit. Everybody else was shouting too.'

203

'Not "Go, go, go" they weren't. Thass what did it. I knew that was you, so I knew that must be her, so I turned round.' She took out a handkerchief and blew her nose noisily. Charles realized there was no point in protesting.

'Well, at least you weren't hurt. I'm very glad about that.' And trying to be consoling, he added 'After all, it was only a race.'

'What you mean, only a race?' Nellie's anger returned. 'There's a fair bit of prize money on that race. It may not be much for a young gen'leman like you, but thass a week's stabling and feed so far as I'm concerned. Only a race, he says.'

'Oh dear.' He had no idea what a week's stabling and feed might cost, but it must be a substantial outlay on Nellie's pay. 'Let me make it up to you . . .'

'I'm not taking your money,' cried Nellie, outraged. 'What sort of girl do you think I am then?'

'I didn't mean that,' pleaded Charles, though actually he had. He floundered desperately on. 'I meant, perhaps I could take you out somewhere?' Then he remembered. 'That's if Mortimer doesn't mind.'

He had made another mistake. 'Mortimer! Thass nothin' to do with Mortimer, who I go out with. Don't you go jumpin' to conclusions, just 'cos he gave me a hand after that fall. He give me the horse for a buthday present and he helps out a bit 'cos he knew me Dad, thass all.'

'Yes, yes of course,' he said hastily. If that was what she believed, it was up to Mortimer to enlighten her, not him. 'He told me, he's just a friend of the family. Anyway, can I take you out somewhere, to make up for that race? The pictures, perhaps?' He assumed she would not even consider it, but he felt he ought to make the gesture. To his surprise, and slight alarm, she hesitated before replying.

'Well, I dunno,' she said. 'Thass *Under Capricorn* on at the beginning of the week. Ingrid Bergman's lovely, but that Michael Wilding, he's terrible wet. I'd sooner see *Samson and Delilah* at the end of the week. Victor Mature, he's really sexy. Or there's Burt Lancaster and Virginia Mayo next week in *The Flame and the Arrow*, that should be quite exciting. I always see his films. But I'd sooner see Victor Mature, he must be smashing as Samson . . .'

Charles listened to this stream of cinematic information in something of a daze. He had not realized that Nellie was such a film buff. She was obviously a regular visitor to the Regal; the company, he assumed, was unimportant, so long as the film was right, and the seat was free. Perhaps he should have suggested a whist drive instead, the other popular form of mixed entertainment in Toftham.

'Well, that sounds quite nice,' he muttered. The ramifications of his hasty offer were beginning to sink home. It was not so much the reaction of Mr Juby to this kind of office liaison, nor indeed the reaction of Nellie's friends in the Golden Fleece, though that might be tricky enough. It was the reaction of the Old Rectory in Remingham that could be the problem.

'I don't mind going on my own if you don't want to,' said Nellie sharply, detecting the lack of enthusiasm in his voice.

'Certainly not,' Charles assured her. It was too late to back out now. 'We'll see *Samson and Delilah*. I wonder who plays Delilah . . .'

'Hedy Lamarr, of course,' said Nellie without hesitation. 'I expect she's a bit old for your liking.'

'I'm not as young as all that,' Charles said a little hotly, then remembered this was a peacemaking mission. 'Which night would you like to go? I expect Saturday's pretty crowded' – it was also the night that Nellie's friends were most likely to favour – 'and Friday's market day, that could be quite busy too. Shall we say Thursday?'

'All right, then, Thursday. If we meet there at seven when they open we can see all the adverts. They're quite

205

good, some of them. There's one for Craven A that's ever so clever.'

Charles promised to be there in time for the Craven A advert. In spite of the potential hazards, he found himself rather looking forward to it. An evening with Big Nellie might prove something of a challenge; 'stimulating' was the word that sprang to mind. And at least it would be economical; he could use the office cinema pass. As he climbed the stairs to his office, Rebecca's letter rustled reproachfully in his pocket . . .

Freddie Pendleton was waiting for him. It was not unusual for Freddie to call in, to advise him of forthcoming funerals. He had not tried his grimaces after that first disastrous encounter and over the months, with their frequent meetings in various churchyards, they had become quite good friends. But Freddie had not called on what he liked to describe as grave business. He was also chairman of Toftham Round Table's fête committee.

'We're looking for a publicity officer, Charles. Very important job. We need to whip up a bit more interest among the populace.'

'Oh, yes?' said Charles vaguely. His mind was still on next Thursday evening and the scenarios that might develop, all of which seemed to feature Nellie's magnificent chest.

'We thought you'd be an ideal chap,' said Freddie. 'You're an experienced journalist, you must know about these things.'

Charles started to pay attention. 'Very flattering, but not true,' he protested. 'I don't know a thing about publicity.'

'That doesn't really matter,' Freddie assured him comfortably. 'All you have to do is slip something into the *Journal* every week until the fête.'

'But what on earth is there I can write about every week? It's just another fête.' And he added feelingly: 'There're hundreds of the damn things.'

'That's just the point,' said Freddie earnestly. 'We

need to make out something different. We need something extra, something exciting and dramatic that'll bring in the crowds.'

Charles's mind went back to his assignation. 'How about Big Nellie doing a strip-tease?' he suggested. 'That should pack 'em in.'

'It's a nice thought.' Freddie paused to savour it for a moment. 'But not quite what I had in mind. We need some sort of professional display, a really spectacular affair, the sort of thing you see at a circus.'

'But why talk to me about it?' asked Charles. 'Shouldn't this be decided by the fête committee?'

'They have decided,' said Freddie. 'They've decided that it's the job of the publicity officer to find the right act. And they've decided you're the publicity officer. You've been elected unanimously. It's all been done democratically. Congratulations.'

Charles sank into his chair. All thought of next Thursday was now forgotten. 'Look here, Freddie, I may be able to write the odd publicity story for the *Journal*, but I don't know anything about booking acts. I don't even know how to start.'

'You start with this,' said Freddie, and passed him a brightly-coloured brochure. There were pictures of men in stetsons brandishing pistols and men in leopard-skins brandishing dumb-bells; small young ladies dressed in spangles hanging from trapezes and large elderly men dressed as Cossacks hanging from horses. There were jugglers and gymnasts and performing seals. There was even a ringmaster, available with or without a whip. It looked like an order form for Barnum and Bailey.

'You just decide which act you want, ring up the agent, tell him what date we want it, and if it's available, book it. It couldn't be simpler. But don't forget we've only got a corner of the Football Ground to play with, not Wembley Stadium. And don't go over fifty quid.'

Charles examined the brochure more closely. 'That rules out the massed bands of the Brigade of Guards, the aerial display team, the troupe of Chinese jugglers and the Four Horsemen of the Apocalypse. Pity about the Four Horsemen; it would be interesting to see the end of the world come to Toftham.'

'I expect they're just members of the North Norfolk Hunt, doing a bit of moonlighting,' said Freddie. 'Don't worry about them, I'm sure you'll pick a winner. And it should give you something different to write about.'

'And if I pick a loser?' asked Charles.

'You'll probably have to pay the fifty quid yourself,' said Freddie cheerfully. 'But it will all be done . . .'

'I know,' said Charles. 'Democratically.'

'Got it.' Freddie rose to leave. 'I should book it today if you can. The best acts probably get booked up quite early.' He peered up the stairs. 'Mr Juby's out. You could make the phone call now. Let me know how you get on.'

'See you in church,' said Charles. 'Or at the graveside.'

He started making a list from the brochure. The fifty-pound limit narrowed the field considerably; the restriction on space narrowed it further. He eventually selected two possibilities. There was a knife-throwing act called Buffalo Bob and Barbara, which included Bob throwing the knives at Barbara while blindfolded on a bicycle; Charles thought he might get a discount if he offered to provide the bike. And there was the Human Fireball, who leaped from a sixty-foot tower into a blazing tank while on fire himself. 'Tower and tank provided', said the brochure. 'Local Fire Brigade should provide water for the tank and be ready to assist in case of emergency'. That gave it a gruesome note of authenticity.

He rang the agent, gave the date of the fête, and asked for Buffalo Bob and Barbara. Alas, said the agent, Barbara was indisposed. And no, he said, before Charles could ask, it was not a knife wound, it was shingles. The Human Fireball however would be happy to oblige.

The agent explained the Fireball would arrive in his lorry on the eve of the fête, and set up his tank. The Fire Brigade would need to start filling it early, while he erected his tower. He would do his first jump at three o'clock, and his second – 'assuming he survives' Charles interjected, but the agent ignored him – a couple of hours later. At fifty pounds the Human Fireball seemed a snip. Charles booked him.

'By the way,' he asked as an afterthought. 'What's his name?'

'You don't need to know his name,' said the agent. 'You make out the cheque to me.'

Charles thought for a moment. 'Could it be possible,' he suggested, 'that the Human Fireball remains incognito because he is actually a member of a distinguished family with royal blood in his veins?'

At the other end of the line there was a loud guffaw. 'I've never asked,' said the agent. 'I suppose it's always possible.'

'Can I say that you will neither confirm nor deny it?'

The agent guffawed again. 'I can see you've been in this game before, mate. You carry on. I might even use it myself.'

'Thank you very much,' said Charles. He was not sure if Mr Juby would approve, but he had got his first publicity story for the Toftham Round Table fête.

At a quarter to seven on Thursday evening Charles finished his third pint in the farmers' bar and decided he had enough courage to confess to Mr Juby how he would be spending the evening. Ever since making the date with Nellie he had debated whether to tell him, or let him find out for himself. But since the Regal Cinema was in full view of the Dog and Partridge it would probably be only a matter of minutes before word reached the farmers' bar. He might just as well get it over; but he needed the three pints first.

'I'll be off then,' he said casually. 'I'm just taking Nellie to the pictures.'

Mr Juby remained calm. He took a sip at his special. 'A great one for the pictures, is Nellie.' He took another meditative sip. 'A great one for all manner o' things, come to that. You mind how you go.'

Now he's going to suggest I visit Mr Pollitt, thought Charles resignedly. As it happened, he already had. His previous purchase had long since been discarded, in case it came to light accidentally in Lambeth Palace. He had decided to get another, in the belief that if he had it he would not need it. So tonight it was not Rebecca's letter that rustled in his pocket.

Mr Juby however was taking quite a different line. 'I'm just looking to get a little work done in the office. Mortimer wastes quite enough time on her and that horse; I don't want two of you gawping after her.'

Charles was no longer surprised by Mr Juby's all-seeing eye. 'There's no question of that,' he said. 'I'm just taking her out to make up for her losing the Ladies' Race.'

'And I believe you, Charlie. She's been moanin' about that "go, go, go" of yours ever since. I'll be glad to hear the end of it. But don't forget the young leddy that won the race, boy. She might not be so understanding.'

'She doesn't have your intelligence network,' said Charles confidently. 'She'll probably never know.'

'Don't be daft, boy. Everyone in Remingham'll know by morning. Nellie's got an uncle there, for a start. You'd better tell the gal Beccy, same as you told me. There hent many secrets in these parts.'

'You're probably right. I'll have to pick the right moment.' He looked at the clock. 'I'd better go now or I'll miss the Craven A advert.'

Mr Juby watched him leave. Maggie handed him another special.

'Nice boy,' she said. 'Do you think he'll be all right with Nellie?'

'He'll be all right,' said Mr Juby. 'He's been to see Mr Pollitt.'

Nellie was waiting for him in the foyer. In spite of the warm evening she wore her imitation fur coat and an extra layer of make-up to go with it. Her hair was massed above her her head like a swirl of candy floss, regardless of anyone who might be in the row behind her.

Her perfume hit Charles when he was still only half-way across the Market Place but it was she who sniffed disapprovingly as he reached her.

'You've been in the Dog and Partridge again,' she said accusingly. Charles felt the effect of three three pints fading rapidly. It seemed he had come from one lecture to another.

'Shall we go in?' he enquired politely.

'What about nuts, then?' And when he looked blank, 'or crisps, or chocolates if you can afford it.' She pointed at the kiosk in the foyer.

'Yes, of course. Chocolates.' The kiosk had nothing smaller than a half-pound box. He bought some Black Magic. 'I like the advert,' he explained to Nellie, and led her up the stairs to the balcony.

'Don't you have to buy the tickets, then?' asked Nellie.

He showed her the press pass, thinking it might impress her. It merely annoyed her.

'Cheap old evening, hent it? You could have bought some more chocolates.'

Mr Juby should be here now, thought Charles. Not a lot to worry about so far.

The usherette greeted Nellie like an old friend, as indeed she was. They had a long chat about Victor Mature's past triumphs, and what his latest offering would be like. As this was Thursday and the start of the run, the usherette would be seeing it for the first time too.

'I see you've got your friend from the office,' she said coyly, nodding at Charles. He had not realized he was such a public figure. Nellie clarified the situation.

'He hent a friend. He just works there.' She turned to Charles. 'Come on then, I like to get a seat in the front.'

Charles found himself in the front row, his knees jammed against the balcony. There was the compen-sation, however, that Nellie's splendid legs were jammed

211

there too, only a few inches away. Her skirt, never very concealing, rode up even higher. She had also removed the fur coat, so he had a close-up of the magnificent contours of her chest. He missed the Craven A advert altogether.

'How did your friend know who I was?' he asked during the introduction to the newsreel. Nellie continued to gaze at the Pathé cockerel as if she had never seen a chicken before.

'She's Brenda Curson. Her mother keeps the shop in Remingham.'

'Oh dear,' said Charles. Regretfully he turned his gaze from Nellie's chest to the screen. One false move, with Brenda Curson hovering behind them, and the details would reach Remingham before he did.

The newsreel was showing events which had taken place a couple of weeks earlier, in places not covered by the *Journal*, and Charles's attention wandered. Thursdays, he knew, were always quiet at the Regal, and the balcony, which was more expensive than the stalls, was almost deserted. Another couple sat further along the front row, already locked in each other's arms. There were a few other pairs dotted about behind him, equally oblivious to their surroundings; but the occasional gleam of torch indicated that Brenda was still on active duty. If anything did develop with Nellie, he decided, Brenda would be the only problem.

'Are you going to open those chocolates, or save them for Christmas?' Nellie's brusque enquiry was enough to dispel any thoughts of romance. He opened the box and she took a chocolate and munched it appreciatively.

On the screen the opening credits of *Samson and Delilah* had begun. Nellie wriggled in anticipation. Charles watched her, quite fascinated. The wriggle was really rather seductive. Then, to his considerable excitement, she leaned towards him and reached across, her eyes still fixed to the screen. He held his breath as her hand hovered in front of him, just over his lap. Here we go, he thought exultantly.

Nellie took another chocolate.

And Charles subsided.

She continued to help herself to chocolates until the box was empty. If the way to a woman's heart is through her stomach, thought Charles, then I must be taking a short cut. On the other hand, she was quite likely to be sick. He put the empty box under the seat and, now that the regular movement of Nellie's arm in front of him had ceased, he started enjoying the film.

Victor Mature was in a lingering embrace with Miss Lamarr in the Biblical equivalent of a boudoir. Mr Mature's embraces were always inclined to linger, but this time he was bent on achieving new records. While Charles watched in grudging admiration, Nellie's hand came over again.

'They're all gone,' he whispered, but the hand kept coming. It gripped him firmly round the thigh.

Startled, Charles looked at her. Nellie was still staring avidly at the screen, breathing rather heavily, and completely engrossed in Mr Mature's *tour de force*. His mind whirled. Was the grip on his thigh an unconscious reaction to the passionate activity on the screen, or was Nellie just using it as an excuse? He was still trying to decide when her hand moved a few inches higher.

He looked round hastily for Brenda, but he need not have worried. Brenda was sitting at the far end of the row, her official duties suspended, watching Mr Mature just as fixedly as Nellie. The bush telegraph to Remingham might well remain silent tonight.

With enormous care Charles placed his hand on Nellie's knee. The grip on his thigh grew tighter.

Keep going, Victor, he implored silently to the marathon lover on the screen, who was still gamely lingering. He moved his hand gently up Nellie's leg; she moved hers up his.

He was making wild plans about taking Nellie back to the office and flinging her across Mr Juby's desk when the film broke.

This was not unusual at the Regal. Its projection

equipment, bought second-hand many years before, was very rough on films, and the films themselves had generally seen long service before they ever reached the Regal. When the screen went blank and the sound faded away, the management merely went into familiar routine. The lights came on, a slide appeared featuring Lyons' ice-cream, and the usherettes went for their trays.

Downstairs there were the predictable catcalls and stamping of feet, but up in the balcony most of the couples remained locked together, hardly noticing any change. Charles, appalled at this unexpected turn of events, withdrew his hand as if it had been bitten. Nellie, rather less dramatically, withdrew hers.

He gave her an embarrassed look. She was still breathing quite fast, and her eyes were sparkling. In the subdued cinema lighting her make-up seemed almost natural. She was really looking very attractive.

'What a pity,' he murmured.

She turned and look him squarely in the eye. This must be the moment of truth. Had she realized what she was doing, or had she just been carried away by the film?

'There you are,' said Nellie. 'I said you should have bought some more chocolates.'

He studied her carefully, but it was no help. She was either being extremely devious, or extremely naive. That's Norfolk for you, he thought. I'll probably never know.

'Never mind,' he said resignedly. 'Let's both have a choc-ice instead.' It took some minutes to repair the film, and they found little to talk about while they waited. Brenda bought them the choc-ices, and from her casual demeanour it was apparent she had not noticed their activities during the Mature embrace; he was thankful for that small mercy.

When the film resumed the embrace had been completed and Victor was busy with more mundane matters, like killing people with the jawbone of an ass. Nellie's hand never even twitched in his direction, and it certainly never occurred to him to move his. All he wanted now was to get safely home.

As they went out through the foyer Charles offered, without any great enthusiasm, to see her home.

'That's all right. You get off to Remingham, that's where you ought to be.' He wondered if the remark had any special significance; again, he suspected he would never know.

'Well, goodnight then,' he said, and hesitantly held out a hand.

Nellie smiled at him. It struck him that this was the first time she had smiled at him all evening.

'Thank you for a nice evening, Charlie. I enjoyed the chocolates, and the choc-ice, and – everything.' She kissed him firmly on the lips, and walked off across the Market Place, two splendid legs under an imitation fur coat and a swirl of candy-floss hair.

Charles watched her go. He was thinking about that final word, 'and – everything.' One day, perhaps, he *would* know.

As he turned towards the office to collect his bike, from the doorway of the Dog and Partridge came a familiar chuckle.

'Fare y'well, Mr Juby,' murmured Charles.

Fourteen

The university term had long since ended, Rebecca had still not returned to Remingham, and the summer was slipping away. Occasional messages filtered through that she had stayed on in Newcastle, then gone to stay with friends somewhere in the north. Charles watched each sunny picnicking day pass with increasing frustration.

So he was quite glad to have something different to think about when Mr Juby suggested that he spent a week in Wettleford while Mortimer took a rare holiday.

'He don't like to leave his patch in case that hent there when he come back,' Mr Juby explained. 'He's a great worrier, is Morty. But I send him off for a week or two every so often, to make sure he gets a break. I usually look after Wettleford from here while he's away, but if you fancy yourself as an acting reporter-in-charge for a week, you can have a go.'

Charles fancied it very much. He was also gratified that Mr Juby felt he could handle it. Mr Juby, however, did not allow him to get too carried away.

'You'll be doing just what you're doing here, so there hent a lot to it. But be a little extra careful, boy, specially with those initials.'

Charles promised to love and to cherish each initial. 'Do I stay in Wettleford or do I have to commute?' There was a spasmodic steam train service between Toftham and Wettleford, but the first train was quite late and the last train was quite early. There would also be the bike ride to Remingham.

'That depends on Mortimer. He's got a little company flat over the office. He may not mind you using it while he's away. Then again, he may. Otherwise there's the Red Lion, but you'd have to pay for that yourself, boy. Our friends in Narridge won't lay out for it, thass for sure. They'd say you should stay here and use the tele-phone. Very careful they are, up in Narridge.'

Charles said he would have a word with Mortimer about the flat, but he had no great hopes. Nothing had been mentioned about his abortive outing to the Regal with Nellie, but he had no doubt that word had reached Wettleford, and in spite of Nellie's conviction that Mortimer was just a friend of the family, he did not expect him to be entirely happy about it, innocent though it turned out to be.

A couple of days before Mortimer was due to start his holiday, Charles loaded his bike into the guard's van on the nine-thirty a.m. train to Wettleford and settled back for the forty-minute journey. The train had come from Norwich and would be going on to the handful of little towns and villages on the coast, but although it was high summer there were very few passengers. The guard had plenty of time for a chat.

'What takes you to Wettleford?' he asked as he clipped Charles's ticket. Charles explained who he was.

'Mortimer taking a holiday, then?' said the guard. 'Thass a rare do.' It turned out he was a Wettleford man himself; he had worked on this line since he was a boy.

'Things are very quiet today,' Charles commented.

'They're quiet every day,' replied the guard gloomily. 'There's talk they'll be cutting back on this line. There's another one goes up to the coast from Norwich, more direct than this. Thass the one most people use; there hent many want to come out Toftham way.'

'But if they close this line, how will anyone get from Toftham to Wettleford, or up to the coast?' Charles enquired.

The guard grunted. 'They talk about buses. But you couldn't put that old bike of yours on a bus. And the days we are busy, say market day, where do people put all the bits and pieces they've bought? We've had wardrobes on this train, and armchairs, the lot. You wouldn't get no more'n a cushion on a bus.'

He went off down the train, still muttering, and Charles made a mental note to pass on the conversation to Mr Juby. He had not known of any talk of rail closures; perhaps he could actually tell Mr Juby something he had not heard already.

The train chuffed gently through the Norfolk countryside. For some time the track ran alongside the river that meandered through the Launford district, the same river he had sat beside with Rebecca at Remingham. He found himself picking out likely picnic spots along the bank, until he forced himself to think of other things. He studied the crops that were ripening in the summer sunshine, the little stations they stopped at along the route – mostly deserted except for the odd porter sunning himself on the platform – and the occasional tractor trundling down a lane, or a fisherman dozing by the river. The train was the only sign of purposeful activity in a placid, unhurried world.

Mortimer was waiting for him on Wettleford station, Charles was not sure what reception he would get, but Mortimer was as friendly and self-deprecating as ever, and insisted on fetching his bicycle out of the guard's van.

'You'll have to get something a little better than this if you're going to stay a district reporter,' he commented as they went out of the station yard.

'I suppose I could graduate to something a little flashier,' Charles agreed. 'Drop handlebars and silver mudguards and a five-speed gear, all that stuff.'

'I didn't mean another bicycle,' said Mortimer. 'I meant a motorbike. It's a big area you've got at Toftham, nearly as big as this. You can't cover it properly on a pushbike.'

Charles had not contemplated anything so ambitious. 'I haven't got the money for a motorbike,' he said. 'I can't even ride one.'

'I might be able to help you there,' Mortimer said hesitantly. 'Not with the money, I'm afraid, but I'd be happy to teach you to ride. That's if you'd like me to. It's very easy really.'

Charles was delighted. 'Mort, that's very good of you. Perhaps once I've got a licence I can talk my parents into putting up the money.' He had had only occasional contact with his parents since his move to Norfolk, but he assumed they were still interested in his welfare.

'You might even get some help from Norwich,' Mortimer suggested. 'You've been with us long enough now to show you can do the job. Otherwise they'd have got rid of you.'

'That's true.' It was something else he had not thought of. Certainly the agreed trial period had long since passed without any complaints from Norwich; he had even been given a modest rise. 'It's worth a try, Mort. Thanks very much.'

'There's one thing I ought to warn you.' Mortimer smiled at him innocently. 'You'll find that Nellie doesn't like riding on motorbikes.'

Charles felt himself blushing. 'You know about the cinema, then.'

'Oh yes, she told me all about it.' *All* about it? thought Charles. But Mortimer seemed quite unconcerned. 'It was a very nice thought of yours, to make up for losing that race. I appreciate it.'

'That's quite all right,' said Charles uncomfortably. 'Let's forget about it. I can't imagine it'll happen again.'

'I don't suppose it will.' Mortimer smiled quietly. 'She doesn't fall off all that often.'

Charles left it at that.

The *Journal*'s Wettleford headquarters was a small office over a newsagent's shop in the High Street, reached by a discreet side door. Mortimer's flat was on the floor above. The office was a replica of Charles's, with dusty files on the shelves, a desk heaped with papers, and a couple of wooden chairs. The only extra item was a battered armchair for the more distinguished visitors, an acknowledgment that as sole representative of the *Journal* in Wettleford, Mortimer had to extend the company's hospitality on a properly lavish scale.

In the flat above, Mortimer made a pot of tea in the tiny kitchen while Charles went into the sitting room and looked out over the High Street. Wettleford was smaller than Toftham, with a population of perhaps three thousand people. Its High Street was much narrower, and the market place it ran into was much smaller, but on market days, Mortimer assured him, it was a busy and bustling place, the centre for an area stretching up to the coast a dozen miles to the north and a similar distance all round.

Mortimer showed him the rest of the flat as they drank their tea. It extended over the adjoining building as well, where there was the bedroom and a small bathroom. It was all spotlessly clean and neat.

'I envy you,' said Charles. 'I wish there was a set-up like this at the Toftham office.'

'You'd have to get rid of Mr Juby first,' said Mortimer, 'but his office would make a nice sitting-room.' Charles looked at him sharply, but he could still never tell when Mortimer was being serious. It seemed a good moment, however, to ask if he could use the flat during his stay in Wettleford.

'I assumed you would,' said Mortimer without hesitation. 'You're very welcome. I'll be glad to know somebody is looking after the place. To be quite honest, I don't really like being away from it.'

It turned out he would not be going very far. He explained that his mother had bought a bungalow near the beach at Hunstanton, which was only about thirty miles away. He would spend the week with her and be back on the Saturday evening.

They went downstairs to the office and Mortimer showed him the contacts book and the diary. Judging by the sparseness of the entries, not a lot was happening in Wettleford. Charles was not too disappointed; even to have sole control over a whist drive report, without Mr Juby looking over his shoulder, was power enough.

At lunchtime they had a sandwich in the Red Lion, Wettleford's equivalent of the Dog and Partridge but without the distinction of a farmers' bar. Charles was introduced to some of the regulars, and he established his credentials by buying a couple of rounds of drinks. He hoped he could justifiably put them down to expenses.

Mortimer had to do some writing and phoning in the afternoon, and Charles occupied the time cycling round the town, getting his bearings. It had one great asset that Toftham lacked. The river flowed round it in a great horseshoe bend – no doubt the Saxons had selected the site for its sound defence – and he was able to take his cycle along the riverside path which led from one side of the town to the other. He lingered by the old arched bridge which was the only access to the town from the south, and the scene of much traffic congestion on market day. This afternoon there was little traffic about, and he was able to sit on the parapet, dangling his legs over the water, and ponder on the delights of his new responsibilities.

When he got back to the office he found Mortimer wheeling his motorbike out of a shed behind the news-agent's shop. 'I'll run you up to the coast. It'll give you an idea of what the area's like – and maybe we can fit in your first lesson on the way back.'

They rode northwards out of Wettleford, through country which became more hilly and wooded as they approached the coast. As they rode, Mortimer pointed out the motorbike's controls and shouted over his shoulder how they worked. As he had said, they seemed fairly simple to Charlie – a twistgrip throttle with the hand-brake on one handlebar and the clutch, like a second brake, on the other. The main brake was down by one foot pedal, the gear change was by the other. Switches for the lights, a horn and a mirror, and that seemed to be it.

They reached the crest of a hill and the coastline was laid out before them, the salt marshes and the broad ribbon of sand, and the sea beyond. There was a narrow inlet winding through the marshes with boats moored along it and others drawn up on the mudflats on each side. At its head there was a cluster of cottages, reached by a lane running down from the coast road.

'That's Branham Staithe,' shouted Mortimer as they cruised down the hill through an area of gorse and heather, with little footpaths and clearings. 'Great place for sailing, if you want to go in for that sort of thing. But this common we're going through is a great place for picnics.' And he added, rather slyly, 'I gather that's rather more your line.'

'Now, now,' said Charles, and gave him a friendly thump. Mr Juby was right; there were no secrets in these parts. But he noted the common nonetheless.

They rode along the coast road for a few miles, passing through little villages where people often waved to Mortimer and shouted a greeting as they went by. They saw little of the sea; although their route was called the coast road it was some distance from the coast, with broad areas of salt marshes in between. But at one point they followed a track through the marshes, right down to the beach itself. They left the bike among the dunes and walked along the wide belt of sand between the marshes and the sea. It was the holiday season, but where they stood on the beach there was hardly a soul to be seen in any direction, just the birds calling on the saltflats, and a few yachts well out to sea. And over it all, as always, the great expanse of the Norfolk sky. For the second time that day, Charles counted his blessings.

On the way back to Wettleford there was a disused war-time airfield, the concrete runways overgrown and the buildings derelict, an ideal place for a little motor-cycle practice. He had problems at first finding the gears and co-ordinating them with the clutch, and the engine seemed a lot more powerful now he had to control it, but it was a successful beginning.

Mortimer congratulated him, but was cautionary too. 'There's a big difference between riding around on an empty airfield and coping with the traffic in Norwich when you take your test. You really need to practice on a bike of your own; you should think about it seriously.'

'I'm thinking about all sort of things seriously today,' said Charles. 'I can see why you don't like budging from this area. I think it even beats Toftham.'

'So do I,' said Mortimer, and he was suddenly subdued. Charles recognised the worried look that he had seen at their first meeting, when Mortimer thought he had come to replace him.

'Don't worry, Mort,' he said heartily. 'I'm not going to take over at Wettleford.'

But it was an attractive thought, nevertheless.

The first couple of days as acting reporter-in-charge were almost idyllic. Charles moved a few clothes and some tinned food into Mortimer's flat, but he took most of his meals at the Red Lion over a pint of beer. His reporting duties were not onerous. He made the routine visits to the clergy and the undertaker and the police, telephoned a few of the names in the contacts book, and dealt with the reports that were put through the door. Mr Juby had made it clear he did not expect any great scoops during his stay – 'Thass a holdin' operation, boy, thass all it is' – so he was happy to adopt the Juby routine and let the news come to him, rather than go in search of it.

The working day, if such it could be called, virtually ended when he strolled to the railway station and handed over his envelope of reports to the guard on the four-thirty train to Norwich. The bus timetable at Wettleford had not been planned with the *Journal*'s needs in mind, and there was no convenient service to Norwich, so the four-thirty was always used by Mortimer as his regular line of communication. Its route via Toftham was not the most direct – indeed the railways in that part of Norfolk never seemed to go directly from anywhere to anywhere – and the envelope did not reach

Norwich until mid-evening, but such had been the system for years and Charles was happy to continue it.

He spent his evenings in the Red Lion, or ambling round the streets to make sure there were no lynch-mobs on the rampage, or just sitting in the office by the window surveying his empire.

On the Wednesday morning, having made a few phone calls and dealt with the modest post-bag, he was debating whether to stroll down to the river to see if the fish were behaving themselves when Len Hedges appeared in the doorway.

He had met Mr Hedges in the Red Lion. Mortimer had introduced him as the secretary of Wettleford Trades Council. 'A bit of a stirrer,' Mortimer told him afterwards. 'The local unions aren't too bothered about the Trades Council, so Len really has it all his own way. A few of his cronies go along to the mettings and they pass a lot of resolutions. Nothing ever comes of them, but it looks good in the paper.'

'Good morning, Mr Hedges,' said Charles brightly, pleased that he remembered the name. 'Nice to see you. Didn't know you'd had a meeting.'

'We hent had a meeting, not yet,' said Mr Hedges. 'This is an individual initiative, like. The Trades Council will consider the matter in due course, and no doubt representations will be made, but I thought you'd like to know about it in time for this week's paper. Today's the last day, you know.'

'Yes, I do know, Mr Hedges.' He was duly impressed. Not every secretary had such an eye for publicity.

'So what's it about?' he asked, ushering the representative of Wettleford Trades Council into the Distinguished Visitors' armchair.

'It's that poor Mrs Anstey. She's being thrown out of her cottage; and she hent got nowhere to go, the poor soul.'

'And why is that?' asked Charles, trying to display the judicious calm of an acting reporter-in-charge, but feeling a little excitement stirring.

'Because thass a tied cottage, thass why. Old Henry Anstey, he used to wuk on the estate. Then when he died a little while back, that Burton feller, he says she got to go.'

Charles sat up. 'Burton? That wouldn't be the Honourable Henry Burton?'

'Thass the son,' said Mr Hedges. 'It's his father's estate, old Baron Burton. He's the man what's responsible.'

Charles was hooked. A wicked baron would be wonderful copy. And the fact that the obnoxious Harry Burton was his son added an extra piquancy. The judicious calm was becoming difficult to maintain. 'Tell me all about it, Mr Hedges.'

And Mr Hedges did, though there did not seem a great deal more to tell. Henry Anstey had worked as a pigman on the Burton estate all his married life. He and his wife had lived in the same cottage for over thirty years. After he died suddenly – Mr Hedges was a bit vague about the date – Lord Burton told his widow she would have to vacate the cottage.

'But that's quite legal, isn't it?' Some of the judicious calm still remained. 'If it's a tied cottage then the landlord is entitled to demand possession.'

'Oh yes, thass legal. But that hent very hoomane, now is it?' demanded Mr Hedges, beginning to assume the style in which he addressed the Trade Council. 'We ought not to stand for it in a free country, thass what I say. That hent right and proper, and I'm going to propose a resolution to that effect at our next meeting.'

'But is it really a matter for the Trades Council?' asked Charles, genuinely puzzled.

'Everything's a matter for the Trades Council if it's a matter that needs putting right,' said Mr Hedges firmly. 'It's the rights of an individual what's at stake, and thass what we stand for. You ask Mortimer, he'll tell you.'

'I'm sure he would,' said Charles. He was getting the measure of Len Hedges. However, it sounded like a good story and he ought to follow it up. He thought of one more question.

'Isn't there anywhere Mrs Anstey can go? Doesn't she have any children?'

'No children at all.' Mr Hedges became slightly emotional. 'She's just a poor widow woman, being thrown out of house and home.'

'Quite so,' said Charles. 'I'll see what I can do.'

Mr Hedges gave him directions on where to find the poor widow woman and her house and home. 'You'd better hurry,' he urged as he was leaving. 'You got to get to get it on that four-thirty train, you know.'

'Yes, I know, Mr Hedges,' said Charles. The secretary of Wettleford Trades Council might be a useful inform-ant, but he was really a terrible pain.

Mrs Anstey lived in a row of farm cottages a mile or two outside Wettleford. Hers was easy to identify – it was the one with the barricades at the windows.

Charles propped his bike by the gate and was making a note about the barricades – he was already toying with phrases about Englishmen's homes and castles – when Mrs Anstey appeared at an upper window. She was a large lady with a flushed face. She held a big enamel jug.

'Don't you come any nearer,' she cried, 'or I'll pour this lot over your head. You won't get me out of here, not unless you blast me out, so don't you try it.'

'Mrs Anstey, I'm from the *Journal*,' Charles shouted back. 'I've heard you're being evicted and I want to take up the matter. I just wondered if there's any com-ment you'd like to make.'

'I've got a comment all right,' yelled Mrs Anstey. 'You can tell that bloody Burton he's a . . .'

Charles dutifully took it down, but knew he could not print it. Apart from the obscenity laws, it hardly fitted the image of the poor widow woman.

Mrs Anstey disappeared from the window with her enamel jug to await further visitors, and Charles rode back thoughtfully to Wettleford. It seemed a straightforward story, another example of Mr Juby's foodal society. But he could have wished for a more sympathetic character to champion, and he did not relish being an ally of Len Hedges. He remembered Lord Remingham's warning about making sure of all the facts; he would have to get Lord Burton's side of the story. But the Burton mansion was up near the coast, well out of cycling range if he was to get the story on the four-thirty. He would have to phone him instead.

He expected the call to be answered by a secretary, or even another butler. But a familiar voice came on the line.

'Burton here.'

Charles stiffened. 'Would that be the Honourable Henry Burton?'

'It would indeed.'

He assumed the businesslike crispness of an acting reporter-in-charge. 'Charles Benson here. We met at the point-to-point. I'd like to speak to Lord Burton.'

There was a pause, then a laugh. 'Of course, the Purveyor of Good News. Well, I'm afraid it's bad news, Chas. My father is abroad.'

That's it then, thought Charles, I'd better drop the story. But he made a final attempt.

'I suppose you don't know about Mrs Anstey and her cottage?'

'That appalling woman? Of course I know about her.' The tone became sharper. 'And it's not her cottage; it's our cottage.'

Charles reached for a pencil. This was more like it.

'You think it's right to evict her, then?'

'Of course it's right. We need the cottage. The sooner we get her out, the better.'

Charles scribbled it down. It was just the quote he wanted. But he offered Harry Burton another opening.

'Is there anything else you'd like to say on behalf of Lord Burton? For instance, why you need the cottage so urgently?'

The voice at the other end became icy. 'We really

don't have to explain our decisions to you, do we? I think you ought to purvey your good news in some other direction.' And the Honourable Henry rang off.

Charles sat staring at his notebook, half-furious, half-exultant. The obnoxious Harry had put him down again, but he had said enough to give him his story. He put aside his misgivings about Len Hedges and the unlovely Mrs Anstey, and started writing . . .

It was Thursday afternoon when the phone call came. It was a sheer fluke that Charles was in the office to take it. The deadline for that week's *Journal* had passed, there was no point in seeking any more copy, and he had decided to spend the rest of the day dozing by the river. So he picked up the phone reluctantly.

A woman's voice came on. 'Is that the *Journal*?' Charles admitted it was. 'This is Lord Burton's secretary. I'll put him on.'

'Wait a minute,' said Charles. 'I thought he was abroad?'

'He was, but he was due back today. He'd very much like a word with you, if you can spare a moment.'

'Yes, of course,' gulped Charles. He was gratified by this courteous approach, but it did not stop his heart from thumping. He reminded himself that he was the acting reporter-in-charge, and a force to be reckoned with.

'Is that Charles Benson?' It was quite a pleasant voice, not the clipped tones that Lord Remingham used. 'I believe you've been having a word with Henry about Mrs Anstey and the cottage?'

Charles agreed that he had. Now, he thought, he'll tell me he's the chairman's first cousin. Here we go again.

'I thought you might like to have the full picture,' said Lord Burton, 'then you're welcome to print what you like. Incidentally, Henry tells me you're a friend of Rebecca Bateman. What a charming girl. But I gather you and Henry didn't hit it off terribly well, he may not have been very helpful in answering your questions.'

'I think he said quite enough, sir,' said Charles rather pompously.

'I see. Then he told you about my new pigman and his family?'

Charles was puzzled. 'No, he didn't.'

'Pity,' said Lord Burton. 'Fact is, I've taken on a young fellow with a wife and three small children. They're living in a wooden shack on the other side of Wettleford. We've been trying to get Mrs Anstey to leave for the best part of six months now, so we can get him and his family properly housed. They're really living in quite appalling conditions.'

Charles had a sudden picture of the Gibson family in their tumbledown cottage at Remingham. It sounded like a similar case – except that this time he was on the opposite side. But there was still Mrs Anstey to consider.

'I take your point sir, but as I understand it Mrs Anstey has no family and nowhere else to go.'

'She has no children, but she does have a brother, you know. They don't get on very well, I'm afraid, and he's been doing all he can to avoid having her, but there's room enough at his place for her to stay until they can make other arrangements. She wouldn't have far to go – he only lives in Wettleford.'

A disturbing thought crossed Charles's mind. It was a thought which shed rather a different light on the affair.

'Would her brother be a Mr Len Hedges, sir?'

'Ah, you do know him, then. In that case you now have the full story.'

He did indeed. He found it difficult to sound calm as he thanked Lord Burton for the call. 'As you say, sir, it would have been helpful to have been told all this before. Please remember me to your son.' And I shall certainly remember him, he said to himself savagely as he rang off.

He looked at the clock. The *Journal* was already with

229

the printers; the first copies were probably coming off the presses. Tomorrow morning he would be the laughing stock of Wettleford – and the Honourable Henry would no doubt be laughing loudest of all. Beyond the local repercussions there was the shadow of Lord Remingham and the company chairman.

There was only one desperate move he could make. He had to find Mr Juby. He phoned the Toftham office.

'Juby,' came the familiar growl. Charles was relieved, but rather surprised. It was unusual for Mr Juby to be in on a Thursday afternoon. 'It's Charles here, in Wettleford.' He tried to get rid of the little shake in his voice. 'I've got a bit of a problem.'

'Thought it might be you, boy. I been waiting for you to ring.'

Charles could not think why, but there was no time to discuss Mr Juby's clairvoyant powers if the presses were going to be stopped. He gave a quick summary of what had happened. 'Is there still time to stop the story?' he asked, almost tremulously.

'No, of course there hent, this time on a Thursday.' Charles's last hopes were dashed. 'Fortunately,' Mr Juby continued, 'thass been stopped already.'

'How do you mean?' asked Charles, bewildered.

'I been checking your stuff all week,' said Mr Juby. 'You don't think I'd let you loose on your own yet without keeping an eye on you, boy? I been taking your envelope off the train at Toftham, and I've gone through what you been up to, then put it on the nine o'clock bus.'

Charles was dumbfounded, and not a little hurt. He had really believed he had Mr Juby's confidence. But he was also enormously relieved.

'Most of your copy was puffickly all right. Quite good even. But when I saw that story about Mrs Anstey I knew that no-good brother of hers had been on to you. He tried it on with Mortimer a couple of months back, but Morty had more sense. Come to think of it' – Mr

Juby gave one of his more prolonged chuckles – 'you been proper Mortified, hent you.'

Charles did not laugh. 'I checked with Henry Burton. It's not my fault he didn't tell me about the new pigman and his family.'

'Thass true, he should have told you,' agreed Mr Juby. 'But if you go round trying to take over other people's girl friends, you got to expect trouble.'

'But why didn't you tell me you'd stopped the story?' asked Charles, a little angry now at Mr Juby's subterfuges.

'I was going to tell you this morning. Then I heard His Lordship was coming back home about lunchtime, so I thought I'd have a word with him instead, and let him tell you. Might make a little more impact, like.'

'It did that all right,' admitted Charles ruefully. But he had to feel grateful. 'That's why you were in the office then, on a Thursday afternoon.'

'Not entirely, boy,' Mr Juby's voice had grown sharper again. 'I wanted to have a word with you about something else in that envelope yesterday, what was just as stoopid as this business with Len Hedges.'

Charles's heart sank again. 'Surely nobody else has been having me on?'

'You can't blame this on anybody else,' said Mr Juby severely. 'Your report of the Wettleford Bingo Club. You said the caller was Mr E. Figgins. Thass David Figgins does the calling; that should be D, not E. What did I tell you to remember, boy?'

Charles almost laughed with relief. 'I'm afraid I left that notice behind in Toftham, Mr Juby.'

'Then you make out another one and put it in your office over there.' Mr Juby spoke slowly and clearly. ' "Initials Are Sacred". You be more careful the next couple of days. I'll see you on Monday.'

In the next couple of days Charles was considerably more careful, and not only with initials. He was very careful how he behaved, for instance, when Len Hedges came into the office on Friday morning, demanding to

231

know why the eviction story had not appeared in the paper. His first impulse was to kick him down the stairs.

'You didn't tell me you were Mrs Anstey's brother,' he said angrily.

'That didn't seem relevant,' said Mr Hedges, a little disconcerted.

'And why don't you take her in until she finds somewhere else?'

Mr Hedges shrugged. 'You've met her, hent you?'

'That's not the point. You're her brother.' Charles took a firmer control of himself and settled back in his chair. He had not offered his visitor the armchair this time, and Mr Hedges stood awkwardly in front of him.

'Now look here, Mr Hedges. There's certainly a story in all this, and I'm very tempted to write it. How Mrs Anstey has been asked to leave her cottage, which is now bigger than she needs, so that a young family can be given a home, but her own brother refuses to take her in, even temporarily, and meanwhile the young family is having to live in squalor, all because of his "inhoomanity".' He emphasised the word.

'But that hent the whole story,' cried Mr Hedges.

'Nor was the story you told me.' Charles was really feeling like a reporter-in-charge. 'I suggest you persuade your sister to leave the cottage, and put up with her until you can find somewhere else for her. Perhaps the Trades Council can help.' And he ushered him down the stairs.

On Saturday afternoon he boarded the four-thirty train to Toftham. He had left a note behind for Mortimer, due back in a few hours' time. 'Thank you for the use of your flat, your office, and your district. I enjoyed it enormously – even though I was Mortified.' No doubt Mr Juby would explain.

It was the same guard he had met on his first journey, and again there was plenty of time for a chat. 'Another quiet day?' he said half-jokingly. But the guard only frowned. 'More's the pity,' he said. 'People round here will soon be wishing they used this line a bit more. They're in for a rare shock come Monday.'

'What sort of shock?' asked Charles, greatly interested, but the guard decided to say no more. 'You wait till Monday. You'll hear soon enough.' And he would be drawn no further.

Charles was still grateful. He had quite forgotten their previous conversation. The hint from the guard might distract Mr Juby if he decided to give him another roasting over the eviction story. But all that could wait until Monday.

He cycled into Remingham, wishing it was more of a triumphal return; he had not exactly distinguished himself in Wettleford. Then he heard a whinnying from the paddock behind the Old Rectory, and he saw Thunder prancing about in a most uncharacteristic fashion. He remembered what Dr Bateman had told him, and his spirits soared.

Rebecca was on her way home.

Fifteen

*Triumph 250 c.c. m/c, only one owner, good runner, needs
a little attention, £35. View any time. Toftham 335*

It was the only motorcycle he could find in the *Journal*'s
advertisement pages, when he returned to the Toftham
office on Monday morning, which seemed to be within
his means. He had decided not to approach Norwich for
a loan; they would probably take a couple of months to
make up their mind. And he was reluctant to go to his
parents for help – they would no doubt disapprove of
a motorcycle anyway. Now that Rebecca's return was
imminent – the Batemans had confirmed Thunder's
forecast and said she was due any day – he wanted to
get his plans for more sophisticated transport under way
as quickly as possible. There was no chance of taking
his test before she went back to Newcastle, but at least
he could demonstrate that he had ambitions beyond
Geo. Perkins's delivery bike.

He telephoned Mortimer in Wettleford, partly to
check that he had returned safely and found nothing
amiss, and partly to ask if he would come and give an
expert opinion on the good runner with only one owner,
needing a little attention.

Mortimer assured him that all was well, and readily
agreed to inspect his prospective purchase. He sounded
rather gratified that Charles was acting so promptly on
his advice.

'Incidentally,' he said, as Charles was about to ring
off, 'I gather you had some trouble with Len Hedges.'
Mortimer had his finger as firmly on the Wettleford
pulse, thought Charles, as Mr Juby had on Toftham's.
But it was unlike him to crow over somebody else's
mistake.

Mortimer, however, had no intention of crowing. 'I do apologise, it's my fault entirely. I really should have warned you about Len and his sister. I didn't think he'd try it on again.' He sounded quite upset. 'I had no intention you should be mortified, believe me.'

Charles realised his facetious note had been taken seriously. He had to spend some time assuring Mortimer that it was just a joke, a gentle pun on his name. One really did have to be very careful with Mortimer. But it was very typical, thought Charles, that he should try to take the blame. Then he heard Mr Juby climbing the stairs; he told Mortimer again not to worry, and rang off.

'Len Hedges bin giving you any more scoops?' asked Mr Juby a little maliciously.

Charles ignored it. He told him instead about his conversation with the guard over the possible cutbacks in the service, and the warning that something was to happen that day.

'I thought that must be coming to the boil,' mused Mr Juby. 'Ben Kingsworthy was in the Dog and Partridge on Saturday night, looking rare gloom. He hent a drinking man normally. He wouldn't say narthin, but I thought something must be up.'

He saw Charles's enquiring look. 'He's the stationmaster,' he explained. 'You nip round there and have a word with him; he might know something he can tell us by now. I'll have a word with Narridge.' Charles realised it must be serious; Mr Juby rarely bothered to ring Norwich about anything.

Toftham station had once been a major centre for freight traffic as well as passengers, but most of the local crops were transported by road now and the extensive goods yards were largely unused. But the station itself still retained some of its Victorian splendour. Elegant cast-iron pillars supported the lofty crenellated roof, each of the sturdy wooden seats was embossed with the station's name, and the splendid weighing machine with its enormous dial was still accurate to an ounce.

The waiting room was decorated with posters advertising long-forgotten outings to the seaside and to London, and a modest coal fire was kept going during the winter, but most people preferred the station buffet. It not only provided refreshment for passengers but also served as a social centre for the station staff, who were not over-taxed by their official duties. Next to the station was a rather grand signal-box controlling the level crossing, where the signalmen could be seen peacefully reading their newspapers in the long gaps between trains. It was all very civilised, thought Charles, but not terribly cost-effective.

He found Ben Kingsworthy standing on the platform outside his office. He was a man of impressive proportions, tall and broad-shouldered and even broader further down; the watch-chain that spanned his waistcoat looked sturdy enough to be used for towing if an engine chanced to break down. As Charles approached he was studying the massive pocket-watch attached to the end of the chain.

Charles introduced himself. 'I wonder if I could have a word about the development affecting the Wettleford line?'

Mr Kingsworthy looked down at him – he was a good six inches taller than Charles – and frowned suspiciously. 'What development's that, then?'

Charles stepped into the unknown. 'The development that's happening today. It's going to cause quite a shock, isn't it?'

Mr Kingsworthy's frown deepened. 'How d'you know about that, then?' So the guard must have been right. Something was happening, but what?

'I'm afraid I cannot reveal my sources.' It was a line that reporters were always supposed to be using, but this was the first time he had had occasion to himself. He had to confess it sounded frightfully pompous.

Mr Kingsworthy however was studying his watch again. 'That'll have to keep for a moment. Here's the ten-thirty coming in; it's two minutes late already. You wait in the office, Mr Benson.'

He strode off up the platform, his braided cap gleaming, as the ten-thirty from Norwich pulled into the station. Charles watched him hustling the waiting passengers into the compartments. Only a handful of people got off, women with shopping bags who had come in from the outlying villages and one or two men in suits carrying briefcases, no doubt with business in the town. There was also a girl with a large haversack over one shoulder and carrying two suitcases. One of them had a tennis racquet strapped on the side.

Mr Kingsworthy blew a mighty blast on his whistle and waved to the driver, and the ten-thirty started on its way northwards to Wettleford and the coast. But Charles was not watching it; he was running up the platform to catch up with the girl.

'Carry your bags, miss?'

Rebecca looked round in astonishment. 'Charles! How on earth did you know I'd be on that train?'

Charles drew himself up. 'I am not permitted to reveal my sources,' he announced solemnly – then added, beaming, 'but I can say that Thunder had something to do with it.'

They laughed together as he took the cases and they walked up the platform together. Rebecca explained that she had arrived in Norwich the previous evening from her holiday in the north, spent the night with friends, and was now heading for Remingham.

'Unless you've fitted a bigger basket on your bike,' she said as they reached the station forecourt, 'I'll need to get a cab.' Toftham's two taxis were parked there as usual – they optimistically met every train, but rarely acquired a fare. This time one of them was in luck.

'That's one of the things I've got to tell you about,' said Charles. 'I'm planning to pension off the old bike. Might even try to flog it to Freddie Pendleton – he was keen enough to buy it at the auction.'

'There are things I have to tell you too,' said Rebecca,

and there was a curious note to her voice. 'Why not come out to Remingham with me in the taxi so we can have a talk on the way – then it could bring you back again. He's got to come back anyway, so he shouldn't charge any extra.'

For a moment Charles was sorely tempted to accept the apple that Eve was offering. But he resisted it. 'I've got to see a man about a railway line,' he said. 'I'll call round tonight.'

He helped to load the suitcases into the taxi, and they stood for a moment beside it. 'See you later, then,' said Rebecca. She kissed him quickly on the cheek, then she was in the taxi and away. With an effort Charles turned his mind back to railway closures and returned to Mr Kingsworthy's office.

The station-master was seated inside, his braided cap on the desk before him. He was studying an official-looking document, which he put aside, though Charles was able to read the heading: 'Notice to All Staff'.

'I hoped you'd gone,' said Mr Kingsworthy bluntly. Charles explained he had been meeting a passenger off the ten-thirty, and at his mention of the train the station-master brightened slightly.

'Got that away pretty sharp,' he said with much satisfaction. 'Saved best part of thirty seconds there. It should make up the rest before it reaches the coast.' Then he slumped again. 'Won't have to worry about that much longer.'

Charles seized upon the reference. 'That's what we were talking about,' he reminded him.

Mr Kingsworthy looked at him sternly. 'Whatever you want to know, I'm not allowed to tell you.' It was an unpromising start. 'This letter says staff must refrain from commenting to the press about the intended closure. There'll be an official statement in due course.'

'I quite appreciate that,' said Charles smoothly. This was now very promising indeed. He had confirmation that the line was going to be closed. 'I wouldn't expect you to comment at this stage. I just wanted to check the facts.'

Mr Kingsworthy was suspicious again. 'I thought you knew the facts already, Mr Benson.'

'Yes, of course. I've got the general picture. I just wanted to fill in the details.' He chanced his arm again. 'For instance, is there an actual date fixed for closing the Norwich line?'

'The Norwich line?' Mr Kingsworthy laughed bitterly. 'Don't you go printing that, young man, that's about the only line we're going to have left. It's the line from here to the coast they want to close. Didn't you know that?'

'Yes, I'm sorry, that's what I meant,' said Charles lamely. But he was getting what he wanted.

'You haven't seen the letter then, that sets it all out?'

'Not exactly. I expect there'll be a copy back in the office – I haven't had a chance to call in yet this morning,' he lied happily.

'Well, I don't know about that. They were only sending it to local councils, not the press.' Mr Kingsworthy's suspicions deepened sharply. 'And come to think of it, they'll only be getting the letters this morning. You seem to have heard about them remarkably quickly.'

He rose, an imposing and rather threatening figure, and put on his braided cap. 'I think you'd better go, Mr Benson.'

Charles did not argue.

As he got to the door the station-master called after him: 'Those letters are supposed to be confidential, you know.'

Charles paused only briefly. 'If I may quote Mr Juby,' he said, ' "there hent no secrets in these parts".'

He did not really expect it, but when Charles got back to the office there actually was one of the 'confidential' letters on his desk. It had been brought in to Mr Juby by his good friend Mr Nicholson of Tittlesham, one of the parishes which would be affected by the closure. Mr

Nicholson not only represented the village on Launford Council, he was also chairman of the parish council. When his parish clerk had shown him the letter his first move had been to call a parish meeting; his second was to give the letter to Mr Juby.

Meanwhile Mr Juby had been on to Head Office in Norwich, who had heard nothing official yet from British Railways. They had asked him to provide the full story for the following morning's paper.

As soon as Charles had returned and reported his revealing conversation with Ben Kingsworthy, Mr Juby marshalled his forces.

'I'll see George Flatt and find out what he's going to tell the Town Council to do, and I'll have a word with that fool of a Clerk round at Launford, though I doubt he even knows we got a railway. Mortimer will look after the Wettleford end and have a run up to the coast – there'll be jobs lost all along the line there, if this goes ahead. You go out and about in the villages, Charlie, find out what'll happen if the railway goes, how they'll get to market, how they'll visit their folks in hospital. Thass the hooman interest we want, boy. That should be just up your street, seeing how you fancied that tale from Len Hedges.'

It was to be Charles's busiest and most exhausting day since he arrived in Toftham. He visited all the villages that lay within cycling distance along the route of the railway. It would have been a lot more comfortable to go by train, but he could not tell how long he would need to stay in each village, and there was only one train an hour each way.

In some villages he was the first to break the news. Not every parish clerk or chairman acted as speedily as Mr Nicholson, and there were one or two – though not many – who actually paid attention to the 'Confidential' stamp on the letter.

Most people were dumbfounded. They had heard the rumours, but they expected just a reduction in services, with perhaps smaller diesel trains instead of steam. The

240

news that British Railways wanted to close their line completely produced some powerful and revealing reactions.

One elderly villager summed it up angrily, 'Thass a funny sort o' progress, hent it? Instead of making the railways wuk better, they throw in the sponge. This'll just be the fust to go. Give it a year or two, there won't be a train running in these parts at all. They're putting the clock back a hundred year, and there's narthin goin' to stop 'em, you mark my words, boy.'

And Charles did mark them. They would make a fine opening to his report.

It was quite late when he wearily climbed the stairs to his office, not a little saddle-sore but with his notebook full. Upstairs Mr Juby was working late, too, and from his frequent calls to Wettleford it was apparent that Mortimer was just as busy. It was very nearly closing time before they had phoned all their material through to Norwich, from the angry reaction of George Flatt, who promised that the Council would organise protest meetings and lobby MPs (he had taken it as a personal affront that British Railways had not consulted him first) to the sad tale of an old lady at Tittlesham who looked forward so much to her weekly outing on the train, in her wheelchair, to visit her house-bound sister in Toftham. Charles had found quite a number of stories like that.

Mr Juby decided to keep their reports separate; he dealt with all the official reaction and comment, Charles provided the 'hooman' touch. Charles even managed to work in a verse he had learnt at school about a country railway station. 'Yes, I remember Adlestrop . . . The willows, willow herb and grass, and meadowsweet and haycocks dry.' Mr Juby had been a little dubious – 'This hent a woman's weekly, boy' – but Norwich loved it. The editor-in-chief actually came on the line to congratulate them on their efforts. Such praise was rare; they hastened across to the Dog and Partridge to celebrate.

It was only after his second special that Mr Juby

realised, with some regret, that they had not sent the story to the nationals.

And it was only after *his* second pint that Charles realised he had entirely forgotten his promise to contact Rebecca that evening. It was the first time that his work had seriously interfered with his personal life.

But damn it, he thought, as he bade goodnight to Mr Juby, it had been worth it.

When Charles called at the Old Rectory next morning, Rebecca was out on Thunder and was not expected home for some time. He left a message with Mrs Bateman apologising for not calling the previous night and saying he would come round that evening. It turned out to be another vain promise; the rail closure story had only just begun.

Mr Juby, amazingly, was in the office ahead of him. Listening discreetly up the stairs, Charles discovered he was making good his omission of the previous night and was now phoning the London evenings. They did not pay as much as the national morning papers but they were always grateful for early stories.

He also found a note on his desk listing the emergency parish meetings that had been called in the next few days to discuss the closure proposals. He was apparently expected to cover them all. He would also have to be at a public protest meeting in Toftham on Thursday evening – George Flatt had arranged it himself and would get the Council to approve it, no doubt, after the meeting had been actually held. There was no word yet from Launford Rural District; if Lord Remingham happened to be away then nothing would be done until he returned.

Charles realised that with all these meetings, the updating of the original story, and the routine assignments that still had to be carried out, there would be very little time to see Rebecca. He had banked on Thursday evening, normally a quiet night before the *Journal*'s publication day, but the Toftham protest meeting ruled that out.

It would happen this week of all weeks, he thought bitterly, but when he opened the Norwich morning paper he felt a lot better. His 'hooman stories' were featured in full on the main news page; they carried the by-line 'By Our Special Reporter Charles Benson'. It was the first time his name had appeared on a story and he had certainly never been called a Special Reporter. Let's hope Rebecca sees it was his first thought. And let's hope that bastard Harry Burton sees it too was his second.

Almost cheerfully he telephoned the Batemans and said he would not be coming round that evening after all, nor indeed for the rest of the week. 'I shouldn't worry too much, Rebecca seems quite occupied,' Mrs Bateman told him, sounding a little offhand, though she may not have meant to. 'She's going to the Toftham Carnival on Saturday. Aren't you something to do with that? She'll probably see you then.'

He had quite forgotten the Carnival. That was another job he had to do, his regular plug for the Carnival and in particular the Human Fireball. After his conversation with the agent he had managed to build up quite a mystery about this sensational but secretive act he had booked. He made great play of the line that royal blood might flow in the Human Fireball's veins, quoting the agent as saying that he could not confirm or deny it. Nellie in particular was quite excited by the vision he created of a daring princeling who divided his time between attending state banquets and setting fire to himself on top of a sixty-foot tower. He had promised to introduce her after his act – if the Fireball met Nellie at close quarters beforehand, he thought, it might spoil his concentration.

While Mr Juby was still dictating away on the phone he typed another and final piece about Toftham Carnival and its star attraction.

'The precise identity of the Human Fireball is still

243

being kept a strict secret, even from the organisers of the Carnival,' he wrote. It seemed unnecessary to add that the organisers did not give a damn who he was, so long as he did his act without killing himself.

'Enquiries at the Palace have failed to reveal any clue to his background.' If anybody queried that, they could check with the Palace themselves; they were pretty certain to get the same answer.

Mr Juby interrupted him before he could add any more imaginative touches. 'They're having a union meeting up at the station. Away you go, boy.' And he was once again immersed in the rail closure story. For the rest of the week he had time to think of little else.

'That don't look bad at all, Charlie. I reckon we all done rather well.'

They were sitting in Mr Juby's office on Friday morning. Mortimer had come over from Wettleford, partly to share in the glory and partly to have a look at Charles's hoped-for purchase, the good runner, only one owner, needing a little attention. In front of them was a copy of the *Journal*, its front page featuring photographs of gloomy railwaymen, angry villagers, and crowded protest meetings. The centre-piece was a map of the Wettleford line, with a sword hanging over it. The art department in Norwich had got quite carried away.

The inside pages were full of Charles's hooman stories, much expanded from the original versions used in the Norwich paper, and bearing the same gratifying byline. It was the most dramatic issue of the *Toftham and Wettleford Journal* since Toftham United had won the Norfolk and Suffolk Football League.

'Thass all a waste of time, o'course,' observed Mr Juby, indicating the reports and pictures of the protest meetings. 'British Railways'll go through all the proper procedures and invite objections and consult committees and all that squit, then they'll close it anyway. There's no changing their mind now.'

He wagged his pipe at Charles and Mortimer. 'If all

these folk what are jumping up and down and passing resolutions about how terrible it is to lose the railway, if all of them actually travelled on it, then they'd never've larst it, would they?'

He leaned back in his chair. 'That old feller you quoted, Charlie, he's got it to rights. There'll be more lines closed, and the buses won't take over if they can't make it pay. People in the villages will have to get themselves a car or move into the town, unless they want to live like harmits. There hent the work in the villages to keep 'em anyway. There's big changes a-comin', and not for the better.'

Then Mr Juby looked again at the paper in front of him and his good humour returned. 'Never mind, thass a good story. And we done it well.'

After more mutual congratulations Charles went down to his office to phone the number in the motorcycle advertisement. It seemed faintly familiar, but the owner's actual identity was as much a mystery as that of the Human Fireball. The mystery was soon solved.

'Frederick Knock and Sons, can we be of service?' He remembered where he had seen the number before – on the card that Fred Knock had given him at the council meeting.

'Do you have a motorbike for sale, Mr Knock?'

'That I do,' said Mr Knock. 'Good runner, that is. Only one owner.'

Charles completed the description. 'But needs a little attention.'

'Well, just a little,' agreed Mr Knock, 'but once you get it a-goin', that'll go really well.'

'You mean it's not actually in running order? You didn't say that in the advertisement.'

'I said it was a good runner,' Mr Knock protested. 'I didn't actually say it was running. Thass fair enough, hent it?'

Charles was tempted to forget about it there and then, but Mortimer had come over specially at his request.

They might as well have a look at it. He arranged for them to call straight away.

'Is that young Charlie at the *Journal*, by the way?' asked Mr Knock before they rang off. 'I hent got no news for those Gibsons you were worried about. Thass a real long shot, that is.'

Charles realised guiltily that he had quite put the Gibsons and their housing problem out of his mind. Another winter in their overcrowded old cottage would be a far greater hardship for them than any rail closure. He urged Mr Knock to keep trying.

Mr Knock's business headquarters were some way outside Toftham, an isolated group of buildings where he kept his lorries. They were isolated for a very good reason; one night-soil lorry could be off-putting at close quarters, but a number of them parked in an enclosed space were quite overwhelming. Mr Knock need not have given any directions; they just had to follow their noses.

When they arrived on Mortimer's motorbike he was waiting for them outside the barns, dressed as always in his black suit and wing-collar with the gleaming pin in his tie. Mortimer might have seemed an incongruous figure on a motorcycle in his old blue suit and flying helmet, but the image of Mr Knock straddling a 250cc Triumph seemed even stranger.

Mr Knock may have guessed what he was thinking. 'Hant done any riding lately, of course, but I always used the bike before the business built up.'

'How long ago was that?' asked Charles. It had just occurred to him that the advertisement made no mention of the bike's age.

'Thass before the war, o'course,' said Mr Knock. 'Bought it new in tharty-seven; never had a moment's trouble. I should've sold it afore, I suppose, but I just couldn't bear to part with it. I need the space for another lorry, or I wouldn't be letting it go.'

Charles and Mortimer exchanged glances. Mr Knock's line in sales patter seemed all too obvious. It was an appropriate moment to leave. But Mr Knock was ushering them firmly into one of the barns and there was no immediate escape.

The atmosphere inside the barn nearly bowled them over. Three of Mr Knock's night-soil lorries were inside it, and it was apparent that they had just returned from a fruitful collection around the privies of Launford Rural District. Charles tried to hold his breath as long as possible; Mr Knock seemed quite undisturbed.

Alongside the parked lorries was something covered in a tarpaulin, which from its stained appearance was also used to cover the lorries. Fred Knock removed it with a flourish, and his two visitors stared at what stood beneath. They had fully expected a rust-covered, dilapidated wreck. Instead they saw a very handsome motorbike, its chromium handlebars and petrol tank gleaming, the paintwork immaculate, the engine without a trace of dirt or oil. Charles heard Mortimer gulp; he felt like doing so himself.

'Thass it,' said Mr Knock with great pride. 'Haven't ridden it for years, but I keep it good and smart. That gave me a lot of good service in the early days, thass the least I can do for it.'

Charles felt he must not sound too impressed. 'What work needs to be done on it?' he asked.

'Well, that hent got any petrol in it for a start. Drained it out years ago, just in case of accidents. And I dussay you'll need a new sparking plug and this and that. Narthin much, I'd say.'

'This and that,' thought Charles, could cover almost anything. He looked at Mortimer, who was still gazing admiringly at the machine. 'What do you think, Mort?'

'I wonder if perhaps we could look at it outside?' asked Mortimer very sensibly. He too had been trying to hold back his breath. Mr Knock wheeled it out of the barn and they followed him gratefully into the open air.

The bike looked even more impressive in the sunshine. Mortimer got on his knees and inspected it closely from all angles, while Charles tried to resist picturing himself on this gleaming monster, sailing majestically through the Norfolk countryside.

Mortimer got to his feet and beckoned him to one side, while Mr Knock ostentatiously refrained from listening.

'Now of course I can't see inside the engine, but the bike itself is in excellent condition. He really has looked after it beautifully. To make absolutely certain I'd need to take the engine down, but that takes quite a time and I haven't got the tools with me. But I must say, unless there is anything drastically wrong, it's a real bargain at £35. I've seen bikes like this at twice what he's asking.'

'That's good enough for me,' said Charles, who had made up his mind anyway. 'I'll buy it.'

'Hold hard,' said Mortimer. 'Don't you give him what he asks. You must do a little dealing with him, get the price down a bit.'

'Even if it's a bargain already?' asked Charles.

'Of course,' said Mortimer, with some surprise.

'Perhaps you'd do it for me, Mort,' pleaded Charles. 'You're a Norfolkman, you know about this sort of thing.'

So Mortimer did. To Charles's embarrassment he offered Mr Knock twenty pounds. Mr Knock, registering hurt surprise, would not go below thirty-two. Mortimer, with a great show of reluctance, went up to twenty-five. Mr Knock, expressing amazement at his own generosity, went down to thirty. Mortimer insisted that twenty-five was his final offer, Mr Knock vowed he could not drop below thirty. They settled at twenty-eight.

Mr Knock shook hands with Charles. He nodded towards Mortimer. 'He's a real dickey dealer, that Mortimer,' he said admiringly. 'Wouldn't like to do too much business with him.'

'Nor would I,' said Charles, much impressed.

Mortimer offered to return as soon as he could with his tool-kit and get the machine going, but Fred Knock said he would deliver it to Remingham in the next few days. He saw Charles's apprehensive expression and explained that he would use a pick-up truck, not one of his lorries.

Charles wrote a cheque and Mr Knock gave him the registration book. 'Of course that hent taxed or insured,' he said as he took the cheque.

'Of course not,' said Mortimer, but Charles had not thought of that. His expenditure as a motorcycle owner was just beginning.

In the farmers' bar of the Dog and Partridge they found Mr Juby having his usual lunchtime special. He was talking to a middle-aged stranger in a London suit.

'This is Jeffrey Palmer of the *Sunday Herald*,' he explained. 'Come up to do a feature on the railway closure.' And he introduced Charles and Mortimer.

Charles was taken aback. He had visualised all Sunday newspaper reporters as dashing, handsome young men in flapping raincoats, with a press pass on their lapel and a bus ticket in their hatband; Jeffrey Palmer looked more like a bank manager. But this was no ordinary reporter, this was the Jeffrey Palmer whose column had appeared in the *Herald* for as long as he could remember, one of the doyens of the Sunday press. He greeted him with respect.

'I read your column every Sunday, Mr Palmer,' he said, not entirely accurately.

'I've read yours too,' said Jeffrey Palmer. He had a copy of the Norwich paper with his byline in it, and that morning's copy of the *Journal*.

'Mr Palmer wanted a word with you,' said Mr Juby. 'He'd like to talk to some of the folk you found in the villages – specially that old leddy in the wheelchair.'

'There are some well-written stories here,' said Palmer. 'That little verse is a bit over the top, but most of it is good stuff. It's just the sort of style for the *Herald*. I'll show it to the editor when I get back.'

Charles blushed, and Mr Juby chuckled. 'Hooman interest, thass what it is. It's Charlie's speciality.' They all laughed, Charles included, but he felt a little excited nonetheless. As he drank his bitter he pictured himself again on his gleaming new bike, but he was not flying through the Norfolk countryside this time, he was dashing to the scene of some great international disaster, to cover it exclusively for the *Sunday Herald* . . .

He gave Palmer the details of his interviewees and where to find them, and was promised that a suitable cheque would be forthcoming for the information. He hoped it might cover the tax on his new bike.

'Make it out to Our Special Reporter,' interjected Mr Juby, who was on his fourth special and enjoying his lunch enormously. Charles smiled dutifully.

'And I meant what I said about those articles of yours,' said Jeffrey Palmer as Charles and Mortimer made their farewells, Mortimer to return to Wettleford, Charles to sit in his office and gaze dreamily into space.

He was still gazing when he heard slow and heavy footsteps on the stairs. He assumed it was Mr Juby, but these steps were much slower and heavier, even allowing for the four specials, and there was much grunting and muttering and heavy breathing.

'Bleedin' steps, they'll kill me,' he heard a husky voice gasp. He waited, fascinated.

In the doorwway appeared a scraggy little man in a dirty sweater and shapeless trousers. The perspiration gleamed on his bald head, and he was having great problems getting his breath. His wrinkled face was very red from his exertions, except for his nose, which was purple. He looked as if he had just climbed, with some difficulty, out of a dustbin.

'Good afternoon,' said Charles. His visitor took a few moments to get enough breath to reply. 'It's them bleedin' steps,' he managed to explain.

'Of course,' Charles tried to sound sympathetic. He hoped the poor chap had not come to visit Mr Juby – the next flight of stairs *would* probably kill him. But it was not Mr Juby he was seeking.

'Are you Mr Benson?' he gasped out.

'Yes I am,' said Charles, surprised he should know his name.

'Pleased to meetcher,' said his visitor as he collapsed into a chair. 'I'm yer Human Fireball . . .'

Sixteen

'He'll never make it,' said Charles gloomily.

He and Freddie Pendleton were on the football field watching the Human Fireball unloading scaffolding from the ancient lorry in which he had spent the night. The story of his dramatic arrival in the office the previous day had been kept as quiet as possible to preserve the mystique which Charles had created with his reports in the *Journal*, but one glimpse of this seedy figure would doubtless dispel any theories about royal blood, so they were keeping the public well away from his corner of the field until the last possible moment.

The only other person present was Station Officer Ketch of the Toftham Fire Brigade. He was observing with astonishment not the Fireball but the tank he had just assembled.

'He bent goin' to dive into that?' asked Mr Ketch. 'He'll break his neck, thass for sure.'

It was certainly quite a shallow tank and Charles shared his scepticism. But Freddie Pendleton was delighted with this reaction.

'It's a marvel, isn't it, Mr Ketch? He'll be risking his life, jumping into that. Do make sure you tell as many people as possible.'

Mr Ketch looked at him suspiciously. 'This hent one o' your practical jokes, is it?'

Freddie regarded him with great solemnity. 'This is no joke, Mr Ketch. This the genuine death-defying Human Fireball, as seen by many of the crowned heads of Europe.'

'I thought he was supposed to be some sort of crowned head himself.' Mr Ketch studied the wizened little fellow again. 'The only crown he ever wore was a pairper one, I'd say.'

Charles felt he had better try to keep the story going. 'You can't go by appearances, you know. I wouldn't rule anything out, Mr Ketch. Now isn't it time to start filling the tank?'

Mr Ketch went off to fetch the pumping equipment from the fire station, and Charles and Freddie watched the Human Fireball erect his tower. They had offered to help, but he assured them he had done it many times. 'I may be no bleedin' good with stairs, but I nip up a ladder orl right. Yer pull up with yer arms, that's the trick.' And indeed he was shinning about on his scaffolding with remarkable agility. Charles began to feel a little better; perhaps he would not have to pay the fifty pounds out of his own pocket after all.

Elsewhere on the football ground, at a respectful distance from the Human Fireball, stalls were being erected and side-shows assembled in the familiar pattern of pre-carnival chaos. To his relief Charles was not involved in that side of the proceedings. Each stall and side-show was run by a different organization in the town, and there was always much debate about location, space, and facilities.

The Golden Fleece Darts Club, for instance, which ran a simple competition for the highest score with three darts, required on the face of it just enough room for a dartboard. They also however demanded storage space for several crates of beer which they insisted were essential to the smooth running of the competition. This meant that the Salvation Army, which had the adjoining pitch for its guess-the-weight-of-the-cake stall, requested to be moved to a less alcoholic location. There was some difficulty in finding anyone prepared to swap, since the Fleece Darts Club was known to become quite boisterous as the afternoon progressed. Finally the Rugby Club agreed to set up their hoopla stall next to them on condition they had a share of the beer.

Toftham Conservative Association caused a problem by demanding twice as much space as Toftham Labour Party, on the grounds that they had twice as many members. The Labour Party argued that this was only because the Conservative Club had one of the few snooker tables in the town, while the Labour Club could only offer table tennis. It all required the judgement of a Solomon or, failing him, Freddie Pendleton, and Charles was very glad he only had the Human Fireball to contend with.

The Fireball was rapidly completing his tower, a flimsy-looking structure made of scaffold poles with some boards laid loosely across the top to form a platform. While Freddie went off to placate the Toftham Horticultural Association who were demanding more space for their seed-boxes, Charles wandered over to the tower to inspect it more closely. He gingerly pushed at one of the uprights, and the whole structure swayed alarmingly.

'Don't do that, mate!' shouted the Human Fireball from one of the upper struts. 'That's bleedin' dangerous.'

The whole operation looks bleedin' dangerous, thought Charles, as he surveyed the lofty tower and the shallow tank beneath it.

'Are you going to jump too?' The familiar voice behind him made his heart give a little jump – and not just at the thought of emulating the Fireball.

'Not unless you leave me for ever and I decide to end it all,' he said jocularly.

'You shouldn't joke about it,' said Rebecca. It was not clear whether she meant her leaving, or him jumping. But he was too pleased to see her to ask.

'I didn't expect you to be here until this afternoon.'

'I knew you'd be busy once things started,' she explained. 'I thought you might have a bit of time to spare before lunch.'

Charles looked up at the little figure still working away overhead.

'I'm supposed to be looking after the Human Fireball. But he seems to be managing very well on his own.'

Rebecca looked up too. 'So that's the Human Fireball. He looks more like a slice of burnt toast.'

'Don't mock,' said Charles. 'Just climbing up this

thing takes a fair amount of nerve.' And he pushed it again to prove his point.

'*Don't bleedin' do that!*' came a furious shout from above. The Fireball was clinging to one of the poles as the tower swayed again. 'You do that once more and I'll pack it in, mate.'

Charles shouted an apology. 'Let's hope the wind doesn't get up,' he muttered to Rebecca, then addressed himself again to the angry little figure over his head. 'Do you mind if I leave you for a bit – you'll probably get on better without me.'

'Too bleedin' right mate,' shouted the Fireball with feeling. 'You take yer bird off somewhere else, before you 'ave the whole lot down.' Charles happily complied.

As they strolled around the ground, watching the stallholders gradually sorting themselves out, he told Rebecca about his new motorbike and how it had emerged in all its gleaming beauty from its unsavoury setting in Fred Knock's barn. 'Mortimer should get it going next week, then I've found a splendid place for a picnic, up on the common overlooking Branham Staithe. I don't think I'm supposed to take passengers until I've passed my test, but I doubt if anyone will worry too much around here.'

Rebecca did not seem to share his enthusiasm. 'That's really what I wanted to talk about,' she said.

'About my driving test?' asked Charles, puzzled.

'No, no. About the picnic, and – all that sort of thing.'

Charles was even more baffled. 'All what sort of thing?'

'Isn't there somewhere else we can talk?' asked Rebecca. They had come to a halt in the middle of the ground, two rather conspicuous figures in the empty area which was being kept clear for the Morris dancing and other delights. Curious glances were coming their way from the stalls all around.

'I'm afraid there aren't many quiet corners in Toftham on a Saturday morning,' said Charles, still with no idea of what she was talking about. 'There's my office, I suppose?'

'I don't think so,' said Rebecca.

'Or there's the churchyard. Freddie's up to his neck with the carnival, so there can't be any funerals today. We could take a turn around the tombstones, if you won't find that too depressing.'

She nodded rather sombrely. 'I should think that's as good a place as any.'

With increasing foreboding Charles led her out of the football ground. They stood aside for Station Officer Ketch to drive in the fire engine, and Mr Ketch rang his bell in greeting but they did not respond. They were both silent as they walked the short distance to the parish church, the scene of Charles's first funeral.

'Go ahead,' he said as he sat on one of the tombs in the deserted churchyard. She sat down beside him.

'I gather from Mummy and Daddy you've been asking about me rather a lot,' she said hesitantly. 'And that letter you wrote. You seemed to have jumped to rather a lot of conclusions. I'm not very good at writing letters, but I thought I ought to clear things up as soon as I got back.'

'Oh yes?' said Charles. It seemed all there was to say.

'You see, there's this friend of mine at college, the one I've been staying with since the term ended . . .'

'A male friend?'

'Of course,' said Rebecca. 'That's the point.'

'Oh dear,' said Charles.

She went on rapidly. 'There was nothing much in it before, but we really had a marvellous time up at his place. I'm going back there in a few days. I thought you ought to know the situation before you suggested any more picnics or – that sort of thing.'

Charles tried to joke about it. 'You mean,' he said portentously, 'this is the end. We must never meet again.'

'Of course not,' said Rebecca a little impatiently.

'We're sure to meet again. We can hardly help it. I just wanted you to know what was happening.'

'But you haven't explained precisely what is happening,' he complained. 'Are you engaged, or what?'

'No we're not.' Rebecca blushed. Charles thought how attractive she looked when she blushed. 'He did ask me, but I said it was much too early to decide, we needed to get to know each other a lot more. So he said he'd wait until Christmas, then ask again.'

'And meanwhile,' said Charles, trying not to sound too sour, 'I suppose as far as I'm concerned it's hands off.'

'That's putting it a little bluntly,' she said, 'but yes, I think that's what I mean.'

'And if you decide by Christmas that he's an absolute stinker, then could it be hands on again?'

'That's really rather dificult to say, when you put it that way,' she said, a little primly. Then she smiled. 'But I did enjoy that picnic. Let's wait and see.'

Charles did not relish this picture of himself sitting on the substitute's bench, waiting for Christmas. He decided to hit back.

'Well, I may not be here by then,' he announced. 'Things have been happening here too while you've been away.'

Rebecca looked suitably surprised. 'Where are you going?'

'The *Sunday Herald* is very impressed with some of the stuff I've written. They may well be getting in touch.' She looked slightly sceptical. 'Their top columnist was down here, Jeffrey Palmer. He saw some articles I'd written and came down specially to see me.' It was very nearly true.

'But would you really want to work on the *Sunday Herald*?' she asked. 'It doesn't seem to be your kind of paper – some of the pictures really go a bit far.'

'It's got an enormous circulation,' he said defensively. 'And Jeffrey Palmer's one of the best writers in Fleet Street.'

'So if they offered you a job, would you take it?'

He scored a quick point. 'Let's wait and see.' Actually he was sure the situation would never arise, but he hoped he had impressed her.

'Things have certainly been happening,' said Rebecca. 'I'm glad we both know where we stand.'

'And we'll know even better by Christmas.' He got up from the tombstone and brushed the lichen off his trousers. 'I'd better get back and see how the Human Fireball's getting on.'

But as they walked together to the churchyard gate he felt so miserable, he did not care if the Human Fireball had broken his bleedin' neck.

'LADIES AND GENTLEMEN!'

Freddie Pendleton's voice blasted out over the tannoys, and the crowds around the stalls and side-shows fell silent.

'Now for the high-spot – and I mean the *high* spot – of this afternoon's programme.' The crowd tittered appreciatively. 'You have read about him, you have heard about him, now you can marvel at him. From the summit of that sixty-foot tower he will make a death-defying leap, on fire, into that blazing tank. For an encore he will dive from the same tower into a wet flannel.' The crowd tittered again. A real card, was Freddie.

'A great welcome please for the amazing mystery man with the nerves of steel and the body done medium-to-rare: THE HUMAN FIREBALL!'

Charles and Rebecca, both trying to look more cheerful than they felt, applauded with the rest of the crowd as the tarpaulin on the back of the lorry-cum-dressing-room was pushed aside, and the Human Fireball emerged.

'Good lord,' murmured Charles. 'How has he done it?'

'Is it a bird, is it a plane?' Rebecca murmured back.

Somehow the seedy little man in the dirty sweater and the baggy trousers had transformed himself into a minature Superman. With the use of some judicious padding his chest now swelled impressively under his tight-fitting costume. Even the arms bulged where no muscles had been discernible before. His bald head was concealed under a multi-coloured version of Mortimer's flying helmet strapped tightly under his chin. Only the legs, in black tights, retained their natural proportions; they looked distinctly spindly under such a magnificent body.

The Human Fireball walked a little painfully from the lorry to the tower; had he not looked such a picture of fitness one might have thought his rheumatism was playing him up. But once on the ladder he became a different character, swinging himself up briskly from rung to rung. Tom Twite and the Toftham Troubadors, who always provided the music at the Toftham Carnival, rose to the occasion, and played the most rousing piece in their repertoire, the Gay Gordons.

As he reached the platform at the top of the tower the Fireball gave a majestic wave to the crowd below. The crowd below waved back. Then the Gay Gordons ended and silence fell over the football ground as he picked up a can from the platform beside him and poured petrol on to his sleeves and chest.

'Let's hope he hasn't forgotten the matches,' muttered Charles, trying to sound nonchalant, although he was as tense as everyone else. This chap's earned his money so far, he thought. But now comes the tricky bit.

The Fireball completed his ablutions with the petrol can and waved a hand towards the tank below. Station Officer Ketch, standing beside it, lit a rag and tossed it in. The petrol on top of the water burst into flames. There was a murmur from the crowd.

The Fireball stood, poised, on his platform. The timing, thought Charles, must be crucial. The petrol on the water must be burning as he plunged in, to give the full effect, but be out by the time he surfaced.

On the Toftham Troubadours' dais Mr Twite personally took over the drumsticks and began a dramatic roll.

'He'll have to jump soon,' murmured Rebecca, trying to match Charles's nonchalance. 'Tom can only keep that going for a few seconds.'

And jump he did. But just before, using some sort of lighter invisible to the crowd below, the Human Fireball became just that. Flames appeared on his chest and arms and even on his helmet. He stood there ablaze for just a second, then leaped into space. There was a great 'Ooooh' from the crowd as he hurtled down into the tank.

The timing, Charles now realized, was not so important after all. As the water splashed up, the flames went out. But even without the flames it was still a very shallow tank. There was not a sound anywhere on the field after the Fireball entered the water. Tom Twite stood over his drums, the sticks held expectantly aloft over the big cymbal.

Then a helmeted head appeared out of the water, two arms were waved, and a great cheer broke out. Mr Twite thumped frenziedly on the cymbal and the Troubadours joined in with whatever instrument came to hand, as the Human Fireball, now safely doused, made his way to the edge of the tank and hauled himself out.

Charles dashed over to congratulate him. Station Officer Ketch had given the Fireball a blanket by the time he reached him, and he was huddled inside it, the sodden costume clinging to his skinny frame, the helmet now removed so that his bald pate was revealed.

'That was marvellous!' cried Charles, and grasped him by the hand.

'In that case,' said the Human Fireball, 'how about a bleedin' whisky?'

Everyone agreed it was the most successful Carnival in living memory. The crowd which watched the Fireball's first jump had nearly doubled by the time he made his second, as word got around the town among the shoppers and the loafers and the late lunch-time drinkers. The second jump proved just as successful, with the added bonus that Station Officer Ketch, standing too close to the tank, got thoroughly soaked as the Fireball hit the water.

Freddie Pendleton persuaded the star of the day to appear on the platform before he left, though he looked rather less impressive once he had shed his wet costume and was back in his sweater and baggy trousers. Freddie insisted on Charles taking a bow also – 'Our Toftham Impressario' he called him, 'the man who made it all happen' – and he too got a tremendous cheer.

'While we have them both on the platform,' cried Freddie, 'perhaps we can ask them now to reveal the secret they've kept so well over the past few weeks. You will have read in the *Journal* about the mystery surrounding our guest. Now it can be told: is there really royal blood in his veins?'

'Royal blood?' muttered the Fireball to Charles. 'What the 'ell is 'e talking abaht?'

'No idea,' said Charles.

'So now I'll ask the Human Fireball,' went on Freddie. 'Tell us, sir, your real identity.' And he handed him the microphone.

The Fireball took it dubiously and looked around at the expectant crowd. Then he shrugged.

'I dunno what all the mystery's abaht,' he announced, 'but I tell yer what, yer can't make a livin' just jumpin' off that bleedin' tower. I'll be back on the dust-cart on Monday.'

And to the cheers of the crowd he shook hands with Freddie and Charles and headed for his lorry. A lot of people followed him to grasp his hand and slap his diminuitive back, while others surrounded Freddie and Charles to congratulate them too. Charles spotted Rebecca on the edge of the crowd, and he remembered the scene in the winner's enclosure at the point-to-point. This time, he thought with some satisfaction, the situation is reversed. As she turned and walked away, he did not attempt to follow her.

'See you at Christmas,' he muttered to himself, then turned to shake another hand.

It was Nellie's.

'That was ever so exciting, Charlie.' Her eyes were gleaming, just as they gleamed in the cinema after Victor Mature's lengthy clinch, and her magnificent chest was heaving. 'Fancy you finding someone like that. Never thought you had it in you.'

Charles held on to her hand. Fate, he thought, must have engineered this encounter with Nellie. He decided not to thwart it.

'Are you doing anything tonight, Nellie?' he asked expectantly.

But Fate had got things wrong. 'Course I am,' said Nellie. 'Always go out on Saturdays. What's it matter to you, then?'

'Never mind,' said Charles. He almost felt relieved. 'It doesn't matter at all.'

'I nearly forgot what I came for,' said Nellie. 'There's a letter came to the office for you this morning. It was marked urgent, so I brought it along for you.'

She handed him the envelope and before he had time to thank her she had disappeared into the crowd. He remembered his promise to introduce her to the Fireball, and he was going to follow her when he glanced at the envelope she had given him. It was addressed to Charles Benson, Special Reporter, and it bore the elaborate logo of the *Sunday Herald*.

As the crowd still milled around him he opened it and read the letter. It was from the Editor's secretary. The Editor wanted him to know that he had been much impressed by the material Jeffrey Palmer had shown him. He thanked him for the assistance he had given Mr Palmer and a cheque was enclosed herewith. Charles looked at the cheque and discovered it would not merely pay the tax on the motorbike, it would probably cover the insurance as well.

But it was the final paragraph that he lingered over most.

'The Editor also asks me to say that he would be happy to meet you when you are next in London. Please telephone me to make an appointment.'

There were great celebrations at the Dog and Partridge that evening as the Round Tablers basked in the success of their Carnival and in particular of the Human Fireball. Nobody celebrated more enthusiastically than Charles; but it was not the Carnival, nor the Human Fireball, he had in mind.

'Do you think I might have a few days off? I seem to have missed a summer holiday this year.'

Mr Juby shrugged. 'I suppose you've been here long enough to qualify. I'll see what Narridge says. Where do you plan to go?'

'I thought I'd go down and see my parents,' said Charles. That was only partially true; it was an easy journey by Underground from Wembley Park to Fleet Street.

'I'll need you back in time to report the Drama Society's play. I seen them so often I hent got anything left to say about them. That'll be good experience for you.'

Charles was rather gratified. He had heard that the Drama Society's annual production was quite a major event in Toftham's social calendar.

'I thought that wasn't until the end of November,' he said. 'I shan't be away that long.'

'But it may take that long for Narridge to let you go.'

Norwich however responded fairly quickly. He could take a week, whenever was convenient for Mr Juby. Charles sent off a letter to his parents and another to the editor of the *Sunday Herald*.

He stayed on in Toftham quite late that evening, as he intended doing every evening until Rebecca had gone back to the north. He decided there was no point in any further meetings until she had sorted herself out. He hoped he could put her out of his mind until Christmas;

certainly there were other matters to occupy him at the moment.

One of them became evident when he eventually cycled into Remingham. On the outskirts of the village he detected a familiar smell. As he neared Lambeth Palace the smell grew stronger; and as he went in the gate it became quite overpowering. In the front garden was a bulky object covered by a very stained tarpaulin. Mr Knock had delivered his motorbike.

John Cranmer was in his study. As Charles entered he ostentatiously held a handkerchief to his face. 'If you're going to do some sub-contracting for Mr Knock', he observed, 'perhaps you could store your equipment somewhere else. In Suffolk, for instance . . .'

Next morning Charles managed to dispose of the tarpaulin on the village refuse tip, but the smell lingered on. The motorbike itself seemed impregnated with it after many years of sharing the barn with Mr Knock's lorries. He and John Cranmer got weary of explaining to passing villagers that there really was nothing wrong with the drains.

During the days before Mortimer could get over from Wettleford to take down the engine Charles obtained his provisional licence and L-plates, sorted out the tax and insurance and optimistically applied for his test. Each of these operations involved further outlay, which not even the *Sunday Herald*'s cheque could completely cover. And the motorbike was not even on the road yet. Perhaps, he thought, he should have stayed loyal to Geo. Perkins after all.

He thought so even more when Mortimer carried out his inspection of the engine and told him what needed to be done. 'I can understand why there was no oil on the outside of the engine,' he explained gently. 'There's none inside it either. Mr Knock must have drained that along with the petrol. It wasn't really a terribly good idea. I don't know whether he tried to run it after he drained it, but there's quite a mess in there.'

He pointed out the various problems, but Charles's

mechanical knowledge was negligible. All he understood was that more expenditure was on the way.

'It shouldn't be too bad,' said Mortimer. 'I can get the parts second-hand in Wettleford. By the time we've finished it'll add up to just about a fair price for the bike. I thought Mr Knock came down a little too easily.'

Remembering the bargaining, Charles did not think he had come down easily at all, but he did not argue. He did argue, however, over Mortimer doing all the work for nothing. Mortimer said he felt responsible because he had advised him to buy the bike. Charles said he knew he had been taking a chance and was prepared to pay for his mistake. Mortimer said motor-bikes were his hobby and he would enjoy doing it. Charles still protested, and Mortimer used the ultimate argument, 'Of course, if you don't think I can manage to do it . . .' Charles gave up, but vowed he would pay Mortimer back somehow; and he also promised himself a strong word with Mr Fred Knock.

Mortimer had still not been able to complete the repairs to the bike when Charles went off to London for his week's holiday. He took the train to Norwich – he had not been able to use it when he first arrived in Toftham, because there was no service on Sundays – and realized why Mr Juby sent the envelopes on the bus. The line took a most convoluted route, stopping at numerous little stations and halts, most of which seemed deserted. It won't be long, he thought, before this section follows the Wettleford line into oblivion. But the train did keep to time, which would have gratified Toftham's punctilious stationmaster, and he comfortably caught the London connection.

It was the first time he had been home since he joined the *Journal*, but as he walked along the streets of semi-detached houses in Wembley Park he felt no particular nostalgia. He recognized none of the people who bustled past him – but he would have recognized very few of them when he lived there. The residents of Wembley Park had little interest in their neighbours; as he neared his home not a single curtain twitched. He could not imagine that happening in Toftham.

His parents were obviously still dubious about his job. He had written every few weeks, but it had been difficult to make the work sound exciting. Even the rail closure story, which had caused such a stir in Norfolk, seemed very remote and unimportant in Metroland.

'So when are you coming back?' asked his father. He was on the brink of telling them about the appointment at the *Sunday Herald*, but thought better of it. By the time that reached his mother's bridge club it would have developed into a personal invitation from the editor to take over the paper.

'I shan't be leaving Toftham for a while, that's for sure,' he told them.

'Well, don't leave it too long,' said his mother. 'You're even beginning to speak like them.' He realized that he had actually said, 'Thass for sure'.

'I don't think that's really very terrible,' he answered rather sharply. 'Don't worry about me going native. They've given up eating missionaries in Norfolk.'

'There's no need to be rude,' said Mrs Benson. 'I am sure there are some very nice people in Norfolk.' And as a special gesture she added: 'I expect some of them even play bridge.'

Charles was glad he would only be home for a week.

Next day, on the pretext of visiting the paper's London office, he took the train into town to keep his appointment at the *Sunday Herald*. It occupied a big building betwen Fleet Street and the Embankment, and although he was determined not to be overawed he could not help feeling a little excited as he watched the massive rolls of newsprint being unloaded from lorries and swung alongside the presses which filled the ground floor.

At the front desk they sent him upstairs to the newsroom. People were rushing about and shouting into telephones and drinking mugs of tea, just the way he had imagined. As the editor's secretary led him through all the bustle and noise he tried to imagine how he would feel as a part of it all, at the hub of a mighty national newspaper. And he thought of his own dusty little office on the first floor of the *Toftham and Wettleford Journal*. The gap between the two seemed enormous.

But he was led into a room which seemed just like his office. It had a desk covered with papers, shelves full of files, a couple of uncomfortable chairs, and a fair layer of dust. Was this the domain of the editor of the *Sunday Herald*?

However it was Jeffrey Palmer who greeted him from behind the desk, and ushered him to a chair. 'I'm afraid he got called away to a meeting,' he explained. 'It happens all the time in this place. But he asked me to put you in the picture.'

Charles was not too disappointed. Indeed he felt rather relieved. It had been a formidable prospect to meet the great man himself; he felt a lot more at ease with Jeffrey Palmer.

The secretary brought in coffee in a couple of large stained mugs, and Palmer got to the point straight away.

'The situation's this. As the editor said in his letter he likes your writing style. I think he also liked what I told him about you. And he thinks you're the sort of chap we could use. But I have to tell you that, first, there are no vacancies at the moment, and second, it would mean starting at very nearly the bottom. You'd be a researcher, a sort of reporter's assistant, to do the digging and the chasing about. It's not very glamorous and it's damned hard work, but it's the way most of us started, and you'd be able to write the odd story on your own after a bit. Then it would be up to you. What do you think?'

Charles was not sure what he thought. Some of it sounded good, some not so good. All of it sounded very different from life on the *Journal*.

'What would the pay be?' he asked, to gain time, and when Palmer told him his jaw dropped. The starting figure was about three times what he was getting in Norfolk and expenses, it seemed, were almost unlimited.

Palmer confided that a lot of reporters managed to live on their expenses and bank their salaries. 'It's not a bad little number,' he admitted. 'We do nearly as well as the printers. Now let's have a drink.'

He took him to El Vino's wine bar in Fleet Street and pointed out various journalists whose by-lines were very familiar. Charles was duly impressed; but he would still have preferred a beer.

'No need to make any decisions today,' said Palmer as they parted. 'But if you're interested, drop a line to the editor and he'll put you on the list. You shouldn't have to wait too long; there's quite a fast turnover on the paper, people coming and going all the time. And once you've got a foot in, if you're any good you can move around almost anywhere. So have a good think about it – and give my regards to Mr Juby.'

'Tha' I will,' said Charles automatically.

As Charles cycled into Remingham a week later, his suitcase in the basket of his bike, there was a bitter wind blowing, Norfolk's famous 'lazy wind'. 'Thass too lazy to go round you, that go strairt through'. Winter was setting in early.

He thought of the *Sunday Herald*'s centrally heated news-room, the comfortable trains that ran so regularly into the City, the snug 'semis' in Wembley Park. On the road from Toftham to Remingham there was just a vista of bleak fields, bare trees and hedges, and a great deal of mud. It was a depressing comparision.

In spite of the wind a little crowd was gathered around the front garden of Lambeth Palace. As he cycled on he heard the roar of an engine, and out onto the road came Mortimer, riding a shining, gleaming, roaring, utterly splendid motorbike.

His motorbike.

'Well done, Mort!' he shouted above the noise. 'That sounds great.'

Mortimer waved to him happily. 'I heard you were

due back today. I've just got it going – shall we try it out?'

Charles jumped off his cycle and climbed on to the pillion. Mortimer revved up the engine and let in the clutch, and as they moved off down the road the little crowd gave a ragged cheer. Charles saw John Cranmer waving and laughing, and Willum was doing one of his little dances. Then they were out of the village and flying through the Norfolk countryside, the wind biting at their cheeks. Charles forgot all about the *Sunday Herald*; this was exciting, exhilarating – real.

But as they turned for home it started snowing, the first snow of the winter. Not just a few flurries; this was thin, driving snow coming straight in off the North Sea, reducing visibility to a few yards and settling quickly on the road. Mortimer slowed almost to walking pace, but even at that speed they slipped and skidded dangerously; only his skill and experience kept them upright.

When at last they got back to Lambeth Palace, Charles was no longer excited or exhilarated; he was soaked, and shivering, and really quite frightened. They wheeled the bike into the shed and Mortimer said it ought to be wiped down, but Charles had had enough of motorbikes for the day. He had also had enough of the Norfolk winter – and it had hardly begun.

That evening he wrote to the editor of the *Sunday Herald*. When a vacancy occurred, he told him, he would very much like to be considered.

Seventeen

Among the crowded rows of seats in Toftham Jubilee Hall there was a buzz of anticipation as the record on the amplifier was faded and the house lights were turned down. The audience stopped chatting, and one or two latecomers hastened to their places. Among them was Charles, who had lingered too long in the Dog and Partridge. He slipped into his reserved seat in the front row as the curtain went up on Toftham Drama Society's production of *See How They Run*.

My Juby had given him a few words of advice. 'Now just remember, boy, this hent the Royal Shakespeare Company you're going to write about, these are amachers. And you hent a drama critic, you're a junior reporter. Don't you go knockin' 'em for six.'

'But I thought they were supposed to be very good.' Charles had heard many favourable comments about the Society's productions from various people in the town; they could not all be relatives of the cast.

'Mostly they are. One or two hent. And it's often the ones that hent that cause the most trouble. Just remember they've all worked hard, and they've got their pride. So thass no good telling 'em how bad they are; apart from anything else, that don't sell papers. Just be sure to get all the names in; and if you say they're all bloody marvellous, so much the better.'

The audience applauded as the set was revealed, the lounge of a country vicarage. In previous productions the same set had been a Victorian boudoir and a City office, but now there were French windows made out of cellophane, an ingle-nook fireplace surrounded by imitation brick wallpaper, oak beams were painted on the hardboard walls, and a flight of rickety steps led up to the doorway. Not many vicarage lounges had flights of steps, thought Charles, but no doubt it gave dramatic effect to the entrances and exits.

A large settee occupied most of the centre stage; there was just room to edge around it. Through the French windows a brightly-lit blue and green backcloth indicated that this was indeed the country. Charles expected a figure in white flannels to enter and cry 'Anyone for tennis?'

In fact most of the figures who entered wore clerical suits and collars. The plot had something to do with a former boy friend of the vicar's wife arriving unexpectedly, and for various unlikely reasons dressing up as a vicar himself. At one stage the real vicar's trousers fell down; at another a Nazi airman appeared with a revolver and shouted at everybody in broken English. It was all quite unbelievable. But Charles was not to concerned with the plot; he was much more interested in the cast. He had not had time to look at the programme, and each new entrance provided a fresh relevation.

The vicar turned out to be Mr Grind, the Assistant Clerk to Launford Rural District Council, freed from his piles of ledgers and the shadow of Commander Bludgen, and remarkably convincing as an unctuous cleric.

His young wife was played by the Commander's very attractive daughter, whom Charles had seen occasionally around the town, but never at close quarters before. From his front-row seat he was able to view her from particularly striking angle. Her amorous friend, predictably, was Freddie Pendleton, hamming it up with enormous enthusiasm and keeping the audience convulsed.

But the star of the show turned out to be Harry Hurn the hairdresser, who had exchanged his white coat for flowing clerical robes and was a comic bishop to end all comic bishops, delivering his lines with great panache in the plummiest of mock-Oxford accents. The audience fell about, and so did Charles. It would not be too difficult to follow Mr Juby's instructions he decided; Harry Hurn was bloody marvellous.

But there were more revelations to come, not quite so pleasing. The village gossip, who was supposed to add another touch of broad humour to the play, was portrayed appallingly by Mrs Godfrey Bleddington, the Chairman of the Bench. She was uncertain of her lines, and those she remembered were delivered in the same forbidding tones in which she passed sentence on offenders. Charles could see he was going to have problems there.

It was the entry of the German airman, however, which provided the biggest and most unpleasant surprise. The man in the ill-fitting Luftwaffe uniform, waving a revolver and shouting in quite absurd broken English, was the Honourable Henry Burton.

Charles glowered up at him as he strutted round the stage. He had to admit the actual part was quite ridiculous; even so, Henry played it very badly. With great satisfaction Charles wrote in his note book: 'German airman: overacts, nervous, shouts too much, uniform doesn't fit.' When Henry leaned against the fireplace and the whole set rocked, to the embarrassment of the cast and the great delight of the audience, Charles's cup was full.

When the lights went up finally and the cast took their bow, Charles applauded as loudly as anybody. It really was a very entertaining show, and the real-life identities of the players added a little extra spice. There were cries of 'Producer!' and it would hardly have surprised Charles if Lord Remingham had emerged from the wings, but in fact it was George Flatt, the Clerk to Toftham Council, who appeared resplendent in full evening dress and bowed graciously to the audience and the cast.

No wonder the production is so efficient, thought Charles, if he organizes the players as firmly as he runs the Council. But how did Mrs Bleddington and the Honourable Henry slip inside the net?

*

'So what did you think of it?' Mr Juby asked next morning.

Charles admitted he had enjoyed it. 'But how did Henry Burton get into it? He doesn't live in Toftham.'

'George Flatt's a great one for keeping in with the gentry,' explained Mr Juby. 'This is the only drama society worth a light in these parts, and Henry fancied joining it. George hent got the guts to keep him out.'

We'll see about that, thought Charles, and started on his report.

The compliments about the main characters flowed easily. He rhapsodised over the Bishop, and devoted considerable space to the vicar's wife – 'whose delightful performance,' he concluded, 'must have enchanted everyone in the hall.' Then it was time for the Honourable Henry.

'Henry Burton, as the German airman, nearly brought the house down, but not perhaps in the way the author intended.' He studied the sentence, the deleted 'perhaps' and inserted 'certainly'. 'Mr Burton did not seem to appreciate that a stage fireplace is there to be looked at, not leant on.' He began to enjoy himself.

'He conveyed the uneasiness and self-consciousness of an escaped German prisoner so convincingly that one could well believe the feeling were genuine. But one does wonder if the author intended this character to appear quite so nervous and stilted. Perhaps Mr Burton is too young to remember what German officers were really like.'

That'll do for Henry, he decided, and turned to Mrs Bleddington.

'Henrietta Bleddington,' he wrote, 'as the local gossip, seemed the victim of an error of casting. Although she was in a very different role from her usual one as Chairman of the Bench, she played it in much the same fashion, except that she sometimes seemed at a loss for words, something that rarely happens in court . . .'

Felling quite pleased with himself, he took the report upstairs to show Mr Juby. The feeling did not last very

273

long. Mr Juby, having nodded approvingly at the complimentary passages, came to the paragraph about Henry Burton. He studied the opening sentences closely.

'Did he knock the fireplace over, then?' he asked.

'Very nearly,' said Charles complacently. 'He leaned on it and the whole set rocked. Quite spoilt the effect.'

'That hent his fault they didn't build it steady. And he won't do it again the rest of the week. That won't mean narthin to anyone who weren't there last night.'

He glared at Charles and read on, with increasing anger. 'What's all this fancy stuff about uneasiness and self-consciousness? He can't help it if he's nervous, everybody's nervous fust time out. He won't get any less nervous reading that. And this squit about being too young to remember – he hent no younger than you are.'

He waved the report at Charles fiercely. 'Don't you go tairkin it out on young Burton in the pairper, just because he did you a bad turn. Thass no way to wuk, boy, thass damn stoopid.'

He scored out the paragraph, then went on more quietly, his accent becoming less pronounced as he calmed down, 'There's something you ought to remember, Charlie. When you're writing for a pairper, you got power.' He saw Charles raise a sceptical eyebrow. 'Oh yes, even on a little local pairper like the *Journal* you got power. You can hurt people and they can't do narthin about it, not in time to do any good. Sometimes it's just a mistake, and we can all make mistakes, so long as we don't do it too often. But sometimes' – and the accent crept back again – 'sometimes thass on parpus, just to show how hully clever we are, like this bit about Henry Burton, and I don't stand for that, boy. They might like that sort o'squit on the *Sunday Herald*, but you don't do it with me.'

Charles seethed silently. He also wondered about the mention of the *Sunday Herald*. Did the Juby all-seeing eye extend to Fleet Street? It would not have surprised him.

But Mr Juby had returned to the report.

'Here's another one. What you've written about Henrietta Bleddington. "The victim of an error of casting". That weren't no error. She always gets a part, and that were the only one going. She's had a part in every play since the Society started, boy, long before the war. Lovely girl she was – "enchanting", no doubt you'd call her. Always played the lead, always did it well. Thass a long time ago, but people remember. And now she's not so "enchanting", and her memory's not so good, and she's not as sprightly as she was, but they make sure she's always got a part, for old times' sake.'

He crossed out the paragraph, and looked up again at Charles. 'If we printed this, boy, they'd have your guts for garters – and I wouldn't blame them.'

'But I've got to say something about them,' said Charles desperately. 'You told me not to leave anyone out. And they really were pretty awful. It's not fair to the rest of the cast if I say they're just as good.'

'Well, we can't have you jeopardising your principles, can we?' said Mr Juby. 'There's an easy way to get round that.' And he wrote at the bottom of the report in a large hand: 'Other parts were taken by Henry Burton and Henrietta Bleddington.'

'I'm afraid,' said Mr Juby, 'you still got a lot to lun.'

In the next few weeks Charles had plenty of chances to lun. He seemed to cover every Sunday School Nativity play, every end-of-term concert, every village concert party. He even sat through an evening of recitations at the Methodist Women's Own. His education as the *Journal*'s drama critic, he felt, was complete.

In Remingham he kept away from the Old Rectory except to establish that Rebecca would be coming home for Christmas. As usual, she had not said when. He occupied much of his spare time on his motorbike, with tuition from Mortimer whenever he could come over. After that early snowstorm the weather had improved and he got in plenty of practice. His test was booked in Norwich at the beginning of the Christmas week; he hoped the examiner believed in the season of goodwill.

Toftham always looked its best during the period leading up to Christmas. The Council provided a tree as the centre-piece, the Chamber of Trade did a deal with Evans Electric, he of the revolving silver ball, to festoon the Market Place with coloured lights, and every shop window was decorated. Even Mr Hurn draped steamers over his Brylcreem posters.

Big Nellie, not to be outdone, removed the yellowing photographs of weddings and garden fêtes, and pinned up green file covers to spell out 'A Merry Christmas To All Our Advertisers'. Up in his first floor office Charles hung a large paper bell in the window bearing the inscription, 'ANOTHER CLANGER', and even Mr Juby entered into the spirit by giving his curtains their annual outing to the laundry.

It was in this atmosphere of general conviviality that things started to go wrong.

The driving test was a disaster. Charles had become very proficient at driving around country lanes, and he could cope with the familiar traffic hazards of Toftham Market Place. He had even driven round it on a market day without killing anybody. But Norwich was a very different matter. In the heavy traffic he had to reduce his speed so drastically that he developed an alarming wobble. He did not dare let go of the handlebars to signal a right turn, and was nearly flattened by a bus. When it came to the Highway Code he was so demoralised he could not even remember in what order traffic lights changed from red to green. He returned to Toftham with the L-plates still on the motorbike, and a deep hatred of Norwich traffic in his heart.

Mr Juby tried to be sympathetic. 'They always fail young fellas the fust time, just to keep you in your place. That don't make much difference – you can still use the bike.'

'But I can't carry a passenger,' grumbled Charles.

'Thass good of you to think of me,' said Mr Juby solemnly, 'but luckily I've got a car . . .'

Mortimer rang up with commiserations. Charles

enquired if he had passed first time and Mortimer confessed apologetically that he had.

'I expect they were impressed by that flying helmet,' Charles observed sourly.

'I'd gladly have lent it to you if you think it would have made any difference,' said Mortimer. Charles, as always, could not tell whether he was joking.

He rode home that evening still depressed, and even the village's festive appearance on this clear December evening failed to cheer him. Lord Remmingham always paid for the church to be floodlit, and its battlemented tower and high flint walls made an impressive sight. Mrs Curson left her shop light on to show all the Christmas fare in the windows, there were coloured bulbs all over the front of the Remingham Arms, and the lights were all on at the village school where they were preparing for the Nativity play next day. Far from being cheered, Charles recalled morosely that this was yet another production he had to cover for the *Journal*.

He parked the motorbike in the shed, alongside the now-neglected delivery bike. He had mentioned it casually to Freddie Pendleton, but Freddie had merely laughed uproariously and suggested he tried selling it back to Geo. Perkins. Mr Perkins also found that very funny. Charles hesitated to put it back in the auction, where it would doubtless be snapped up for a few shillings by Mr Futter. He still had a certain attachment for the old machine and he hesitated to see it disappear into the Futter scrapyard. So it still lay there, and rustmarks were beginning to appear on 'Chas Benson, Purveyor of Good News.'

Inside Lambeth Palace John Cranmer looked up from his desk and could see the little black cloud over his head. 'Bad luck,' he said.

Charles grunted an acknowledgement and collapsed in a chair. 'I can't take the test again until sometime in February. We'll probably have three feet of snow by then. Might as well go back to using the pushbike.'

'I was going to mention that,' said John. 'I assume

you're not really going to use it again. If you want to get rid of it, I'd like to buy it.'

'What on earth for?' asked Charles, astonished. 'We can't have the Rector visiting his parishioners on a delivery bike.'

'Oh, I don't know.' John grinned. 'If I just altered your name to mine on the name-plate, the rest of the inscription would be highly appropriate. Rather more than it is for you, most of the time.' And Charles had to accept that was true.

'But actually,' he continued. 'It's not for me. It's for a Christmas present.'

Charles was still puzzled. 'I can't imagine anyone would want a battered old delivery bike for Christmas. Unless they actually wanted it for deliveries.' He paused, and light dawned. 'Hang on . . .'

'That's right,' smiled John. 'It's for Willum.'

Charles laughed for the first time since the examiner had given him the failure slip. 'What a splendid idea. Willum'll love that; he can pension off that old handcart at last.'

'It's a sort of thank-you for all his help at the family services,' John explained. 'I doubt if the children would bother to come if it wasn't for Willum and his guitar.' He paused for a moment, then added: 'It'll be a farewell present as well.'

'Farewell? Where's Willum off to?'

'He's not off anywhere,' said John gently. 'But I am afraid I am.'

Charles was no longer laughing. First the driving test, now this.

'I haven't told anyone yet, so please don't spread it around – and certainly not in the *Journal*. I'm seeing Lord Remingham tomorrow, and Dr Bateman. But I thought you should know as soon as possible because you'll be directly affected, I'm afraid. I doubt you'll be able to stay here once I go; the next rector will probably have a family, he'll need all the space.'

'But why are you going? And where? And when?' Charles could not take it in.

'I've been asked to take on a parish in North London. It's quite near the one I came from and I know some to the people already. Quite honestly I think I'm better suited to a town parish than a village. I don't think I could go through anything like that business with the Brownings again, and that sort of thing doesn't happen quite so much with a bigger congregation.'

He paused, and smiled a little ruefully. 'I'm sure there's a lot to be said for Mr Juby's "foodal society", but I need to feel I'm ministering in the twentieth century, not the eighteenth or nineteenth. Perhaps I'll come back one day, but I have things I need to do, and I shall never be able to do them here.'

Charles knew very well how he felt. There was no point in arguing but he was deeply sorry that their pleasant coexistence at Lambeth Palace was to end. He asked when John would be leaving.

'Not for a month or two. These things take a little time. But it might be as well to start looking around for some digs.'

'I don't think I will just yet,' said Charles, but he did not explain why. If the *Sunday Herald* made me an offer there would be no need for any digs – not in Norfolk anyway. Perhaps, he thought with a faint flicker of hope, John's departure was A Sign.

He remembered John's enquiry about the bike, and had a pleasant thought.

'I'm not going to let you buy that old bike to give to Willum,' he announced. John looked taken aback. 'No, you can have it for nothing. But I insist on changing the name-plate myself. I can't get Willum's name into the *Journal* every week, but I can put it on his bike for all time . . .'

One of the youthful shepherds, leaning on his crook at the back of the stage while his companions discussed the strange light in the sky, yawned enormously. Charles, perched on one of the tiny infants' chairs in the auditorium, knew how he felt. The Remingham School Nativity play was being greatly enjoyed by the parents, but it was the fifth he had been to in a fortnight, and he longed for the closing tableau.

He became slightly more interested when he recognised Mary and Joseph as the two youngest Gibsons. But then he remembered there was still no news from Fred Knock about a pair of council houses becoming available. It seemed sadly appropriate when the stage innkeeper turned them away and directed them to the stable. If he was writing a book, Charles mused, then Fred Knock would appear on the Gibsons' doorstep on Christmas Eve, wave his magic tiepin, and their new home would miraculously appear. But Launford Rural District Council had already shut its offices for Christmas.

At last the entire cast was assembled in the stable around Mary and Joseph and the manger. There was also a real sheep, the pet of the Chief Shepherd (which was why he had been made the Chief Shepherd). It received a special round of applause as it was led on to the stage. The sudden noise seemed to disturb it, and the applause turned to cheers as it relieved itself over the feet of the sleepy shepherd, who was yawning no longer.

'You little bugger,' exclaimed the shepherd in a clear and penetrating voice.

At last, thought Charles with relief as the audience dissolved around him, something different to write about a Nativity play . . .

He was feeling quite cheerful as he made his escape from the school. Then he heard a familiar whinnying from the paddock behind the Old Rectory and his gloom returned. Rebecca was on her way home; he would soon know the worst.

Back in the office Mr Juby was browsing through the week's diary. Mercifully there were no more Nativity plays; the remaining Christmas-tide events were the

Christmas Eve carol service in the Market Place, the Christmas Day visit to Launford Old People's Home by the council chairman, and the Boxing Day meet at Remingham Hall. To Mr Juby's surprise, Charles volunteered for them all.

'Hent you got any celebrating to do yourself?' asked Mr Juby.

'I very much doubt it,' said Charles.

Mr Juby studied him carefully. 'The gal Beccy not home yet?'

'Any time,' he replied, 'but it won't necessarily be a celebration.'

'Ah,' said Mr Juby thoughtfully, 'Well, never you mind, there's always a bit of a knees-up in the Market Place after the carol service. You might enjoy that.'

'And I suppose Launford Old People's Home is a real riot once the chairman's been round,' observed Charles.

'Well, that can be a bit depressing,' Mr Juby admitted. 'But you have a good enough time after the carol service, you'll hardly notice. And you can look forward to a nice glass of port from His Lordship on Boxing Day.'

'Sounds like a really jumping Christmas,' said Charles gloomily, and went off to think of something terribly amusing to write about the misbehaving sheep.

He hastened back to Remingham that evening, hoping to find that Rebecca had arrived home. Instead there was a message from her parents. She was due home on Christmas Eve, and would he care to join them for a little celebration party?

He tried to read between the lines. Did the invitation mean that Rebecca had asked for him to be there? Would they have troubled to invite him if they were not expecting to see more of him? Or was it just another Christmas invitation?

He cursed volunteering for the carol service, but there was no urgency about writing the report with no papers on the following two days. He could escape promptly.

As it turned out, he quite enjoyed the service. The

281

evening was cold but clear, and the lights on the Christmas tree and in the shop windows, and the people carrying lanterns and torches, made the Market Place look welcoming and festive. It had been kept clear of cars and the crowd was able to spread out from the tree, across the roads and into the shop doorways. Most of the upper windows were lit too, with the occupants leaning out and exchanging greetings with friends below. In the doorway of the Dog and Partridge was a group of customers with Mr Juby, grasping a special, in their midst. Even the customary group of youths outside the Golden Fleece seemed on their best behaviour.

Two areas had been roped off near the tree, one for the Salvation Army band, the other for local dignitaries and the press. George Flatt and most of the town council were there with their families; so was Mrs Godfrey Bleddington and some fellow magistrates, and Clarence Burney, the Clerk. And there was a group from the Launford Council offices, headed by Commander Bludgen and Mr Grind.

They all gave him a friendly welcome; Mr Bleddington, who always ignored his existence in court, wished him good evening, and even George Flatt mustered a smile. It might have been just the Christmas spirit, but Charles warmed to it nonetheless. A few months earlier they would not have given him a second glance. For the first time he mentally thanked Mr Juby for cutting out his comments on Henrietta Bleddington.

A girl came up beside him and tapped him on the arm. 'Excuse me.' she said, 'are you C.B.?'

She was dressed in a long coat with a collar turned up round her ears, and her hair was hidden under a big fur hat, but he recognised the face. It was the Commander's daughter, the vicar's young wife in *See How they Run*. The 'C.B.' became clear; Mr Juby had put his initials on the report.

'Yes, I'm Charles Benson.'

'I just wanted to thank you for the nice things you said about me. That stuff about "enchanting the entire audience" was a bit over the top, but I thought you were very kind about me anyway.'

'Not a bit,' he protested. 'You deserve every word. Especially "enchanting". You really were.' He tried to remember her first name. Was it Debbie? Fanny? Ellie?

'Well, thank you anyway.' She smiled, and he smiled back. There seemed nothing else to say. Was it Mandy? Cindy? Melanie? Then the Salvation Army band burst into 'Good King Wenceslas' and further conversation was impossible. By the time the carol ended she had moved away and rejoined her father.

He did not wait for the vicar's final blessing. If anybody decided later to blow up the tree or assassinate the Chairman of the Bench, Mr Juby could report it. He was still in the doorway of the Dog and Partridge, but Mavis had obviously kept his glass replenished. He waved cheerfully to Charles, and put his thumbs up ostentatiously, for no obvious reason. Charles waved back, mouthed 'Merry Christmas' to him across the Market Place, and edged off into the crowd. A few minutes later he was on his motorbike, heading for Remingham.

The Old Rectory was almost as brightly lit as the floodlit church across the road. Dr Bateman had wound the coil of coloured lights around the big fir tree in the front garden, and there were more lights around the front door. There were also a great many cars in the drive and the road outside. This was a much bigger party than Charles had expected. He wished he had paused at Lambeth Palace to smarten up.

Dr Bateman greeted him at the door. 'Glad you could come. It was all arranged at rather short notice, I'm afraid. Beccy didn't give us much warning.'

He ushered him inside and gave him a glass of mulled wine. Charles was still puzzling over what he had said. The Batemans had known for some time that Rebecca would be home for Christmas; they could have arranged the party weeks ago.

He caught sight of her in a far corner, with a large

group clustered around her. So I'm on the outside again, he thought, just like that damned point-to-point. And sure enough, the awful Harry Burton was in the group, and some of the others who had been at the races. It did not bode well.

He crossed the room and joined them. Rebecca spotted him, and smiled and waved. He smiled and waved back. But he was looking at the young man who had his arm around her waist and was waving casually too, through they had never met before. He did not need to see the ring on Rebecca's finger.

'Congratulations,' he shouted over the heads of the group. 'Thank you,' she shouted back, and looked as though she might come over to him, then changed her mind. 'Are you all right?' she called.

'Absolutely splendid,' he called back. 'Probably see you later on.' But he knew he wouldn't.

Instead he drank a couple more glasses of mulled wine then made his apologies to Dr Bateman, explaining he was on duty next morning, and left. He thought for a moment of returning to the knees-up in Toftham – what *was* her name? – but it seemed too much of an effort. Instead he spent the rest of the evening at the Remingham Arms, to such good effect that when he did get back to Lambeth Palace he could only collapse in an armchair, where John Cranmer woke him next morning on his way to early service.

'Happy Christmas,' said John.

Charles looked at him, bleary-eyed. The memory of the previous evenings returned, and he clutched at the solitary straw.

'At least,' he said, 'it's not Harry Bloody Burton.'

Looking back afterwards, Charles decided it was probably the most depressing Christmas he had ever known.

Launford Old People's Home, even with its rather forlorn Christmas decorations, was as dreary as Mr Juby had predicted. And for once his advice turned out to be wrong – a hangover made it seem even worse. He trailed after Lord Remingham and the other councillors as they visited each of the sitting rooms. Lord Remingham paused occasionally to have a word with one of the residents, much as an inspecting officer would have a word with the men in the ranks. Or, thought Charles grimly, much as a Victorian squire might have a word with some of the peasantry.

The contrast on Boxing Day at the Remingham Hall Meet depressed him still further. Elegant riders congregated on the drive in front of the steps where he had once parked his bike and been advised to move it by the butler. This time the big door was wide open, with Lord Remingham waving greetings to his friends while the butler served stirrup cups in little goblets from a massive silver tray. Against the backcloth of the Hall, and with the rolling parkland all around, it could have been an eighteenth-century hunting print, thought Charles, except that the handful of villages who had turned out to watch were dressed in serge donkey-jackets instead of smocks, and their trousers were not actually tied with string below their knees. But the atmosphere, he mused, could hardly have changed in two hundred years. He was not surprised to find that he did not get offered a glass of port.

New Year's Eve had been a little more convivial. Freddie Pendleton asked him round with some other Round Tablers. There was much hearty drinking and reminiscing, and Charles received more congratulations on the success of the Human Fireball. But all the other Tablers had wives or girlfriends with them, and when it came to forming a circle for 'Auld Lang Syne' he was the only odd man out. He finished up clutching the hand of Freddie Pendleton, which Freddie found very amusing but Charles did not. It had also been difficult, when greetings were exchanged and he was wished good luck in the New Year, not to confess that if the *Sunday Herald* came up trumps he might well spend the New Year elsewhere.

But it was now the end of January, and there was still

no word from the *Herald*. Charles had dropped back into the *Journal*'s normal routine, with the additional dubious honour of being appointed deputy sports reporter. Mr Juby had always covered Toftham United's matches and Charles enjoyed having most Saturday afternoons free during the winter. But one of Mr Juby's New Year resolutions, he announced, was to broaden Charles's reporting experience, and he delegated him to take over the football. Mr Juby, as it happened, was beginning to find that his rheumatism played up after ninety minutes on a chilly touchline.

Which was how Charles now found himself standing there instead on a bitterly cold afternoon in a wind which could no longer be called lazy, since it was trying hard to blow down the club's flagpole. Charles huddled among the handful of spectators, wearing two sweaters under his duffle-coat and a scarf wrapped round his ears, and still numb with cold.

He had pleaded in vain that his school had only played rugby and he knew nothing about football. 'This hent got nothing to do with football,' said Mr Juby. 'This is Toftham United.' Such subtleties as the offside trap were therefore quite beyond him. He had learned however to stand behind the more knowledgeable spectators and note down their observations. He was thus able to include an occasional intelligent comment in the fifty words he had to phone at half-time to the Green 'Un, the company's Saturday evening football special. He also learned to refer to the ball as 'the leather' and the goalkeeper as 'the custodian', which added a further touch of authenticity. Whenever nothing much seemed to be happening on the field, which was quite a common feature of Toftham's matches, there are always the magic formula, 'End-to-end play then ensued.'

This afternoon end-to-end play seemed to ensue almost continuously, with the players galloping up and down the field in a desperate effort to keep warm. Nobody put the leather past the custodian in the first half, which made Charlie's fifty words all the more difficult. A detailed description of a goal, with X beating Y to centre to Z, who then headed into the rigging – another useful word – could easily use up half his allocation. Instead he wrote at some length about the wind, which was becoming gale force. 'Conditions were not conducive to skilful play,' he dictated to Norwich from the phone box, implying that Toftham were usually skilful. It was over-generous, but Charles was learning.

When he emerged from the box the icy blast that hit him was so unpleasant he thought of deserting his post during the second half and picking up the result at the end. But there were so few spectators his absence would be noticed and no doubt reported to Mr Juby. And it would be just his luck if the flagpole blew down and killed a couple of players while he was lurking in the office.

So he stayed on. The flagpole did not quite blow down, there was still no score, and at the final whistle the players disappeared as fast as the spectators. And it's only the end of January, thought Charles miserably; another dozen such Saturday's stretched ahead.

He phoned the results to Norwich – 'N-n-nil n-n-nil' was how it came out – and thankfully mounted his motorbike and headed for home. The wind buffeted him so violently he was nearly blown off the road. Pieces of broken branches were flung at him, and a few flurries of snow got in his eyes. It was a most unpleasant ride.

Lambeth Palace was empty. John Cranmer was in London, visiting his new parish; he was not due back until late. He was going to move in mid-February, and Charles had started looking in earnest for other accommodation, but nothing seemed available. The spectral figure of Mrs Abbs loomed ever closer.

As he opened the front door the wind caught an envelope lying on the mat and blew it along the hall. Only after he had hung up his duffle coat, taken off his gumboots and put on the kettle did he bother to pick it up. Then he saw the *Sunday Herald* logo.

There was a vacancy for a researcher, wrote the editor's secretary, available in six weeks' time. The salary offered, as Jeffrey Palmer had promised, was about three times what he was getting at the *Journal*; there would also be adequate expenses. In view of the many applicants on the list, his reply in writing would be appreciated within the next few days.

Charles sat in the kitchen, the melting snow dripped out of his hair, his hands and feet still numb. This is the day, he said to himself, when the course of my life changes; a new world lies ahead. And he looked at the calendar to note the day that it happened. As he did so there was a mighty banging on the front door.

Mr Juby was standing on the doorstep, wrapped in an enormous coat, his hat pulled down over his ears. The wind howled past him. Behind him in the lane was his beautiful Flying Standard, normally never out in bad weather, its paintwork already mud-stained from the drive out from Toftham. The engine was still running.

'Come on, Charlie. Jump in, boy. There's all hell breaking loose up on the coast. I'll tell you on the way.'

The date on the calendar stuck in Charles's mind as he climbed into the passenger seat, his wet duffle-coat staining the immaculate leather and his gumboots muddying the floor.

It was January the thirty-first, nineteen fifty-three.

Chapter Eighteen

'It's the wind and the tide together, thass what's doing it,' explained Mr Juby as the Standard headed towards the coast, labouring quite noticeably against the force of the gale. 'We've got higher tides than usual anyway, this time of year, and now this wind's got up from the north and thass pushing along behind it. Heard it first from the dockmaster at King's Lynn; we've known each other a long time. The water was coming up over the quay. He said our Norridge people didn't take much notice of him, but I had a word and put 'em right. Then I checked along our part of the coast, and the same thing's happening there, even though we usually get high tide a little later.'

'But that doesn't sound too bad, just washing over the quay,' said Charles, still wishing he had had time for a cup of tea and a warm-up. 'I've seen that happen down on the South Coast; it just washes back again.'

'This hent the South Coast, this is the East Coast,' said Mr Juby. 'And that hent the Channel out there, thass the North Sea. But you miss the real point, boy. It's still another three hours to high tide.'

'Three hours?' Charles began to appreciate what was happening. 'So it can go on rising for another three hours?'

'The last time anything like this happened,' said Mr Juby grimly, 'there were floods right along the coast. There's a church in Lynn that's a hundred yards or more from the quayside, that had five feet of water all around it.'

'Do you remember it then?' asked Charles.

Mr Juby chuckled. 'Not quite, boy. That were 1883. But I've heard tell of it many times. You can still see the mark on the church porch. And from what I can gather, conditions are much the same tonight.'

They drove through Tittlesham, the inn-sign outside the Hero swinging almost horizontally in the wind. It occurred to Charles they were entering Mortimer's territory. 'Does Mortimer know we're coming?' he asked.

'No, he don't,' said Mr Juby. 'He don't know because he hent there. He's gone over to his mother's at Hunstanton. She gets worried when she's on her own and the wind gets up. He phoned me this afternoon and said he was going. We didn't know then it was going to get this bad.'

'Well, it may die down,' said Charles, a little too nonchalantly.

'You don't know narthin about it,' snapped Mr Juby. 'That won't die down, and that tide is going to keep on a-comin'.'

They reached Wettleford and drove past the *Journal* office and the empty flat above. The High Street was deserted; they nearly collided with a dustbin as it was blown past them, rolling crazily from side to side of the road. As they passed the Red Lion Charles saw some faces in the window. They were looking at a tree which was creaking ominously as the gale blew it against the side of the pub. The life-size metal lion which stood over the porch seemed to be rocking too.

'This must be a hell of a wind,' said Charles, much impressed.

'That hent dying down a lot,' agreed Mr Juby drily.

They drove on northward, on the same road that Mortimer had taken him in the summer, and climbed the hill that looked down over Branham Staithe. As they reached the summit they were hit by the full force of the gale howling in off the North Sea. The Standard rocked, and Mr Juby braked to a stop and peered through the windscreen.

Below them they could make out the lights of Branham Staithe, and there were the headlights of one or two cars moving along the coast road. In their own lights they could see the trees alongside the lane lashing from side to side in the wind; the road itself was littered with small branches. And beyond the noise of the wind Charles could detect another, more ominous roar, the sound of the breakers beyond the salt-marshes.

'Thass a wild night, and no mistake,' muttered Mr Juby. 'There's folk going to need help down there before long.'

He drove slowly down the hill, trying to avoid the debris blowing about on the road. At one point a large branch had snapped off and was almost blocking the lane. Mr Juby bumped up on to the verge to get past it and the wheels flung up clods of mud over the Standard's windows. Mr Juby ignored them, and drove on.

When they reached the coast road and turned along it towards Branham Staithe the roar of the breakers became stronger, even though there was half a mile of salt-marsh between them and the sea. Or rather, there should have been. As Charles peered through the darkness, the white lines of the breakers seemed a lot closer than half a mile.

'Thass broken through.' Mr Juby had seen them too. 'There's only a ridge of shingle between the beach and the marshes on this stretch. The sea must be through that and into the marsh. That'll be up to the road come high tide. And Branham lies level with the marshes.'

Charles remembered how the village had looked that summer, a picturesque huddle of flint cottages and shops at the head of the winding estuary where the yachts were able to sail up and moor at high tide. The sun had sparkled on the placid ribbon of blue water and the brightly-painted boats pulled up on the mud-flats beside it. The lane that led down from the coast road to the quayside had been full of holiday-makers, mostly sailing folk in shirts and shorts, mingling with the local fishermen in their more workmanlike black sweaters and caps. It had been an idyllic scene.

They drove over the little hump-backed bridge where the coast road crossed a tiny stream that flowed into the estuary, and turned down the lane that led into the village. And this was a very different picture.

Nearly every cottage had its lights blazing. People with torches were propping boards and sandbags against the doorways. Others were huddled in little groups, looking down the hill towards the quayside. The wind was blowing straight up the street, and in a heavier gust some slates came flying off a roof and crashed into the road, scattering one of the groups. Behind it all there was the continuous roar of the sea.

Mr Juby pulled up at the top of the street and surveyed the scene. 'That won't be a good idea to take the car down,' he told Charles. 'There's no telling how high that sea's going to come.'

He backed a few yards and drove into the playground of the village school, which stood at the top of the slope and led down into Branham. He parked the Standard by the main door of the school.

'Come on boy, thass time to take a walk.'

They struggled down the village street, the wind almost taking them off their feet. Through the windows of some of the cottages, as they neared the quay, Charles saw people carrying pieces of furniture upstairs – chairs, tables, cupboards, even rolled-up carpets. 'That won't do a lot of good if that really comes,' muttered Mr Juby.

Down on the quayside they joined a group of fishermen who were gazing out along the channel. A surging mass of water already covered the mud-flats and was only a foot or two below the level of the quay. Some yachts were tossing crazily at their moorings; others, which must have been drawn up on the mud, had failed to right themselves as the water rose and were still on their sides, partially submerged, with each new wave breaking right over them. Pieces of timber, duckboards, hatches, all manner of debris which had been swept off the decks were being flung about in the water. The noise of the wind and the sea was quite deafening.

'What's the situation?' Mr Juby shouted to the man beside him, a fisherman in high boots and a heavy jacket, and a cap pulled down hard over his eyes. The men turned and recognized him. 'Thass Mr Juby hent it? You got here fast, then.'

'Only just in time, I'd say.'

The fisherman nodded. 'Thass comin' in hell-for-leather over the marshes. The bank at the entrance to the channel must be still holding up, but that can't last much longer. And there's still a fair time to high tide.'

Charles hung on to a bollard to keep himself upright as the wind swept in over the marshland. He had never known anything like it.

'Must be over a hundred-mile-an-hour,' shouted one of the men. 'They never said it would be that strong.'

'Lot they know,' growled one of the others.

A big white bundle floated out of the darkness and thumped against the quayside just below Charles. It was the body of a sheep.

'Thass one of mine,' said the man who knew Mr Juby. 'I've got a hundred more out on the marshes. They'll all be gone by now.'

'Let's hope we don't lose no more except sheep,' said Mr Juby.

'D'yew be quiet,' said somebody sharply. 'Thass a rum noise a-comin', hent it?'

From out of the darkness beyond the channel came a rumbling, roaring sound, like waves breaking on shingle but magnified many times. The water started rising sharply and ran over the quay and round their feet.

'The bank's gone,' shouted the man next to Mr Juby. 'Get back up the street, fast as y'like. Thass a-comin'.'

Charles paused for only a moment. He saw a great white wall of water advancing up the inlet, flinging the moored boats against each other so that the sound of shattering wood merged with the roar of the massive wave. Then he turned and ran as he had never run before. As he passed the first cottages he heard doors being slammed shut and yells of warning from one window to the next. He caught up with Mr Juby, now panting heavily, and put a hand under his arm to help him along, but Mr Juby shook him off. 'I can manage, boy,' he gasped.

Then the wave hit the quayside and swept up the street behind them. Charles turned for a second and watched, horrified. The front walls of the cottages on the quayside took the full brunt of the wave and crumbled into heaps of flint. The roofs crashed down on them. The shouting turned to screams.

As it surged up the street the water smashed down doors and burst through windows. The plate glass in a butcher's window disintegrated and sides of meat were flung about inside the shop and washed into the street. A parked car was turned over and hurled against one of the cottages. And still the sea kept coming.

It only stopped when it was level with the village school. The group from the quayside, and others who had run up the street with them, stood in the lane outside the playground, the water swilling around their feet and the air full of spray. They looked, appalled, at the shambles just down the road which a few seconds before had been the village of Branham Staithe.

The water receded a few feet, then the second wave came and washed into the playground and around the wheels of Mr Juby's car. They waited tensely for the next, but it did not come quite so far. The marshes on each side of Branham were lower-lying and the water took the easier route and swept around the village to the coast. It had reached its limit in Branham itself.

'Right lads, give a hand.' Mr Juby's acquaintance was taking command. 'One of you find the schoolteacher, see if she's all right, ask her to open up the school. The folk from the quayside cottages can come up here. Some of you see if you can find a boat that's still in one piece. The rest of you come along o' me.' And he splashed off down the street and into the village.

Charles turned to Mr Juby for guidance.

'You go with 'em, boy, lend a hand. You'll be more use than me. I need to find out what's going on along the coast – that's if the road hent under water. There's some blankets in the boot; I'll leave 'em here for the folks in the school.'

He gave Charles the blankets and climbed into the car. Charles was still finding it difficult to think straight.

'Give it a turn, then, Charlie.' Mr Juby was waving the starting handle. As he took it and cranked the engine he realized he would have no way of getting back to Toftham, and pointed this out to Mr Juby.

Mr Juby was unsympathetic. 'There's neither of us'll get back to Toftham tonight,' he said. 'I'll come and find you in the morning.'

As he drove gingerly through the water that covered the playground, Charles had another, more disturbing thought.

'What about Mortimer?' he called out. 'Do you think he's all right?'

Mr Juby pulled up in the gateway of the playground, and looked down the lane into the flooded village. 'If it's as bad as this here,' he said sombrely, 'then God knows what it's like in Hunstanton. Thass one of the things I got to find out.'

Charles watched him drive off into the darkness. The wind still howled around him, the air was full of spray. He felt as though he had been left in the middle of a nightmare.

'If you're not a-goin' with Mr Juby, then you can give a hand in this boat.' The fisherman who had taken control of the rescue operation was standing up in a small rowing-boat, floating a few yards down from the school.

'I'm not very good with boats,' said Charles nervously. His only experience of them was on the Serpentine many years before.

'Thass not boats you need to be good with, thass people,' the man shouted back. 'Come you on, lad, make y'self useful.'

Charles peered down the lane to see the best way to get to the boat; it seemed to be in quite deep water. For the first time he noticed there was a phone box next to the school, its light still on. Suddenly he remembered the *Sunday Herald*.

'Are you comin', or hent you?' demanded the boatman. 'There's wuk to be done here, boy, I can't hang about.'

Charles still hesitated. This is crazy, he thought, this is the biggest story I shall ever have in Norfolk. The Sundays will love it. Then he looked down the hill at the shattered cottages, men floundering about in the water trying to drag people through broken windows, the gaping holes in the walls, the sagging roofs, and the shouting and the crying echoing above the howl of the wind.

'Coming,' he yelled, and waded into the water. As he approached the boat it got deeper and came over the tops of his gumboots, soaking his feet. He hauled himself clumsily over the side.

'Sorry to hold you up,' he said. 'Let's go.' And throughout the rest of the night he never thought of the *Sunday Herald* again.

In most of the village the electricity supply had been cut and the only lights came from torches and candles. They passed the higher cottages, where the water was only half-way up the front doors. 'They'll manage to get out if they want to,' said the boatman, 'or they can stay on the top floor for the present. The real trouble is down by the quay.'

As he rowed down the street men splashed about waist-deep in the water beside them carrying sticks of furniture or holding bedding above their heads. One man had a little girl in his arms who was gazing fearfully about her as if the end of the world must have come. But in one of the upper windows a couple of children, apparently enjoying all the excitement, waved to them cheerfully as they rowed by.

When they approached what had been the quayside Charles could see the full horror of the flood. The water was level with the bedroom windows of those cottages still standing, but there were gaps where the force of that first wave had demolished entire walls and brought roofs down on the people inside.

Another boat was already there. The men carried flares and they were searching in the water where a cottage had stood. In the back of their boat lay an old woman in her night-clothes; the waters must have swept in on her as she lay in bed. Charles looked closer as they passed, then looked away. He had not seen a dead body before.

They came level with a top window where a woman was looking out, ashen-faced and trembling, with a baby in her arms.

'Come you on, m'dear,' the boatman said to her gently, as he manouevred the boat alongside the window. 'You're all right now gal. Let's have the bebby first.'

Silently she handed the baby out of the window to Charles. From her drawn expression he feared that the baby must be dead too, but to his relief its eyes were open and it glared at him balefully. He rocked it awkwardly in his arms and it started to yell mightily.

'Thass a great job you're doin',' grinned the boatman as he helped the woman climb out of the window and into the boat. Charles grinned back.

In the next cottage an elderly couple were seated by their window, watching the activity all around them. The boatman edged the rowing-boat against the sill.

'Come on then, missus, we've room for two more.'

'We hent movin', Jimma,' said the old woman, the man beside her nodded agreement. 'We've lived here ever since we were married; that old sea hent a-goin' to shift us now.'

'Don't be daft, missus,' said the boatman urgently. 'We don't know what state the cottage is in under the water. That can come down any time.'

'Thass steady enough,' said the old man. 'If that were comin' down, it would have come down when the others did. That'll be all right now, you leave us be.'

Nothing would budge them. Finally Jimma shrugged,

and wished them luck, and rowed on. 'Stubborn folk,' he said to Charles. 'But I expect my old people would say the same.'

They took another two women on board, as many as they could hold, and Jimma rowed back through the village street and grounded the boat in the roadway outside the school. The door was open now and there was smoke coming from the chimney. The electricity was still connected here and the school's outside lights were switched on. Charles carried in the baby while Jimma helped the women through the few inches of water that still lay there.

There was a roaring fire in the schoolroom, and a score of people were gathered around it on the little school chairs, with blankets around their shoulders and mugs of soup in their hands. To Charles, with the water squelching in his gumboots and his clothes now sodden, it all looked most inviting.

'Come on lad, there's others waiting for us,' called Jimma. Charles followed him outside to the boat, and they rowed back into the village.

He did not give the telephone box a glance.

'We'll make a boatman of you yet, boy. You done well!'

It was three o'clock on Sunday morning and Charles and Jimma were sitting at last in front of the big fire in the schoolroom. The men from the other boats were there too. Charles had taken off his sodden trousers and was wrapped in one of Mr Juby's blankets. Behind them, people lay asleep on mattresses among the desks.

'Have another nip of this, lad,' said one of the men round the fire, and passed him the bottle of whisky that was going from hand to hand. The village pub had escaped the worst of the flood and the landlord had contributed the bottle to the team of rescuers; there was another one waiting by the fire.

Jimma had decided there could be nobody left in the village who did not wish to remain there. They had stopped by every cottage, and shouted through every window. It had been a night of grief and fear, but there were lighter moments too. They had helped one old man out of his flooded cottage who insisted that his goldfish should come along too. He ignored Jimma's joking suggestion that it could swim around in the bedroom until he came back. And there was the lady at the top end of the street, where he had been able to wade through the front door to fetch out her bedding, who called to him as he splashed down her submerged garden path, 'Mind you don't step on my geraniums!'

He hoped he would remember all these little details when he came to write the story for Monday's paper. He realized rather guiltily he had not taken a note all night.

'So what's your name anyway?' asked Jimma. He had not got around to it before. Charles explained who he was.

'You got a story tonight, thass for sure,' said Jimma. 'You be certain you tell it right, Charlie lad. There's folk away from these parts who won't believe all this.'

They chatted on for a while. The second whisky bottle was opened, and whether it was the heat of the fire, or the companionable atmosphere, or just the whisky, Charles forgot the horrors of the night and dozed off peacefully in his chair.

It was daylight when he woke, and Mr Juby was standing over him. Jimma and the other men were in the kitchen with the villagers who had been sleeping on the floor, and a pleasant smell of toast was wafting through.

'Up you get, Charlie.' He got up so sharply that his blanket fell to the ground. Mr Juby eyed him up and down. 'You'd better get your trousers on before the leddies come back.'

The trousers had dried beside the fire and Charles struggled into them. He had a crick in his back from the chair, and a thumping headache from the Scotch. He felt in urgent need of a wash, a shave, and several hours' decent sleep.

'Time we were off, boy. Get y'self a cup of tea and a bite of toast, then we'll be away. There's no more you need to do here.'

'And how did you get on?' asked Charles. 'Did you get very far along the coast?'

'Far enough,' said Mr Juby cryptically. 'I'll tell you in the car.'

Charles went into the kitchen for his tea and toast, and was startled to find himself being greeted as something of a hero.

'Here he is,' cried Jimma. 'He hent much good with boats, but he's all right with people.'

One or two of the villagers they had rescued in the boat came over and shook his hand. The woman who had been marooned with her baby was no longer looking drawn and haggard. She smiled at him happily as she brought the baby to him. The baby took one look at him, and started yelling.

'Not so good with babies, I'm afraid,' said Charles.

'Never you mind about that,' said its mother, and to his embarrassment she kissed him warmly.

Charles made his farewells, and Jimma went with him to the door. 'We'll get the village to rights again, you'll see,' he told him. 'And you know you'll always be welcome here, Charlie lad.'

When he climbed into the car beside Mr Juby, still munching a slice of toast, his headache and the crick in his back seemed much better. He settled back comfortably in the leather seat. But the feeling of well-being quickly passed. As they reached the coast road he began to realize how widespread the devastation was.

The little humped-back bridge was no longer there. Instead a broad swathe of water covered the road and stretched back into the fields on the landward side. Mr Juby turned in the other direction to make a detour, and as they drove alongside the salt-marshes Charles saw that most of them were now under water. In the next village they drove through the water had subsided, but mud and shingle were piled high against the scarred walls and the smashed windows of the cottages. And as they turned inland and started climbing, there was similar damage and flooding all along the coast for as far as he could see.

Mr Juby had hardly spoken, except to tell him to keep the crumbs off the seat – to that extent at any rate, normality had returned. As they reached the top of the hill and headed for Wettleford, Charles asked him again how he had fared during the night.

Mr Juby took a little time to reply. 'I got as far as Hunstanton,' he said.

Suddenly Charles guessed why he had been so subdued since they had met. Hunstanton was where Mortimer's mother lived.

'Is Mortimer all right?' he asked.

Again Mr Juby took some time to reply. He kept staring straight ahead. Then eventually he answered.

'That were all over before I got there,' he said quietly. 'That were far worse than at Branham. Whole rows of bungalows swept away. Waves around fifteen feet high, they reckon. No chance to run, even if they'd known what was coming.'

'And Mortimer? And his mother?'

Mr Juby shook his head. His eyes were moist.

'Both gone, boy. They didn't find the bodies until nearly daylight, washed up half a mile down the beach. They asked me to identify them.'

He stopped speaking, and gripped the wheel more tightly. Charles was silent too. Then Mr Juby went on.

'Thass a bad, bad business, Charlie. There's many more gone besides; nobody knows yet how many. They're still trying to find some of the bodies. We never thought it could be this bad.'

They drove on into Wettleford. The tree which had been threatening the Red Lion was still standing, but the metal lion had been blown off the porch and was lying on its side by the door. As they drove along the High Street Charles could not bring himself to look up at the empty office and the empty flat above.

Mr Juby dropped him off in Remingham. Charles climbed out of the car, its beautiful paintwork covered in salt-stains and mud, and stood for a moment beside it. Mr Juby leaned over towards him.

'It's been a hell of a night, Charlie,' he said quietly. 'You get some sleep, and have a bath and a shave. I'll see you in the office this afternoon and we'll put the story together. Narridge is sending another man along the coast to look after things today, then tomorrow morning we'd better get up there again. That'll take a long time to clear up the mess, and there's a lot more to be written. Now get you on, boy. You look terrible.'

They looked at each other sadly. Both of them were bedraggled and weary, but they were not thinking of their own discomfort, or of the story that had to be written. They were thinking of a kindly man in a rumpled blue suit, with a gentle manner and a self-deprecating smile, who had gone to comfort his mother in case she was frightened by the storm, and had died with her.

By Monday the great clear-up had begun. The death toll in Norfolk had been a hundred, with Hunstanton the worst hit. Five thousand homes were damaged or destroyed, forty thousand acres of land were flooded, the county's sea defences had been breached in two thousand places. In Great Yarmouth ten thousand people were evacuated from their homes; in Kings Lynn the floodwaters rose higher than in 1883. It was Britain's worst flood disaster of the century.

The Norwich morning paper devoted nearly all its Monday issue to the story. Charles's account of the events at Branham Staithe was printed at length; this time the by-line referred to him as Our Special Correspondent. But he did not celebrate. In the centre of the page, in a black surround, were the names of the dead. They included Mortimer Thirkle and his mother.

When Charles returned to Branham Staithe that Monday morning the waters had retreated back to the quayside, revealing the smashed walls and the rubble of the demolished cottages. On those that still stood there was a thick layer of grey mud. The main street was as busy as on a summer Sunday, but these were not holiday-makers, they were groups of volunteers from Wettleford and Toftham and elsewhere, come to help with the clearing-up and the scrubbing-down.

The villagers were moving their furniture down to the lower floors again. Those who had lost their homes had been taken from the school by relatives and friends, and the school itself was being used to supply hot drinks and food for the helpers. It was a great community effort, and Charles hoped his report would do it justice.

Mr Juby had suggested he used the Wettleford office to write it, so that he could provide a gathering point for news that came in from other villages on that part of the coast. It also meant that he had a steady stream of callers coming to express their sympathy and grief over Mortimer's death. He stayed on into the evening as they continued to come, some of them in tears, all of them with stories of Mortimer's kindness and willingness to help. He coped as best he could, but at times he was close to tears himself. Mortimer had been a much-loved man.

By seven o'clock he could take no more. He telephoned Mr Juby that he was leaving and locked the office. He decided to have a quick beer at the Red Lion before he headed for home.

The metal lion was back over the porch as Charles went in. He found the bar packed with total strangers. As he edged his way through them he gathered from their noisy conversations who they were. The Fleet Street press corps was in town.

He tucked himself in a corner, trying to ignore the loud voices and the laughter around him. Then somebody tapped him on the shoulder.

'The chap behind the bar tells me you're on the local paper,' said a stout man with a pork-pie hat on the back of his head and cigarette ash on his lapels. 'Seen anything much of the damage?'

'Just a little,' said Charles curtly.

The stout man breathed gin into his face. 'A lot of people killed, I'm told. Can't understand that; why didn't they get out of the way?'

Charles looked at him in blank amazement. 'Have you the faintest idea what it was like up on the coast on Saturday night?' he asked.

The stout man shrugged. 'Quite a bit of wind, I suppose. Big waves, all that sort of thing. But you get big waves anywhere. Kids have great fun dashing in and out of them. Perhaps people are a bit slower up here.' And he grinned knowingly.

Charles tried to keep calm. 'Have you been up to the coast and had a look for yourself? You might have a better idea of what you're talking about.'

The stout man stopped grinning. 'I'll have a look round tomorrow. There's no hurry – I don't have to file until the end of the week.'

'You're on one of the Sundays then?' asked Charles, and an unwelcome thought struck him.

'That's right. The *Sunday Herald*. All the news that's fit to print – so long as the lawyers pass it.' And he guffawed.

'My God,' said Charles.

. And left.

By Wednesday the Toftham office of the *Journal* was getting back to somewhere near normal. It would be months before the scars along the coast were healed, and some of the mental scars would take much longer. But Charles had returned to his normal duties, and in his pocket when he arrived at work was the letter from the *Sunday Herald*. He could not delay answering it any longer, but he wanted a word with Mr Juby first.

When he went up to Mr Juby's office he found him talking to Fred Knock. It was obviously the wrong time to discuss the letter and he turned to leave, but Mr Juby called him back.

'We've got some good news for you, Charlie. Tell him, Fred.'

Mr Knock came straight to the point. 'Those Gibsons,' he said. 'We've found a place for them.'

Charles listened with delight as he explained how it had happened. A family had left a council house in Remingham to move to the Midlands. The tenant of the adjoining semi asked if he could exchange it for one which had just become vacant in another village where he actually worked. Mr Knock would be proposing at the next housing committee meeting that the exchange be agreed, and the two houses in Remingham be converted into one for the Gibsons.

'That's marvellous. I'm really most grateful,' said Charles. Indeed he was so excited by the news that Mr Knock had bade his farewells and left the office before he remembered the matter of the extra work and expense involved on the motorbike. But in the light of other events it now seemed unimportant.

'That'll make a nice little story about the Gibsons,' commented Mr Juby. 'But you hold on to it until next week, after the committee meeting. There'll be no room for narthin but the floods this Friday.' And he added casually, 'The Sundays won't have much room for it either.'

The reference reminded Charles what he had come for. He took out the letter and put it on the desk. Mr Juby glanced at it, but did not bother to pick it up.

'They've offered you a job, then.'

'You don't seem very surprised,' said Charles, disappointed that his bombshell had failed to explode.

'I'm not daft, boy. Nellie told me about the letter you got from them with "Urgent" all over it, so that couldn't have been just a cheque and a pat on the head. Then next thing I know, you're asking me for time off to go and see your parents, when you hent bothered about seeing them since you came here. I'd have known what you were up to, even if they hadn't told me from Narridge.'

'Norwich?' Now Charles was really put out. 'How did they know anything about it?'

'That Jim Downing, the personnel man, he spends a lot of time in London, saw you in El Vino's with our friend Mr Palmer.' Mr Juby snorted scornfully. 'Fancy you in a wine bar! Thought I trained you better'n that.'

'So Downing told Norwich, and Norwich told you.' Charles still did not understand. 'Why should they bother to do that?'

'Perhaps they don't want to lose you, boy. I tell you, they're rum folk in Narridge.' Mr Juby chuckled, and started filling his pipe. 'They wanted me to get on to you, find out what you were up to. I told 'em I'd do no such thing. Thass your business, I told them, not mine, nor theirs.'

Charles indicated the letter in front of Mr Juby. 'I appreciate that, but they've made an offer now and I'd be glad to have your opinion. It's only a researcher's job but Jeffrey Palmer says it's a good way to start, and the money's incredible. What do you think?'

'Thass not what I think, thass what you think, Charlie. I can't decide that for you.' He lit his pipe slowly. 'Basically, I suppose, thass a matter o' pools.'

'You mean it's like winning the pools? I wouldn't put it that high.'

'No, no, lad. It's big pools and little pools. And big fish and little fish. Depends what you fancy, a big fish in a little 'un, or a little fish in a big 'un.'

'I'm hardly a big fish in this pool,' said Charles, a little ruefully.

'Thass very true, Charlie, very true.' Mr Juby puffed meditatively on his pipe. 'But you're a-growin' all the time.'

Charles decided to broach a delicate subject which had been in the back of his mind for a couple of days. 'It seems awful to mention it,' he said hesitantly, 'but I suppose there's Mortimer's job going at Wettleford.'

'Don't you bank on that, boy,' said Mr Juby sharply. 'There hent no guarantee they'll put you in Wettleford.

306

Just as likely to bring in some London feller they take a shine to. If you decide to stay, you assoom you stay in Toftham. You be quite clear about that.'

I asked for that, thought Charles. He picked up his letter. 'I ought to reply to this today. Things have been so hectic since Saturday, I haven't had a chance to think it all through, really. Would it be all right if I had a little time out of the office to sort things out?'

''Course you can,' said Mr Juby expansively. 'Just get a bit of a move on this morning, get all your calls done and check through all those village paragraphs, and see George Flatt about this flood relief fund he's starting up and what sort of reaction there is, and make sure there's nothing new happening up on the coast, then if you've cleared all that up by lunch-time you can take the afternoon off.'

Charles smiled wryly. 'Why, thank you, Mr Juby, that's very generous.'

Mr Juby was already sorting through the papers on his desk. 'The pairper's still got to come out, boy, whatever personal problems you got. I'll be in the Dog and Partridge this evening. Let me know what you decide.'

Charles sat on his motorbike on the brow of the hill overlooking Branham Staithe. There was no vestige now of the weekend gales; it was a fine, clear afternoon. Around him was the now familiar vista of rolling fields, and isolated farm buildings, and the silhouettes of churches on the skyline. Just ahead of him was the common where Mortimer had suggested he might picnic; the lane which ran down through it to the coast road was now passable again. A temporary Bailey bridge had been erected where the little hump-backed bridge had been swept away. Some of the salt-marshes were still under water; beyond them lay the beach and the sea, now quite placid in the sunshine.

And there was Branham Staithe, the village he had come to know so well, with work already under way on rebuilding the smashed walls and the fallen roofs. 'You'll always be welcome here, lad,' Jimma had said. He had made some good friends that night.

But others had gone. Nobody could replace Mortimer, and he was losing John Cranmer, and Rebecca had already been lost. In London there would be new opportunities and no doubt new friends. He would be working on major assignments with people like Jeffrey Palmer – though there was also, he reminded himself, the stout man he had met in the Red Lion. In Toftham there was the tedious round of jumble sales and garden fêtes and darts club dinners, the freezing Saturday afternoons on the touch-line, the little snubs and irritations that kept cropping up in his 'foodal' and sometimes primitive society, where people like the Gibson family had to live nine to a tumbledown cottage . . .

He had quite forgotten about the Gibsons. And he wanted to be the first to tell them the good news. He started up the bike and drove fast to Remingham. He did not know that Mr Knock, who enjoyed such moments also, had been there before him.

Betty Gibson saw him riding up the lane and by the time he reached the front door she had assembled all the family in the sitting-room. As soon as he knocked she flung it open and turned to the children.

'Three cheers for Mr Benson,' she cried. The hurrays might have been heard in Remingham.

All that Charles could think of doing was to hug her, and she hugged him back. Dan Gibson grasped his hand, and the children gathered round and hugged him too.

'It's really Fred Knock you should be thanking,' he protested.

'But he'd never have thought of it without you,' said Mrs Gibson. 'And anyway, I don't think I could hug Mr Knock.'

They had a celebratory cup of tea, then Charles set off back to Toftham. As he rode through Remingham he met Willum cycling towards him on the old delivery bike. Willum waved to him gleefully.

'Hent this a fine bike, marster!' he cried.

'That it is, Willum,' said Charles happily. Willum rode on past him, singing one of his little songs. The name-plate, which Charles had repainted, now read: 'Willum Eke: Purveyor of Good Will.'

When Charles arrived at the office Mr Juby had already left and Nellie was just locking up. He had hardly had a chance to speak to her since the weekend, except to tell her how sorry he was about Mortimer. She had not seemed too upset; he was glad Mortimer would never know.

'They say you done really well up at Branham on Saturday night,' said Nellie as they passed in the doorway. He murmured something about just trying to help out.

'No, I heard all about you in that boat,' Nellie persisted. 'Very good with the baby, Uncle said.'

'Uncle?' asked Charles. 'Not another uncle?'

'Thass right,' said Nellie cheerfully. 'My Uncle Jimma.'

'Of course,' said Charles. 'Who else . . .'

He went up to his office, and sat for a while, thinking. Then he typed out his reply to the editor of the *Sunday Herald*. As a postscript, he sent his best wishes to Jeffrey Palmer. Then he added a further one, saying he hoped the *Herald* reporter who was covering the flood story had found his way to the coast.

He posted it on the way to the Dog and Partridge.

Inside the farmers' bar Mavis was already pulling his pint. Mr Juby was beaming at him from behind his special.

'You made the right decision, boy. I'm glad you're staying.'

Charles did not attempt to understand. He just raised his glass and touched it to Mr Juby's.

'Anyway,' Mr Juby continued, 'if you're as good as I reckon you are, that won't be the last offer you'll get. And maybe later on that'll be right to go. But just now, I reckon you're right to stay.'

'I know what you're going to say,' said Charles.

'Thass right, boy. You still got a lot to lun.'

Mr Juby made only two more observations of note that evening. As he supped his second special he commented: 'Now you've made up your mind, I think we should tell Narridge about that letter, but we needn't tell 'em you've replied to it. I'll say you're thinking seriously about it, and if they want to keep you, maybe they should offer you the Wettleford job. If they don't, there's no harm done. And if they do, I dussay you'll manage.'

And as he supped his third, he told Charles: 'That Bludgen girl you were talking to at the Carol Service, she's a nice girl, even though her father's an idjut. You might do a lot wuss.' And Charles remembered the thumbs-up sign. But Mr Juby had not finished.

'She telephoned about that report of yours on the flooding at Branham Staithe. Seems she does a lot of sailing there, knows most of the local folk. Thass a very moving report, she says.' Mr Juby sipped at his special. 'That hent as good as "enchanting", I reckon, but that hent bad. Said she'd like to tell you herself.' And he added as an afterthought: 'In case you still can't think of it, her name's Penny. And don't look so startled, boy. I saw you mouthing names to yourself after she'd gone . . .'

It was quite late when Charles left. He said his goodbyes and headed for the door. But in the doorway he turned and looked back at Mr Juby, perched on his stool at the end of the bar, another special already in his hand. He took a chance.

'Fare y'well, Mr Juby,' he called in his best Norfolk accent.

For a moment Mr Juby frowned. Then the frown went, and out came the familiar chuckle as he waved his glass in gentle salute.

'You'll never be a Norfolkman,' he called. 'But fare y'well, boy.'

A Selection of Arrow Books

☐ No Enemy But Time	Evelyn Anthony	£2.95
☐ The Lilac Bus	Maeve Binchy	£2.99
☐ Rates of Exchange	Malcolm Bradbury	£3.50
☐ Prime Time	Joan Collins	£3.50
☐ Rosemary Conley's Complete Hip and Thigh Diet	Rosemary Conley	£2.99
☐ Staying Off the Beaten Track	Elizabeth Gundrey	£6.99
☐ Duncton Wood	William Horwood	£4.50
☐ Duncton Quest	William Horwood	£4.50
☐ A World Apart	Marie Joseph	£3.50
☐ Erin's Child	Sheelagh Kelly	£3.99
☐ Colours Aloft	Alexander Kent	£2.99
☐ Gondar	Nicholas Luard	£4.50
☐ The Ladies of Missalonghi	Colleen McCullough	£2.50
☐ The Veiled One	Ruth Rendell	£3.50
☐ Sarum	Edward Rutherfurd	£4.99
☐ Communion	Whitley Strieber	£3.99

Prices and other details are liable to change

ARROW BOOKS, BOOKSERVICE BY POST, PO BOX 29, DOUGLAS, ISLE OF MAN, BRITISH ISLES

NAME...

ADDRESS ....

....

....

Please enclose a cheque or postal order made out to Arrow Books Ltd. for the amount due and allow the following for postage and packing.

U.K. CUSTOMERS: Please allow 22p per book to a maximum of £3.00.

B.F.P.O. & EIRE: Please allow 22p per book to a maximum of £3.00.

OVERSEAS CUSTOMERS: Please allow 22p per book.

Whilst every effort is made to keep prices low it is sometimes necessary to increase cover prices at short notice. Arrow Books reserve the right to show new retail prices on covers which may differ from those previously advertised in the text or elsewhere.

Bestselling Fiction

☐ No Enemy But Time	Evelyn Anthony	£2.95
☐ The Lilac Bus	Maeve Binchy	£2.99
☐ Prime Time	Joan Collins	£3.50
☐ A World Apart	Marie Joseph	£3.50
☐ Erin's Child	Sheelagh Kelly	£3.99
☐ Colours Aloft	Alexander Kent	£2.99
☐ Gondar	Nicholas Luard	£4.50
☐ The Ladies of Missalonghi	Colleen McCullough	£2.50
☐ Lily Golightly	Pamela Oldfield	£3.50
☐ Talking to Strange Men	Ruth Rendell	£2.99
☐ The Veiled One	Ruth Rendell	£3.50
☐ Sarum	Edward Rutherfurd	£4.99
☐ The Heart of the Country	Fay Weldon	£2.50

Prices and other details are liable to change

ARROW BOOKS, BOOKSERVICE BY POST, PO BOX 29, DOUGLAS, ISLE OF MAN, BRITISH ISLES

NAME..

ADDRESS...

....

....

Please enclose a cheque or postal order made out to Arrow Books Ltd. for the amount due and allow the following for postage and packing.

U.K. CUSTOMERS: Please allow 22p per book to a maximum of £3.00.

B.F.P.O. & EIRE: Please allow 22p per book to a maximum of £3.00.

OVERSEAS CUSTOMERS: Please allow 22p per book.

Whilst every effort is made to keep prices low it is sometimes necessary to increase cover prices at short notice. Arrow Books reserve the right to show new retail prices on covers which may differ from those previously advertised in the text or elsewhere.

Bestselling General Fiction

☐ No Enemy But Time	Evelyn Anthony	£2.95
☐ Skydancer	Geoffrey Archer	£3.50
☐ The Sisters	Pat Booth	£3.50
☐ Captives of Time	Malcolm Bosse	£2.99
☐ Saudi	Laurie Devine	£2.95
☐ Duncton Wood	William Horwood	£4.50
☐ Aztec	Gary Jennings	£3.95
☐ A World Apart	Marie Joseph	£3.50
☐ The Ladies of Missalonghi	Colleen McCullough	£2.50
☐ Lily Golightly	Pamela Oldfield	£3.50
☐ Sarum	Edward Rutherfurd	£4.99
☐ Communion	Whitley Strieber	£3.99

Prices and other details are liable to change

ARROW BOOKS, BOOKSERVICE BY POST, PO BOX 29, DOUGLAS, ISLE
OF MAN, BRITISH ISLES

NAME...

ADDRESS..

....

....

Please enclose a cheque or postal order made out to Arrow Books Ltd. for the amount
due and allow the following for postage and packing.

U.K. CUSTOMERS: Please allow 22p per book to a maximum of £3.00.

B.F.P.O. & EIRE: Please allow 22p per book to a maximum of £3.00.

OVERSEAS CUSTOMERS: Please allow 22p per book.

Whilst every effort is made to keep prices low it is sometimes necessary to increase cover
prices at short notice. Arrow Books reserve the right to show new retail prices on covers
which may differ from those previously advertised in the text or elsewhere.

Bestselling Humour

☐ The Ascent of Rum Doodle	W E Bowman	£2.99
☐ Tim Brooke-Taylor's Golf Bag	Tim Brooke-Taylor	£3.99
☐ Shop! or A Store Is Born	Jasper Carrott	£2.99
☐ Cat Chat	Peter Fincham	£3.50
☐ Art of Coarse Drinking	Michael Green	£2.50
☐ Rambling On	Mike Harding	£2.50
☐ Sex Tips For Girls	Cynthia Heimel	£2.95
☐ Tales From Witney Scrotum	Peter Tinniswood	£2.50
☐ Tales From A Long Room	Peter Tinniswood	£2.75
☐ Uncle Mort's North Country	Peter Tinniswood	£2.50
☐ Five Hundred Mile Walkies	Mark Wallington	£2.50

Prices and other details are liable to change

ARROW BOOKS, BOOKSERVICE BY POST, PO BOX 29, DOUGLAS, ISLE
OF MAN, BRITISH ISLES

NAME...

ADDRESS...

....

....

Please enclose a cheque or postal order made out to Arrow Books Ltd. for the amount
due and allow the following for postage and packing.

U.K. CUSTOMERS: Please allow 22p per book to a maximum of £3.00.

B.F.P.O. & EIRE: Please allow 22p per book to a maximum of £3.00.

OVERSEAS CUSTOMERS: Please allow 22p per book.

Whilst every effort is made to keep prices low it is sometimes necessary to increase cover
prices at short notice. Arrow Books reserve the right to show new retail prices on covers
which may differ from those previously advertised in the text or elsewhere.

Bestselling Thriller/Suspense

☐ Skydancer	Geoffrey Archer	£3.50
☐ Hooligan	Colin Dunne	£2.99
☐ See Charlie Run	Brian Freemantle	£2.99
☐ Hell is Always Today	Jack Higgins	£2.50
☐ The Proteus Operation	James P Hogan	£3.50
☐ Winter Palace	Dennis Jones	£3.50
☐ Dragonfire	Andrew Kaplan	£2.99
☐ The Hour of the Lily	John Kruse	£3.50
☐ Fletch, Too	Geoffrey McDonald	£2.50
☐ Brought in Dead	Harry Patterson	£2.50
☐ The Albatross Run	Douglas Scott	£2.99

Prices and other details are liable to change

ARROW BOOKS, BOOKSERVICE BY POST, PO BOX 29, DOUGLAS, ISLE
OF MAN, BRITISH ISLES

NAME..

ADDRESS...

....

....

Please enclose a cheque or postal order made out to Arrow Books Ltd. for the amount
due and allow the following for postage and packing.

U.K. CUSTOMERS: Please allow 22p per book to a maximum of £3.00.

B.F.P.O. & EIRE: Please allow 22p per book to a maximum of £3.00.

OVERSEAS CUSTOMERS: Please allow 22p per book.

Whilst every effort is made to keep prices low it is sometimes necessary to increase cover
prices at short notice. Arrow Books reserve the right to show new retail prices on covers
which may differ from those previously advertised in the text or elsewhere.